TWIST OF FATE
A TRUTH WRAPPED IN A BEAUTIFUL LIE

WRITTEN BY NIKKI FLOWERS

outskirtspress
DENVER, COLORADO

Outskirts Press, Inc.
http://www.outskirtspress.com

ISBN: 978-1-4787-6974-3

Outskirts Press and the "OP" logo are trademarks belonging to Outskirts Press, Inc.

PRINTED IN THE UNITED STATES OF AMERICA

ACKNOWLEDGMENTS

A lot of different processes went into birthing *Twist of Fate*. It took 9 months to create something as perfectly planned as Egypt. I always wanted to write a book, but I couldn't sit still long enough to finish the process until God granted me the opportunity. So, first and foremost, I want to thank God for giving me a second chance to do things right and walk into my purpose. Unfortunately, this process took place in prison, but without having been incarcerated, I wouldn't be writing this.

I also can't thank you enough, Shammek (BOY) Johnson for sharing the first four chapters of your book with me. It wasn't until I read these that I formed the goal of not just starting, but finishing my own novel. I am also truly blessed for the advice that Delicious Jones drilled into my head: to take my time, finish what I start, and learn how to live like I'm poor. Every time my pen hit the paper, I wanted her to read the words. She isn't here to see the finished copy, but she read many of poems and short stories that I created. She is my angel, shining down on me always.

I also want to thank Jarisa White for giving me so many dictionaries, thesauruses, and writing materials like paper and pens while getting on my nerves. You definitely motivated me when I didn't want to write and listened when I needed a shoulder to lean on. The best piece advice that you gave me was, "Don't go looking for love, go looking for respect." I didn't really get what you were trying to say until I put the final touches on this project.

I can't thank you enough, momma Catherine "CatDog" Famularo, for typing 529 pages into my computer when I needed to send the manuscript out to my editor. I don't know what I would have done without you. I probably would still be typing with my slow butt, lol. Another big thanks goes to my family for supporting me when I was away and to my handsome grown man, my son Elijah. I didn't just write this for me: I wrote this for you as well. I wanted you to see that your mother could do something besides sell narcotics. You're the backbone of this project, and you kept the pen in my hand.

Last, but not least, thank you to all of the women in the Cambridge Springs Correctional Facility who contributed to my process. You did everything from reading a couple of chapters, to putting up with me banging on my typewriter, to buying me typing paper and typing ribbons, to giving me all of the hugs that I needed even though we weren't allowed to touch. Thank you…

CHAPTER ONE

Ms. Lola James... Yeah, that's her... The woman I love to hate. My mother. As I sit in the back row of the church listening to her preach the word of God to us devils, water builds up in my tear ducts. Her full length hair lies perfect around her neck and her high cheekbones make a glow come about her face as if she found it, her calling to God. The night air is chilling to the bone yard, awaiting the Candyman to come through the streets and bless the addicted. It was a must I got off the street for just a second as my feet ached from the cold. I could picture myself in the front seat of his vehicle rather than listening to a woman who left me at birth, but what choice did I have? I needed to get warm.

The words spilling out of her mouth bring about butterflies in my stomach as if she's talking directly to me, even though the church is packed and you can hear the amens bouncing off the walls. I can't hear or see anything else but her face. Does she notice me sitting before her as she speaks? Can she recognize me sitting in the back row? Of course she can't! I'm invisible in her eyes, and I blend in with ever other face in this church. The manifestation of a man is how I carried myself for the last five years of my life, being an aggressor. Hell, no, she don't recognize me! My life, my life isn't shit!! I've received the fucked up hands of life dealt to me and I've sucked it up, in and out. Her daughter, her little girl, that's what I was the last time she laid eyes on me, held me in her arms and saw my face. Today, I stand before her a grown-ass dike with issues as she stares past me. She hasn't changed a bit from the photo I gazed upon so many nights in distress wanting her to come back for me. She was beautiful to me then and more beautiful to me now. My stomach muscles turn from calm to reflexed, ready to chuck up the 40-ounce beer I drank a half hour ago. As I tweak for another hit of crack, my head spins out of control. I turn about in my seat as my mother goes on to preach louder. "The only man you need in your life is Jesus."

She walks back and forth across the pulpit holding up the Bible in her hands. "He is my rock, my faith, my best friend, and my only un-conditional love when it all falls down. He is my mother and my father when I need guidance. I want my people in the church to really listen to me now." She points out into the congregation with her right index finger and rubs her ear with her left hand. "I know some of y'all just walked in off the street to get warm and so the police wouldn't harass you for loitering." She wipes the sweat from her forehead and takes a sip of water from a glass resting below. "And I want you to see and know, we as a church don't care where you're from, but we care about you, and you are welcomed in the house of the Lord. Can I get a amen right now!" The congregation shouted their amens following up with applause. "That's why you're here! The Lord can work in mysterious ways and means." Wiping her forehead once again, she stomps around the pulpit. "The Lord needed ya'll to know today that he loves the sinners as well as the church folks, and maybe even more, 'cause ya'll don't know any better." The congregation stood to their feet praising the Lord, clapping their hands and stomping their feet, giving the unfamiliar faces a glance over before sitting back down.

"Damn!!!!! She's on the money with the preaching thing. She got these old-ass ladies getting ready to split their wigs trying to get to their purses to hand out a donation to a God that don't exist." I ut-ter my words under my breath as I begin to sweat from head to toe. With my body temperature on the rise and my stomach turned down right spoiled, I give my mother one last look as the crack takes over my body for its next fix. I can hear the words, the conversation she is having with God and her people, but I can't see her face anymore. Everything is a blur.

"Don't walk out the door too soon, young ladies and gents, you just might miss your blessing walking out the church doors and walking out on God. He doesn't like ugly and he isn't too fond of pretty neither." I get up from my seat and rush to the exit with tears streaming down my face. I can barely take a breath, gasping for air. I'm going to miss my blessing anyway, chasing the get high. I walk out the door, turning my back on everything I loved and once upon a time wanted to love me back.

I stand outside in the front of Hillcrest Seventh Day Adventist Church in a standstill. I want to walk but I can't move. I ask myself out loud, "How can she be saved by God?" Wiping the tears away with the back of my hand, I shake my head in need of answers. I scream into the cloudy night sky with my hand raised, wanting an answer from somebody. "So far, but so damn close, why wouldn't you come back for me, Momma?"

The naked tree branches shake as the wind whips around, smacking me dead in the face as I wait on the curb for a miracle. I can hear the people inside the church saying "Amen" crisp and clear. I want to return to my seat, but my hatred towards my mother and God won't let it be. There isn't any God and I never had a mother... It was just me, myself and I...

The night air is even thicker with a blanket of cold as I shut the door to the old-school Caddy. An hour passes while I suck dick for money. The old man rode around the block of the church as I did my business and my mother continued to preach while I committed acts of prostitution. I can't believe I let an old man do me in the back of his car in front of a fucking church. Better yet, I can't believe God let me do that. Time and time again I prove this crazy world wrong—there isn't a God. And if there is, he doesn't know me. But what I do know is I want to get high with the last $20 I just made sucking and fucking.

I can't believe I let that old fart do me, but the deed is done. I know he had more money in his pocket, but I can't get down with robbing. For sure that's some crack head shit and I don't want any part I'm just a hustler that smokes for fun, you dig me?

"SHIT!!" I shake my head in disgust.

"This should be her, not me! She should be the one drinking a fifth of Vodka to sleep at night!"

Yelling at the closed double doors of the church, I hear the people inside getting louder and louder.

"Preach, pastor, preach on!!!" The congregation shouts and sings, joining in the background as my mother closes out with prayer.

"I can't believe it!" I shout at the double doors in disgust. The woman I wanted to see my whole life is a few steps away, but tonight I will not speak on it; I'm just ready to get high.

My mission begins as I follow the hill down Wiley Avenue to Centre Avenue behind the church, not looking back at my mother or God. Three for $20 was the mission impossible, and I'm on it. Someway, somehow, I get the job done, sweet talking the dealers into what I need. It isn't a long stroll or a walk in the park reaching the middle of the hill out of breath and chilled to the bone. Throwing up beer and whatever else I have in my stomach didn't make it any better. I run the rest of the way downhill, seeking out a sucker from afar for the gain of the product.

From the streetlights to the flashing red and blue lights of the police cars, the ballers stand out with the big body trucks and the floodlights ruling the streets. The ballers drive through the streets nice and slow, catching the eyes of the woman as well as the police. Nonetheless, no one gives a damn because everyone was breaking the law. It's on, and cracking on this Friday night, even though the temperature is icy.

Majority of the women sport chinchilla furs and wipe-me-down-fuck-me dresses, but the top-notch niggas don't care as their wives roll through in nothing but the best. Everybody loves to pull rank on the street with who got the hottest whip to the hottest chick, and who can be the biggest gangster of all.

Broke as hell with only a couple of dollars in my pocket, you can't tell from my dress code and the swag in my walk. I'm known for getting money in the streets and flashing everything I had for a bitch. I'm the biggest trick in the world. I just don't trick with women, though. I do it with cars, clothes, popping bottles and so on. I live and party like a rock star. I'm not going to lie, quoting that I run the city and have keys of coke because the truth of the matter is, I was small-time compared to the ballers roaming the avenues. The most coke I ever flipped in this game—in a roundabout way—give or take, was 500 g. I'm proud to claim that status being a female in the game, too.

Cars, I had a few; chicken heads, I done plucked them all, and shopping sprees I spared no expense, experiencing the most elaborate boutiques money could buy. I bought so many sneaks I should have made an investment in the Foot Locker shoe store chain. One-half kilo wasn't bad, but just as I made the money, I spent it on bullshit. Hey, they say it isn't tricking if you got it, and it just didn't feel right not spending it after standing on the block throwing bricks at the penitentiary.

So there she is, the most beautiful bitch in the world. Moet leans up against her restored, tricked-out, all black 5.0 Mustang. The 20-inch rims make it tasteless; nonetheless, I want to ride it. Better yet, I want to ride the car and its owner can ride my face. Moet is flawless, adding to the fact that the bitch is loyal and a moneymaker against all odds. It makes her the Head Bitch in Charge in my eyes. Bringing beauty to the dope game with style and elegance, Moet is Bonnie and everybody wants to be her Clyde. Holding her man down—who would never see the light of day again—she took over his day-to-day operations and made a killing. Accustomed to the lifestyle, Moet hit the block buying her first quarter ounce off me. "She is so fine …" I utter under my breath as I approach her beauty, the car and her face. Her complexion is a signature chocolate without a blemish in sight. Those big brown hazelnut eyes are enough to melt one's heart as she keeps me under her influence. I stand there lusting over her petite physique, licking my lips. I'm tweaking hard for her crack and to suck that fat-ass pussy willow she has between those long, luscious legs.

"What are you looking at, Nikko?" Moet asks, placing her hands on her hips. "I can feel you staring a hole through my pussy." Throwing her head back with conceit, she chuckles. "You want some of that, don't you?" She laughs at her own question, knowing the answer to it.

Placing my hands in my pocket, I give her a glance-over once more." Don't ask questions you already know the answers to, woman. Please! You know what it is, lil' momma." Giving her the flicker of my tongue, I turn myself on.

"It's not fair to let me see and not touch."Grinning from ear to ear, she unlocks the passenger door requesting I enter to conversate further. Catching the smell of her expensive perfume, I go in for the kill, seeking a kiss. Mugging me in a playful manner, she states that I speak my piece.

"What do you want from me boy? And please try to keep your hands with all your other body parts to yourself." Moet smiled flattered by Nikko but couldn't give in to a woman's touch. She was strictly dickly.

"I want you woman, however, since you're not going to give in to me tonight, I will settle for a double up for twenty dollars."

"Are you serious Nikko? You slowed me down for twenty dollars? Why are you outside anyway, without any work, boy? It's Friday night and the first of the month."

"I just came over here for pleasure and ran into a business opportunity to make a couple of extra dollars to spend on the ladies. Anyway, I just wanted to say hi to your fine ass. And I know how you feel about time wasting." We look at each other because we know what I mean by the saying, "If it don't make dollars, then it don't make sense." We quote the saying together, laughing at the code we lived by.

"Don't think you know me like that, playboy, because you don't," Moet says while she sticks her hand down the seat of her jeans. Pulling up a plastic baggy, my stomach fills with gas instantly, feasting my eyes on the melt. "Can you smell it?" Moet asks, rubbing her finger under and over my nose. I can smell the product as she open the bag, but pussy I can't smell, though I would've loved to. "I wish you were a real boy sometimes, Nikko," she goes on to say, counting out dime pieces of crack. "I would take you home with me and give you this wet-ass pussy. Sike, sike, sike and sike again. I need to stop talking shit; I'm too damned scared you might turn me out."

Placing the coke in my hand, her beauty is no longer existent. All is good and I'm ready to step the fuck off. "Didn't you hear what I just said to you?" Moet asks, confused by no response. I heard what she said, but the words don't mean shit to me after I got what I paid for, so I play it cool.

"Okay, ma, let's play the game." I speak with a devilish grin. "How about we just take this car and park it on a side street to make shit happen? You can cum all over my face if you give me my money back." My devilish grin rises.

Giving a roll of the neck, Moet replies, "Nigga, please! That was a good come back line."

Laughter fills the car as the transaction comes to an end. "You were close, but no cigar for asking for your money back with a no-refund-policy bitch like me." We both start laughing again as we give each other a pound. "Take that shit, Nikko, and stuff it before them boys in blue come knocking and get gone before people start to think I'm diking it now." Giving me two more dimes that look like twenty pieces, she kisses me on the cheek, letting me know it's time to go. I open the car door getting, my body halfway out when I go in and grab a handful of Moet's breast. "You make me sick boy. Stop touching what doesn't belong to you!" she yells with a teasing voice as our eyes say good-bye.

Picking up a slow jog down Centre Ave., half my mission is complete. Now, all I need is a place to chill and lay. The townspeople of the Hill District don't know the facts about me getting high, so I have to be careful about choosing a spot. Cutting up a side street, my mother and her words crept across my memory bank. "Don't walk out the door too soon; you just might miss your blessing." Over and over it resonates in my mind, but my body is tweaking for what I have in my pocket, so I don't listen. I block my mother and her voice from my mind. Not aware that I cut down Kirkpatrick Street, I come across an old hangout from back in the day. If memory serves me right, every nigga in there wanted me for one reason or another. Not stepping on this side of town for a moment, I could run up in the spot and make them weak-ass niggas meet my demands. A sexy face and a tight pussy get me what I want when it comes to men, for the simple fact they think with their dick and their cash flow. And since no dick is running up in me, as well as I get my own money, I'm nothing but a challenge to a standard nigga. Every nigga thinks one shot of dick would make me straight,

Touching the rail as I walk up the steps to reach the door, my mother's voice overwhelms my consciousness. "Don't walk out the door too soon; you just might miss your blessing." It rings loud in my ears as if I'm back in church sitting in the last row.

The old house stands alone on the corner of the block. Trash and tall shrubbery consume the landscaping. The fractured cement moves unsteadily from side to side as I do a bounce from uneasiness trying to find a door bell. With no doorbell available, I hurt my knuckles knocking hard on the cold steel door.

From the outside you would think the house was abandoned. The trees and the broken glass surrounded the place. It made the house appear like something out of a horror flick.

Standing there tweaking, my stomach cramps up, needing that get-high stashed away in the corner of my pocket. I pound on the door harder while my mother's voice haunts me on and on. My body is defiant, ready to get a blast to take the pain away. I need to escape my thoughts, if only for a minute. I bring my hand to the door to pound on it once more when I hear a voice call out from behind the door.

"Who dat?" spits an unfamiliar tones "Nikko," I respond with a low pitch, disguising my voice to sound like a man.

"Who? Speak up, if you want to get in this mutherfucker!" I catch the voice the second time he throws it at me and yell out, "It's me fool! Nikko! Is that you, Boo?"

"Yeah, it's me," he replies, opening up the door.

"Long time no see, nigga. God damn, you're still as ugly as the day I met you. That was about three years ago, wasn't it?"

Boo stands six feet tall was and is skinny as a bean pole. Hair nappier than an African booty scratcher with skin were as black as the midnight sky with no stars. He is so black looking blue, he favors the man we all know and love as Flavor Flav. I couldn't help myself as I yell out "Yeah, boy," mocking the voice of the old-school rapper and giving him a pound.

"Take ya ass upstairs!" Boo demands as he rolls his eyes at me like a straight bitch.

"I'ma let that shit slide for now." I slide past his body structure over the threshold in need of heat. "Everybody got jokes nowadays." He closes the door behind me. "Where your sexy ass been at anyway? I don't give a fuck about you looking like an Usher mini-me, I'll still fuck."

"Whatever dude. You're tripping. I look like me, not no fucking Usher." Looking around the downstairs area, there isn't a soul in sight.

"I haven't seen you for a minute 'round here. Where you been at?" Boo asks, leading me upstairs to the next level of the house.

"I've been doing me, and I think you should back the fuck up and continue to do you," I state firmly. Reaching the top of the stairs, I can smell the get-high in the air with laughter and many voices talking shit. I think, *Why should I give this up? Right here is the parties of all parties, the get-high.*

I enter a large room filled with smoke, with Boo behind me. I stop in my tracks, taking in the unknown faces that fill up the room in the rapture of the thick smoke. My mother's voice comes back again, this time louder and stronger, and I can feel her presence taking over my body.

"You know you have to pay house before you sit and do anything, Nikko, so pay up," Boo says, pushing me from behind and bringing me to reality. I hang my head and tell the voice to shut up.

"Boo, don't worry about me! I got this, you booty scratcher." I shoot at him with nothing but laughter, his comeback line is weak as hell as he calls me a fucking dike.

"I see why you don't have a man. Your mouth is smart as hell, bitch."

"You know I'm just playing with your black ass. Stop crying and take me to the cut. Fuck house rules; me and you can get high with this shit I got from my girl Moet." I lean in closer, just wanting Boo to hear my plan. "We need to be alone; I want to get high, and I want you to bust a nut at the same time."

The look on Boo's face is priceless. He is shocked by my statement, with his mind made up from the door. Boo speaks in a whisper, up close and personal to my earlobe. He looks around as he makes sure no eyes pay attention to his next move. "Come on, follow my lead then. There's nobody back in the laundry room. I got a good idea on how I can lock it down so we won't be disturbed."

I nodded with acceptance and begin to follow Boo to the back when we hear a voice scream out, "Who the fuck is that with you, Boo?"

"Don't worry about it, nigga. I'm doing me, so I think you should do you," he screams back, giving me a diabolical grin in the process.

Walking down the hallway, we pass two doors. The first one was cracked open, and the sight is hideous, as well as the smell escaping from it. A small television and a full-size bed reside in the tiny bedroom. The stench is ridiculous, damn near downright offensive.

"Padussiefa," came out of my mouth with laughter behind it. Boo looks back at me as if I were crazy.

"What the hell is padussiefa?"

"Pussy, dick, balls, and feet. It's stanking up in there, homie. I hope you don't sleep in that space we just passed up." I answer his question holding my nose while waving my hand back and forth.

Boo busts out laughing, informing me that the laundry room was around the corner. The last door is shut and I'm guessing that funky-ass space must have been his because he doesn't deny it. The hallway was dark and gloomy. The dim lit path makes me happy because I don't want to look at Boo with that ugly-ass face. The laundry room is in the cut just like I want. I walk in behind Boo and watch him secure the door by pushing an old dryer in front of it, keeping us in and others out. Turning on the lights, I am forced to look directly at Boo and his mean mug shot. As we stand there eyeballing each other, the laundry room becomes smaller. My mother's voice has returned with the calling of the crack stashed in the corner of my pocket.

"The only man I need in my life is Jesus," rings loud in my ears. I pull the crack out of my pocket and give it to Boo.

"Roll it up in some weed 'cause I'm ready to get high. Do you got a box of blunts?"

"Yeah yup," he replied, pulling an apple-flavored cigar from a box he confiscated out of the pocket of his jeans.

"All I want to do is get high, Boo! I've been tripping for the past hour, and I'm going crazy, nigga."

"No, you're not." Boo speaks as he cuts open the cigar to dump the filling. "Well, maybe you are, the way you coming at me." Talking with conviction he grabs his crotch and massages it slow.

I watch him roll my get-high, thinking to myself I hope his ass can eat pussy, 'cause with a face like that, it's his only hope. Handing me a perfectly rolled blunt, I spark the flame to it with the quickness, tasting the apple flavor mixed with the weed and coke; it is the righteous. It tastes so sweet, and I am thankful.

"Boo?" I say, inhaling deep on the get-high.

"What's up, mami, or should I call you papi?" Boo replies with a smile.

"Shut up and roll the rest of the get-high. Break them fat-ass dimes down to two pieces and roll four more blunts. Moet and her dimes are like twenty pieces of crack, the bomb. You can face one, because this good mutherfucker right here you rolled is to the dome."

"You're so bossy, Nikko," Boo says, but follows my demand.

"I know you can watch me touch myself until I'm ready for you to dive in." As I call the shots, it gives Boo a straight blood rush to his man hood. I can see the bulge skyrocketing in his pants.

Sitting in the corner of the laundry room on the floor, I hit my blunt and feel my heart race. Moet has the fire, as I desire to take hit after hit. I was high after hitting the smoke four times, taking small drags. Boo is hooking up the last blunt, smoking one in the process while waiting on me to give him the go ahead.

"Girl, you still got ya pants on?"

"Boo, don't bug me! Let the get-high handle it." I give him a look that could kill.

Boo sits down next to me, giving my body the glance-over like I'm a piece of steak licking his lips and shit. I know I'm high because the nigga started looking okay in the face. I had to look once, then again, as I realize, *Nope, he still is an ugly mutherfucker.*

"Nikko!" Boo calls out, demanding attention.

"What, nigga? You are going to blow my high asking questions and shit."

"I want to know what you are doing back here getting high with me instead of getting money? You still making money, I hope?" His eyes are sincere as he takes a drag of the get-high. "What's up with you coming at me with that weird shit? You letting this get-high shit get you off your square, girl?"

Before he can utter another word, I'm blazing my second blunt and my boxers are on the floor.

"Shut the fuck up, nigga, and do what I told you to do!" Boo focuses his eyes on me sitting in that corner with my legs open wide, touching myself. His eyes fix on my pussy, and I can see his mouth thirsty for the juices that would follow after his touch.

"I never thought in a day of this lifetime you would be so serious." His eyes broaden when I stick my middle finger inside my moisten hot spot pulling it out and in slow. "I was just trying to get high with you, Nikko, but I'm going to give you what you want."

"Please do," I say annoyed. "You talking too much, ugly." From that moment on, it's popping. Boo has my ass out of the corner with my back to the floor as his tongue strokes me from the back to the front. I puff that blunt in one hand and with the other guided his head as my back arches with pleasure. His ugly ass isn't playing any games either. I should have known his ugly ass was going to have the bomb.

That's the last thought I have before I feel strange. I hit the blunt once more, but this time my heart isn't racing with the rush of needing more. My body is numb. I can't move a muscle. I try to say stop, but nothing comes out of my mouth. *Am I too high?* I think, feeling this tingling sensation taking over my body? I'm screaming "I'm cumming," but nothing is coming out. Boo stands up, looking down on my body, and I try to move once more. I can only feel the warmth of a teardrop fall from the corner of my eye. Standing over me, he unzips his pants.

"Who the fuck is ugly now, bitch!? Talk shit now, you dike-ass bitch! You can't. Your body is numb as hell from that heroin you just blazed up, stupid. You couldn't smell that shit?" Boo pumps his fist in the air, declaring victory over me.

"This here is too easy; your pants are already down. You're so fucked up you can't even fight me back. Me and my niggas been waiting to fuck your tight pussy for years, and now they will have the power."

He keeps talking shit with his raspy-ass voice, and I can't do anything. He ties my hands to some old pipes running alongside the wall and then duct tapes my mouth. He must have done this shit before with his ugly, crazy-looking ass. He was too prepared.

"You just might miss your blessing." Over and over I can hear my mother's voice as Boo stuck his flesh inside me, thrusting against my walls as hard as he can. My body can't feel any pain, but my mind is racing with thoughts of my so-called life. Yes, I can believe Boo would do something like this, but not to me. I guessed wrong as I lay here being raped. Boo is fucking me so hard he brought the feeling back to my canal. I could feel my pussy going dry as he is killing my insides. Two minutes later this nothing-ass nigga marks the top of my snatch with his salty manhood.

"That's what the fuck you needed, bitch. You need a real man to fuck that pussy hard. I'm going to watch while my niggas pound you out, plus make a profit. I'm charging twenty dollars a head. I can make some get-high fare off ya ass." Boo has a look in his eyes I never saw before.

I know I'll never be the same as I watch Boo orchestrate play by play. He leaves the laundry room, and I tried to escape. I'm so high I began to nod from the dope. My eyes feel heavy when I hear someone come back into the room and cut off the lights.

"Just relax, baby. Daddy gonna take real good care of you." The unknown man smells like a bar; V.S.O.P his drink of choice. I cry for help and even try to move, but I'm not going anywhere. As he entered me I couldn't escape from him or the laundry room. So my mind detaches from reality, sending me into a dream... a beautiful nightmare...

CHAPTER TWO

Born June 2, 1976, at Magee Women's Hospital, eight pounds, ten ounces, I slid out the canal splitting my mother from cooch to anal. She gave birth to a Hershey dark-chocolate baby girl name Egypt Winters. Yeah yup, that's me, and I was something kinda magical. I was sexy way back when the doctor slapped me on the ass and while the nurse cut the cord detaching me from my mother's womb. My mother couldn't wait for me to come into this world to prove to my father that I was his child. Nine months and sixteen days she carried the seed while enduring verbal, physical, and mental abuse from my father. I was a curse to my mother before I was even born into this world. My father's whereabouts were unknown at that moment, but my mother knew he would show up after the deed was done.

My mother's side of the family was a no go as she had me by herself and all alone; however, two nurses and a doctor had to stop by to help her out. She held me in her arms as if I was the best thing that happened to her in years, staring into my deep brown eyes. But the moment was surely ruined when my mother heard the voice of my drunken father cause a scene. In the process, tears of embarrassment streamed down with each step he took toward the room.

"Where my baby boy at?" he yelled at the top of his lungs, resting his forearm against the doorframe. Sitting on the bed, my mother shook her head and my drunken father finally entered the room.

"What's wrong with you?" He spoke rudely, ready to cause havoc. His words slurred, his body staggered toward the bed to look at my face. How dare this mutherfucker come see me fresh out the womb drunk as hell, talking shit to my mother? He had the nerve, as if she didn't just bring a part of him into this world by her damn self. Taking me from my mother's arms, he looked down on me with a smile on his face and a tear in his eye.

"He is so beautiful, Lola," he said, cradling me in his arms. This fool was so drunk, he never noticed the pink blanket the nurse wrapped me in. He just really wanted a boy.

"It's a girl, Carter. Now give me back my baby!" my mother yelled, holding her arms out. My crazy father went to curse my mother when the nurse interrupted. "I will take her sir," in all politeness.

"The hell you will, lady! This here is my child and it stays with me!" He left the nurse on stand with her arms extended for him to place me into them. The nurse looked to my mother for assistance with my father, but my mother's look let her know she was on her own.

"Can you please help me obtain the child, Ms. James? I have tests to run to make sure the baby is healthy."

"Damn, it's a girl?" My father was stunned. "I thought it was a boy." He stood there with a stupid-ass look on his face while every-body else in the room wanted me out of his drunken hands. But before my mother could say a word, my father snapped back to his reality.

"Here, you can take the little bitch!" He pushed me out of his arms into the next set of close-by arms.

"Why the hell do you have to come in here drunk, embarrassing me, Carter?!"

"I'm embarrassing you! Fuck that!! I'm embarrassed by you, bitch! Shut the hell up, woman. You don't know anything! I only had a few beers. Ain't nobody drunk!!" Slurring his words as he talked made sure that my mother wasn't okay to be left alone with his crazy ass. I can't believe he called me a bitch, though.

My father noticed the nurse's presence. Ready to curse my moth-er, he instead cursed her first.

"What the hell you still standing there for, bitch? Go take care of the damn baby." He talked in a tone that let the nurse know to put an egg in her shoe and beat it. She left the room, shaking her head in disgust at our dysfunctional family.

My father talked to my mother like she was a piece of shit. The nurse overheard and couldn't believe a man could be so cruel to the woman who just gave birth to his child. It was one conversation she wished she never heard.

"Can you stop yelling at me for one minute, Carter? Please! Before the man come and put you in jail for public intoxication. Can you, Carter? Please, please baby?" My mother begged that drunken, crazed fool to act civilized.

"Yeah, I can do that," he answered in slurred words as he took a seat in a nearby chair next to my mother's bed. On the real, he needed a second wind to rip into my mother's ass once again and she knew it. She laid back in her bed while my father sat and the nurse took watch on the room. Besides the chatter of the hallway, it was quiet in the room for the moment. My mother went to shut her eyes from the exhaustion of the day when my father spoke a kind word from his drunken lips. "She looks just like me. I'm sorry for all the pain I've put you through." He placed his hands over his face ashamed. "I can't deny our child any longer." A drunken tear fell.

"I told you, Carter, you got damn drunk. She is a perfect reflection of you. You can't keep doing this to me, to us, and now, to our family. You, me, and Egypt Winters, we can start over. You know we need a fresh start, a new beginning, honey." My mother gave a smile, even though she forced it. She wanted things to be right between them. Having little belief that my father would change, she still had to try for the sake of our family.

"How did you come up with such a beautiful name?" my father asked, pleased with my mother's decision.

"Egypt was a well-known place in the Bible for fallen soldiers in God's army, and with parents like us, she needs all of God's help just as Egypt did." My mother smiled from the thought. "I don't know why I gave her your last name. You won't be around that long to claim her anyway." Her smile faded, turning into a mask of anger. "You treated me like shit the whole time I carried your seed, you abusive asshole! All the other women you slept with, throwing them up in my face; the countless beatings, and all the nights I spent alone while you ran the streets drinking and drugging. I'm surprised Egypt made it to see the light of day. I was so unhealthy, carrying your baby." My mother finished expressing herself on feelings long overdue, and she hung her head low awaiting the aftermath.

"What the hell am I here for then?!" my father responded with fury. "Every time I try to be nice to your dumb ass, you piss me off!" He got up from the chair and threw it across the room. Dry mouth suddenly arose from the true words spoken from my mother. He had no choice but to chase the drink.

"Go ahead and run, you fucking coward! Me and my daughter don't need your sorry ass. Go and get a drink, you drunk mutherfucker!"

My mother yelled at the top of her lungs, crying so hard she could barely catch her breath.

Pushing those words out she thought to herself, *This can't be life, this can't be love, there has to be more then this shit she endured.*

My father walked out the door and down the hallway hearing not a word and not turning back. The attention was on my mother from every doctor and nurse that resided on the floor; they couldn't help but overhear the argument. The floor was quiet once again, only to hear my mother's pain as she sat alone wallowing in her tears.

The nurse returned shortly after the incident, consuming me in her arms as she thought we needed each other for strength and love. When she approached my mother's bedside to place me in her arms, her first born child, she turned her back on me and denied her daughter.

"Get her away from me. She is not a part of me. She was made from the devil himself! She looks just like him."

The nurse tried one more time to put me in her arms, but my

mother just screamed louder in denial. The nurse stood there, not knowing what to say or do. At last pulling me close, she walked me to the door. "It's not this child's fault who her parents are. She wants the same love and affection you do."

"Shut up, lady, and get that devil child away from me. You can keep your comments to you, yourself, and nobody else!"

"My name is Ms. Shirley Williams, not lady, Ms. James," the nurse replied, leaving the room in a hasty fashion.

The nurse looked upon my face with sympathy, wondering how such a pretty baby have no one to love her back. Disappointment set in as she thought about sending me to social services if my mother didn't have a change of heart by morning. But she thought it would be the best thing for me.

Cradling me close on the walk back to the nursery, she hummed a classic tune to soothe me and her soul. Placing me in my little crib with many blankets, she kissed my forehead goodnight.

I never shed a tear or gave a whimper as I laid in my crib in peace. I was even a soldier way back when, you feel me?

"Just give her some time, Egypt, she will come around. You're too beautiful not to love, baby," the nurse said, walking away from my crib to check on her other patients.

It had been a long day for Nurse Williams. She was appalled by the way young women were having babies, thinking it would keep a man. *If he didn't do you right, or love you before you got pregnant, what the hell makes you think he will after the baby is born? Oh, when will they learn, Lord, when will they learn?* The very thought made her stomach turn.

Nurse Williams soon left the hospital, needing the rest from a twelve-hour shift of pure hell. She wasn't about my parents' upbringing, but she knew they were unstable and unfit to raise a child. She felt obligated to make sure that my well-being was safe with both of them. My parents didn't look fit to take care of themselves let alone me. Nonetheless, she didn't want to pass judgment.

Trying to relax at home with her own family, she tried to stop thinking about me and my situation. The whole ordeal was too much for her. With her mind made up right, she decided in the early a.m., she would return to work to check on me.

At 6:43 a.m., Nurse Williams rushed through the double doors to the east wing of the hospital. She was hoping, wishing, and praying that me and my mother were okay and picked up her momentum to second gear. The elevator was crowded as usual on a Monday morning as she pushed past the work rush hurrying to press the twelfth-floor button. Getting frustrated at the slow movement of the elevator, she pressed the twelfth-floor button once again. She couldn't understand the connection between the two of us or why she cared so much, but she couldn't shake me from her soul. The crowded elevator seemed to stop at every floor, as a strange feeling of something wrong overwhelmed her body. People exiting and entering the elevator—and taking their good ol' time to punch the clock—made matters worse. She hit the twelfth floor with anticipation. "Finally," Nurse Williams said, passing through the work traffic and rushing out of the elevator.

Walking into the nursery, she scattered about through the cribs until she came across mine, as I lay alone. Sighing with relief, she picked me up and held me close.

"Your mother should be taking care of you right now. It's your feeding time, little one. I thought about you the whole time I was at home and have to thank God you're okay."

As she looked around the quiet room, Nurse Williams realized I was the only one there. Shaking her head sympathetically, she said, "I'm happy you're okay, Egypt." Sighing once again, she rocked me back and forth close to her bosom.

I squirmed about in her arms, giving off a smile, a burp and a shirt full of vomit. She laughed, placing me back down to clean me and herself off while reflecting on why my mother hadn't come for me yet.

"What is your mother's problem? She got me upset, ready to curse her out myself, and I'm a God-fearing woman. Please God, have mercy on my soul and keep me in my place as a nurse." Picking me up all nice and clean, she wrapped me up in another pink blanket to take me to my mother. Approaching my mother's room, the on-call nurse from last night walked past us, then suddenly stopped.

"Is that the Winters' baby you're holding?" she asked, turning around sharply.

"Yes. Why do you ask?" Nurse Williams replied.

"Because the mother went outside for a cigarette last night and never returned."

"You mean she never came back?"

"That's what I said," she responded quizzically. "I'm leaving for the day. I worked all night. I'll leave it up to you to call Child Welfare." And as quick as the on-call nurse appeared, she disappeared even faster into the stairwell.

Nurse Williams held me in her arms as sorrow overwhelmed her heart. She couldn't bring herself to call Child Welfare on me just yet. She had to figure out something else to do with me or my time at the hospital would be up. Turning to take me to the nursery, an idea crept into her conscience that just might work.

Magee Women's Hospital—where most of the inner-city women have their children—meant she had a shot at finding my mother. She thought she could check the medical records and convince her to come back for me or find a relative. Whatever the nurse was going to do, she had to move fast. In twenty-four hours, the hospital would step in with Child Welfare. Nurse Williams held the phone to her ear as it rang, searching her memory bank for the young lady's name in charge of the department. She couldn't recall the woman's name to save her life. *How can you ask someone for a favor when you can't remember their name?* she thought to herself. A young man—instead of the young woman—answered the phone, throwing her off track.

"Medical Records, this is Mr. Thorn. Can I help you, please?" He waited for an answer from the other end of the phone. "Hello? Can I help you?" His voice grew aggravated waiting for an answer.

"I apologize for the delay, but I was expecting Karyn White to pick up the phone." *Okay, that's her name,* she thought as she continued to talk. "By any chance, is she available?"

"No, ma'am, she won't be in today. Is there something I can help you with?"

"No!" The nurse slammed down the phone in his ear. "Dammit, she was supposed to be there," she thought out loud, considering her next move.

Forgetting about her duties as a nurse, she remained determined to find me care, custody, and control, at whatever cost. She left the room and headed for Medical Records to retrieve the information herself. Before going down the back stairwell to avoid co-workers, she peeked around the nurses' station to find my mother's chart. Lady Luck must have been on her side because my mother's chart was right there in plain sight, and there wasn't a soul in sight to ask questions. The nurse picked it up and was on her way. It was exactly 11:00 am when she reached the department in hopes of an easy quest. Nurse Williams stood outside the door, preparing herself to handle the situation and remain professional with her feelings so involved. What she really wanted was to run through there as if her hair was on fire, demanding everyone's expertise and understanding.

Putting on a calm face, she entered the office where a lot of familiar faces were doing their jobs. Looking around, she spotted a young woman no older than twenty-one in the far left corner. "You are the weakest link," Nurse Williams said with a smile that flashed all of her teeth.

"Ms. Tate, how are you doing today? You're looking busy this morning." The nurse put it on thick so the young woman would feel important and want to help her out with anything she needed. As the saying goes, you can catch more bees with honey than vinegar.

"Yes, ma'am, I've been busy all morning, but I'm getting ready to break for lunch," she replied graciously, happy someone even knew her name.

"Can you break for lunch a little later to help me out with something very important? It should only take about twenty minutes of your time."

"Sure. What is it you need me to do?" With a smile, Ms. Tate waited for instructions.

Handing Ms. Tate the chart, Nurse Williams told her to find out everything she could on my mother and relatives of any sort. "Mr. Thorn needs this information fast." Ms. Tate nodded and got right to it as the nurse gave details on why she had to have this done. "She has an outstanding medical bill that we need to get cleared up as soon as possible. We also think insurance fraud has played its part. So please go through the file quickly, but carefully, okay?"

"Yes, ma'am, I'm on it."

"I'll be back no later than half an hour to see what you come up with. I want to get that paperwork to Mr. Thorn as soon as possible." Walking away, Nurse Williams wiped the beads of sweat from her forehead with the back of her index finger. Going back to the twelfth floor, she decided to give my mother a call on the number from her chart. She knew it would do no good.

My mother wouldn't be found. She figured if my mother was going to come back for me, she would have done it by now.

Finding a phone close to the nursery, Nurse Williams felt safe to make that call. But deep down in her heart she knew it would be a dead end. "What do you say to a woman who has run out on her child?" The words danced on her lips as she dialed the number, but she didn't have to worry about what to say. The number was disconnected. "I hope and pray Ms. Tate comes up with something downstairs." She held back tears as she faced the fact that Child Welfare might end up with me.

Checking her watch every couple minutes until exactly twenty minutes later, she made a mad dash back to Medical Records check on things.

"I hope she found something to rescue this child from a system that has no love for our black children." The nurse muttered while dashing down the stairs. "Maybe I could take her." She shook her head so lightly, knowing her family would never approve. "Maybe Ms. James will come back… Oh, what should I do, dear Lord?"

Opening the door to the medical records department for the second time this morning, a sudden calm submerged her being. Walking toward Ms. Tate, she just knew something good had come across her desk.

"Ms. Tate, honey, what did you come up with?" the nurse asked brightly.

"I got a number and address," she replied with a huge grin. "It's someone who signed Ms. James' discharge papers not too long ago when she came in to get some x-rays on some bumps and bruises that magically appeared. I think it's her sister, a Diane Kingston James. She lives at 255 East Ohio Street, in a housing complex called Allegheny Commons, East Apartment 103-F."

The nurse couldn't believe what she had just heard—she heard hope in the making.

"I can fall to my knees, Lord, right here and now. When there is a will there is a way, when you trust and believe." Holding the information in her hand, the nurse thanked Ms. Tate with a hug.

"I will tell Mr. Thorn personally to thank you when he gets the chance."

"Excuse me, ma'am, can I ask you a question?" Ms. Tate asked, intrigued.

"Go ahead, honey."

"Did Ms. James really do what you said? It really doesn't matter now because the deed is done, but I don't want to lose my job by helping you out."

"You will not lose your job Ms. Tate as long as you keep this between you and me." The nurse parked her rump on the edge of Ms. Tate's desk. "No, Ms. James didn't do what I accused her of; it was something worse. You just saved her daughter's life, giving her a home maybe." Ms. Tate smiled, pleased with the nurse's answer. It was all she needed to hear.

"Hopefully it works out for the sake of the child. I'm glad you came to me," Ms. Tate said, nodding her head with respect.

Rushing back upstairs, Nurse Williams ran head on into her boss. "Excuse me, sir, there is a patient that requires my attention a.s.a.p."

"Well, I need to talk to you when you're not so busy," he said as she brushed past him.

Ignoring his request and skipping steps, she was out of breath when she reached the twelfth floor again. Returning to check on me, she questioned the staff on my well-being.

"Did she eat?" Nurse Williams asked.

"Yes she did," the on-call nursed answered.

"How much?"

"About four ounces of formula."

"Any problems with a bm?"

"No, she went fine for me about twenty minutes ago. I do know how to do my job," the on-call nurse said sarcastically.

"She is perfectly healthy," both nurses said, drawing the same conclusion.

"Just keep an eye on the James' child while I make a run for some lunch. And for the record, I know you know how to do your job. I apologize if I've made you feel incompetent."

"It's okay. It seems to me that you're under a lot of stress right now, so no offense taken. I can hold this down here. Just remember to bring me back a cheeseburger with everything on it."

"I can do that," Ms. Williams replied, heading out the door.

Deciding to talk to Diane James in person to discuss the matter at hand, she prayed to God that everything would work out in my favor. "Please, Lord, guide my words as they fall from my lips when representing little Egypt Winters' case to Ms. James, who just might be her aunt. Amen!"

Nurse Williams couldn't keep quiet for long behind the wheel of her car, putting God first in everything she did. Sounding more like a lawyer in court than a woman praying to the Lord, she had a good feeling that everything was going to work itself out. Not calling first wasn't the brightest idea, but if there was no one home she could always leave a note, Nurse Williams thought.

The complex was beautiful from the outside. Following the building numbers, she came across 103 shortly after pulling into the parking lot. Parking the car, she said one more short prayer before exiting her vehicle. Checking the door numbers on the townhouses, she realized she had to walk another flight of steps to reach 103-F. Catching her breath, she knocked hard standing more nervous than a hooker in church. No one answered, so she knocked again and again until her hand was tired. Reaching for the zipper of her purse to retrieve a piece of paper and a pen, she closed her eyes and took a deep breath. Going through her purse, the nurse never saw the tall, slender woman walking up the steps.

"Can I help you with something?" the woman asked, startling the nurse.

"Yes, you can. Do you know Ms. Diane James?" the nurse replied nervously.

"Yes. Who wants to know?"

"I'm Nurse Williams, and I'm trying to find a Ms. Lola James. She's missing, and I need to talk to her."

"She was having a baby the last I heard. I'm her sister. What do you mean she's missing?" Diane asked placing her hands on her hips.

"So you are her?? Diane, I'm so happy to see you!" Nurse Williams' eyes lit up, hugging Diane and going into detail before the woman could unlock her door and invite her in.

By the end of the story, Diane was in tears, telling the nurse she would meet her at the hospital around four o'clock to see her niece. Nurse Williams thanked Diane for taking time out to hear her. Giving one last hug, she left to finish her lunchtime mission.

It was four o'clock on the dot when Diane stepped off the elevator with another woman who was both Lola and Diane James' mother. Diane had called her mother as soon as she could get the door open, giving all the details the nurse had given her. Not surprisingly, Nurse Williams was right there by the elevator ready for the meet and greet. "I'm so happy you showed up. Who is this with you?"

"This is my mother." Diane spoke with pride.

"How are you doing today, ma'am?" Nurse Williams asked with her hand extended for a formal greeting. Ms. James pushed past her hand and embraced her. "Thank you for what you've done for my family. You didn't have to do all this, but you have, and I'm so grateful to you." They all walked to the nursery, where Nurse Williams handed me to Diane, who held me for the first time with tears in her eyes.

"Meet Egypt Winters, your niece, and your grandchild. Your daughter named her before she took off."

"Her name is so adorable, Momma, isn't it?" Standing there holding me, my Aunt Diane couldn't believe what her sister had done. Handing me over to my grandmother, she shook her head in disgust.

"Thank you for this nurse, thank you…"

I MAY WALK THROUGH THE VALLEY AS DARK AS DEATH, BUT I WON'T BE AFRAID. YOU ARE WITH ME, AND YOUR SHEPHERD'S ROD MAKES ME FEEL SAFE.

PSALM 23:4

CHAPTER THREE

Every day of the year I'm reminded of my mother's abandonment, but my birthday was the worst. My mother left me in the hospital the day I was born to defend myself. My grandmother told me the story way too often and her words never changed, not one. Nurse Williams will always be the nurse God sent to protect me, let grandma say.

It was June 2, 1992 and my sweet sixteen. Happy birthday to me, myself and I. Hanging around the house with my grandma listening to old wive's tales on how shit was way back in her day, I sat restless. I should be grateful, she said, every day of my life that we had each other in our lives. Waiting for Diane to pick me up for shopping, I grew weary fast, sucking down my second cigarette. If she didn't come through soon I was heading for Downtown on my own to steal me a birthday suit.

Diane wouldn't let me get too far, as she always rode my heels, never going too far herself. She felt she had to keep an eye on me becoming a woman and hate on me enough to keep me a virgin; now picture that. A woman is going to do what she wants when she wants.

Nobody ever said anything about my parents or their whereabouts, even though I asked repeatedly. And then one day, I just stopped asking because I didn't care anymore.

My grandmother quoted herself on many occasions that she will hate my mother with every breath in her body for leaving me the way that she did. I don't think she really felt that way about her own child, but she didn't want me to feel alone or wrong in my perception of her neither. My grandmother always tried so hard to make me feel comfortable and loved in her household.

Nope, the bitch never came back for me. No phone calls and no letters. My grandma hasn't had a number change since the day she left. At one point in time, my grandma had it out with the phone company just for that reason. And she wouldn't change it. They offered her a free month, but she wouldn't budge. I don't know why they wanted her to change it, but it was a no-go. Late nights—and there were many—both me and my grandmother would wait by the phone for a call, but there was nothing. We both thought maybe one day she would pick up to call, and when she did, my grandma wanted her to get through on the line. My grandma will die in this house awaiting that phone call.

I grew up to become a nice-looking young lady, but I always felt better about myself running around tomboyish. I pulled hoes either way it went down that morning, no matter what dress code I was rocking.

"Chile, you still waiting on your auntie?"

"Yes, ma'am, I don't know where she at with her drama-having ass."

"Watch your mouth, chile! Watch your mouth!"

Anyway, me and Diane been drinking buddies since I was about fourteen years old and she schooled me on how not to keep a man. Diane lived three doors down from my grandma, so we spent a lot of time with each other, good and bad. I often watched her daughter, my cousin Chase, who is six years younger than me. I did that to hang out in her apartment and play grown-up with my boyfriend. Diane had a schedule that revolved around two things: her job and fucking, which left no time for her own daughter. She was such a damn hoe.

Me and my cousin Chase were close, only for the reason of me feeling bad for her. She had a mother who didn't care, and me, I had a mother who was the unknown. My aunt didn't pay that girl any attention, unless I included her, which was rarely. I envied my cousin for having a mother and I didn't. I sought all of Diane's love and affection, even though I couldn't stand her. I was selfish and only out for me. I always got what I wanted and moved by playing the best friend role. And I was seen just as that. What me and Chase didn't know was we were pawns and rooks in the chess game Diane played with our lives.

So many nights Diane would come in with a random date that went to hell, sending her daughter to bed without a hug or a kiss. But me, I was the bartender to the bar she had set up in her kitchen. Diane introduced me to the drinking game early in life. She taught me how to cover the pain. On those nights, we took shots back one by one, downing 100 proof gin.

Taking away the agony weighing down our hearts, we sang slow jams by the one and only Mariah Carey while swapping broken-hearted stories. At the age of fifteen, I was a professional bartender who could drink a grown woman under the table and kill the mic at karaoke.

Through laughter and tears, Diane and I opened up to each other. Sharing our different experiences we had in life and men. I let her do most of the talking though, controlling the conversation so I could learn from her mistakes. Diane thought she was smart, but not smart enough. Always on my toes, going off my gut feeling, I knew she was setting me up for the kill every time she tried. She always wanted me to reveal steaming hot details of my love life; however, she showed me that wasn't a smart move.

I was drunk constantly, but not stupid, staying two feet ahead of her game at all times. I was fifteen years old doing what grown wom-en do, and my auntie was thirty-two acting out like a teenager in heat.

My grandmother could never understand the connection between us two and would have killed Diane dead if she knew about my drink-ing sessions. The only thing we let Grandma in on was the shopping sprees we had so often, compliments of the Double D boys and their pockets. It was to the point that my friends and my man were com-plaining about how much time we spent together up in her apartment.

RING! RING! RING!

"Holla at the birthday bitch!" I scream into the telephone, hoping it's for me.

"Happy birthday, baby." A suave voice took over the phone.

"Where the fuck you been at all morning? You all calling up here with that sexy shit, so I know your ass is up to no good." Talking a mile a minute, I don't let the suave voice get a word in. "I was hoping your dumb-ass was Diane so I can get to the mall. Anyway, I've been on your heels all morning, calling your house since nine o'clock! Let me find out you been creeping up Brandy's again and I will fuck you and that bitch up, you dig me A.J.? I don't give a fuck about her being your baby mama!"

"Damn, girl! Can I get a hello, a how you doing, better yet, a thank you, before you start talking shit!? I wasn't even with dat girl! I was out buying your dumbass a birthday gift!"

"All morning, A.J.??? Nigga, please!"

"Yeah, all morning!! Soften up your tone of voice and get at me later." CLICK!!!!!!!!

"No, this mutherfucker didn't hang up on me!" My shout echoed off the walls of the kitchen.

"Didn't I tell you to watch your mouth, chile?" It's so funny how my grandma always appears when I want to curse someone out.

"Yes, ma'am, you did," I answered in a respectable tone.

"Then watch your mouth in here, in this house! I'm not going to tell you again. You're getting too grown for your own britches, young lady."

"Grandma... Please roll off... Please." My attitude was shot as I raised my voice.

"You love that MF word too much and you always have, Egypt. Be a lady in the mouth, chile," my grandmother replied, eyes upturned with a sly smirk.

I stood there holding the phone, listening to Mr. Dial Tone sing me a lullaby in my ear. I kinda feel bad for not saying thank you to my baby A.J., but what the fuck, he ain't 'bout nothing.

A.J. was just a knockoff of my ex-boyfriend, Trap. I wanted to marry him and have kids with a big house and a picket fence. I spent time with A.J. to keep my mind off of that sexy-ass man known as Trap. And A.J. with that magnificent head game he had, with that tongue, always kept me coming back for more. Damn, that nigga can eat some pussy with all jokes aside. His peanut-butter skin and that short, stocky, football-body structure was appealing to my eyes, and he had a smile that could bag any woman's ass he wanted.

His baby momma was twenty-five and counting, and A.J. was only seventeen, having his first born at fifteen. Yeah yup, that nasty trick Brandy was breaking the law for real when she opened her legs for him. And what grown-ass woman wants to have a baby by a baby? A dumb one, that's who. She must have been hooked on that tongue just as I, but feelings I don't have, and I don't think I ever will in this lifetime. All in all, he was mines, and I don't share my shit with nobody else. What's mine is mines and what's his is mines, too.

Taking a deep breath, I lit a cigarette, picking up the telephone to call A.J. back to apologize for two reasons only: my birthday gift and some of that bomb-ass head game to make the rest of the night the shit. Reaching to hit the last number, guess who comes through? Diane, snatching the receiver out of my hand and hanging up.

"Happy birthday, girl!" Diane shouted with haterism all in her voice. "I had to get my hair done. That's what took me so long. I like it, Egypt, do you?" I stand there with my hands on my hips and my eyes to the sky. Her hair looked like a nappy bird's nest. "Your girl hooked me up in 108-E. Whatcha think?"

"You should go right back over there and fight her," I answered with a devilish grin, anticipating the next question she would ask.

"Why you say that, smartass?" Diane asked, patting her fucked-up hairdo.

"So you can whip that ass for her fucking up your hair like that." As soon as the words fell off my lips, grandma was laughing with me at Diane.

"Chile, she do have a point. Your head is a hot mess. I done told you to start acting your age and not your shoe size. Calm your body down, chile, and act your age, Diane… act your age."

"Whatever, Ma. Ya'll opinions don't count anyway, as long as my man like it," Diane replied, looking over her hairdo in the mirror that was hanging over the couch.

"Since you out there getting your hair done, I hope you got my money you owe me," Grandma spoke while parking her rump in a seat on the couch.

"Dang, Ma, I got it!" Diane yelled back disrespectfully. "I was gonna give it to E like you told me to."

"Well, I want to see you put it in her hand so the both of you can get out of my hair." Diane pulled a bank envelope from her pocket with a sick look on her face. Peeling off three crispy one hundred dollar bills, my eyes grew bigger and bigger. Placing them in my hand set off the fireworks as I screamed thank you to my grandma hugging and kissing on her.

"All this for me? I can't believe it, Grandma. This is the best birthday present ya'll could have gave a sixteen-year-old teenager."

Running to Diane's car ready to get my shop on, I had to laugh once again about the fucked-up hairdo Diane sported. It wasn't really fucked up; it was just an old-school hairstyle dumbed down completely. The hair style itself was just too young for my aunt. Lady did it as a favor to me, plus she wanted to get back at Diane for fucking her man. She was going to make her hair fall out, but I begged her not to. I knew Diane would try to out shine me on my day, but I shut shit down, always two feet ahead of her game.

The parking lot was packed at the mall, even in the mid-afternoon. Everybody normal should be at work, but it looked like everybody is selling drugs nowadays. Nonetheless, we managed to find a close parking spot next to the entrance of the shopping center. Hopping out the car after occupying a handicap spot, Diane looked around and busted out with a limp as if she needed a cane. As we both laughed out loud, we hit the entrance with force, making our presence known. I had five large ones in my pocket—three from Grandma and two I'd stashed away for this very day—and I was ready to spend every last red cent to make sure I looked excellent. That's what I always strived for, excellence. It would have been enjoyable, though, to hit the downtown area to check out the chocolate boy wonders comb the streets to get dope-boy fresh, but what the hell, you never know what lurks around these department stores. I just might catch a date. Diane going her way and me going mine, I didn't have a clue on what to wear. Mary J. Blige was fresh on the scene with a new wicked b-boy, but sexy, smooth and direct style of her own that was taking over the summer and it was hot. I love her jam *Real Love*; it's the shit. Everybody wants to be in love, ya dig me?

Foot Locker was packed from wall to wall with bodies as I walked in to see what I could come up with. Every type of male figure you could think of was standing around waiting to place their order for a pair of Nike Air Jordan's that just hit the sales floor. If you wanted a date, be in Foot Locker the day a new pair of them was hitting the stands and you will succeed in your mission every time. I wasn't prepared to find a date. My one-track mind was on striking gold with the perfect outfit. Window shopping the unfamiliar faces, I started my search for a pair of Air Max. An authentic Pittsburgh Pirate's baseball jersey cut me off in mid search, creating a picture of myself as Mary J. Blige in the video *Real Love*. It would have to match up perfect to the queen of R&B and hip hop if I wanted to pull it off. And who else would you want to look like in this day and age? The girl is young, black and beautiful. Thinking to myself, I visualized the achieved goal, grabbing up a fitted hat to match, a black sports bra and a pair of all white Air Max.

Approaching a sales rep to get my shoe size, I run into my ex boy-friend Trap. What fucking bad luck do I got!? Very bad luck just to see his face, period. Trying to turn around quickly to go the other way, I could feel his breath on the back of my neck.

"Happy birthday, sexy." He spoke smooth and passionate on the rim of my ear, his warm breath made me want to take my panties off right there in the store.

"Please, go 'head, Trap." The words trembled off my lips in fear of his touch.

"I just want to know how you doing. Don't push me away, boo."

I stood there with my back to him. I was scared to look in his smokey brown eyes. As his words hung in the air between us, I couldn't speak or move.

"Long time no see, but I do know today is your birthday. How can I forget that? We Scorpios and Leos have very passionate sex, don't you agree?"

I fluttered with anger when the word sex came up. He left out one minor detail on why we weren't having it anytime or anywhere. I turned around feisty and my body language spoke loudly. He had struck a nerve.

"You're a foul-ass nigga, Trap. Don't talk any sex shit to me. You know you fucked that all up, so don't reminisce on nothing that can never be."

"Damn, you can't say thank you for me wishing you a happy birth-day?" He stood there looking like a double scoop of Morris Chestnut, nibbling on his bottom lip with that Nino Brown running the city sex appeal. I wanted to kiss his full-sized lips while he held me in that strapping frame of his. I can imagine just how good his tantalizing neck smells. "Why you standing there sizing me up? What's on your mind, boo?" As he stood there licking his lips, my heart skipped a beat and my middle spot splashed. I knew then I had to disengage myself from this situation.

"Thank you for the happy birthday and goodbye, Trap." As I walked away, he grabbed me, forcing our eyes to lock.

"You've forgiven her, but why not me? You running around with that lame-ass nigga A.J., who playing you anyway." The left side of his lip flared up with anger. "I know I look better than his no-money-getting ass, plus I seen his bitch-ass creeping this morning from Brandy's nasty-ass house."

"What-the-hell-ever, Trap. No matter what you say to me, I can't forgive you for what you did. Didn't nobody owe me shit in our relationship but you. You did what you did and now it's over."

Looking me up and down, he gazed his puppy dog eyes at me. He reached in his pocket, giving me a reason to watch him as he pulled out a fat knot of money. Placing five twenty dollar bills in my palm and turning my hand over to kiss the back, he winked his right eye, disappearing back into the store crowd.

Standing there all moist between my legs, I didn't realize my mouth was hanging open or the mousey little white girl asking me if I needed anything else. The cashier counter was hidden behind people and the line was ridiculous, but I saw no Trap. The manager came over the loud speaker requesting everyone to leave if they were done making their purchases or security would be called for safety purposes. The dudes tried to play it hard, still hanging around only for moments to impress the females, but most of the drug-dealing crowd moved on. You could tell the niggas with no money in the store. Those were the ones acting like they had major dollars to spend with their loud mouths.

"Did anybody help you today?" The mousey girl had returned to my vision just as sweet with a pleasant tone.

"Nope, but I'll take this Air Max in a size six."

"Okay, I can take you next over here at the counter." As I followed her lead, I glanced over the store once more for Trap and that thuggish walk.

"Did you find everything you were looking for okay?"

"Yeah yup." I put my stuff on the counter and reached for the dough in my pocket. My brain was on freeze, wanting and needing my ex back in my life.

"With everything plus tax, you're looking at one hundred and eighty-seven dollars."

Paying the sales clerk, I grabbed my bags off the counter, heading for the exit with the quickness, trying to catch one last glimpse of the forbidden fruit.

A straight thug from the streets, he was playing the part of 2Pac in *Juice* to the fullest. I wonder if Diane has seen him yet with her nasty ass. I can't believe she fucked my man. What kinda person gets her niece drunk to the point of pass out and sleeps with her boyfriend? How did I not investigate when I heard the moaning? How could she be so foul, and how could I be so stupid to leave a hoe around my man? Where that nasty bitch at anyway? I stretched my neck and opened my eyes wide, putting out a red alert on both of them.

He will always be my first love, my first relationship, and my first lover. "Damn!" I stomp my feet as the tears roll down. Now I'm crying, and it's supposed to be my day. Rushing to the restroom, passing everybody in line, I couldn't hold the tears back. I pushed past an elderly woman about to occupy a bathroom stall, slamming the door shut in her face. Sitting on the diseased toilet seat my face fell into my hands as my emotions took over my being. I wish my cousin Chase would have never told me that heartbreaking shit. That little bitch had a motive of her own for letting the truth be known. I can't knock her, though, because if I had the card I would've played it also. She wanted her mother to herself by any means and me out of the picture. I can understand my cousin and her motives of wanting the love and affection she deserved from her mother.

I would have rather shared Trap without knowing a thing than knowing and having to let go of him completely. How could I compete with Diane without me knowing? She was far more experienced than me and I couldn't win that game, only having sex for a year or so. I wonder if he goes past her house and still hit that off? I swear if I catch the two together I'm going in hard. I'ma have lockjaw on somebody's neck like a pit bull in attack mode. I lit up a cigarette in the non-smoking bathroom to release some tension. I promised myself to never get caught slipping again. Never trust your man around friend or foe; it's a no-no. That was the first rule I had to learn the hard way when it came to relationships.

"Oh, God, I can't believe I'm still in this bathroom stall breaking down!" I yelled at myself as I got up and pulled it together, reminding myself who's day it was. Giving myself a pep talk, I washed my hands and splashed water on my face. I got to be that bitch. I don't have any time for tears.

I'm ashamed that Trap can pull me out of character even though he's been out of my life for a couple of months. I made it up in my mind at that moment it wouldn't happen again. The mall bathroom suddenly became small as my red eyes calmed down. It was time for me to get back to shopping.

The shopping center was clearing out with no sign of Trap or Diane for that matter as I finished shopping for my outfit.

"Let me catch them two together and I swear…"

"You swear what?"

"Damn, Diane, you scared the hell out of me! Don't be sneaking up on me like that."

"You don't need to be talking to your damn self neither. You got people looking at you all strange and shit. Where you been? I've been looking for you over the last half hour."

I held onto my anger in search of an answer. "I was just doing my thing. You see the bags? I bet you you will never believe what I did."

"What your bad ass done did? You better not have been in here stealing out of these stores."

"Shut up, Diane!" I said sarcastically. "I ain't stole shit today but some thug-ass nigga's heart. I copied Mary J. Blige's whole get up. I bought everything she wore in that video. Diane gave me a curious stare, checking my bags. Giving them a quick glance over, a burst of laughter came about as she discovered I even bought the knee pads to make the outfit complete.

"I can't believe you, Egypt." Diane chuckled once again. "You in this outfit is a must..."

On our way back to the car I had to ask the question. "Did you see Trap in the mall?" Diane cut her eyes at me opening up the car doors.

"Nope, I didn't see him at all, and I'm glad."

That's it? That's all she got to say about it? She lying, but I'm gonna let it fly for now. She ain't even ask me why. A dead fucking giveaway that she had seen him. Straight sneaky-ass bitch!

Warren G came on the radio as we rolled down the street and I tried my best to consume myself with his hit record.

"You know what?" I spoke up over the radio, and I could see Diane taking a deep breath. "What girl?" she replied, annoyed.

"I forgot to call A.J. back. We got into it earlier and he hung up on me." I threw that information out there just to ease the tension I seen creep across her face when I mentioned Trap's name. "That's who you clicked off when you came in the door raving about that fucked-up hairdo you got." I could feel the evil stare Diane gave off without even looking her way.

"Serves his bum ass right anyway. I don't know what you see in him."

Yeah, he was a bum-ass nigga indeed, but he made time for me when I needed it. Me and A.J. (always known as (aka) Action Jackson, real name by his mother, Andrew Jones) had a relationship which caused us to be angry at each other most of the time. Many of the fights we endured were from the insecurity Trap placed over my heart with his betrayal. Sometimes I know I drive him right into the arms of Brandy to find peace. He had shown up six months before I ended it with Trap and when I did, he was the comfort zone as he licked all my pain away. I was always looking for someone to spend time with as Trap became more loyal to the streets. And A.J. caught my eye just being the opposite of him.

Living in the Commons, everybody knew everybody and we who lived there stayed there. It was a middle-class project with our own park, basketball and tennis courts and a neighborhood pool to seal the deal. Everyone from Manchester to Northview Heights came down to the Commons to play. A.J. would come through and play craps with the niggas who lived down there; nonetheless, he earned his respect and cool points by lighting up the hoop court with a three-point shooting game that was insane. He would work the basketball court until the late hours of the night to make it possible to crash at someone's house. After about a year of hanging out down our way, he convinced his mother to become an official resident of the Allegheny East Commons.

At twenty-two, A.J. was childish as hell, keeping up appearances in every young buck's face. I often sat on the sidelines, watching him at work. He had all the game on the court, however, none with the ladies. He had no game, no car and no money to flash around. I liked that he had to be himself and couldn't hide behind the streets. He didn't have anything to hide his true self. The nakedness showed his true character, whatever the hell it was.

Sneaking out the house in the middle of the night to meet Trap, I was thinking no one was watching. Nonetheless, A.J. was in the shadows of the night doing his own dirt. That's how our paths crossed, and I became the object of his ridicule. He would always find a way to clown me around my girls, cracking jokes on my late-night rendez-vous. It really didn't mean shit to me about what he saw. Nobody ever laughed at what he said, so I just waved him off. I had to put his name on the top of my stalker list.

"When you gonna stop letting that nigga use you for a booty call and get with a real nigga?" A.J. would say. "How come whoever you're meeting can't pick you up at a decent hour?"

I would roll my eyes and stomp my feet at the questions he always threw at me. He made me sick acting like the hood reporter for the Channel Six News. On the real, I wanted to curse him out for putting me on blast, but my girl got fed up first and called the shot.

"If you want her nigga, speak ya peace. If not, ease up, playboy! We tired of you gossiping like a woman!" Sasha was my girl, and I remember this shit like it was yesterday, waiting on dirty Diane to get me to the crib so I could get ready.

Anger painted A.J.'s face red, but his response played it cool when he invited us to his crib to chill and lay while drinking. He was the sexiest Super-Nintendo, spades-playing, crap-shooting, 40-ounce-drinking, no-hustle-game-having, broke-ass, lame-ass nigga I had come across. Truth be told, I liked him from the door. He was lame and on the low. I was too, but I would never live up to it.

A.J. didn't comment on the remark that my girl Sasha made, and he didn't deny the facts of either accusation as I smiled on the inside, not wanting him or others to know I was digging in the dirt on him hard. Declining his invitation the first night didn't stop him. We managed to become friends, spending a lot of alone time in his bedroom playing video games and watching old gangster flicks.

"Egypt, what you doing over there? You don't hear me talking to you?" Diane shouted, bringing me back to reality. She ice grilling me hard, as if I stole something. "You always daydreaming, Egypt. Wake the hell up!"

"I hear you now, so what?"

"So what," Diane replied with upturned eyes. "Your mouth is so smart sometimes, but I'm still going to be nice since it's your birthday and buy you ten bottles of Sisco to show off with your friends." My face lit up once again with a huge smile requesting my favorite flavor.

"Strawberry, baby, you know that's all I drink." I hopped around in the front seat of her car like a kid in a candy store. My face turned from a frown to a smile, loving Diane for the moment. But my heart wouldn't let me get too excited. I question her motive behind her charity. It wasn't nothing but a petty move for doing what she did with Trap, nasty bitch.

"You better not tell my mother or go home drunk as hell, disrespecting. If you can't stand, you better rest your neck where you party at."

In my mind, I had to react to her bossy tone with a bitch please, but I answered back with a "Yeah, I got you, Dee, and thanks for the bottles. You should be grateful you got a thank you. I haven't been giving them out at all today."

"Ain't that about a bitch? You got it fucked up!" Diane played a sly smirk upon her face. "It's always please and thank you when it comes to me." Diane pulled up into the liquor store parking lot and we went back and forth with sneeringly remarks.

Diane was in the liquor store for damn near a half hour. I knew when she returned it would be about some nigga. I could see her from the car window putting her big ass titties in the cashier's face as she smiled from ear to ear, working him over slow. Bell, Biv, and Devoe tried to school these dumbass niggas, telling them never trust a big butt and a smile. But something about Diane I got to give her, because she can have any man she wants by using what she got to get what she wants.

Next thing I see is this old head carrying all the bags plus a box of flutes, which I love to pop off with. Opening up the back door, he placed the bags on the floor and the glasses in my hands as I reached for them, telling Diane he would stop pass later on this evening. Diane couldn't even get the car door shut before she spilled the beans on how she gamed him into only paying for five bottles of Sisco and getting the champagne flutes for free.

"You gave him some pussy, didn't you, Diane?!" I cut into her speech, shaking my head in disbelief.

"I sure did. Let him lick me from the back to the front!" She screeched while the car swerved to the left, scaring the hell out of both of us.

"So why did you pay for anything?" The car filled with laughter as I doubled over in pain from giggling so hard. "You know you lying woman. You gave that old dude some pussy." I continued on laughing as Diane slammed on the brakes to keep from hitting the car in front of us.

"You're always talking shit, Egypt! You need to learn when to shut the fuck up! If I did give him some pussy, you're benefiting from it and I did this shit here for you. Anyway, we had to make it look good for the camera, so stop laughing you little bitch." I can't believe she would try to pin her promiscuity on me, embarrassed about what she done because we both know she doesn't care. She's a Burger King bitch— you can have it your way.

"Me and you are having the first drink before you act an ass. I want to make a toast to my favorite niece. After you get dressed, make sure you stop by my apartment before you start your evening." Diane pulled into the housing complex with an attitude, but I overlooked it.

"Yeah, right, Diane. Favorite niece my ass; I'm your only niece." She pulled up in front of the house, slamming down on the brakes once again. This time she was being smart, causing me to hit my head off the dashboard.

"Why do you always have to have the last word with that smart-ass mouth? Go ahead and get up out the car. Go pull yourself together while I go handle some business." I should have punched her in the face for causing me to hit my head, but I let it pass since she did buy the alcohol. I exited the vehicle with style and grace, happy as hell I had mad shopping bags. Speeding off into the sunset, I couldn't even get the door shut before Diane pulled off with my arm. Checking out the crib, I discovered Grandma wasn't home. I felt a jam session coming on, with Mary J. Blige's name written all over it. The coast was clear and Mary sang *Love No Limit* loudly from the bleeding speakers. I stood in front of my mirror in my room creating the outfit to look just like Mary in *Real Love*. It came together too fast after I shit, showered and shaved. I put on some Mac lip gloss to make a smooth transition complete. Grandma must have been at church praying to her God that never answers when she down on her knees knocking at the door. I've knocked at his door down on my knees asking him to bring my mother back to me for years. And what happens? Not a damn thing. It's been sixteen years today, and I've come a long way from those crying nights I used to have.

I remember gazing into my mother's eyes in her beautiful picture my grandma kept close to her bedside. So many nights I've spent alone wondering why she doesn't love me. My heart ached for her in the morning on the first day of school, noon and night, when I had bad dreams and grandma couldn't come for me. I couldn't do nothing else but pray through my tears of pain and agony. You need a license to drive a car, even to shoot a rabbit, but they will let anybody become a parent.

My mother would always be dead in my grandma's eyes and I felt her on that comment. I respected her feelings but I would do anything to feel her embrace around my being. Today is a new day though. I'm leaving all this shit in the past as I come into womanhood with a lot of different emotions which I will unleash in due time.

The love I once yearned for from Lola is no longer needed. It's been consumed by hate wrapped in pain and sorrow. Looking at myself in the mirror, I felt Mary J. as she sang the track with her and her man, K.C., from the hit group Jodeci, *I Don't Want to Do Anything Else*. I sang along with the track, gawking at my own reflection, as if I just stepped off the *Real Love* video shoot. From my hair, hanging out of the top of my fitted hat, to the knee pads covering up my caps, I had pulled it off.

"What's the 411?" I shout at me, myself and I at the top of my lungs. I couldn't wait until somebody saw me in this outfit; it was the bomb.

"Egypt, are you crazy, chile? Look at you in that get up and go. You look crazy as hell."

My grandmother shook her head. "I want you to go down there in that living room and cut that sad music off."

"I didn't hear you come in, Grandma, I'll go turn it down, but why do I have to cut it off? You know Mary J. is meant to be played loud in surround sound."

"That's why you couldn't hear me come in. You couldn't hear the door open over the loud music, chile. If somebody wanted to come in here and kill you, or steal your milk and cookies, it wouldn't be hard to get you because you can't hear anything but Mary J. Blige. Now tell me what the knee pads are for? You got a lot of things running through this old lady head right now."

"It's Mary J. Blige's style, Grandma, and everybody is gonna want to bite my style in the next couple of days. You know how small the Commons is. It's going to spread like wildfire, just watch and see."

"Ain't you sick of Mary J. Blige, Egypt? Ain't you!? I'm not liking you dressed up like her. You should want to be yourself." Grandma shook her head with a smile. " You don't have to turn it off, just turn it down and play something else on my stereo. Give that chile a rest on that tape!"

I ran down the steps because that was it for my girl Mary J. Anyway, it was time to go. Grandma had spoken, giving the last say of the matter and wanted the music off. It was true, though—I do play the tape way too often. I would come home to my girl later and sing myself to sleep.

Taking one last look in the mirror, I blew a kiss to myself. I kissed my grandmother on the cheek, told her she was the only woman I loved in my life, and I was out the door. Then I realized I hadn't called A.J. back from earlier today when I hung up on him. Going back through the door, I checked with Grandma to see if he had called back, but he hadn't. I picked up the phone and dialed his number. I felt bad on how I acted out earlier, willing to apologize for my actions.

"Hello, Ms. Jones, may I speak to A.J. please?"

"Who is this calling?" My nostrils flared up by her question as well as her tone of voice. What does she mean by who's calling, as if I don't call there every day?

"It's me, Ms. Jones, your daughter-in-law." I answered calm, even though I wanted to scream.

"Oh, baby, I'm sorry, I couldn't catch your voice. I heard A.J. talking earlier about some party he was going to. I'm guessing he is there with those hoodlum friends of his he hangs out with."

"Do you know where the party is at, or who's throwing it, Ms. Jones?"

"No, I didn't hear him say anything else about it, but if he wanted you there or wanted you to know he would have taken you with, don't you think so? Today is your birthday, right?"

Oh, no, this bitch didn't read me like that! ran through my mind. I clenched my fist, ready to hit the wall. I swallowed my pride slowly, taking a deep breath so I wouldn't curse the bitch out. She was A.J.'s mother, so I had to respect her.

"Yes, it is my birthday, ma'am, and you are right, so I gotta go now." Slamming the phone down, I kept my composure as my grandmother taught me to respect my elders.

RING! RING! RING!

"Who is this? Speaking is the birthday bitch," I answered the phone temperamental, ready for a drink to calm my nerves the hell down.

"It's Diane, Egypt! Where the hell are you at?"

"I'm three doors down from you. Didn't you just call the house?" We both laugh at my smart-ass comment, moving passed the sarcasm.

"You're so smart, smartass! Now hurry the hell up and come get that drink. What are you doing over there? Trying to call Mary, I bet you, but guess what, E, you don't have the number. HA HA HA." The bitch laughed at her tired ass joke as I shake my head in disgust.

"You think you're so funny, bitch. I'll be there in a minute."

"Watch your mouth and save your teeth, young buck. Hurry up!"

The door was locked as I checked the knob to Diane's apartment and the music was on blast. I swear this female is nuttier than a fruit-cake. What is she up to? She never has the door locked, on the prowl for a suspect to come walking in to catch her naked. She is such a hoe.

"Why you didn't knock on the door, stupid? You just standing there looking into space." I grab my chest and swallow my heart as Diane caught me by surprise.

"First off, you scared the hell out of me swinging the door open like that. Why would you tell me to come over and then lock the door on me? And what's up with that?! You never lock the door. Just move out the way, Diane, I need a drink, A.J.'s mom done pissed me off." I push past her heading straight to the bar. "I still have to find somebody to party with. I refuse to be in the house getting drunk with you on my sweet sixteen."

Diane followed behind me as I walked into the kitchen. "Don't worry about it, Egypt." Diane handed me a champagne flute filled with Strawberry Sisco. "To my niece." We raised the flutes, and I had nothing else on my face but a smile. "I give you all the love your heart can take. You've reached a point in your life where nobody can tell you nothing, and you don't believe your shit stink. So on that note, sip slow, get money, keep your head up, eyes open, thong on ice and get a hustle. Happy birthday, woman, this night belongs to you." Clinking glasses and giving hugs, Diane stood back to capture the reaction as I heard many voices scream "Surprise! Happy birthday, Egypt!!"

Real Love bounced off the walls on blast, and me, I played it off cool as I moved through the apartment in shock for what my aunt had done for me.

Everybody on my everyday status graced my presence with a bottle of Sisco in one hand and a 40-ounce in the other, pumping to the bass of the sounds ready to get their house party on. A.J. was posted up by the stereo system playing D.J. to the many CD's that Diane had with the same Pittsburgh Pirates jersey I had on. Staring at me with those big brown, wanting eyes, my pussy got wet instantly. His demeanor was extremely sexy and I could have peeled his clothes off right there in this crowded room, dropping down to my knees to please him most definitely. I walked over with lust set in my veins, approaching my prey.

"Why are you standing over here all alone? Don't you have a date, playboy?" I'm in his left ear seductively wanting to role play.

"My woman played me. She went to a party without me, turning sixteen and all... So what's up with you?" A.J. was right on the money, playing into my hand, making me want him more.

"I'll do something that your girl wouldn't do. Meet me in the bathroom when you see me hit the bottom of the steps." Giving a nod to my invite, those wanting eyes gave off the sexiest energy, heating up my middle spot. I shook the look off, mingling amongst the mixed crowd of my friends, with Diane becoming the life of the party. There she was with a couple of the girls we hung out with at least four times a week at her crib in the open bar acting a damn fool. We all knew it was coming—with all the young dick in the air, as well as the liquor she could blame it on in the morning. She could be so immature at times. The spotlight she creates malfunctions under the influence of alcohol and she comes out on the front page of the gossip column every time. One day she will learn bad bitches move in silence, but until then, I will hear about my aunt and her lewdness off the lips of the townspeople.

That's what excited me the most—the gossip and the evil things women do. I had quit hanging out with females my age, wanting to be in this space, wanting to be grown up and do grown-up things, becoming an adult with everything and anything that came along with it.

(Singing) "You, you remind me of a love that I once knew. Is it a dream or is it déjà vu? I just had to let you know, so I got to sing it for you, boy, I don't know. The way you walk and the way you talk, I really like your groove and the way you dress the way you dance, I really like your moves, baby. You remind me, yes you do."

"Check you out in here, singing your little heart out, dressed to impress, lil' Mary J. Blige. You're rocking that shit hard girl, and you know I'm all in that next week for the skating party since you too grown to make an appearance." I turned around from the bar to see the face of the only friend I had my age. We gave smooches to each other, conceited, falling into an embrace. "What up, bitch? I thought you was Mary for real, girl, ya hot like fire."

I posed for the imaginary camera taking a cover shot as she handed off a blunt she was smoking. I hit up my stash of the Sisco bottles I had hidden under the sink in the kitchen, passing her one off with a devilish grin.

"I know, boo, I do look too hot for TV. And no, you can't borrow it for a lame-ass skating party. Please wear it to the underaged club at least." We gave each other a pound as we began to laugh.

"I know you right about that, silly. You know my momma ain't going for that. Anyway, what's up with you and A.J. having on the same shit? Who in the hell came up with that bright idea? Ya'll look so cute wearing the same colors and shit to the party. For real, ya'll need to stop that." Sasha talked shit, cracking up about the matching shirts, and I let her get her shit off, knowing the play was kinda weak and I had no comeback line.

"Okay, Sasha, the funny is over, and I didn't plan any of this. I think Diane and A.J. put this thing together, and Diane told him what I bought when we were at the mall today. I ain't gonna front on him, though, it's kinda weak, but I think it's real cute he did that for me." I hit the blunt a couple more times, passing it off and guzzling down half a bottle of Sisco, recounting the conversation me and A.J. had a moment ago.

"You know you my girl, Sasha, but I got to go thank my man right now. I'll catch up with you later and don't do anything I wouldn't do." The corners of my mouth glowed a devilish grin once again.

"Aiight, Egypt, but don't be thanking him all night," Sasha shouted over the hood music as I left the kitchen. Back towards the crowd I felt A.J. and those wanting eyes all over my being as my foot touched down on the very first step leading to the upstairs. Only if I would have had the info on Diane in the cut lying like a Band-Aid watching both of us creep off, I wouldn't have made my move.

Opening the bathroom door, A.J. professed he wanted to taste me in a whisper to my ear. "So what is it that you think my woman won't do?" Thirsty, he pulled me close grinding on my backside, his hands traveled down my spandex pants, pulling my second pair of lips apart, plucking my guitar string. I moaned with pleasure, gyrating against his fingertips hungry to release orgasmic excitement. I pulled his hands away from my middle spot with all my might, turning about to lock eyes with A.J.

"To answer your question, I present to you a grown woman." I raised my hands to the top of my head and follow the silhouette of my being sinking as low as the waist, coming face to face with the beast. I undo his pants, wrapping them around his ankles as I take a deep breath. Reaching inside of his boxer shorts, I take in his rock hard muscle I pulled from behind the cotton. I wish I could have seen his face as I stroked his hardness in and out of my mouth, but I was afraid to look him in the eyes, being it was my first time giving anyone oral sex. He pumped my mouth, gently gripping my neck with force, moaning in satisfaction. My pussy splashed with every stroke I took, and I enjoyed this feeling of pleasuring my man. His legs began to tremble and his grip around my neck struck pain as the gentle stroke turned into a thrust.

"I'm about to shoot, Egypt. Let it go now, baby. Let it go now!" Ignoring his warning, I gave it the deep throat, sucking every bit and every drop of his manhood that leaked from his muscle. I got up from my knees and A.J. fell to his, clenching my ankles, shaking his head.

"What did I do to deserve that, girl?" I untangled myself from the cuffs of A.J., taking a few steps to the sink. I spit out everything I took in. Reaching for my toothbrush to freshen up, I was crazed by my doing.

"I'm a woman now, baby, doing grown-up things. It was a birthday present to me, and you just reap the benefits in my becoming, but don't flatter yourself."

"I will always be flattered being the first. I don't think I'll ever be able to help that." Taking a deep breath, he wiped the beads of sweat from his forehead. "So you a grown woman now, doing big things, you say. Well, I wonder if you can handle this, birthday girl." A.J. picked me up, placing me on the sink. Pulling my pants off on an attack, I knew what I was in for. The thrust of his tongue drove me to say his name in an insane rage as I popped quickly. My baby couldn't beat up the pussy to save his life; you know, a one-minute man, but the skills his sly tongue possessed was out of control. He made me feel every stroke as he aroused my soft spot with the gesture of affection. A.J. massaged his manhood while sucking my pussy harder and harder, sending my body into a convulsion. I could hear voices outside the door as we brought out our sexual heat. We had drawn a crowd occupying one of the most popular spots in the house and the spectators stood there patiently listening for the highlights of the show and to put faces to the voices. Hearing the "oohs" and "aahs" from the other side of the door turned me on deeper, reaching my peak. I embraced the climax, banging my head off the medicine cabinet, embarrassing the shit out of myself.

"Are you okay, baby?" A.J. chuckled looking me in my face with those eyes and lips I couldn't resist. Placing his face into my hands to kiss them, I tasted my own juices sucking on his bottom lip.

"I guess you cool." Answering his own question, he glanced over my body.

"So... Moved your ass off the sink, can I wash my face?" The sarcasm set into his tone, letting me know the moment was over.

"Don't be mad, baby. I know I should have called you back earlier, but Diane..."

"See, stop right there, Egypt. Diane what? I go with you and Diane now? It's always that bitch before me. That's why you came in here putting my dick in your mouth."

"What, nigga? You tripping for real, talking to me like that!" I rolled my eyes with a vengeance, turning my back on him.

"We can talk later, enjoy your night, and I'll give you your gift in a minute." Planting a kiss on the back of my neck, I gave in to A.J. and his smart ass remark. We fixed each other's clothes to make sure we were presentable to the crowd and cleaned up the bathroom, leaving no traces of sexual acts. The door opened and our audience gave their approval by clapping. Pushing past the crowd, I could feel Diane on my heels. She's talking shit with her hot-ass, drunken breath demanding for me to meet her on the patio a.s.a.p.

Ignoring her request, I found Sasha with two full bottles of Sisco, dancing to some new cats from down south called Outkast. Sasha moved sexually to the bass, dropping in between two male figures as I cut in. I rode her hips while all eyes combed over our collision and the alchemy of the liquor took over. Drunk as hell, I grab a bottle of Sisco from Sasha's hand, popping the top and tilting it back, giving a ten count deep throat style.

The male figures caress us as we caress each other coming into the next song. Feeling a bulge rise from behind provoked me to turn around to expect A.J., but falling into Trap's arms. I knew right then and there I was in trouble. Fresh to death from head to toe, his fragrance captivated my being to a point of no return. He placed his lips on mine, spinning the room quiet around us.

If what I'm feeling is wrong, I don't want to be right, so I didn't let go of his strapping frame. Our hearts moved as one to the bump-and-grind segment of the music, developing a rapture between him and I. So caught up in the moment, neither one of us saw A.J. creeping on a come-up until the bottle came crashing over Trap's head. Smacking me down with his next move, Trap tapped his chin, but it didn't faze A.J. one bit. A.J. picked up another bottle from the floor, thrashing Trap again in the head, this time knocking him out. A.J. jumped on my ass like a wild spider monkey, and the people just stood around and watched as if it was a movie. I felt every punch and kick he gave off repeatedly as he kicked my ass. Diane came out of nowhere to save the day with her twenty-two handgun, giving A.J. a straight-dome call saving the day.

"Get the fuck out now A.J., and if you put another hand on my niece, I swear I'll use this." Pausing with his hand in midair, he backed off, realizing what the hell was about to happen.

"You lucky I don't smack you bitch for pulling a gun out on me up in here." Diane cocked that little mutherfucker back, giving off a look that I wouldn't even test. "You right, you right." A.J. stated raising his hands chest length. "Your wish is my command. I'm up out this mutherfucker!! Fuck you, Egypt! I'm gonna have Brandy beat that ass on sight."

"You threaten my niece again and you're going to Allegheny General Hospital tonight, punk." Diane never flinched, standing their holding that gun with a look in her eye that was scary. A.J. left the apartment and the party was over, taking my high with it.

"You okay, Egypt?" Sasha came from the left after I got my ass kicked, asking me a dumb- ass question I really didn't want to answer.

"Yeah, I'm cool, but I wish I would have got my gift first before all this shit went down. Now move out my way before I punch you in the face. Does it really look like I'm okay, stupid?"

"The only person getting punched in the face is you, Egypt!" Diane spoke, gripping me up with force by the neck of my shirt, pushing me with all her might through the patio doors.

"If you would have come to talk to me when I told you to, hot ass, none of this would have happened! You never listen to nobody girl! A hard head makes a soft ass! Just wait and see. You will learn, rock head." My head began to spin and the words Diane spoke became unclear.

"The only man I need in my life is Jesus."

"What did you say, Diane? Why are you talking about Jesus?"

"What the hell you talking about, Egypt? I think A.J. must have hit you harder than I thought. Come back in the house and clean yourself up." Walking back into the house, it was damn near empty and my baby Trap was nowhere to be found. Diane kicked out the remaining few left throughout the crib, leaving us with a lot more to drink. I licked my wounds, falling out on the couch.

"You look like you should be on *America's Most Wounded*, Diane joked, sitting next to me on the couch.

"You're not funny, Diane," I replied in laughter as we both sat shaking our heads, recapping the events that took place. I checked the time on a nearby clock.

"It's two-thirty a.m., that's it and that's all... Niggas do know how to fuck up a party."

"Shut up, Egypt. You drunk and you sound stupid. You fucked up your own party being grown and nasty. The reason why you didn't come to see what I wanted was because you thought I was going to trip about you in my bathroom fucking your little boyfriend. All the way around, young buck, you played yourself." In a way, she was right about the whole ordeal, but I could never admit it.

"Whatever, Diane. I don't know what you're talking about. My night ended just the way I didn't want it to. I'm sitting here with your old ass, so bust out them slow jams to go with this liquor. Make me cry with some Mary J., please, or play that old-school shit you like."

I believe in my heart Diane knew what the deal was before Trap even showed up to my surprise party. I can't prove it, but I know her. What happens in the dark must come to the light. She's the devil in disguise, always creating mischief.

Finishing off another bottle of Sisco, I listened to *Sweet Thing* a million times over, thinking about Trap and A.J. fighting. I couldn't shake this voice I felt inside.

"The only man I need in my life is Jesus." It kept growing and growing inside me. The voice was so loud inside me I had to let it out.

CHAPTER FOUR

My body is sprawled out on the cold, hard, linoleum floor, tied up. I lay in my own feces, grotesque to my nose as I snap back into reality. No longer intoxicated from the heroin forced into my veins, I lay dope sick. The room is empty, whereas a haunting aura surrounds the darkness and my heart beats fierce with fear. I am overcome with fear for what could happen next as I begin to pray. I begin to pray in the name of a man I never knew or believed in. I'm rusty, but I try, searching my soul for the right words to say. I can't get it right. It's hard to figure out the right words not talking to the guy upstairs since I was thirteen.

"Have mercy on my soul, dear God." A calm sweeps over my body so sudden remembering a bible verse from Sabbath school we made into a song so us kids would pay attention—for I raised hell in church as I did at home.

"Don't punish me, Lord, or even correct me when you are angry. Have pity on me and heal my feeble body. My bones tremble with fear and I am in deep distress. How long will it be? Turn and come to my rescue, show your wonder love and save me, Lord, please. If I die, I can't repent or even remember you. My groaning and my lifestyle has worn me out. Can you hear me, Lord, even though I cursed you so many times before? Hear my cries, Lord, make me a believer."

Saying "amen," a small ray of light comes into view as the laundry room door cracks open. I try to remember the distant voices, but I can't remember how I became a hostage in this dungeon. The door opens and a shadow of a man appears. He shuts the door quickly and stands over me. A lump arises in my throat. At that very moment, I remember the diabolical plan Boo overloaded on me and my body.

Raping me slow, he seized my power from out of my hands, placing it in his. Taking my strength gave him strength.

The room is in total darkness again. I only hear a voice of masculinity degrade me with words. "You smell foul as hell, shortie. I can't see you, but I can smell you!" As quick as he came he is gone. He slams the door extremely hard, cursing at the top of his lungs and demanding a refund immediately. Embarrassed by the words coming from out of his mouth, I begin to fight. Using the last of my energy, I try to break free of the ropes until I break down in tears. Bound to the pipes, exhaustion sets in swiftly, breaking the fight in me.

I can't deny it. I want to ride it——the thrill of my vein popping with the ecstasy Boo subjected me to. I want it. I want the pain to go away. I just want the nightmare to be over. I can't lie to the fact when he stroked my arm slow the injection was overwhelming as the drug took over my being. A warm sensation granted me serenity, taking away every moment of agony I've endured in my so-called life. It was a moment of clarity, giving me an adrenaline rush that I will forever chase.

"Smack her again, dammit!"

"I hit her so hard, the bitch should still be seeing stars." Boo says jokingly, as his partner, General, takes a shot at his chest.

"What the hell you hit me for?" Boo asks with labored attempts to breath.

"Dis here ain't no joking matter or no game, nigga. Look what ya dumbass done did, Boo."

General cuffed Boo by the back of the neck, causing him to look closer at the mess he made. "You gave her too much junk to the vein, stupid! Knowing she don't shoot up, you should have only slid her ten units and that's still a lot." General knocks on his head with a closed fist. "She was already smoking crack. Come on, you got to think, man."

"That's what I did, General! What you talking 'bout?" Boo breaks free from General's hold, shaking his head with a mask of anger.

"I'm talking 'bout the fact I got all this piss and shit on my floor, stupid. You lying to the dope boy himself, nigga, and I know these things. Look at her!" General's shout goes up another two pitches and the bass makes Boo's heart pump with fear. "She damn near looks dead to the world."

"Well, maybe you should check her pulse."

"Shut up, stupid! You can't even tell a lie 'cause your face gives it away." General sighs with disappointment. "Man up, bitch, for real!"

"I just thought…"

"Don't think, Boo. Leave dat to me, stupid! I don't want you to hurt yourself! I'm going to take her to the shower so I can clean up your mistake. You can mop up the piss and shit. Understood?"

"Yeah, you got it, dog, but you don't have to talk to me like that." Boo hesitated to speak, but forced the words to be spoken.

"Yes I do, until you man the fuck up! Now get to work, nigga, before I hit you so hard you'll be seeing stars." General grabs me from the floor, slinging my body over his shoulder.

Filling up a bucket of soapy water to clean up the mess on the floor Boo did as he was told. His stomach in knots, pulling tighter and tighter, enraged with hate building up in each one of his bones, Boo slings the mop back and forth, doing what he was told. Boo knows he can't go against General.

General would never claim Boo to be his brother in the known worldly eyes of man. When he did, rarely, he would refer to themselves as the descendants of Kane and Abel, implying that one day Boo would raise his hand to kill him for his birthright. Being the envious brother who didn't have a psychopathic bone in his body, however, he wanted to be in charge.

"I was a bitch, a homo and a sucker to him my whole life. Every day I try harder to please him, to become him, to be better than him. One day soon I will earn his respect, but until then, I will do as I'm told and be my brother's keeper." Boo gave himself an out loud pep talk, shedding some light on his dim future.

Hatred and fear submerge Boo's brain with racing thoughts to kill General. He is in dire need to be feared by others, as he fears General.

"I could say my heart won't let me do it because he's all I got, but the truth of the matter is, he's right——I got to man up."

Growing up in one of the toughest city projects on the North Side of Pittsburgh, our feet often touched the concrete beating the pavement to eat. Our grandmother adopted us, not giving a rat's ass about nothing besides the monthly check from the state. I was too young to remember what happened to our parents; nonetheless, the newspaper clippings hidden up under General's bed helped me create my own story.

Supposedly my father set the house on fire by setting himself on fire basing cocaine. My mother was burnt to a crisp in her bed asleep, doped up off of heroin, so the police thought.

Then the autopsy report showed there was no smoke in her lungs. She was murdered by a hot shot injected into her jugular vein.

Me, of course, wanting to know more about our parents, went to General in search of answers. I lost my virginity to a pit bull that night as my brother held a gun to my head. "That's what happened to me when I tried to hug the bastard I knew as our father. The trifling piece of shit you're asking questions about." I can smell the stench of his breath still to this day as General spoke in a whisper. He had tears in his eyes when he seen my manhood leaking from my flesh. The tears quickly turned to anger as he struck my face. It was the first and last time I seen my brother drop a tear for anybody or anything. General raped me that night in the basement of our grandmother's house. He stole my innocence, and I lost a brother as the ill-will words still play in my mind. "You are no brother of mine, but if you do what I tell you, you will always eat." Do as I say and not as I do, was the first lesson I learned in the world.

"Boo, what are you doing?" General asks furiously. Giving Boo a two-piece to the chest, he damn near causes him to fall.

"I'm doing what you told me to do, G." Boo grabs his chest, catching his balance. His head hangs low, with his eyes to the floor.

"I've been calling your ass for over five minutes. Who the hell you mind fucking?" General is up close and personal as his saliva rains on Boo. "You better snap back to reality. I moved the bitch into the back room after I got her to wash the stink off that ass. I tied her back up and she keeps asking for you. She needs the dope, Boo. Only give her ten units. Only ten! Understood?"

"Yeah, man... understood."

"When you finish, untie her and bust a nut. That's an order, funny-looking-ass nigga. You need to bust a nut anyway, ugly. This is the most pussy you'll ever see. You still sticking niggas in the ass or are you a recovering addict?" General laughs at his own twisted joke, smacking Boo on the back of the neck.

"Shut up!" Boo shouts and follows up with an outrageous swing, trying to hit General. "It's all because of you, mutherfucker!"

Those were the last words Boo spoke before being knocked out with the butt of General's chromatic forty-five glock.

"Look what you made me do, silly-ass nigga." General circled around his body as it lay on the floor, wanting him to get up so he could knock him down again. Noticing his body is still, General turns the light off in the laundry room and shuts the door behind him.

"I'm going to pull the tape off your mouth, and you better not scream. If you do, I will stick something in your mouth you won't like. Understood?" The words came from his mouth in a whisper to my ear and the voice sounded so familiar to my soul. I almost feel safe as he removes the tape from my lips. "I'm sick, and I can tell by the cologne this voice can't be Boo. Who are you?"

"Don't ask me no questions; just answer them. Understood?"

"Understood."

"I wonder why women sleep with other women. Ya'll can't help but to be scandalous towards one another. It's in a bitch's nature. How could you not want this hot, thick, dick up inside you?"

"Who said I didn't, stupid?" I quote him sarcastically, causing him to smack the shit out of my face.

"See, bitches don't know how to listen to nothing. Didn't I say don't ask me shit!" The whisper of his voice becomes a bark.

"I didn't ask you anything. I was just saying."

"Don't cut me off again when I'm speaking!" The bark became the roar from the mouth of a lion, giving me two body blows to the kidneys. My body cringes from his loud voice and the pain from the blasts of his fists. All I want is to get high.

"Now, how can you call me stupid when you know nothing about me?" I can hear him pull up a chair as he gives off this sinister cackle. "What's your name anyway?" When the silence grows long, he gives me permission to speak, stroking my face with his fingertips.

"I'm sorry for insulting you," fell from my lips.

"Apology accepted. Now run me that name." The bark has calmed down to a suitable voice.

"They call me Nikko, but my momma name me Egypt. That's the only thing she ever gave me." A deadly calm comes through the passing as I wait for him to respond. Forever had gone and come back when I hear the wrapper of a cigar break open. I can't see it, but I know what it is from smoking so much dope.

My body begins to crave intoxication. Anxiety set in as my thoughts take over. Maybe he is preparing my next dose to satisfy my hunger.

"Are you there?" I ask, knowing the answer to my own question; just wanting to hear his voice.

"I'm here woman, but didn't I tell you not to ask me shit? I'm going to have to show you that I'm the fucking general of this camp and everybody in my camp must obey or suffer the consequences. Since you can't be quiet, I got something to shut you up. I want you to put my dick in your mouth and suck me off as if your life depends on it."

His touch is demanding, dropping me down to my knees. I can hear the zipper of his pants go down. Pulling me closer to his being... I think to myself I should bite it off when he climaxes. I hear the cold, hard steel of his gun cock back and he rubs it against my face, giving dismissal to that thought quickly.

"Now, now, now, don't get any crazy ideas rolling around in that smoked-out little brain of yours. I will splatter it all over these walls." On my every thought, I take his words to heed doing what I was told to do. Complimenting me on my skills with the ooh's and the aahs, he hammers my mouth hard, releasing his tension down my throat. I want out of this situation, but there is no way out as tears form in my eyes from gagging on his salty manhood. Pushing me to the floor with the palm of his hand, a sense of familiarity comes across strong.

All of a sudden, I feel a sigh of relief with him being in the room, even though he is having his way with my body. I have to be sick in the head because I have the nerve to be turned on by him instead of being frightened. I want out of the situation, but I want to get to know the voice that is in the room with me. Always having a soft spot for men with authority who can control and run shit, I break down. Making money with power moves is enough to make any woman's pussy wet.

My stomach is back on crave mode, sick for the drug and I want more, more and more.

"Why you rubbing your stomach? I just gave you a healthy-ass serving of my nut on a platter."

"I ain't hungry, nigga. I want whatever it was you pumped in my veins earlier. I want to feel that rush again."

"The power of drugs is what I love the most. It's always been my first passion to single handedly destroy people's lives." General laughs.

"I don't mean to interrupt you, but I don't want to hear about you and your shitty life. I got my own life story that ain't shit."

"What? You don't want me to get ugly in here, Egypt." His voice has come back to a whisper in my ear and it is intimidating, but it doesn't stop my tongue.

"What kinda kidnapper the fuck are you!? Yo, for real man, I'm sick!" I yell at the top of my lungs, thirsty for intoxication.

"Do whatever it is you came to do, just dope me up, please!" The words spill out in a cry. I need the mystery man to bless my craving. I didn't care about his reaction to my outburst.

"You're a bold bitch to talk to me like that. I will excuse you this time for you don't know who I am or what I'm capable of doing. Just remember this woman, I'm that nigga who will torture you slow. When you get the brilliant idea to escape, you better hope, wish and pray you get away or bitch-ass Boo catch you, cause if I do "BOOM!" The gun went off loudly close to my left ear. "You're fucking dead, bitch!"

Damn near jumping out of my skin from the sound of the gun, I can hear the door open and shut, leaving me alone once again with my own negative thoughts.

As soon as General steps out the door, he stands toe to toe with Boo. Ice grilling him hard, General can smell the dried-up blood covering Boo's face. Breathing erratically, Boo wants the war to come out of him right then and there. He wants the nerve to strike first, going blow for blow. Boo can't do it though; he can't man up and he knows it. Knowing in his heart General sees no brotherly love towards him, why provoke a fight he can't win. He's not ready to kill. Standing down for the moment, he decides to make peace and not war. Boo holds out his fist to dap up General.

"Did you let her see your face?" General gives Boo eye contact on the note of, *Do I look dumb or what?*

"What do you think, Boo Boo the bear? Oh, hold up, I told you not to think. Wasn't you paying attention when I blindfolded the bitch in the laundry room before I threw her over my shoulder? Or did that bump rising on your head make you forget?" General folds his arms across his chest. "I thought for a minute you were ready to stand up and quit acting like a woman, but I thought wrong, nigga." Pushing Boo's fist down, General shows nothing but disrespect, doing what he does best, instilling fear.

"Get your little-ass fist out of here, nigga! I don't dap up no bitches! Let me know when you stop wearing a thong and I just might let you into the all-boys club. Get your ass in there like I told you before and get her ready to make this money! Understood?"

"I got you; don't worry about shit." General flexes his muscle to make Boo flinch and just as he thought, Boo did.

"Hey, Boo," General says, walking away from him.

"What?" Boo replies, ready for his command.

"Wash the blood off ya face first before you go handle that." Watching General walk down the hallway Boo, is relieved I'm still alive after hearing the gun go off, which awakened him from the deep sleep General put him in.

Boo let the warm water run into his hands, gazing at the reflection staring back at himself in disbelief, his conscious in panic mode for what he had done to impress General. My death will rest on his shoulders and he knows it. *And all she wanted to do was get high...*

"Fuck it, I did it! Another day, another dollar. I can't be Mr. Super Save a Hoe."

Approaching the door, Boo braces himself for what lies beyond the pass through. He stretches his earlobe against the wood to take a listen. Opening the door slow, he stands in the passage, skepticism setting in on what really happened in the room. I'm laid out on the floor without a bruise in sight, still breathing. He stands puzzled by the actuality I'm not even bleeding.

"What happened in here?" Boo asks, removing the blindfold General had perfectly placed over my eyes.

"Are you going to let me go, Boo?" I cry out in pain, dope sick.

"Who was that crazy-ass nigga with the gun? You gotta tell me something."

"Don't ask me no fucking questions about nothing. This ain't no question-and-answer period."

"The mystery man made me suck his dick!" Throwing attitude in my shout, I scratched my arms like a dope fiend. "I'm sick Boo. This shit here ain't right." I doubled over in pain, gripping the dirty mattress. "What did I do to you to deserve this? I was trying to get you high for free. If I ever make it out of here, I will personally beat shit down your leg."

"Shut up, bitch, you ain't gonna do shit! And you're in no position to tell me what will happen in the future. Your future is in my hands, so remember that, bitch. I don't give a fuck about you and I guess I will never find out if your statement is true because you're not going anywhere no time soon. You didn't talk to my nigga like that, and I know it for sure, so don't think ya gonna do it to me. Now, what happened with the gun? I thought you were dead, all jokes aside." Boo's holla turned soft as butter. Taking a seat in the only chair in the room, worrisome eyes took over.

"You almost sound sorry for me. What's up with that?" My words hung in the air and there was no response. "Your nigga told me if I try to escape, he would kill me, aiight." Boo looked up at me with fear in his face, but still no response. "I can't believe you got the nerve to come in here demanding answers from me after what you've done. Standing over me like you won a million dollars, calling me a dike. Bitch-ass nigga, I know what I am." My blood has started to boil, but my veins are thirsty, causing my mouth to become fearless. "If you needed pussy that bad, you should have just asked. You didn't have to dope me up to get it. I was giving you free get-high and pussy. Why you so quiet, punk? Oh, you don't have shit to say now. Then you let another nigga come in and do the same shit to me, charging twenty dollars. I know my pussy is worth more than that. I got that

NIKKI FLOWERS

come-back pussy. Well, that's what your momma said when she gave me head." The more Boo paid me no attention, the more I talked shit.

Boo never had lets his eyes fall off of me as I run my mouth. I can't understand why he hasn't punched me in the face yet.

"Are you planning to kill me, Boo?" His stare becomes hair-raising and my own question strikes fear in my heart.

From what I know, Boo is no killer, but people do change. Nobody knows where I am, and nobody worth caring will come to look for me. I'm shit out of luck and they can do whatever their hearts desire. I got myself into something I can't get out of. More and more thoughts rush me full speed until I am out of breath. I'm so worried about getting high, dying never crossed my mind.

My mouth tensed up, asking the question again. "Boo, are you going to kill me?" The silence was a death sentence. Boo puts his hand in his pocket, removing it holding a plastic bag.

"Not today." I watch him quietly while he sets up the works on a small table. I see a sudden change in his eyes that brings about pain. The expression on his face says he needs to escape, yet from what and from whom?

Getting up from his seat he walks towards me, slowly picking up the duct tape from off the floor in his step. He places his index finger on his lips. "Sssh," was the sound he made, taking up the slack on my braids. Pulling my head back, he slaps tape on my lips in a painful manner. Shaking his head, he returns to his seat at the small table to indulge in whatever drug of choice he wants. Seeing the dope makes my stomach bubble for the narcotic Boo blazes in my face. I have to witness his lips wrap around the homemade pipe as he rides the high. It is unbelievable. My eyes bug out as he puts the flame to the old antenna he made into a stem.

"Don't fucking judge me! You don't know anything about me or where I'm coming from. I ain't no crackhead, and I don't do this all the time." Boo spits, going back and forth in a conversation with himself. My stomach aches for a blast, watching the flame melt the rocks.

I'm thirsty for a hit of anything to put the craving on the back burner. Fuck smoking it in the weed! I can suck on that homemade pipe to.

"I got to man up he says. I can kill if I have to. He's not the only one who can run shit in the game." Back and forth he paces, my eyes watching his every move as he trips the fuck out. "Punk mutherfucker ain't no career criminal mastermind. I put this shit right here together."

Boo stops dead in his tracks, looking at me in deep thought. His eyes are no longer in pain. They bulge out like Wyle E. Coyote who just seen the road runner. It was almost the same look when he raped me in the laundry room.

He goes back to the table, blocking the narcotics with his body. I can hear the substance being sucked up by his nostril as his back arches with pleasure. Cracking a smile, Boo puts his attention back on me as the dope calms him down some. Arrogance spills out of his mouth, rambling on to himself once again. His eyes don't leave me, and I don't like the look in his eyes.

"You want to feel like I feel right now, don't you?" Boo lets out a bitter laugh and rolls a perfect blunt, teasing my addiction, setting off a conflagration inside me. I moan and groan as he puts the fire to the smoke. The melt in the blunt overpowers the weed, leaving a sweet aroma to my nose. Relaxing his body, he falls under a spell, inhaling the fumes. It appears so tantalizing to my hungry eyes.

In the mist of the smoke, a text message alert snapped him back into reality. He snatches the phone from his clip, annoyed from the disturbance, checking the message in awe. Reading the wire, Boo squashes the cherry on the blunt, sucking his teeth. "You ready to dream, baby?" Boo asks the question, placing his index finger to his lips. "You can drift through infinite time, boundless, with no regard to the past or future messing with this here." My body goes into a sigh of relief watching Boo at work. I know it's my time to fly. The transformation is absolutely beautiful to my eyes.

The flicker of the flame turns the powder mass into a liquid substance. Drawing back the needle, consuming the narcotic, my sweet spot splashes.

"You want this, don't you?" Boo asks, and I shake my head yes. Boo throws my face down into the soiled sheet and my ass in the air. I didn't hear his zipper go down, but the spit he choked up was disgusting. Spitting in his hand, he massaged his muscle, forcing it inside me. Pounding my dry walls and squeezing the back of my neck this time, I can feel the total wrath of him inside me. His muscle brought tears to my face as I feel my insides rip. As quickly as it started it ends, with him collapsing on my back out of breath. I feel like Celie from The Color Purple at that instant when she opened up to Shug Avery about Mister. He just climbed on top of me and did his business. She had no control and neither do I.

The light is cut off as I'm blindfolded again and flipped on my back. I'm in agony. Boo has his face between my legs seconds after stroking my sweet spot with his tongue. I hate to admit it, but his wet mouth feels good on me. Feeling a sharp pinch to my clit followed by his hot mouth, my being oozes with warmth once again. My body relaxes and my thoughts are in static, enjoying the high as I die trying.

CHAPTER FIVE

The summer had come and gone once again as the seasons began to change. Early morning dew laid across the grass as the creeping sun peeked over the many buildings, shops and restaurants along the busy East Ohio Street. The clean, crisp breeze flowed through my box braids awaiting the 6:25 am 54c Northside to Oakland bus to carry me off to Schenley High for the first day of school.

Revved up engines scattered throughout the long street from the working-class people down to the Double "D" Boy's showing off their speed. The drug dealers of the community had to outshine one another on this special day of reckoning to let the cat out of the bag for the sideline spectators. Showing off their money, power and respect they had earned over the summer for the young and dumb upcoming hoodrats, you could hear them loud with the phrases "That's sweet" and "That's cold" while the working class went on with their everyday routines.

By the time the sun came up, East Ohio Street was crawling with labels from block to block; not with designer clothes, but with social economics. School was nothing but a mere fashion show to those who hung out this morning and by the end of the week, the glitz, as well as the glamour, will have faded to black.

The early mornings would start to cramp the Double "D" Boys late-night lifestyles as they couldn't bring themselves to make the eight o'clock homeroom classes. The hoodrats came in all different shapes and sizes, a dime a dozen and down for whatever with a ferocious demeanor surrounding their aura. They took their pick of the litter while the getting was good and the block was hot on the young, black and noble steeds within fifteen minutes of the drive-by. They put claim to the near future on the fuck buddy of their choice. With their parents at work, their young daughters work toward becoming ready-made whores. You didn't catch another hurried momentary look at them at the bus stop again until a Double "D" Boy dumped her or she just played herself out.

"What's up, girl? Standing here mean, mugging everybody, looking all cute. Let me hit your squed, E, or are you still mad at me?" Sasha placed her hands on her hips, waiting for an answer. I hadn't forgiven her on how things went down at my birthday party with A.J. and Trap, but deep down in my heart I missed the only real friend I had to talk to.

"Take the squed to the face." I handed over the rest of my cigarette with a pleasing smirk. "Ya jeans are hot, too." Complimenting her on the all-white Guess jeans she had on one size to small, plumpish around the ass, I held my arms out to embrace my girl I hadn't kicked it with all summer. Holding a grudge I should have been let go, we fell into arms, teary-eyed, missing each other's company, conversation and late-night rendezvous when nobody else was looking.

"I missed you, E. I can't believe you avoided me all summer behind some shit Diane directed, starred in and produced at your surprise birthday party." As she put an emphasis on the words "surprise birthday party," the rolling of her eyes intensified. "I love you, E, like a sister I never had. We go way back, and we have come too far for me to just reach out and hurt you deliberately. How I look like, letting some nigga in your party you used to mess around with without telling you? Dat shit got Diane's foul ass written all over it."

I couldn't make eye contact as Sasha spoke the truth off her lips, and I couldn't believe how I let Diane get past me with that one.

"Pick your head up, E. You know you still my homegirl no matter what."

"I'm sorry, girl, for fronting on you like that, but you got to know I'm too stubborn to admit when I'm wrong."

"It's cool, it's cool," Sasha spoke nonchalant, grabbing me close and squeezing me tight.

The bus was crowded from the door approaching our stop with everyday working people, leaving a handful of seats for us high-schoolers to compete for. Off to the races they went when the double doors opened to let us enter. Sasha didn't have no problem pushing past the elderly to be the first to step foot on the bus as I fell back to let the townspeople do what they do, but not on my brand new kicks. I read her lips through the big square window of the bus as she claimed her seat and held one up for me.

Diane introduced me to Sasha three or four years ago when she and Sasha's mother became good friends. Two women knowingly God's gift to men were bound to bump heads sooner or later with both of them on the prowl. What started out a simple friendship of you be there for me and I will be there for you, ended in treachery. Jealousy set the tone two years later in their sister-to-sister relationship when the honey-tongued and extravagant Marco Struthers walked in the Alpine from off the cold street.

Tall, dark and handsome, he stood six-foot-two, wearing a size thirteen shoe. You know what they say about men with big feet—they got big dicks, too. Every woman who laid eyes on the prize wanted to witness his magic stick within their own extravaganza.

His reputation took women and their minds beyond the limits.

The cream-colored suit demanded respect from the men and was appealing to the naked eyes of the women as it clung to his every movement throughout the dimly lit bar.

Dapping up all the fellows who hated on the game with his head held high and his chest out, you could feel his presence no matter what corner he stood in. His persona was cool and intriguing to most, catching everyone's attention as the spotlight always shined down on him.

The ladies flocked to the highly respected man everyone knew and wanted to know with nothing but love. Sliding his Gucci frames up to rest upon his head, the predator unleashed on the hunt for something to taste and turn out. Didn't do relationships, but had a thing for being the destroyer when it came to others, the women flocked for a taste disregarding the consequences.

The bar was packed to capacity with an ass on every stool as the hottest jukebox played. Diane worked the small dance floor, popping that nasty cock on every baller on the move while Shane sat at the bar sipping on a drink to gain enough confidence to just say hi to Marco.

Shane had the hots for Marco, laying sight on his skin-tight muscular physique as he ran a full-court basketball game down the Commons awhile beforehand. Flexing his skills, she mastered his moves, placing her own into rotation, lusting after his feel.

Confiding her fantasies to Diane, they made it official that Mr. Struthers was Shane's mark, and if she couldn't have him, Diane couldn't neither. He would be off limits and nobody would come in between their relationship.

Ordering another drink, Shane picked up the smooth thread from the corner of her eye making its way towards her.

"Let me guess—you're drinking something soft like a wine spritzer, I bet you." Just the sound of his voice created a splash down below as Shane turned about to face her destiny. Buying her drink, Prince Charming had her eating out the palm of his hand. Hanging on his every word, her heart throbbed for him.

Laughing at every joke he told, she stared beyond those big brown eyes and her thong was soaked from the juices he created from licking those luscious lips of his.

Everything fell into place as they talked for over an hour. You wouldn't believe there was over fifty people in their space as they conversed. It went on for about fifteen more minutes, then the time came to exchange numbers and move on to the next victim. Diane, in the limelight shaking her ass on the dance floor, watched the two with piercing eyes and schemed to make her move on Marco as soon as the opportunity presented itself.

Just as she expected, a bathroom break would have to occur. Soon Marco broke free from Shane, heading downstairs toward the restroom. It was the perfect opportunity to catch him alone, and if she couldn't get the job done there, the next quick thought-up scheme would have to be to follow him to his car.

Grieving with envy, Diane always wanted what she couldn't have, and there was no competition when it came to what she wanted. All that sister-to sister shit flew right out the window when she yearned to taste his loins. Diane was the type of person who could accomplish anything by putting a dick in her mouth, so let it be written.

Shane stood alone by the bar in amazement. Diane scoped her out for a hot second, making sure her eyes weren't on her as she pursued the mark. Leaving the unworthy on the dance floor to follow the gifted, she trailed behind him, slow to camouflage the obvious.

Giving him a minute or two to pull his muscle out to take a leak, Diane walked in the men's bathroom as if she were one, cocky and conceited.

Marco turned around, smelling the scent of a woman with his flesh in his hands, and Diane locked the door so there wouldn't be any disturbance.

"Can I help you with something, baby?" Marco asked, voice suave with a sly smirk. Diane shook her head yes, making eye contact with the inevitable. Marco shook his head in denial, staring down at his genitals, then turning about so she could get an eyeful.

"Is this what you came for, baby?" Marco asked his last question as Diane dropped to her knees, taking his breath away.

The soiled floor didn't stop her from swallowing his dick as if it was the last meal she would receive. In and out, she stroked the tip as her middle spot splashed out, always watching his facial expressions.

His ass cheeks clutched as he tried to fight the tingling sensation, but he couldn't escape it. Grabbing her head, he brought it up and down on his shaft until he released the tension. He tried to pull out, but her mouth swallowed every inch, taking in every drop of his salty manhood.

Marco's eyes bulged with stupidity as she sucked the life out of him. Standing there speechless, his mouth hung open.

"I will let you fuck Shane first before I tell her you came over my crib the same night you gave her your number, fucking my brains out into the sunrise."

"Is that an invite, baby?" Marco put his dick back in his pants, quick smoothing out his suit pants as if nothing ever happened.

Climbing up off her knees, the mission was complete but the grand finale would come later.

Diane smoothed out the wrinkles on her dress, washing down the last bit of evidence with a beer, she sat on the sink before action took place. Patting herself on the back for a job well done, she unlocked the door and scuffled back out into the dimly lit hallway, falling up the staircase to rush back to the bar to check on Shane. Shane was on cloud nine. She had men surrounding her, buying up the bar when she noticed Diane coming from Lawd knows where with stank hoe written all over her face.

Shane glanced around her, setting as the predator stare Diane had on her face gave it away when Marco was nowhere in sight. Not wanting to jump to conclusions, Shane finished off her drink, dismissing the entourage, glancing around for Marco's body once more.

His face didn't appear under the dim lights, and Shane became furious, instantly placing her focus on her nasty-ass friend who couldn't look her in the eye. Shane spun around to get up off the stool to investigate the scene when slick-ass Marco slithered up.

"Can we talk in private?" Marco grabbed Shane by the hand and led them to the dance floor. Looking into Shane's eyes, he hung his head low, pulling her body close as the DJ spun the old-school classic by Keith Sweat, *Make It Last Forever*.

Shane's arms draped Marco's neck as her head laid on his chest. Inhaling his masculinity, she melted like butter all over a hot dish. They held each other while all eyes watched them dance to the rhythm of their heartbeats.

"So what was it you wanted to talk about?" Shane asked as others read her lips.

"This was it right here, baby. I wanted our bodies to talk to each other through song. Does that sound corny to you?" Marco replied, brushing his hardness against her middle spot.

"Hell no, you don't sound corny, and I'm digging on you hard."

Diane downed her third rum and coke as she decided to have the last laugh, feeling disrespected by Marco and the situation she created in the restroom. She walked past the two, catching the stare of Marco as she put on the seductive saunter, leaving every other man in the bar grabbing their crotch as he just grinned. He nibbled on Shane's earlobe, never breaking eye contact with Diane, and it sent her over the edge.

"You got my number, sweetheart, and I hope you use it since you are digging on me hard." Sliding the small piece of paper in the back pocket of Shane's mini-skirt, he placed a wet kiss on her forehead.

"I got you, Mr. Struthers, if it's the last thing I do, it will be you," Shane replied in a sexual nature.

The lights came up and the DJ faded out back to the jukebox. The bar was filled with loud talk and a thick cloud of smoke as the small crowds dispersed.

"Last call for alcohol!!" the bartender shouted with apathy. Hearing those words, the drunks swarmed the tiny woman behind the bar, counterpulling close the female for the evening to grant their last request, securing that their dicks get wet later.

Shane and Marco finished their dance with a few words between them, pushing against each other's succulent lips.

Diane crept out the bar as the lights became high onto the cold street not to be seen by anyone. Shane knew the rules to the game too well and they both always followed them to the T.

Posting up in the cut, Diane had a bird's eye view of the entrance to the Alpine. Across the street from the bar, she hid in the comfort of the shadows, awaiting her mark. Animal instinct intact, the predator was on the loose, sniffing out its prey.

Ten minutes later, the shining light on the Alpine's name went dark. The staggering alcoholics gleefully fell out the door one by one onto the sidewalk. Five more minutes passed and the outgoing crowd from the bar had gradually faded as Diane's patience wore thin.

"Where could they be?" Diane muttered to herself as she noticed the door opening back up for a departure. Shane and Marco stepped out on the curb hand in hand as if they were a couple for years.

A smattering of goodbyes bit into the dead silence as they parted ways.

Watching Marco hit down the side street, she kept a close eye on Shane until she pulled off in her car to go home. And Diane stepped out of the shadows, following Marco's footsteps. The sound of Diane's shoes hitting the pavement caught his attention, pressuring him to turn around.

Marco let a sly smirk play on his lips, smitten by the girl fight that was in the making, when he laid sight on the deep-throat beast.

No words were spoken as Marco hit the car alarm to the Cadillac coupe and opened the passenger side door. He checked his pager, walking back around to the driver's seat as Diane slid in on the other side. Taking a seat in the car, it was noticeable that someone was missing from the passenger side, and it only meant one thing. Diane was in the back of the coupe with her legs spread eagle waiting for penetration.

"Is your girlfriend this promiscuous?"'

"What is that supposed to mean? You can ask her yourself after handling business."

Marco stared down at his flesh as it grew harder and harder. Asking no more questions and wasting no more time, he plunged inside her without a care in the world.

Shane sat at the final red light before reaching her destination, but something told her to go back and check on Diane. Something didn't sit well with Shane about Diane leaving the bar unannounced. Diane was on point when it came to flossing some dick. It wouldn't be right if the women didn't see her pull another baller for the taking.

The red light turned green and Shane had made a U-turn as her brain throttled with nothing but Diane and her motive for stardom this evening. It was after two in the morning and there wasn't a car in sight to prolong her destination back to the Alpine. She circled the block, coming back to the bar once again, praying the chick had her drawers up. Not once or twice, but three times Shane had caught Diane drunk in a dark alley exposing her lewdness, and she always paid the price playing super save a hoe.

The moment she drove past the bar, butterflies swarmed her stomach as she approached the small side street Marco walked down to retrieve his car just a half hour ago.

Shane spotted the rocking vehicle with a quick glance down the street. Turning off the headlights to her car, she turned around and went back to the side street to get a closer look. Shane crept up on the caddy quietly, knowing in her heart she was going to witness—Diane once again ass up.

Shane's bare-skinned legs were covered in goose bumps in the cool night air, but the closer she got to the care, the more she felt the heat rise between her legs. You could hear the moans and the groans echoing off the cold bricks as the car rocked harder.

"Marco, baby, I'm cumming, I'm cumming! Hit it right there, boy, that's my spot." Diane squealed loud and clear with every thrust of flesh pounding her insides as she put on the show for Shane to watch.

Shane's rage grew once she heard the name. She wanted to bust every window on Marco's two-door coupe, yelling loud, "I didn't like you anyway, you pretty mutherfucker!" But the fault didn't lie with Marco—he was just a man being a man, and she realized at that moment, he wasn't the man for her.

Stomping away from the car her heart shattered in a thousand pieces. Shane felt defeated by Diane and wanted revenge. *Bad bitches move in silence,* she thought to herself, returning to the shadows from which she came.

Despite the fact that Diane gave her word to her best friend to keep her hands off Marco, Shane blamed herself for getting so close with a woman everyone warned her about. She was burnt by the fire Diane afflicted on her pride. When you lay down with dirty-dog bitches, you come up with fleas was the lesson she learned.

Pulling off in her car, Shane wasn't surprised that not one tear had fallen as she sped by the two lovebirds making it known she had seen them.

Shane knew Diane couldn't be trusted, but she also thought if she showed her how to be a true friend that maybe she could teach an old hoe new tricks.

"You's a nasty bitch, Diane, but I'm going to give you an ass beating that's long overdue!"

I heard those words lying in bed while talking to my boyfriend on the phone, thinking to myself, *Whose man my aunt done fucked now?* I could hear the blows thump against someone as I told Trap I would call him back to fill him in on the Commons Soap Opera.

I hopped up off the bed, taking my good ol' time, hoping Diane was getting her ass kicked because homegirl needed it on the real. I have to give respect, though, to where it's due, and my aunt had taken many bitches out who got in her way about her hustle.

Breaking my neck to see what was going on in the front of the apartment, the outside crowd gave up the score. Shane was serving

Diane two pieces like she was Colonel Sanders himself. Diane tried to handle her own, but the iron fist couldn't fight with the fury of a true friend scorned.

Weave was flying, fingernails were popping off and the screaming grew louder as the two of them threw blows and the instigators refereed the fight, calling the blows out Vegas style.

I stood there in awe, mesmerized by the combinations Shane was throwing when I stepped down off the last step in front of the apartment. To be so prissy, ol' girl could hold her own. She beat on Diane for about fifteen more minutes and would have kept it up if my grandmother wouldn't have rudely interrupted.

"That's enough now, Ms. Shane. I think my daughter has had enough." The old spiritual voice was heard throughout the midst of the cheering.

Shane stopped right there in her tracks, letting go of Diane, but before she walked away, she made a grand exit by spitting in Diane's face.

"You and that walking mattress," Shane turned and pointed at me, "stay away from me and my family. The apple don't fall far from the tree, and I'll be damned if you burn my daughter with your whorish ways you learned from this bitch." Giving me and Diane the look of death, the tears fell as she walked away.

My grandmother returned upstairs without saying another word. I helped Diane to her feet as the instigators disbanded.

"What happened, Diane? Are you okay?" I asked sincerely in search of some answers.

Diane pulled away from my helping hand, biting my head off quick. Cutting off all small talk, she gathered her belongings from off the ground and headed towards home. I felt bad for a split second, then I plotted on how to get her drunk to find out the scoop.

A couple days down the line, I would soon hear the truth with no holds barred. In scheme for the info from the loose-lipped drunk, I poured the shots of gin until every detail was out—my bottom jaw on the floor, ears on fire and heart aching for Shane.

It seems like me and Sasha became thick as thieves when our parents disapproved of our friendship.

"Dang, E, why you so quiet this morning? You nervous about this being our first day?" Sasha tilted her head with a smile to put my attention on her.

"I'm just sorry for how I dissed you all summer, girl. On the real, I missed you so much. Hanging out with Diane all the time keeps me depressed and drunk. It's like I don't want to do anything else besides listen to Mary J. and get drunk. Trap disappeared after the ass whipping A.J. put on him, and A.J. doesn't want anything to do with me, unless my ass is up and my face is down." I tried to hold up the tears, but Sasha saw right through me. "Turning sixteen was supposed to be something special, you know, a turning point in my life. I was supposed to be happy, but there is nothing happy going on in my life." The clear, salty fluids hurt my inner being as they fell down. "I know your mom was happy we weren't speaking, wasn't she?"

"I'm not going to let my mother and your aunt come between us, never." Sasha turned about in the small double seat of the bus and placed my hands inside hers. "I love you, E. You're my homegirl. I would never do anything to hurt you, and I hope you feel the same. Maybe we both were being a little stubborn about squashing the beef with each other, but I couldn't give in to your spoiled ass." Sasha smiled as she held my hands tighter. "I just wanted you to come to your senses about the shit that went down at the party, ruling me, your best friend, out as a suspect. I am not grimy. I don't want to be a spokesmodel for that. Not at all!"

"Okay, I get it now. You can shut up." I couldn't do anything but smile, knowing I had my best friend back in my corner. I had forgotten about how good it felt to be around someone my own age.

"Anyway," I said, sucking my teeth, "you know you wanted me to apologize to your stuck-up ass."

Sasha flung her head from side to side, egotistically poking out her lips as she said, "Yup."

"Did you work on that speech all summer?" Embracing each other, we laughed so hard my tears of sorrow turned to tears of joy.

"No, I didn't work on that speech all summer. I was planning on not talking to you ever again." Sasha dropped her head, displeased. "What I said was from the heart."

Almost missing the bus stop, Sasha got back on point, pulling down the stop request, yelling at everybody else to catch their attention.

"Ya'll ready for this fashion show?" Sasha yelled throwing up a Crip sign. "Well, if you are, rep your hood to the fullest." Sasha spoke with such confidence as insecurity shook my being. Even though I didn't show any fear, my heart was in my throat as I exited the bus. Being from the North Side, where the gang strip was blue, we came all the way to the Hill District, where the bitches' gang banged as hard as the dudes, and their gang strip was red.

From 7:45 am until 2:30 pm, I would reside on the battleground of Shenley High School on a promise to learn something. The Crips and the Bloods were the least of your worries, as Pittsburgh was divided from hood to hood and color to color, and we all was about to face each other.

School consisted of nine periods with two lunches and us horny teenagers following a schedule of whose number to get next. Caught up in the mix quick, Sasha blended into the crowds as I went my own way. Every female from the Hill was dipped in gold, and the young men were on the paper chase or the gangster hunt to start trouble.

I watched my best friend cling to a fella on her way to homeroom, and I retired to the first bathroom I saw to smoke me a squed. Even in a room full of people, I felt alone like a little girl lost. It was only eight o'clock in the morning and I had all day to go until I could reach the comfort zone of a liquor bottle. But the day went on and it was mesmerizing as everybody formed a clique. Now, you have me trying to get in where I fit in, but the complex groups in high school had me questioning who the hell I was.

The categories become a lot more complicated within the groups, and it was nothing like middle school. It was no longer the popular ones and the nerds with everybody else in between, the in between had cliques also.

Me and Sasha didn't have one class together, and our lunch period was even different from the educational programs we were taking up. As I walked into the lunchroom, the cheerleaders had shit on lock. All eyes on them, their hips sashayed back and forth as their loud mouths yelled out the ancient Rock Steady cheer.

When finished, the lunchroom was in an uproar and the cliques appeared focused to the naked eye as they fell into position around the cheerleaders.

The good girls followed behind the cheerleaders, putting themselves on the map to become head cheerleader someday to lead the line. It would look good on any college application to rule the hallways, sidelines and halftime shows. That could lead to a scholarship, if you got the skills to pay the bills.

Skirts that don't come above the knees, sweater dresses and reading glasses rest on their noses as they turn them up at the goodies; they're the sophisticated bitches and the biggest freaks. Hair done up in French twists or buns, but never caught with a ponytail or too much makeup for its uncouth is what their parents would say, but we around here call them stuck up. Following behind, but not far you got the Double "D" Boys, wanting the rights to turn any sophisticated girl into a prize possession, a trophy wife of some sort of a bad girl. And you know what they say about a good girl gone bad? Once she gone, she gone forever. At one time or another, a girl wants to live the dangerous life. The Double "D" Boys prey on these girls until they hit a weak spot to boost their bragging rights.

You could hear the gangs chant throughout the hallways, their blood calls daring a nigga or a bitch to step out of character. But the other gangs kept it low key, knowing they were outnumbered. They would wait a couple days until some of the Bloods soldiers dropped off to their street duties before creating a war, giving them a chance. These crazy mutherfuckers are the reason why we have metal detectors statewide in the schools.

Everything was just twisted up when it came to the football players hanging out with the nerds, exchanging one service for another. The football players made all A's and the nerds got to live to see tomorrow. Straight mafia shit, I know...

The hoodrats tried to creep on a come up, the preppy tried to prove they're not homosexual, and last but not least, here was me trying to figure out who I wanted to be.

Dysfunctional from birth, I had more friends in my head than I had in real life. Always under the influence, I created characters and killed them, celebrated their birthdays and visited the hospital when they were sick, dredging up lie after lie to fit in, to be noticed, for someone to ask questions, crying to seek the attention I didn't receive at home. I asked myself many nights, *Why do I do the things I do?* Sitting in a hospital waiting room for nobody to come out and the only answer I can come up with is *I'm trying to find a cure for my loneliness in need of affection.*

If my best friend knew half of the unnecessary lies I've trumped up just to have something to say, she would put me in a clique all by my lonesome called C.C.C.—Certified Crazy Clique. I rule myself out to be a wannabe because I want to be each and every one of them. Anyone was better than being myself. I wanted to be accepted.

A long drawn-out day with teachers whose breath smelled like hot shit and stale coffee came to the end as I sat in last period daydreaming. It was 2:25 pm, and it was finally over as my English teacher gave out writing journals. I managed to make it through the whole day not having one conversation with anybody, not one single person besides Sasha this morning on the bus ride to hell.

Sasha was socially economic, running the hallways putting her name on the map as the class clown reputation came about rapidly. And me, I declared myself a social misfit, chalking my first day up as a failure to communicate with others.

"Diane, what are you doing here? You know I hate seeing your face first thing walking in the door." I rolled my eyes, slamming the front door to the apartment. "I had a fucked-up day at school, so I'm not in the mood for your bullshit. I coasted to the kitchen, thirsty for something to drink as Diane followed behind on my heels.

"I'm here to talk to you about Trap, smart ass. And if you think you're having a bad day, wait until you hear this." Diane pulled up a chair to the dining table and took a seat.

"Oh, my God. Here we go, like I said, with the bullshit. What can you possibly have to talk to me about when it comes to him?" I take a seat next to her furious. "I know you didn't come over here to tell me you're still fucking him."

Diane stood up from her seat quickly. "No, bitch, I ain't fucking him, but I know about somebody else, and it ain't no bitch."

Our eyes became one as we both took a seat quietly for the first minute while I tried to piece together what it meant.

"So, what are you saying, Diane? You have my undivided attention, and I want to know what's up." I was confused and needed answers in a matter of seconds. I could see the look on Diane's face, and it wasn't good as she bit at her fingernails lost for words.

"I come to you in peace, Egypt, and I need you to really listen to me. I know we haven't always been on the best of terms..."

"Get to the point, Diane. What's good with my nigga, Trap?" Cutting Diane off, I got real close and personal within her space.

"Okay, you smart-ass bitch, you want it, you got it!" Diane spat loudly. "Your man be hitting other niggas off in the ass up Northview where he lives. I heard it through some guy I'm talking to for the moment. But I'm keeping him close until you find out everything."

"Yeah, right!" I twist my lips with disbelief, laughing with a bitter tone. "He don't live up Northview Heights, he lives with his boys across the way on Cedar Ave. What kinda shit are you trying to start up now?"

"I know you think I'm talking out the side of my neck."

"You're damn straight, Diane!"

"But I seen it with my own eyes, Egypt, and that's not even the worst part. My boy told me it's his brother."

"He doesn't have any family at all! You musta got the wrong person or something because we talked about that all the time."

"Shut the hell up, E! You don't know that nigga or nothing about him. Everything he has told you is a lie, girl. I'm telling you I seen it with my own eyes. Just hear me and hear me good. I know you know we did something..."

"I don't want to hear this shit!" I got up from the table with clenched fists, ready to strike blows.

"Well, you're going to hear it, Egypt! He raped me after knocking both of us out from hotwiring our drinks. Go back to the night at my house. We can drink anybody under the table, and Trap don't drink all like that. We didn't even smash half the case before it was lights out."

I stopped in my tracks as I tried to walk away, going back to recall the night.

"Who made the last drinks?" Diane asked with confidence.

"I can't remember shit that happened that night, but I do know this much—I heard you moaning. It didn't sound like no rape to me."

"You're just being smart in the mouth and not in the head. Try and remember. Did you make those last drinks? I know for a fact I didn't, because you had me looking for a CD, as usual. It was him, E. That's why your ass is so quiet right now. Shit, I don't even remember how I got upstairs."

By this time I had sat my black ass back on down, hanging on Diane and her every word in deep thought as she continued to speak. "I know we were drinking, talking shit and having a good time, then the next moment, I wake up with a dick in my ass. I thought it was one of my freaks and you know how I get down, so I didn't ask no questions because I thought I didn't have to."

"You knew it was him. You're always fucking somebody else's man. I just can't believe you did that shit to me, your niece."

The verbal dialogue ceased as Diane placed her face in the palms of her hands, shaking her head. It gave me a minute to be absorbent to the story that was starting to make sense, even though I didn't want to admit it.

"I swear I didn't notice anything wrong until he started to pound me out." Diane's voice cracked with tears, but she gave me no eye contact, I think from being embarrassed. "I don't like it like that when I'm going anal."

"Aiight aiight, too much info, Diane."

"I'm just saying, Egypt, he had me begging for him to stop. It was as if he had the devil in him or something. Where were you at, then? He pulled out a chunk of my hair pumping me full of his seed, screaming out he was the fucking man. I couldn't sit down for a week without crying. , He gave me five hundred dollars to keep my mouth shut. Threatening me on the low, he threw out the words, 'Who is she going to believe? Do you think she gonna believe a trick like you or her man? You're known too much for fucking someone else's man, you pigeon.' He spit on me and went on his way."

Diane's face was beet red and her eyes were swollen from the tear-jerker she produced. I almost felt sorry for her, but pride wouldn't let me show it. She tried to keep eye contact on me, to catch a reaction of some sort from her brokenhearted niece, but I didn't submit to her doing.

"I didn't want to tell you how this nigga Trap was getting down until I had proof. He be fucking niggas in the ass! Do you know how many diseases that dirty-dick nigga can be carrying? Nowadays, faggot-ass niggas is infected with the HIV and AIDS. There ain't no cure for that, Egypt. You and I both need to get tested as soon as possible."

The conversation had come full circle and we were back on the reason why we had to go down memory lane. My heartbeat erratic, I couldn't catch my breath, hearing the abbreviation for death.

"Please, Diane, tell me this is a joke. Let up off the marked-for-death story. If this was the way for you to tell me about how shit went down between you and Trap, let it be known now."

Diane sunk lower in the chair, shaking her head as she cried a river. I knew then it wasn't a game, falling to my knees.

I was disgusted from the whole story, ready to shoot the messenger, when my body inflamed with rage.

"This punk-ass nigga gives me a buck on my B-day, but gives you five hundred. I guess my pussy was trash compared to a good ol' hoe like you."

"Little girl, who do you think you're talking to?" Diane dismissed the tears and stood to her feet. "If you disrespect me like that one more time, calling me out my name, I'm gonna beat that ass, and you can put that on my life. A matter of fact, I'll whip on that ass like your momma should." Diane gave off a sad face, sarcastically placing both of her hands on her cheeks. "Oh I forgot, momma don't give a fuck about her young tramp, seeing how she left you and all."

Diane never seen the chair coming until her body felt the impact. In a matter of seconds, her body hit the floor with me standing over it, swinging bows from the left and the right. As she laid in a fetal position, Diane didn't attempt to hit back.

Diane felt the hits, chalking it up to justification for an ass kicking that was long overdue. She yelled out "I'm sorry" over and over again as each blow took her back to the past.

Lola and Diane were only three years apart, growing up as thick as thieves. They spent more time being best of friends then sisters, sharing everything from clothes to their first boy kiss. Inseparable they were, until Diane entered high school. She had fallen in love with a upper classman who only had eyes for Ms. Lola James. The moment she laid eyes on the strapping frame of Carter Winters, Diane thought they were destined, despite the age difference and the love he had for her sister. She tried every trick of the trade to put the eyes of Carter upon her fully developed, voluptuous body, but nothing ever worked. It made her bitter against the one she called her sister, forced to watch the couple in bliss. Their storybook romance filled the hallways in school and often spilled over on the homeland where Diane couldn't escape the sounds of the lovemaking.

Always in demand for what she couldn't have, Diane waited for the perfect opportunity to bounce on what her life could be if she got Lola out the way. And that's exactly what she did— she waited.

Two years later, her sister nowhere to be found, Carter cried on Diane's shoulder. His father had killed his mother and then himself, crazed from drug addiction. Carter discovered their bodies coming home from work early to surprise his mother on a raise he had got on becoming department head at some grocery store. Showing up on their doorstep on wounded knee, Diane opened her arms and her legs spread eagle.

This gave Diane perfect timing, knowing her sister was working overtime trying to save enough money to buy a car for the summer. A shoulder to cry on led to something else, quick as Diane made her move. Carter was the first man she performed mouth to mouth re-suscitation on, bringing his flesh to life for her liking, and she enjoyed every moment of pleasing her man. Carter gave in to the newness of her lips, escaping the long-term pain for just a little while. With each stroke, a tear fell, for he knew what he was doing was wrong, but he couldn't stop falling victim to Diane's poisonous venom.

She replaced her suction-cup lips with the tender tight of her virginity, putting the finishing touches on her man-to-be as he sobbed uncontrollably from the hurt feel good. Losing his parents and his woman wasn't on his agenda for today and getting caught by the head of the household didn't make things any better. Diane broke her mother's heart, giving witness to the unspeakable act as she pointed the finger at herself for not raising her children right.

It was a deep, dark secret mother and daughter kept to themselves. She didn't want to expose the ugliness of Diane's wicked ways, subjecting her other daughter to the hurt from a betrayal of someone as close as a sister. The silence laced an unspoken warning of secrecy throughout the room of and her momma held her head low, leaving the unspeakable act where it lay.

Things changed for the worst as the secret had a spirit which lingered in the house. Carter continued to sleep with both Diane and Lola as he watched his life go down. His mind wasn't right after the death of his parents and soon after he picked up his father trait of abusing alcohol and drugs. Every chance in the making, Diane painted a perfect picture of her sister being unfaithful, but made sure to pledge her undying love, keeping Carter close to the flame. The flame blew out the day I was born.

"Go ahead and take your frustration out on me, but I'm not the one you should be fighting. Trap is the foul-ass nigga in play, not me," Diane shouted, undergoing the blows from my heavy-hitting fists against her head.

"This is for you fucking my man, disrespecting me and my momma, telling lie after lie and just being a hoe. I hate you, I hate you, I hate you," I spat, giving off three kicks to Diane's midsection as the adrenalin rush ran its course. She huffed and puffed out of breath, falling to her knees in tears. Diane wiped the blood, sweat and tears from her face with the T-shirt she was wearing, ready to bring the truth to the light.

She looked down on me, shaking her head in pity, knowing what was once good was no more. Diane picked up the phone, dialing a witness to confirm the story.

"When you started spreading your legs, you took on feelings you couldn't control, young buck. This here is some grown woman shit for your ass. No teenager should have to go through this, and I'm sorry for what you're about to hear." Diane spoke her peace, calling a spade a spade, waiting on a voice to pick up the other end of the phone. She tried to console me in her own twisted mind.

"I'm going to come through your crib later on and you can tell your so-called proof to meet me there. Get out before Grandma gets home. I don't want her to see us at each other's neck; it will just bring about too many questions." I spoke in a whisper, but it was enough to be heard across the dining room floor.

"Hello, yeah it's me, and I got E with me, too. I need you to come down the Commons real quick so we all can have a sit-down."

Whoever was on the other end of the phone agreed, and Diane hung up the phone, nodding her approval of the meeting.

"Aiight, Diane you set it up now before Grandma gets here." A sinister look crept along Diane's face as her eyes narrowed with hate. She turned her back to me, walking towards the front door, and I felt defeat quiver my body structure. As Diane walked out the door, she flipped off the world in agreement with a truth she held onto tightly. I was a curse to this family from the second I took a peek out of the birth canal coming into this world. And the sooner she could get rid of me, the better.

I tried to clean up the mess before Grandma came in, but the insane thoughts that were planted ran through me until I was out of breath. What was I to do if the allegations against Trap were true and I had a death sentence taking over my veins?

Being exposed to numerous infections from having unprotected sex was the least of my worries an hour ago coming home from school. Holding my head in hands, I cried for someone to rescue me from this life I was living.

"A loving family is what the nurse thought I deserved. If this is the way they love me, I would hate for them to hate me. Why didn't that nosy bitch just mind her business and call child welfare? Someone who cared could have wanted me. Somebody rich in a big house with a backyard and a pool. Someone who discussed how their day was at work and asked me the same while we ate. Being able to depend on someone other than myself would be nice once in a while. Momma, I need you! Where could you be, dear Momma? How come you ain't come back for me? Dear Momma, don't you ever think about your daughter?"

I could feel the mask of anger I wore peel off layer by layer answering my own questions.

"Hell no she don't care about me, 'cause she only thinking about her damn self! I hope you somewhere strung out on drugs so I can accept the fact addiction runs your life.

"WHERE ARE YOU? WHERE ARE YOU! WHERE ARE YOU?" I yell out in a fall to my knees once again in a heavy sob.

"Baby, are you okay? What brought all this on, chile?" My grandmother came from the shadows and wrapped me in her arms. "I know my daughter didn't do right when she walked out on not just you, but us, but we got to get passed it and move on. I know it's hard, baby, knowing she out there, but we just got to move on. It hurts so bad, and I hurt for you all the time. I could hear you preaching from outside, chile." She pulled my hands away from my teary eyes and cradled my face in her hands.

"What the hell is going to happen to me, Grandma? Why doesn't she love me? I need her so much right now in my life."

The words crept out of my throat as my grandmother searched my eyes. She stared at her misguided and unwanted grandchild trying to find the right words to say.

"Egypt, baby, you got to focus on the good and pray about the bad. I can't answer those questions about your mother, but good things are going to come to you. You're the kind of person who can accomplish anything you put your energy towards. You have to trust in God, Egypt, and stay strong."

Hysteria came from within, and out of anger, I cursed my grandma and her God. The first thing to go up against the walls was my angry fists followed by my head. I clawed my face and arms, breaking the skin, snapping out as if I was possessed by the devil himself. I beat myself until I plunged into the long length coffee table resting in the middle of the floor. The table shattered in tiny pieces, cutting away at every exposed part of my body frame crashing through the double glass.

A constant cry of excruciating pain let my grandmother know I was still alive as she rushed to the telephone to dial 911. Darting to my aid, the broken glass cut through the skin of my grandmother as she got on her hands and knees to give me the intimacy my soul ached for.

Rocking me in arms calling on the Lord through blood, sweat and tears, our flesh leaked all over each other and our hearts were in despair.

"Dear Lord, my grandchild is seeking the love and affection of a mother who is neither here nor there. Only you can heal her pain. What if I could speak all languages of humans and of angels? If I did not love others, I would be nothing more than a noisy gong or a clanging cymbal. What if I could prophesy and understand all secrets and all knowledge? And what if I had faith that moved mountains? I would be nothing unless I loved others. What if I gave away all that I owned and let myself be burned alive? I would gain nothing unless I loved others.

"Love is kind and patient, never jealous, boastful, proud, or rude. Love isn't selfish or quick tempered. It doesn't keep a record of wrongs that others do. Love rejoices in the truth, but not in evil. Love is always supportive, loyal, hopeful, and trusting. Love never fails! Everyone who prophesies will stop and unknown languages will stop, and unknown languages will no longer be spoken. All that we know will be forgotten. We don't know everything, and our prophecies are not complete. But what is perfect will someday appear, and what isn't perfect will then disappear. When we were children, we thought and reasoned as children do. But when we grow up, we quit our childish ways. Now all we can see of God is a cloudy picture in a mirror. Later we will see him face to face. We don't know everything, but then we will, just as God completely understands us. For now, there are faith, hope and love. But of these three, love is the greatest.

"Please give me the strength to give her the love she yearns for to get through, Lord. Don't let this be it for my grandchild. She needs to learn the value of love to forgive her momma just as well as I do."

1Corinthians, 1-13

CHAPTER SIX

The EMS workers stormed the apartment door within minutes, asking a whole lot of questions about me and my extracurricular activities. My state of mind lying in the broken glass went from hysterical to catatonic in a matter of seconds. My ripped flesh made the EMS workers nervous checking over my body to make sure that no main artery or vein had been cut too deep.

Bandaging the wounds, they placed my body on the gurney as the white cotton soaked up the blood quickly. The crowd that gathered in front of the door made a hole for the victim as my grandmother followed suit behind the paramedics to ride alongside her granddaughter.

In the back of the ambulance, she held my hand in silence with the Bible in the other.

"Ma'am, did you say that she done this to herself?" The police officer asked with disbelief written all over his face.

"I don't know anything more than what I told you, and my answers are not going to change. My name is Ms. James, and this chile here is Egypt Winters, my granddaughter. I don't know why she done what she done to herself. I don't know if she is all jacked up on drugs or not. And I didn't lay a hand on her, you hear me, Mr. Policeman. Can you understand the words coming out of my mouth, son? Because I refuse to answer these same questions one more time."

Worried to the point of no return, Ms. James copped a squat continuing to listen to the police and doctors on different theories on what happened behind the closed doors of her apartment.

The most severe wounds were to the arms and head. I had protected my face well on the fall down as my mask only suffered minor bumps and bruises. Eighty-eight stitches were applied all together in the head and both arms, making me whole again.

I laid in the hospital bed, heavily medicated. Once I realized I was on the move in the ambulance, a force to be reckoned with had risen. I flew into another outrage, thinking my grandmother was taking me to a mental hospital. Biting the paramedic on the arm and damn near taking his pinky finger clear off, he had no other choice but to put me to sleep.

"How long are you going to keep her, doctor?" my grandmother asked, grief-stricken.

"We are keeping her here under observation for tonight. We want to talk to her when she wakes up to see where her mental state lies. We ran tests on her to check for any drug use and disease which came back in the clear, so we can rule them out as suspects. I will also run a brain scan to make sure there is no internal bleeding once the swelling goes down." The doctor was sincere in his tone, looking over his clipboard.

"What do you mean by 'we want to talk to her'? Who is 'we,' doctor?"

"When I say 'we,' Ms. James, I'm talking about me and a mental physician. Do you know anything that would have sent her into a rage like this? Anything minute would help."

"All I know is I came in from the shopping center, and I see my grandchild on her knees, crying and talking to herself."

"Has she been depressed lately?"

"She's a teenager, doctor; they're always going through something."

"I know what you mean, Ms. James. I have a teenager myself. That will be all for now, unless you have more questions for me."

"No, sir. I just want to sit with my chile alone for awhile. I don't want her to wake up all by herself. I don't think that will be good for her."

"Take as much time as you need, Ms. James. I agree with that."

The doctor nodded his head, giving his approval as he dismissed himself from the room.

I lay in the hospital bed stiff as a board. If it wasn't for the heart monitor reminding you that I was alive, you would've thought I was dead and that God called his child to sit next to him on his throne.

"Momma, is she okay? I'm on my way right now," Diane yelled into the phone in shock, guilty for what happened to her niece.

"No you will not, chile! Don't you dare come here! I feel it in my old weary bones that you're at the bottom of this. Your ways are going to catch up with you sooner than you think. I swear they will and when they do, I hope the Lord has mercy on your soul."

"What about you, Mom?! You ain't no fucking saint neither, old woman!" Diane scornfully spoke her piece before hanging up the phone.

A thousand and one thoughts ran through Diane's small, seductive brain, contemplating her next move, but not one of them was in my best interest. Knowing the secret of Trap's indiscretions to be true, Diane decided to take the honey from the beehive in the most treacherous way. A twist of fate with a splash of lime on the side; it's time to ride on the next nigga's dime.

"Honey, if you can hear your grandmother, I'm sorry, chile, I'm sorry. I just wanted the best for you and your mother. Hell, all my kids for that matter, but that damned Diane, she's a bad seed. There are so many skeletons surrounding why your mother left, I keep tripping over old bones all the time. The time will come for the truth to come out, chile, and when it does, I will lose you forever. I'm getting so tired, baby, mentally, physically and spiritually, I'm broken down. I pray every day for my downfalls and where I fell short, but I hope when my time comes I can sit with the King. You're only sixteen and baby, you're not equipped to handle this struggle that lies before you, but I pray now for strength for you and me both."

Rubbing my hand, my grandmother spoke out loud and prayed

silently while the doctor stood in the midst of the shadows listening to every word.

"I know where your daddy is, and it's time for him to put them drugs down so he can help you. Grandma is going to make it right, chile, I promise you that. I will return in the morning to make sure you're okay, baby. I love you with all my heart."

Kissing me on the forehead and letting go of my limp hand, my grandmother had a chill run through her body. Blowing another kiss and whispering good-bye, she headed out the door to face her demise.

KNOCK! KNOCK! KNOCK!

"Who is it?" Diane shouted at the front door.

"It's your mother, chile."

"What do you want, Momma?" Diane asked, opening up the door with an annoyed look on her face.

"Well, for starters you can ask about Egypt. And you can also invite me in so I can talk to you."

Diane rolled her eyes, walking away from the door, leaving it ajar.

"You know what, Diane? You ain't nothing but a bad seed." Her mother walked through the threshold, slamming the door behind her.

"I've let you manipulate your way through this dysfunctional family long enough. Spreading your poison and laying a plague of hate in our hearts towards each other has made our house a broken home. Do you understand that me being a Christian, I'm not supposed to hate? But your malicious ways makes me feel otherwise. You've set out to destroy every and anything you touch by any means necessary, having no conscience and suffering no consequences for your actions, but you've crossed the line messing with my baby."

"Get to the point, Mom. I don't need you to tell me no life story about something I care nothing about. I know what I am, and I don't care. I do what I do, Momma; I don't give a fuck."

"When did we start disrespecting mothers around here, Diane?"

"When you walked in my house passing judgment on me. Now,

if you're done telling me everything I already know, you can leave. And tell that niece of mine to get a HIV test while she laid up in the hospital."

"What you mean by that?"

"You know what I mean by that. What, you thought she was gonna be a virgin forever? I guess she's not the only walking mattress in the family, huh?" Diane's tone of voice turned sour as her face painted red with anger.

"I despise you for coming in my house acting like your shit don't stink. That's why I can't walk in your house now, because I'm a constant reminder of the shit you let me get away with. What about the plague of hate you installed in this dysfunctional family, old lady? You know me, Momma—I haven't changed! I will always have a pretty face with a killer head game that can cut any man I want down to my size."

"If you don't die first, chile!" Her mother stared into her eyes hurt. She cut Diane off, not wanting to hear more. Taking a seat, Diane did the same right next to her on the couch.

"You may be right about all that, but it's going to take a turn for the better today. I decided to tell Egypt about her father and my conclusion on why her mother left in the first place."

The room fell silent, the tears hitting the floor from both Diane and her mother. Nobody wanted to tell the secret that haunted the James' family, and the old wounds being cut open were going to hurt like hell.

"It's time we work through this, Diane, with the little bit of family we got left. We have to help Egypt save our souls so she can have peace within hers."

My grandmother dropped her head, weeping in her own heartache she caused, putting one daughter before the other instead of trying to help them both. What kind of mother would hide the secrets she had and raised another in the midst of them?

"My soul don't need saving, Momma, because I'm fine with me. Do what is best for you, but leave me out of it. You must really think that's a good idea to do right now, but I think not, with everything that just went down." Diane wiped the salty water falling from her eyes, feeling she deserved an Academy Award for her performance. "I say we say nothing until this passes over."

"She deserves to know the truth, Diane. You should try telling it sometimes, you know….."

"You know what, Momma? I need to be tested for HIV, too. You want to know why? Because I slept with Egypt's boyfriend, Trap, and he sleeps with men. I'm a whore; a walking mattress just like you called me. Look what you've spoke into existence, old lady. That's why she snapped out, Momma. Yeah yep, because of me. That's some honesty for your ass now, ain't it?"

In total shock, her mother stood to her feet with an expression of pain, disapproval and disgust. She couldn't do nothing else but raise up and walk out the door. It was shameful to her to raise a daughter so viscous, but who could she blame but herself?

"What, Momma? You have nothing else to say to me?" Diane was in a rage as she shouted, "Are you going to tell her or not? Momma, I know you can hear me talking to you." By the time Diane noticed how far she had followed her mother outside the door screaming, Shane and Sasha stood close by with unexpected looks.

"I wonder what you done did now," Shane uttered, rolling her eyes up and down Diane.

Diane's eyes were focused dead on Shane's lip movement as she picked up every word Shane thought she whispered.

"I fucked your man again, bitch, that's what I did." Diane responded, fiercely placing her hands on her hips. Shane stared around, confused, appalled, as if Diane was even speaking to her. "What, you thought I didn't hear you? Well, I did bitch!"

"I will beat the brakes off that speeding pussy again! You ain't nothing to me, you chicken-head bitch," Shane snapped back in pre-hype mode, ready to wreck something.

"Come on, Ma, don't do this in front of Ms. James. It already looks like she crying. Shit, Ma, just let it go. Diane going to get what she deserve, you wait and see." Sasha pulled on her mother's arm, trying to put the spark out on the fireworks Diane lit the fuse to.

"You lucky my daughter with me, bitch, or it would be me and you out here again. And, oh yes, your mother would see you kiss the pavement."

"Naw, you lucky, trick-ass bitch." Diane spoke in a lower tone as she looked around to see where her mother was at. Once she observed her mother wasn't in bird's eye view, she slammed the door, not really wanting a confrontation.

"Sasha, I hope you don't be hanging out with her niece. Them chicken-head bitches are bad news, and I don't want you nowhere around when the chips fall down."

"Mom, you tripping right now. I told you Egypt wasn't Diane, and I'm not going to stop being friends with her. She need me. I'm the only friend she got. I'm sorry..."

"There is no need to be sorry, baby, but you my child, and in the future you will learn to never go against family. No matter what, boo, you will learn. Diane is a snake-ass bitch. Everything she touches turns to shit. You just watch and see that the apple don't fall far from the tree."

What am I going to do? my grandmother thought to herself, pacing back and forth across the living room floor. The sight of glass and blood brought a flashback before her eyes. Turning out the living room lights to black out the tragedy, she retired to sleep. This was a day that needed to be forgotten.

CHAPTER SEVEN

"General, I'm not trying to go there with you, nigga. I'm really not feeling this bullshit tonight." His runner is begging him to stall him out for coming up short once again on the package money.

"Whatcha going do then, Craze? You got my three hundred you owe me for coming up short?"

"Naw, man, I don't have dat shit 'cause the count is right. It's always right, nigga. You just be trying to get me. I make you mad money, so squash that shit!"

General stands at ease, with his head cocked to the side, ice grilling Craze.

"Oh, today we decided to man the fuck-up huh?" General replies, pulling his gun from the small of his back. "If I say you owe me, nigga, you owe! Now, you got two options, muthafucker, since you grew some balls today: one, you can pay me my money and drop ya fucking boxers, or two, you can shop for this gat in your mouth."

The ice grilling turns colder as General tucks his chin. Craze stands there, watching the gun in his hand swing back and forth, taking a glance into his eyes, quickly hoping General don't see the fear. But fear creeps up in Craze knowing that he has to take one of his commands. If he has to go out, he should go out swinging.

"My time is money, and you're costing me a lot of both right now, nigga. I no longer give you a choice," General says, raising the gun to Craze's dome. "I want what I want, and it's your ass, nigga." General continues stroking Craze on the side of the face with his gun. "So bend over like a good little bitch since you don't have the heart to man the fuck up."

Not saying a word, Craze gives in, dropping his pants to his ankles.

Bending over, he places his right hand on the wall to give his body support for the wrath that is about to come.

"You taking so long made my dick limp. I'm gonna need you to handle that for me," General says, laughing his head off while Craze festers. With further due, Craze is ready to get it done and over with, turning about and dropping to his knees.

"You better not cry this time neither. Man up, nigga, and if you think about doing something to my jimmy, you going to shop for this gat if you follow through."

General's voice is a whisper. Craze stands eye level to his manhood with a dry mouth. Gagging from the head of his flesh touching his tongue, General moans out a sigh of relief.

Watching Craze go up and down his shaft with a stroke of genius drives General insane on the power he has over men. He is awaiting his arrival all day for the simple fact Craze is getting better and better at handling business. On that note, General decides to push the bar and humiliate Craze further to install fear. Pulling out, he smacks his shaft on his forehead and serves up his testicles in the palm of his hand.

Craze can't hold back the tears. "Please don't make me do it" was uttered before they are forced upon his mouth.

"That's what I wanted to see, nigga, you cry like a woman. Now be a good little bitch and do what you were told." Craze's tears disassemble his manhood as General holds his fate in his hands.

Putting the finishing touches on a sexual experience well deserved, General gives Craze the grand finale, pounding him out. He even calls out his name, devouring his anus as if it was a piece of pussy. As his salty manhood leaks all over the floor, General hasn't realized he kissed Craze on his back when he pulled out from inside. Craze turns around furious, pulling away as General laughs, satisfied with the nut he was given.

"You's one sick muthafucker, and I'm done working for you."

Craze's heart was beating uncontrollably in fear for his life, but he would rather die than endure being raped one more time.

"Are you breaking up with me, bitch?" General speaks calmly.

"I mean it, General, I'm done with you, and I'm going to kill you if you ever put your hands on me again." A fully dressed Craze gives eye contact, speaking his mind.

"Kill me now then, Craze. Right the fuck now because I don't take kindly to threats."

"Naw, you got it dog. I'm going to fuck you like you fucked me, nice and slow. You just watch and see." Craze drops a grand to the floor in a rubber band knot and heads for the door. Before he can open it, General stands close, giving a direct order for him to be present at work bright and early. He swears on his dead mother's grave if Craze doesn't show up for work in the morning, he is a dead man walking.

"Damn, Craze, where you going?" Boo shouts out, already knowing what went down.

"We got some pussy in the back, homie."

Craze pays Boo no mind, leaving the rundown apartment in a two-step. He slams the door so hard, the walls shake.

Boo is fresh to death this Friday night, putting the next nigga's bullshit on the back burner as he shakes off Craze and the meeting with General.

All ready to hit the club to take a load off, Boo sparks up the get-high in relaxation. Hoping General will stay behind to do what he does best, which is himself, Boo wants to keep his outing to a hush.

Niggas are beginning to talk about the weird shit going down in the apartment with me, as well as the drugs. Boo is becoming down-right petrified to make moves, thinking the cops are going to bust down the door any minute, giving out life sentences at any given moment.

But still, General calls the shots, making it painfully clear that he will keep me as long as he likes.

General walks around as if he knew something about me nobody else knows. When he talks to me it's like no other way you see him speak to a woman. It is damn near civilized.

General treats females worse than a dog. He starts off as Prince Charming until they're nice and comfortable, and then Jack the fucking Ripper shows up, shutting shit down. Boo had witnessed it on more than one occasion, often being put in situations by General His dear brother struck fear in most men, and the other small fraction would fear him if they knew the hate he carries around in his heart. A woman who falls victim to him doesn't have a chance.

Boo believes his brother has no soul. He was spawned by Satan's seed, making him think twice about there being a God. If so, where he at? And why is this crazy mutherfucker still breathing? Why do I have to witness all the despicable acts he carries out?

Boo asks himself questions he will never know the answers to, sitting on the broken down couch, finishing the spliff he fired up. The Lox played low on the *Rap City*'s old-school *Friday* episode as Boo's eyes fall sleepy. The get-high overpowers his beanpole physique as he tries to block out all the horrible acts General bestows upon himself, his brother and the hood.

It is what it is around this neck of the woods, so watch your back and your front if you don't want to shop for that gat…

CHAPTER EIGHT

Washing his main body parts at the sink in the bathroom, General glares at the mirror in recognition of himself. Cracking a smile, he can't find a trace.

"You's a handsome devil," General says aloud, winking at himself.

"Niggas ain't shit but ho's and tricks. They think dey hard till I make them suck my dick. I pull dey hair, and I make dem my bitch as dey love to fall victim to my gat and shit. I'm a ruler of all rulers. Ya better man up quick or you will be another bitch sucking my dick. G's up, bitches down, I can make the niggas bounce to this."

A rapper General isn't, but a cold-blooded killer and a rapist amongst men he is. Can the actions of one's parents make their children what they are when they become adults? Should the parents be punished for the havoc their offspring creates walking the world? So many questions, but not enough answers…

The tree branches hit strong against the twelve-year-old boy's window. The wind ripped through the night air howling like the wolves. He lies in his twin0sized bed with the covers tucked under his body so tight in dire need to keep the monsters away that visit him in the middle of the night. Too scared to close his eyes, he hung on every word Marvin Gaye sang loud and proud through his parent's speaker.

Downstairs you could hear the voices of many singing along with the track, too. Laughter filled the air right along with marijuana smoke while they danced into the wee hours of the morning. Ma Dukes and Pops were the party animals of the block. Everyone who was somebody could come through to get high. Selling shots of Nikolai Vodka after the bars shut down at two in the morning drew a large crowd, creating an after-hours spot for the drug dealers. Where there's drug dealers, there's drugs, and that's what Ma Dukes and Pops counted on when they came up with the idea of selling the liquor. A small amount of cocaine and heroin to satisfy their craving would make them open up the door with welcoming arms.

The twelve-year-old boy clenched a big butcher knife under the covers with heavy eyes, but caught a second wind when he heard the music cut down. His hands begin to sweat as the tears fell, knowing the monster would come to his room soon. No way, no how would he endure the pain of the monster another second, minute or hour. He would kill it dead first. The monster would die for sure tonight if he tried to come into his room.

He could hear his Ma and Pops thanking the people that came and wishing them a safe trip home. The party was over, but the twelve-year-old boy's nightmare was about to begin. Pops never helped the boy when he called on him for protection from the monsters and when he reached out for a hug, Pops would just call him names, telling him to be a man about it.

The boy laid in fear with his eyes shut tightly, hearing footsteps near his door. Cracking the door to check if he was sleep, Ma yelled up the steps for Pops to come back downstairs to set up her works. Pops shut the door back gently with his plan in motion to gain a huge score that would sit him pretty for a while.

Down those stairs, Pops worked out many drug deals to keep himself and Ma Dukes thick in intoxication. He sold his first-born son into prostitution to ensure his habit wouldn't go dry. Pops had no love or loyalty for family—only drugs.

The first time the monster visited the boy's room, he was only eight years old. So tired from playing street football in the summer heat wave, he never felt his underwear come off. He only felt a man on his eight-year-old penis sucking it so hard it hurt. Street football wasn't quite the same for the boy.

Nothing was the same for him as the monsters kept coming, creeping under the covers, telling him this is what little boys do for fun. His hopes and dreams turned into nightmares, awaking him often in cold sweats. And when he yelled for his parents in dire need of comfort, they never showed up, too busy getting high on their son's dime.

For the last four years, the boy had been afraid of any bump that comes and goes through the night. But tonight, this night here, on October 30, 1978, the boy decided to change his fate.

The knife the boy clenched tightly in his hands under the covers became more than a comfort, giving him strength as the tree branches hit strong against his window. This was the night, devil's night, when all means would come to an end.

The night started off pretty good, being a twelve-year-old boy out there in the streets playing jokes on the working class. You only get one night to do childish pranks so you don't get labeled the problem child of the neighborhood, and the kids took advantage of that. The boy threw eggs at cars and lit brown paper bags of shit on fire with his friends until the last one had to go home to make curfew. Kicking rocks in the street on his way home, he asked God for someone to abduct him because anything had to be better than his home life. But before he knew it, he stood in front of his own door dreading the fact he had to go in.

Walking in the house in a hurry toward the stairs, past his pop's drinking buddies, he couldn't walk fast enough as he heard his name ring out.

"Come sit down, boy, for a minute. You know it's rude to walk in the house and don't speak!"

Hearing Pops' voice, the boy knew the bullshit was about to begin. Trying to tell Pops he had to study, his old man ordered him to sit down and tell him and his friends a joke.

Pops favorite saying—in dire need of military status—was that he was the Colonel and his kids obey as troops do. Do what he say and not as he do or suffer the consequences, because he rules.

"You're not in the mood to make me laugh?" Pops asked, throwing a joint on the table that stood between them. "Come on, take a seat, young buck, and fire that up like grown men do."

Following his Pops command, the boy took a seat and introduced himself to the get-high. Inhaling deep, the boy didn't cough, but the marijuana turned his frown into a smile by the third hit.

Heart pounding, the boy sat with the big dogs, getting high until the night was thick with darkness. He never told a joke because the joke was on him being introduced to cocaine, as well as marijuana, as he toked away on the joints. Pops and his buddies smoked and drank with the boy until he passed out with a smile on his face and not a care in the world.

Pops laughed at the boy and his limp body as it fell from the couch to the floor. It was time for the boy to put on a show for him and his buddies. Ma Dukes had joined in for the fun, amused that the boy was passed out, until she became the final act of the joke.

Pops pulled out the boy's penis and grabbed Ma Dukes by the hair trying to force her to suck her own son off, but she wouldn't do it. Not following orders earned her a beating for a solid thirty-five minutes while his buddies watched and egged him on.

The only thing that made him stop giving them body blows was he blew his own high and his hands began to hurt. Ma Dukes ran to safety while Pops threw the boy over his shoulder to take him upstairs.

Marvin Gay cut back on with the next group of party animals coming through for the last call to keep their drunken buzzes until the morning. As soon as the boy's head hit the pillow on his bed, he jumped up running to the bathroom to throw up. He lay between the tub and the toilet, turning on the tub water to splash water on his face. After a couple of minutes, he returned to his bed, still high and scared as hell from his rapid heartbeat pounding out his chest.

The tree branches hit against the twelve-year-old boy's window as the wind whipped through the trees howling like the wolves. He laid in the bed with covers tucked under his body so tight in dire need to keep the monsters away that visited him in the middle of the night. With a big butcher knife clenched in his sweaty palms he felt it was safe to shut his eyes.

Moments later, the monster appeared, climbing on top of his twelve-year-old body, pinning him down and covering up his mouth. Frantic as hell, the boy bit down hard through the flesh of the monster's hand, causing him to take a more desperate measure.

Letting himself up to smack the boy to show him who was in control, the twelve-year-old boy's hand came up swinging the butcher knife clean across the monster's neck.

The monster strangled himself, gasping for air as the blood leaked out fierce all over his body. The boy didn't stop there, stabbing the monster twenty-two times. The blood was very thin and dark red as the boy stood over his fear, satisfied with the job he had done.

Watching him bleed out, a smile crept upon his face, feeling exonerated as the monster took his last breath.

Pops couldn't hear the cries from the monster over the loud speaker blaring Marvin Gaye while he pushed cocaine in his nose and heroin in his veins. The boy stood over the dead body, not even scared of what he done. He felt justified for all the wrongdoing he endured over the last four years getting his innocence taken away. But what the twelve-year-old boy didn't realize was taking the monster out created a monster inside himself. Seeing the man struggle to take his last breath gave him the most exciting feeling throughout his body. Death made the twelve-year-old boy tingle all over.

Checking the monster's pockets for whatever he could find, the boy worked fast in static by all the blood. The pockets were empty but his socks were loaded with a bundle of dope and fifteen hundred dollars. The .38 Special holstered to the man's leg was a bonus as the boy held it in his hand. It made his twelve-year-old penis rock hard as the cold piece of steel made him invincible.

The .38 Special replaced the butcher knife in question and a voice in the boy's head told him to finish the job. *Leave nothing for the police to find.*

Pops intoxication was full blast when the boy crept downstairs, walking into the smoke-filled room where him and two more of his drinking buddies dwelled. They never saw him enter the room as they spun their forty-fives with backs turned. He thought to himself why not blow out their brains right then and there while they plotted out the next scheme, but he grabbed up a joint and a beer instead. Dancing to the tune of Oran "Juice" Jones, the boy crept back upstairs with a newfound confidence putting fire to his joint.

Returning to his room, he kicked the dead son of a bitch in the head and jumped on his bed without a care in the world. Tucking the gun under his pillow, he took a long drag off the get-high and exhaled slowly. Getting full contact, not even a hint of vomit traced his throat. Heart pounding and mind racing, the thrill to kill overwhelmed his twelve-year-old body.

Nobody can make you evil, you have to embrace it, the boy told himself, realizing the choice he made within the next hour would change him and his life forever. There is only good and bad, but only he can choose the path to walk.

Preparing himself for one more chilling moment, the boy drank the sixteen ounce can of beer without taking a breath. The laughter in the air faded with the music downstairs. And the boy listened close to see if anybody would ask about the dead man's whereabouts.

Without a struggle in mind, the boy sat back in the dark, waiting for the last call for alcohol to be shouted. Sustaining his position, the boy listened to the falling rain hit hard against the window pane in disgust.

He couldn't understand why Ma Dukes wouldn't leave a man who beat her for sport. The constant black eyes, broken bones, and cuts to the flesh should have made it possible. And Pops selling her first born into prostitution should have been reason enough alone.

Having a little brother didn't claim him from the hatred instilled in his little heart, for Pops praised him like new money. In Pops' eyes, the older boy was beneath his little brother. He wasn't allowed to be around his brother or his mother.

Pops said that they were fallen soldiers, and he would be the one to lead the troops when the time came for war in the streets. *They would taint him and poison his mind with one touch*, Pop's thought, keeping little brother on lockdown. The monster wouldn't dare haunt his room. Would his eyes ever lay down on the vicious cycle that played day in and day out in their house of madness? No, he was the chosen one in the Colonel's eyes.

The house fell silent, but you could hear the cries of Ma Dukes in need for the dope to lace her veins. Pops sat back in a wicker chair with his dick in her mouth and a base pipe in his hands. Sneaking downstairs to get a better look, a sinister look came across the boy's face, ready to go to war. He stood in the shadows listening to Pops degrade Ma Dukes with his harsh words choking her out on his shaft.

No fear made the boy calm as he came into the faded light. Pops never seen the gun coming. He only heard the shot to the back of the head before his brains splattered all over Ma Dukes. Ma Dukes took cover running in the corner of the room, shaking fiercely as his blood fell from her head.

The boy stood back watching Pop's bleed out like a stuck pig and threw Ma Dukes three bags of dope he had found on the dead body. The boy commanded Ma Dukes to go to her room while he cleaned up the mess that he made.

"I graduated real fast to fucking General killing the Colonel dead. I will reign over the streets with nothing but terror in my heart. I will never love another, not knowing what love is, and I will see you in hell, but not before I create one for the soldier you placed upon me."

The pleasure the twelve-year-old boy possessed watching the plasma run from Pops' body satisfied his appetite for destruction. Scared but excited from the bang of the gun, the boy felt no remorse for what he had done and what was to come next.

Ma Dukes sat on the edge of her bed thinking about what she just saw her son do, wishing he had done it a long time ago.

"I hope he's not waiting for me to get him a Band-Aid 'cause I'm about to shoot this dope." Ma Dukes said craving the rush.

The smell of the dope melting down made Ma Dukes dance to a melody that played only in her head.

"That's right, take care of your mother, baby…"

She put the belt around her arm, pulling it tight to pop a vein. She was ready to inject the medicine when General made himself seen. He stood in front of her, staring down with piercing eyes grabbing her hand.

"Not quite yet, Ma."

"What cha doing, son? I need my medicine baby, I'm sick. You don't want your ma to be sick, do you, baby?"

Smacking Ma Dukes across the face, he commanded her to strip down bare ass. He placed the gun to Ma Dukes head and shook his in disbelief.

"It's all over, Shelly… I give the commands around here now!"

Giving Shelly a glance-over, General became aroused from her exposed body. Climbing on top of her, he raped his mother, repeatedly taking out all the pain she inflicted on his soul. The more he beat her, the more the rage kept coming, but she never begged for mercy. She took the beating without a doubt, not giving one scream to boost the boy's ego. Knowing that he was going to kill her for not protecting him from the evil things men do, she accepted her fate. Death.

She prayed that her soul would rest in peace for the things she did and didn't do. She also prayed for her sons and the world, because spawned from Satan's seed, they would both need saving from the wrath that was soon to be. Mixing ammonia with the heroin the hypodermic needle sparkled with the cure—the medicine his mother craved—Ma Dukes lay naked in dire need of intoxication as General climbed on the bed next to her to put her out of her misery.

He stroked her hair, placing the needle in her jugular vein, watching another act of his work. Who would have known those hood classes his father forced him to pay attention to would pay off.

Her body twitched violently. She foamed at the mouth in a matter of minutes and her eyes rolled to the back of her head. Without a doubt, you could feel death's presence in the room. It was done.

The past would affect the future, infecting the minds that would be controlled by the chain of command. A General was born that night as he stood before the mirror.

"What the fuck you doing in the bathroom, nigga? I gotta go!"

"Beating my dick, nigga, and I don't need no help. Back up off the door, homie," General says with authority.

General opens the bathroom door and looks Boo up and down.

"You's a well-dressed nigga this evening. Where the fuck you think you going?"

"I thought I might go to the club," Boo answers, looking down at the floor.

"Well, you thought wrong, bitch boy. You ain't going anywhere."

"Why not?" Boo replies with bass in his voice and a puzzled look.

"Don't ask me any fucking questions and I won't tell you any lies. Get that bass out your voice, too. You don't want to see me. You already casket sharp with your Friday's best on."

General pushes Boo in the chest. "Why do people continue to test me today? You do what I say, boy, and I say no going out. You stay and hold the crib down. I got business to attend to. Watch the bitch."

"Let that dope-fiend bitch go. I had my fun and so did the homies!"

"You ready to kill her, Boo? The only way she leaving out of here is in a body bag. She can die right now if you want to go to the club. Put the bullet to her brain, Baby Boy Boo. You's so hood, right?"

Boo stands there for a moment not moving. Trying to decide to take a life for the club or let me out when General leaves. Boo didn't have the heart to kill me. General would have to do it himself if he wanted me dead.

"So once again you bitch-up, dude. Sit the hell down and get high on me. When I come back, we can have some fun with the bitch."

"I don't want any part in that anymore." Boo says, walking down the hallway to avoid General's facial expression.

"You started all this shit, nigga, and you will be the one to end it when the time comes. MAN THE FUCK UP NIGGA! DAM-MIT!! YOU MAKE ME SICK WITH THAT PUNK SHIT!" General breathes down Boo's back, running up on him.

"Whatever, man…" Boo replies, sitting back down in his spot on the couch in the living room. General walks back towards the bath-room. "His punk ass is always telling somebody to man the fuck up. What he needs to do is stop stealing nigga's manhoods."

Boo thought he mumbled his words until he hears General tear down the hallway like a gorilla in the midst. With a fist of fury, Gen-eral grabs his throat in a blink of an eye.

"I'll stop stealing when somebody lay me the fuck down."

General slaps Boo across the face so hard he falls backwards over the couch, ass up. General bounces on him with no shame. "It's like taking candy from a baby."

I lay in the room listening to what I can hear. I thought the same thing as Boo—*this nigga has to be stopped some way, somehow.* Question-ing my life decisions, I realize I don't want to die at the hands of an-other or the intoxication. How much longer can I blame the actions of others for the lifestyle I chose to live? Cold, hungry and covered in semen, I swear I won't accept my fate but change it…

CHAPTER NINE

"You need an adult to sign you out of the hospital, Ms. Winters. You just can't get up and go," the nurse stated firmly.

"I'm my mom and my dad, dammit! I don't need anybody to sign me out of here because I'm leaving with or without your permission," I spat at the nurse, putting on my clothes in pain from the sutured wounds covering my body. "If someone slips and falls, they got to be crazy, and if they're having a bad day, they have to be clinically depressed. Now ain't that a bitch? How dare ya'll think my grandmother had anything to do with this? She's such a sweet old lady. And for the record, there's nothing wrong with my head; it's my heart, and I got it all under control, dammit."

Fed up with all the questions from the doctors and the police, all morning I was ready to go.

"Look at yourself. Your grandmother was the one who told us you threw yourself into a coffee table in your living room. You didn't just slip and fall, Ms. Winters. You're suffering from a mental illness, Manic Depression Disorder, known otherwise as Bipolar Disorder. We need to talk to your grandmother about the medication you'll need to take. So please, just calm down and give her a couple more minutes to get here."

"Why do you keep calling me Ms. Winters, like I'm some old-ass woman? You can call me Egypt, you know," I yelled, falling back down on the hospital bed and picking up the phone to call my grandmother once again. When she didn't pick up, it caused another outburst on the nurse. Cursing like a sailor, loud and vicious, I punched the bed with my fists.

"Calm down, Ms. Winters, calm down!" the nurse shouted, ducking a pillow being thrown at her head.

"Didn't I tell you don't call me that, bitch?"

"You need to chill out in here, Egypt. I can hear you screaming all the way down the hallway. What's your problem?" Diane stood in the door with her hands on her hips.

"Don't say shit to me, Diane. Where the hell is my grandmother at?"

"Watch your mouth and save your teeth. You don't want that pretty face fucked up. I have some bad news to deliver also."

The nurse removed herself from the situation to get out of harm's way.

"Diane, I swear to God, if you don't go ahead with that bullshit I'm gonna..."

"The old lady is gone, Egypt. She's dead..."

"You better stop playing with me, girl," I said, laughing really hard, as if somebody told a joke.

"There's nothing funny, E. She's dead and gone, for real." Diane hung her head, and the room fell silent. Diane came to me with open arms for comfort. For some reason, I grabbed Diane and pulled her close, wrapping my arms around the only family I had left. We had our moment together, sobbing very quietly. Diane looked me in my eyes as if she was holding something back. Her eyes were filled with sorrow.

"Me and mom had a fight yesterday. I said a lot of things I didn't mean to her. So I went over to her house this morning to clean up the mess and apologize. I didn't want you reminded of what happened, and I felt really bad for disrespecting the only mother I had. After cleaning up, I noticed she hadn't come downstairs to put me out the house, so I went up to check on her."

Tears streamed down Diane's naked face as the words begin to choke in her throat.

She laid at the top of the steps, face down on her stomach. When I turned her over, she was blue in the face and her eyes were still open.

She held a picture in her hand of me and your mother. She had a smile on her face, like she knew something we didn't. I held her body close to me in my arms, telling her over and over I'm sorry for the pain I caused her."

"What are we going to do now? We don't even like each other, Diane. Where am I gonna go, and what's gonna happen to grandma's stuff?"

"Don't worry about all that right now, Egypt. We going take this one step at a time, but first we got to get you out of here."

"Where is grandma's body right now?" I asked, but I don't know why.

"I put her in her bed at the house and came to get you."

"Can't you get in trouble for moving dead people?" I said in a frantic whisper.

"I did it so you could say your goodbyes before they came and took her away."

"You're crazy for that, Diane. I don't think that was a good idea, woman."

"I don't care, E. She was my mother and your grandmother, and I wasn't ready to let her go yet."

The tears kept coming down, and unexplainable fears overwhelmed me and Diane. How would we get passed this?

Diane never took responsibility for anything in her life. She was only twenty-one in her mind, acting as if she was sixteen, living in the moment. And for me, this would be my cross to bear.

Working in the hospital, Diane knew most of the staff. She did a lot of whispering to the nurse and the discharge papers appeared out of thin air within ten minutes. The doctor tried to explain my illness and my need for therapy to me and Diane, but nothing could register in our minds. The words went in one ear and right out the other.

Noticing the look on Diane's face, he knew she wasn't listening, so he gave her his card to inform him if I had another episode. Giving his condolences, he extended his arm for a handshake, confirming he was finished.

For the first time in years, Diane and I felt compassion for each other. Walking hand and hand out of the hospital to do what needed to be done, we held each other down.

Walking into my grandmother's house, I could feel the loneliness from the door. My legs shook as I followed Diane upstairs. My mouth grew thirsty approaching the bed, and then there I stood. I looked down on the rock that held the little bit of family I had together. Peace was still in the room with all of her things surrounding her. Her body was still warm as I brushed my hand across her cheek, and even though I was sad, I couldn't cry a tear in front of her.

After reporting my grandmother's death, Diane disappeared while I said goodbye.

"I don't think I'm gonna make it out here alone grandma. But I guess it's time for me to be what I've been saying, and that's grown."

"The hand we was dealt in this lifetime… seems we was destined to fail, ain't it, E?" Diane came from the shadows, scaring me to death in a cold sweat. Sniffling from the cocaine she had put up her nose, her face was beet red.

Thinking I was unaware of her substance abuse, Diane had got more careless with her habit. Doing it on the low, she thought, but to the naked eye anyone could observe she did some sort of drug.

"Maybe your mom will get word that our mother died and show up for the funeral. What you think, E?" Diane asked, really hoping for the best. She couldn't give me what I needed—a mother she could never be to her unwanted niece. The only thing she needed from me was a babysitter. Abandonment ran through the family, whether they liked it or not, so why not embrace it?

"She ain't never coming back for me, for you or her mother. I already faced that fact a long time ago. But you know what?"

"What?"

"I can feel her presence around me sometimes when I'm alone. It's like we're thinking about each other at the same time. We could walk past each other on the street and she wouldn't even know who I was, though, and that's fucked up."

"Do you think you would know her if you saw her?" Diane asked glassy eyed.

"Yeah, I would know my mother. How 'bout you?"

"Hell, yeah, I would know her. She would be the one coming at my neck quick if we were ever to bump heads. It's an ass kicking I'm willing to take, though, to have my sister back in my life."

"I wish I had a sister," I replied with disappointment.

"Just might have one running around here wit me. I think she has another family, Diane. I don't think it's drugs or drinking that keeps her away, it's her other family."

Diane gave me a disturbing look as the EMS workers entered the bedroom. And I knew it was the last time I would see my grandma's face.

"Can you please excuse me?" Diane asked, running to the bathroom with crocodile tears. But I knew better; she needed her dose to handle business.

I stood there in awe as the police and the EMS workers asked me questions I didn't understand. Diane finally joined us, but by then she was high as a kite and couldn't talk without her lip shaking. Her forehead was covered with beads of sweat, and her face was flushed.

I noticed the way her eyes kept rolling in the back of her head, and I wanted to know if anybody else in the room noticed it. At any given second, she was going to pass out. The coroner came through quickly, pronouncing my grandmother dead at such and such time, placing her body in a black bag. Asking for instructions on how to take care of the arrangements, Diane swayed to the left.

"SPLAT!" Diane fell hard to the floor. It was true just as I knew it——she passed out. *Ouch, that had to hurt,* I thought to myself, watching the EMS workers come to her rescue.

Diane started to shake and foam at the mouth while the EMS workers yelled questions at me fast. I spilled the beans telling them she was blowing coke all morning so they could find a way to help her dumbass.

I was in panic mode. If Diane went into a hospital or a treatment facility, where would I go from here? Foster care is not an option for me. I'm grown as hell and I can do this. I would rather run now than to be caught up in the system until my eighteenth birthday.

In the midst of the coroner taking my grandmother's body and my aunt sprawled out on the floor overdosing, I took it upon myself to disappear. I packed a bag quick, hauling ass out the door and not looking back. Why not run when everyone else does?

I crept out the door and fled the scene without a trace. I missed everything from the funeral to school and even myself. I thought I had made an escape from my life, but I trapped myself within my own misery. I couldn't escape the thoughts that ran through my mental when I lay in the arms of a strange man. And I couldn't escape from myself. I did what I had to do to eat. This can't be life.

CHAPTER TEN

"**C**hase, what the fuck are you doing in the bar looking older than me?"

I was surprised to the fact how my cousin had grown "How old are you again?"

She stood before me beautiful, resembling her mother from head to toe. Had I been gone for that long, I asked myself in awe. Chase looked at me confused for a moment, and then her eyes recognized me.

"Egypt?" she said, squinting her little beady eyes. "Damn, cuz, is that you? What's up and where you been? It's been a long time."

"It's been too long," I added, giving her a hug. I could tell she was excited, scared and worried all in the same note. I could smell the liquor on her breath from a mile away, causing me to back up.

"I see you're all grown up and already drunk."

"Whatever, big cuz, I'm doing me now. My man is a baller."

"And your mother? Where she at?"

"Diane all fucked up on that crack shit. You ain't heard about it? Oh, of course not, because you've been MIA, as usual. Remember Grandma would always say that shit about you?" My head dropped with sadness for just a second, knowing that my little cousin was right.

"You really don't know how much shit done changed since you left, do you?"

"I've been gone for what, three years? So that makes you a whole fifteen, hanging in a bar when you should be getting ready for school. I do know that much."

"She gonna make it to school in the morning, I can promise you that."

Turning around to curse out whoever it was that wanted to jump into our conversation, I got a rude awakening. I couldn't believe the face that stared back at me.

"I know you're not in here with him, Chase?"

"You better say it, baby," Chase replied, waiting for her big cousin's approval.

My stomach turned to the left, and I needed a drink. I cracked a smile not giving into my emotions about her man. In disgust, I kept my composure, buying a round of drinks for Chase and A.J. without no further discussion on the matter.

I couldn't believe this nigga was in the bar with my cousin. He was sporting her like a Gucci bag on some revenge-type shit. She don't know that used to be my piece. She was too young to remember, I think. But I wonder if A.J. told her that? And if so, she's bold as hell to fuck behind me. Like mother like daughter, though, so don't be surprised if it comes out like that.

A.J. was clean from head to toe. His peanut butter skin had a hint of a tan, making his eyes stand out against his complexion. He looked damned good, even though I didn't want to admit it. All the old feelings between him and me resurfaced. I couldn't get the thought out of my head of A.J. giving my cousin that bomb-ass head.

Throwing down a shot of gin, I came to the conclusion that I was jealous. I wanted to scream at the top of my lungs at the whole bar about A.J. sleeping with a fifteen-year-old female that was his ex's cousin.

If I snap, I'm a jealous bitch within reason because Chase is family. On the other hand, I can be looked at as Diane for causing an embarrassing scene in a public place. She was known for that from bar to bar.

Reaching my decision, I gulped down another shot, playing the situation. I walked over to A.J. and Chase, demanding a drink. Shooting Chase disapproving eyes, I couldn't help myself. Jealousy took over.

"I'm glad you found happiness, Chase. I'm on something new. I got me a girlfriend; I'm officially gay. But I have to say I'm hurt a little bit about you and A.J.'s relationship, and I feel he's using you to get back at me."

"Don't be so sure of yourself!" Chase fired back quicker than I expected, giving me a two-piece to munch on.

"We talked about you and his relationship and not once did he bad mouth you. Yes, I knew ya'll fucked around and I don't care. He told me he loved you, but you didn't know how to trust him, and that's why the relationship fell apart. Catching you in another man's arms at your sixteenth birthday party sent him over the edge. Beating up your ex-boyfriend and smacking your ass to the floor was just too much for him. If he had to hit you, why be with you, he thought. He cried in my arms when he seen you kissing that girl at the bus stop, too. You fucked up with him, cuz, 'cause he was really feeling you. Well, he used to be. I handled that for you, though, making him mine. And you can be on something new all by yourself because being with another woman is just downright nasty."

Giving me a sinister look, I could have kicked her ass off that bar stool. But she reminded me too much of me, myself and I, reading my rights. I had to remember who raised us, and she was a perfect mural of me and Diane both.

What adults fail to realize is their kids are always paying attention to them. They hide out when you're drinking buddies are over and listen to life's experiences unrated and without deleted scenes. They sip the leftover beer and smoke the weed roaches in the ashtray, listening to their mother's favorite song while nobody is home.

"You know what, Chase? I'm going to do you a big favor. I'm not going to smack the hell out of you in here in front of all these people. But remember this, cousin—it's a cold world out there, baby girl. When you need me, I'll be here no matter what."

I excused myself from the situation, but before I walked off, I drank Chases' shot and mine. A.J. wasn't in sight, and that was a good thing. I posted up three seats from the jukebox, ordering five shots of gin to take my mind off the pain I carried around with me in my heart.

Chase was right. A lot had changed in the last three years with me and the little bit of family I had. Me bailing out on Diane, I put my feelings on hold about my grandmother's death. I didn't attend the funeral neither. How fucked up is that? When I walked out the door, I left behind every good and bad memory I had of her and drank enough to stop the guilt from creeping into my dreams.

As I sat at the bar, the gin didn't take my mind off my troubles; it brought them into focus. What a tangled web I weaved trying to find myself.

After I watched Diane overdose, I walked out the door and set out to find Trap. I needed to know if there was any truth to Diane's rumor, plus I needed somewhere to stay. It wasn't hard to find him with his ability to hold the block down in one of the roughest projects around. In Northview Heights, everyone knew of him and wanted to be him. He was a ladies' man on and off the scene, controlling the premises with just that: pussy. He made thousands of dollars pulling coke out of female's insides all day, every day.

Gun shots rang out as soon as I reached the first row of houses looking for Trap that night. It sounded like the Fourth of July as bullets flew past my head at some niggas sitting at the corner house. I couldn't move, stunned by the crossfire. I saw Trap with my own eyes come from out of the woodwork with blazing guns. Everyone who saw him coming from the flickering street light tried to take flight, but couldn't escape the bullets that dumped out of his gun.

I opened my mouth to call out his name and nothing came out. Not even a scream as I saw two of the bodies drop to the ground. He walked up on the porch with no mercy, and I could hear the cries from the niggas begging for him to spare their lives. It reminded me of a movie called *Boyz N the Hood*. Trap wanted to be that nigga who pumped fear into the hearts of men. He wanted his respect by any means necessary. I'll never forget the night after we made love and he held me in his arms with nothing but whispers. In my ear he uttered he will be feared by all men and his enemies, knocking down every door of opportunity being enforced as the law. It wasn't great pillow talk, but it made me feel safe. Knocking me to the ground, Trap's boy Bootsie laid on top of me to protect my body. I walked right into my first gunfight not blinking an eye, watching four people die and my ex-boyfriend transform from a man into a gangster. The gunfire ceased soon after and Bootsie rushed me to their spot as if he was an FBI agent doing his duty to protect and serve the innocent bystander. "Why would you come here without paging me first, Egypt?" Trap kicked in the door to his spot in a rage. Snatching me up by the collar of my shirt, I could see his tonsils as he yelled ferociously.

"I could have killed you, girl. Don't you ever show up here unannounced again."

I couldn't answer him from staring at a vein going straight down the middle of his forehead. It had a pulse, and his eyes were beady red, scaring the hell out of me and his crew that was behind him. When he unarmed me, my mouth went dry, but I pushed the words to the top of my throat.

"I have to talk to you in private about something, and I couldn't call because I had nowhere to call you from. I'm sorry, Trap."

Seeing the tears form in my eyes, he pulled me close.

"Naw, baby, I'm sorry you had to see me in action like that." In his arms, I melted and forgot about the four people I just saw him kill.

"I haven't seen you since your party back in June. What's so important you had to come here to find me on the late night?"

Pulling me off into the distance of the room, his crew disappeared, and we stood in each other's arms as I let go of my pain. Trying to tell everything that happened to me in one breath, Trap pulled my face to his eyes, recognizing some of my scars. He kissed my face sympathetically.

"What happened to you out there? Did A.J. do this to you?"

As quick as he asked that question, I snatched away from his arms, accusing him for the display I wore on my face and the rest of my body. I glanced around from hearing voices, growing angry.

"I told you before we needed to talk in private. Tell your flunkies to fall back and rest their necks on something sharp."

Calling the shots brought a smirk to his face as he dismissed his crew in under a minute.

"I see you've gained a lot of power since the last time I saw you, and you're using a gun as your fist...."

"Nope Egypt, you don't know what the fuck you're talking about, so pick another subject."

I couldn't bring myself to ask the questions running through my mind walking back and forth. Are you gay? No, I can't come right out and say that. He'll smack the fuck out of me. Have you ever had sex with a man, Trap? No, no, no, hell no, he'll shoot me...

"What happened to your face, and why the fuck are you here? You keep walking around, talking under your breath and shit."

"And how can you be so calm after shooting four people?" I spat, trying to avoid the situation I wanted on the table.

"That's my business, woman, and I won't say it again. Now answer my question before I lose my cool!"

"I fell through Grandmomma's coffee table in the living room at home, tripping off you. Well, what used to be my home."

"What? You ran away from home?"

I sat down on the floor Indian style, placing my face in my hands. "Diane told me she saw you with another man and you might have AIDS."

Trap's facial expression never changed. He grabbed up some floor sitting next to me, causing our eyes to contact each other.

"Let's take this one step at a time. Why can't you go home?"

"Grandma died last night while I was in the hospital, and when the coroner came to pick up the body, Diane overdosed. She ain't got no love for me nohow. I was scared that the police would see her unfit, putting me in a group home or something like that."

Trap rubbed his imaginary chin hairs in deep thought for a moment, then he laughed a sick laugh. "Is this before or after she called me an ass fucker?"

I was afraid to answer him from the look in his eyes, but I put my head down answering, "After."

"And you believed what the fuck her nasty mouth had to say?" I tried to answer him, but he continued to talk, getting angry. "Her mouth so nasty I don't even want to talk after her. This is the same Diane who drugged your drink so she could seduce me by sticking her ass on my dick. She bounced up and down on me like I was her man. She told you I was fucking a man, the same Diane that's in debt to me for over a thousand dollars, fucking all my boys. She told you about all that, too, I bet you. Hell, no! You're so stupid, Egypt. You let that woman pull all the strings and take all the credit shitting all over you. I would have gave her ass a dome shot, but for the love of you, I chill every day. I'm a killer on the prowl wanting the number one spot. I don't even have time to fuck a woman, let alone a man. The woman I want to fuck wants to fuck lames, you feel me?"

I cried hard and long while Trap rubbed my back. I recounted his conversation in my mental, wanting him to touch me on the inside.

"I need you to tell me it's not true. I need to hear you say it, baby..."

"It's not true, Egypt, I swear it ain't so, and I'll get tested with you. I could kill her right now with a hot dose for spreading some shit like that. That shit can get me killed out here on the streets. Niggas wouldn't even want to do business with me."

"Please don't kill her, Trap. She the only family I got, even though she ain't shit. And your magic stick is cool because I got tested in the hospital and my results came back negative. You got to think about my little cousin Chase, too. She won't have anybody. I don't want her not to have a mother like me."

Trap turned his back to me, not wanting to hear the words I said. He wanted to kill Diane and I knew it. I felt the same way, but I can't be like that. She family.

"If she ain't smoking by now, Egypt, she will be soon, so she already dead and your cousin don't have a chance."

As Trap spoke, his words were at a whisper and his demeanor was ice chilling, but so warm to his gentle touch. The dangerous had me in demand to be held, caught up in the rapture. I believed him and in him.

"Her telling you them lies got your face mangled like that? Look at your hands and arms. You need to get with your man right here."

I smiled, giving Trap a nudge while we both resided Indian style. It felt like old times as I fell under his spell once again.

"What little bitches you got up here sucking on ya dick? Don't think that line got passed me, because it didn't, baller."

"Shut up, E. I was just making a point. But for real, you can't be mad. Ya ain't fucking ya boy."

He grabbed my hand, placing it over his heart. I looked him dead in his eyes once again as his lips parted.

"I'm sorry for how your aunt spun us, and believe me it will never happen again. I don't even drink anymore; it's a sign of weakness in my book. That's how your weak-ass man got the best of me. For one, I was drinking and for two, you were smelling too good for me to pay attention to anything else. I was slipping, drunk as hell not, watching my own back. But only because of you I let that nigga breathe, Egypt." Trap stood up, pulling a gun from his waist, putting it to my head and quoting, "I would have deaded them mutherfuckers if I didn't love you from afar, I kept telling myself, and now you need me as much as

I need you. I hope you're not afraid of me after what you saw tonight."

He put the gun back in his waist when I didn't flinch. I was turned on, and I know he seen it in my eyes.

"I thought I was scared, but not at all. I'm just wondering where the hell the police is at."

Laughing out loud, I lightened up the room as we began to play around, getting familiar with one another's moods. I really couldn't believe that he shot them boys and their cries will linger in the back of my mind, but I wasn't afraid of Trap or his gun. Getting comfortable, I peeped my surroundings a little more closely in awe. The walls were painted all red and on the ceiling there were angels. Hell's Angels was painted in old English letters, black and gold, bold and beautiful. It fit the spot and the people who chilled there. The carpet was plush, taking my shoes off as my toes melted into it. I took the energy of the room in feasting my eyes on a bar. In the middle of the carpet, setting everything off where I stood, was Trap's name wrapped In Drugs We Trust.

Trap had disappeared to handle business while I helped myself to a drink. I walked through the spot, further discovering in the next room a big screen TV and my thing, a stereo complete with CD's.

A double gin and juice with lots of ice resided in my left hand while my fingers did the walking through the CD collection. I felt right at home coming across my bitch, Mary J. Blige, as I slid her into the CD player. Mary J. was the closest person to a best friend I had in my life. She always gave great advice and she always sang to me when needed, not missing a beat. Laying up under the speakers, I sang the hooks word for word, sipping my drink slow.

I was feeling sexy around my third double gin and juice. I was feeling Trap's sexy ass, too, even though he was nowhere to be found. Drink after drink I convinced myself Diane was a liar and the truth wasn't in her. Whatever happened to her and her daughter would be her own fault, crossing Trap and tainting his reputation.

Why should I care anyway? She never cared about me. And the only person who truly loved me is dead and gone, six feet deep. I'm on my own now.

I fixed another drink and went through my possessions until I found my Cheryl Pepsii Riley tape. I decided to switch the track to an old song called *Thanks For My Child*. I didn't get past the first verse before the tears fell, and I realized I was drunk. I thought about my mother and where she could be in my time of need. I felt a hand touch me from behind, but I couldn't turn around to face Trap. I was hurting, but I needed his touch. I was empty and needed to be filled, but with what? I wanted to experience the love Mary J. Blige sang about. Putting his arms around me, I felt at ease until I smelled the scent of another woman. The scent embraced my pain as we hugged. Trap had went and got my best friend in the real world, Sasha, from her house to be with me.

"How you doing, Egypt?" Sasha asked, running her fingers over my wounds. The question was stupid, but I couldn't care less; I was hurting. I cried for at least half an hour, but of course with a drink in my hand. Sasha held me in her arms while I kept uttering, "Grandma is dead... she's really dead..."

"I know she's dead and gone, Egypt, but me and my mother are going to take care of you."

"Your mother hates me and everybody in my family." I replied, laughing through my tears. Sasha smelled so good as she held me. I felt like I belonged in her arms. The feeling was comfortable to me, needing a woman's embrace, and it felt mutual the way she stroked my pain.

"Does anyone need a drink? I know my baby can use one."

Breaking our emotional bond, Trap brought a round of drinks to our attention. He changed the CD to something upbeat and it made the mood more simple.

That was the night I fell in love with my best friend.

It all started with a dance. Biggie Smalls pumped through the speakers and the drinks never stopped as me and Sasha tried to out drink each other. For the moment, I was happy and the liquor was bringing out the beast.

Drunk as hell, I danced with Sasha and Trap, placing all my focus on her sexual body language. I caressed her skin and kissed her body parts without any objections and her sighs released the tension as I continued to explore.

When it was all said and done, Sasha and I blessed Trap's carpet with the scent of our bodies. Rolling around, exploring unfamiliar territories, I caught on quickly, enjoying myself, but I wasn't the only one. Trap watched us like a television set from the sidelines and his eyes didn't make me feel uneasy. The fact he was sitting there with his eyes glued to me turned me on, making me go harder and harder.

Every thrust I made with my fingers inside her created a sensation between my legs that I couldn't ignore. Sasha's reactions was deep and intense. I was in a passionate rage, feeling a violent emotion.

Trap came from behind, entering my walls slow, giving me strong and profound strokes that forced me to suck Sasha's clitoris into a climax frenzy. My life as I knew it changed right before my eyes without me even knowing it. Sasha and I said each other's names all through the night and nobody sucked Trap's dick at all.

"Last call for alcohol!" the bartender announced loudly, bringing me back to reality.

I was good and drunk, but still thirsty. I staggered to find A.J. and Chase and when I did, they were engaged in a kiss. It made me sick to my stomach to see the two suck face.

"We got a baller in the house! You got my last drink, don't you A.J.?" I was very loud and unruly in getting my point across. I wanted them to stop touching and they did, putting their attention on me.

"Yeah, I got you, Egypt and then I'm taking your drunk ass home.

I've watched you all night lick the bottom of the glass. You still drink like a fish, but that ain't nothing new and I see nothing has changed."

"Don't act like you don't know that shit already, baller. I ain't brand new and don't act like we ain't never fuck around neither. You know me, and you know me very well." My words slurred, but I made my point.

Chase's face perplexed with anger hearing the disrespect in my voice. "Rule number one, Egypt—conduct yourself as a lady at all times."

SLAP!!! Chase hit the floor and hit it hard from the backhand I served his ass. I couldn't keep my composure any longer. It was calling me to smack her like it was calling Pookie to hit that crack in *New Jack City.*

I was in my glory for only one second as A.J. came to her rescue. He damn near choked the life out of me before I could get to her nappy-ass weave. The bartender saved me by pulling a gun from under the bar. Putting it in eye view of A.J., he let me go.

"You just lost your ride home, drunken bitch!" A.J. screamed, pushing me to the floor.

"I don't give a fuck about you or ya car. I'll walk..."

"Do it then, drunk-ass bitch. I hope you get arrested for public intoxication."

Chase got out the line of fire quickly, and I needed one more drink, picking myself up off the floor. I should have waited for my drink from bitch boy baller before I decided to wild the fuck out.

The bartender shut shit down and nobody got a drink, and she kicked my ass out before I could start anything else. I had did exactly what I said I wasn't going to do. I embarrassed myself and Chase, being drunk and obnoxious. I learned from the best—Diane.

I don't know what came out of me and Sasha's relationship besides good sex. From beginning to end, it was nothing but obstacles and hurdles which turned into learning experiences. But what did I learn besides hurting the one I love? Nothing...

After becoming porno stars in the eyes of Trap, me and Sasha was inseparable. I had hid out in Trap's secret layer for about two weeks and Sasha kept me company most nights. That quick, in the blink of an eye, my life had changed having sex with a woman. I no longer desired Trap or any man for that matter, gone off the sweet nectar of a woman.

I questioned myself time and time again. Were these feelings always there, and I came up with the same answer each and every time—you are what you eat. I really didn't have an answer on why I felt the way I did, but I knew I liked the feeling when she said my name. Her moan tickled my fancy...

I could have cared less for the extra pair of hands caressing my bottom in the middle of the night, and Trap learned fast running up in sandpaper. My middle spot wouldn't splash for him, and he got tired of brush burns quick. Envy and jealousy set in as he watched my body react to Sasha's touch, but he never stepped out of line. He watched on the sidelines with a drink in his hand.

When I looked in his eyes the day I left to move in with Sasha, I could see his pride was hurt as I left him once again, and this time for a woman. It took exactly two weeks for Sasha to convince her mom to let me stay despite Diane and her trickery. The money she came into for taking care of me didn't hurt neither.

Ms. Shane, Sasha's mother, handled all the proper papers my grandmother left behind with Diane to gain control of my annuity. Her old ass was cool, though, and she was very fair with me. We split the cash for the next year and a half, turning eighteen.

Sasha had a live-in girlfriend and nobody knew it. It was the shit. We slept together, bathed together when nobody was looking, and I often cooked dinner for the whole family. If the walls could talk in Sasha's bedroom, our sexual relationship in casual conversation could make ears burn. We explored each other's bodies for six months straight, only taking a breath when we bled. We were so close we got our periods together and Shane's cycle blended with ours. This made her very happy because she monitored our flow for paternal reasons of her own.

Sasha continued to go to school and keep her male friends in demand at all times. She didn't want anybody to know her dirty little secret while I skipped school and hung out in the local bars.

Sasha had her dreams of becoming a lawyer so she could keep me out of jail with my dope boy ambitions, and me, I didn't plan on getting caught by the police because I was going to control all that, becoming the first girl kingpin.

I had talked to Trap from time to time to make sure he was all right, but what I really wanted was to be a part of his team. He had shit on lock and I wanted a piece. He kept putting me off and playing with the game hoping, wishing and praying I would give in to his immature ways. I couldn't buy the coke; I had to work for him, serving up my pussy as a mule and that was a definite no-no. I wasn't capable of holding down my own block he said time after time, but if I would have spread my legs, it could have worked. I never gambled with my pussy before so I didn't see it as an option and moved on.

I could have been in the dope game by now, with Trap supplying my every need, but he let his dick do the thinking, so no product for me. I couldn't explain if I was a dike or not, but the thought of Trap touching my body repulsed me. I couldn't shake what Diane said to me that night I went ape shit, and I was afraid of his dick.

Becoming a kingpin was harder than I thought, trusting no one else with my money. I knew a lot of boys who liked to play with toys and were very disrespectful to girls who wanted to do boy things. I didn't want to get beat or gang raped, so I had to wait for the opportunity to knock.

Living in Homewood on the east side of Pittsburgh didn't help none neither, because the boys over here was a new breed of killers. The North Side seemed so far away, and that's how I liked it. I didn't want to run into any old ghosts, and I wasn't up for making no new friends trying to get away from my old ones I was running from.

But the seasons had changed and the months kept up their appearances, taking all of us into the New Year. Sasha was head of the class and Shane had paid her house off with the extra cash she was giving and me, they both was tired of trying to make me go to school.

It was May 16, 1995. The weather was breaking and summer was right around the corner. I had a birthday coming up, but today it was my baby's birthday and I bought both of us a present. Sasha had a man I cared nothing about, but I always found myself in competition with Mr. Money Bags. He had the one piece of equipment I didn't that she wanted. That was her sole purpose for dating him, besides keeping up presentations for her mother and friends. It only took her mother to say we were too close one time while we were watching *Ricki Lake* on people coming out of the closet. I'll never forget Sasha's face when her mother looked over at us sitting too close for comfort, asking, you two don't have something you want to tell me?

She was only joking, but we took it literally, putting some space between us in the house. But tonight we dine alone. Shane was working late and her man was going over his partner's house to play poker. I got to give her my birthday present over and over again. I wasn't born with eight inches between my legs, but today I hung low like a pimp ready to handle business.

It made my pussy throb watching my woman get fucked from the back, and I wanted to do the same. So one day I skipped my bar session and introduced myself to sex tools. I traveled downtown to the 24-hour novelty store and expanded my mind sexually. Thanks to the bartender at the Honey Dewdrop, I was about to make a baby tonight. *Once she feels me, Sasha won't need a man for anything*, I thought. That's my mission, and I need it accomplished. I couldn't tell her I fucked her piece-of-shit man while she was studying after school, because she might not have liked that. It wasn't my fault neither; he came on to me. I didn't mind, though. I wanted him out the picture by any means necessary. If I had to fuck him to get my point across, it was worth it. I just had to play my cards right. He surely did. I knew it was wrong, but so did he. I got what I wanted and so did he, that bomb-ass pussy between my legs.

I don't know why he was at our house anyway. The nigga had motive walking through the door when I firmly stated Sasha wasn't home. Being a good host, I got him something to drink and I came back to the living room shocked by what's on the television. What do horny teenagers carry around in their book bags? This one had pornos, because that's what the hell was on my TV set.

The light bulb came on above my head. I fucked that boy three days from Sunday and he had it like Burger King, his way. He moaned my name as he had me bent over Shane's brand new plush-leather couch. It didn't make my body melt like when Sasha said it, but it did turn me on. That's when I first spotted the strap on dildo. The porno moaned in pleasure and my pussy got extremely wet watching the oiled-up white girl pound out the Spanish fly. It was beautiful and I had a bomb-ass orgasm.

Yeah, the dick was alright, but seeing what I saw on that porno set my yearning free. I was in dire need to touch her on the inside.

Today was the day. Her birthday would mark the beginning of a new sexual high for the both of us. I got everything to set it off with and make it special. I was such a devil, a sweet devil. Spending twelve hundred dollars on a pair of diamond earrings alone should get me some pussy, as the dope boy's would say. I had everything planned out perfect, so I thought.

I hooked up our bedroom with apple-scented candles, with a trail of rose petals from the bed to the bathtub for after we were through. I placed the box which contained the diamond earrings in them in the center of the bed to spark the mood off right.

Now all I had to do was figure out how the hell to put the strap on.

I was so dumb not to ask at the store, but it was too late to cry over spilled milk. Checking the time I only had ten to twelve minutes to get it right or I would be caught with my dick in my hand.

It wasn't rocket science, so I played around with it a bit, getting a perfect fit as I heard the downstairs door open. Sasha was right on time. I could hear her feet skipping steps to get to me and her gift. Flying in the room with all smiles she jumped on my waist, giving me hugs and kisses.

"You did all this for me, baby?" Sasha asked, looking around the decorated room.

"Oooh, what's in the box? It better not be no ring, girl..."

"What, Sasha? You tripping and you tripping hard. Open it up." Opening the box, her eyes reacted casually until the bling blinded her.

"It's better than a ring, and you got two, baby."

My plan was working. She danced around the room holding the earrings up to her lobes. She was just as happy as a kid in a candy store. It made me feel good to make her smile. It was always a highlight in my day. I turned on the stereo and my niggas poured out singing that do-it to-me music. Sasha slowly took her clothes off to the beat of Jodeci.

I was afraid now to just spring the strap on her, so I decided to work it in slow. I didn't want to fuck up a good moment, and I didn't know if she would protest, so I cut out the odds. I blindfolded her.

"Just lie down on the bed and let me take control. I needed to blindfold you to see how much you trust me." I uttered the words seductively, removing the rest of her clothing.

"I trust you, Egypt, and I love you."

I didn't say a word. I went in for the kill, kissing her navel. I licked it up and down as I watched her midsection flex from my touch. I turned the stereo up louder for the bass to bounce off the walls. I took down my sweats that was camouflaging my strap, ready for action. Sasha's body laid there on the bed, so tempting, I had to have it.

I kept the kisses light and passionate all the way to her hot spot, resting my face in it. I sucked on her pink, stretching her lips wide so she could feel every stroke. Reaching her climax quick, fast and in a hurry, I slid in the dildo, removing the blindfold at the same time. I wanted to look into her eyes, feeling my first stroke, and that's what I did.

She grabbed me by the waist and guided me in and out, loving me being inside of her. I pumped on and on like I had a dick for years to the sexual vocals of the song *Feenin'*. The oohs and the uuhs of our lovemaking was so in tune, neither of us heard Shane come into her house. The key word in the last sentence was HER house. She was already walking around in a groove about being off from work for the next couple of nights. I shouldn't have had the music up so loud, but I did, and now we both were about to be embarrassed as hell.

One stroke, two strokes, three strokes, beat it the fuck up.

"Oh, I see ya'll having sex in my house, up under my roof." I really couldn't hear the words coming out of her mouth, but her mother's face wasn't too happy. I paused in midstroke, catching the glimpse of light from the hallway. After she said what she said, she closed the door politely.

"You want me to keep going, baby?" Why would I ask that dumb question? It didn't matter because the words had already left my lips and Sasha's hand was slapping me off her. The door opened again. "I can't believe you had the audacity to do this nasty shit in my house!"

I stood there ass naked with a strap on dildo in front of her mother, humiliated.

"Shut the door, Mom, please!" Sasha cried out, in dying need for this embarrassing moment to end.

This time her mother slammed the door so hard she damn near tore the poor thing off its hinges. I still wanted to be nasty, but the moment was gone as Sasha dropped to her knees in shame. Holding her face in her two hands, she cried harder by the second.

"What is my mother going to think of me now?" Sasha asked, sobbing. I didn't know what her mother was going to think about her, but me, my black ass was out the door for corruption of the mind. And for banging her daughter with a rubber dick.

"You done fucked up my life, Egypt..."

"What you talking 'bout, baby? All I want to do is love you. I love you, Sasha, and I'm sorry this happened."

"I have to go talk to my mother right now. And you, take that fucking dick off and get out before my mother kills you."

I stood there in front of my woman, speechless. And the only thing I could say was, "Was it good though?"

We both fell to the bed laughing, and I felt a little better.

"She will get over us being together, you know. I swear she will."

"I can't believe this is happening to me. All the times I've had sex with Money in this house and never got caught and the day my girlfriend decides to take my virginity, we get caught."

"Don't forget all the fucking we did in this bitch neither."

"Stop being jealous, Egypt. And yes, it felt good. It felt like the real thing. But all jokes aside, I'm going to need you to get dressed and leave while I talk to my mother. I don't want you in the middle of our fight."

"But the fight is about me, too."

"Let me do this. I have something else I need to say to her."

"What you got to tell her? You better tell me first, or I'm not going anywhere. It's me and you in this relationship, not me and you and your fucking mother." I kept pushing her buttons, and I knew I was on her last nerve.

Sasha looked at me and rolled her eyes. Fully dressed, she stood over me.

"You remember when I told you the reason why I was throwing up everyday this past week is because I got food poisoning from the school lunches?"

"Yeah, I remember Sasha. I gave you a hundred dollars so you and your friends could eat lunch at the Rib Shack."

"Fuck it, Egypt! Long story short, I'm pregnant. I took a pregnancy test with the money you gave me and it came back positive."

"Well don't look at me, because the baby ain't mine." I had to say it and when I did, laughter fell behind it.

"This ain't no time for jokes, punk. I realized I wanted to keep the baby, and you know my moms ain't having it. She just ain't kicking your nasty ass out; I got to go, too. If I'm grown enough to fuck In her house and get pregnant, I'm old enough to be on my own. You know my mother is from the old school."

"Do you think it's wise to hit your mother with a double whammy like this? She might have a heart attack. She just might keel over on the spot. If I was your mom, I would have to ask if you're having a girl or a boy or a goddamned Chucky doll." busted out laughing once again, but my baby didn't think it was that funny.

"I'm telling you smartass, say one more joke and you won't smell this pussy for a long time. And if you think I'm joking, fucking try me." Sasha's face was long and strong with anger.

"You tell Money Bags?"

"I told him, and he told me to tell you. He claimed you get more pussy than him."

"When did all this happen, Sasha, and why are you keeping big-ass secrets like this from me? I could have been there for support. You didn't have to go through this alone."

"The same reason why you didn't tell me you fucked Money. Don't try and fucking lie about it neither, because I know it's the truth. I set you up, Egypt, and you fell for the bait, failing miserably. You can't be trusted just like my mother said, but I love you…"

"Wait a minute, baby, you got it all wrong. I did that shit to show you he wasn't shit. If he would fuck your best friend, he would fuck anybody on you behind your back. I didn't give a fuck on how you were going to feel until after it was done. I was just so focused on getting him out the picture. It was a bad decision on my part, and I acted very selfishly.

Tears swelled up fast and my heartbeat was even faster, thinking me and Sasha was done for real.

"Calm down, Egypt, and shut off the tears. If I was going to leave your black ass, I would have been done it. You right, that's why I cut Money the fuck off after I told him about the baby. Guess what?"

"What?" I wiped my face with the back of my hand like I'm a damn eight-year old and sound about six.

"Your loving is way better than any man I've been with. Your shit is like dope, and I always need a fix. Now give me a kiss and get out of here so I can handle my mother. I don't want her busting in here again, because next time she might have her gun."

I thought about it for a second and got dressed in a matter of minutes. I didn't want to die tonight. We wiped away each other's tears and gave kisses goodbye as Sasha went to her mom.

Sasha and Shane's mother-daughter relationship was never the same after what went down. Shane couldn't accept the fact her daughter was a pregnant lesbian. Sasha wouldn't get rid of me or her baby.

She had to tell her mother quick she was pregnant because Shane came out swinging and yelling what the hell did she do wrong. Shane's room sounded like the *Friday Night Fights*.

"You know that shit is a sin. I know her nasty ass exposed you to them nasty ways. And you pregnant, too? Where the hell is the goddamned daddy? What are you going to tell this child when it asks you why I got two moms? Do your baby daddy know you a dike bitch? This is too much for me, Sasha."

"Hold up, Mom. Don't call me no dike; I'm still your daughter." I wanted to cry myself outside the door eavesdropping I couldn't play Captain Save A Bitch this evening because Shane just might shoot my dumb ass. "You don't have to come at me like that. This is my life and my choice."

"Look at what choices you're making. They're not good ones…"

"Let me finish, dammit!"

"Oh, we cursing at mothers now?"

"Mom, please shut up and listen. I'm sorry for being disrespectful. I love you Mom, but unfortunately I'm in love with a woman. I love Egypt and this baby I'm carrying. I'm getting along very well in school with my grades, and I know I'll get accepted to a good college if I stay focused. I can make it on my own, if you don't want to support me on this."

The room fell quiet for a couple of minutes. My ears burned from the silence. I needed Shane to answer right and support us or Sasha might blame me forever about the baby not having a grandmother.

"I can't support you on this, Sasha. I just can't. It goes against everything I taught you. I didn't raise you to become this. But I do have something to start you on your journey to adulthood. The money I was getting from your girlfriend. I can't believe I just said that. I've been saving up for these past couple months, and you can have it. The account has your name on it at Mellon Bank, and all you have to do is show you're ID. Sasha, you and your dike friend have to go. I will sign for you an apartment as soon as possible."

"So we have nothing else to say to each other?"

"There's nothing else to discuss about the matter, baby. It's a done deal."

"But you're my mother…"

"I was your mother, but there will be no child of mine coming around here diking it. You can't be embarrassing me in front of my friends and co-workers. Now get out of my room."

I crept away from the door in tears for my baby. Her mother didn't even say happy birthday to her daughter; now ain't that a bitch. I walked back to Sasha's room with her on my heels, and I was happy I didn't leave her alone.

When she opened her door, I stood there with open arms. As I hugged her, I locked the damned door. There was nothing to say about anything because Shane hit and hit hard.

I consoled Sasha with only a warm hug and my heartbeat while I cursed her mother to the floor in my head. There was no reason why I had to respect her ass now. She disowned her own child. My thoughts were unpleasant, but I kept them to myself. I didn't want to feed fuel to the fire, and I didn't want Shane to hear my voice.

From that day forth, we never had a kind word to say to each other. Shane kept her word, too. Sasha wasn't allowed in her house as long as she was with me. Shane did keep her word about moving Sasha into the projects, though, where we've been living ever since. The apartment was rather small, but filled with joy, giving us the freedom we needed.

"It's damn near three in the morning, Egypt. You're such a fucking drunk. Please don't come in here with that loud shit, blasting Mary J. Blige until five in the morning. I don't want to hear it, and the people next door don't want to hear it, neither. And if you wake up...."

"Okay, Sasha, baby, I get it, now shut the fuck up. Oh, yeah, how was your day honey?"

Drunk as hell, the wall in the kitchen held me up. My feet were tired from walking home from the bar and my neck still hurt from A.J. choke slamming me. Sasha looked at me with disappointment in her face, but her eyes told me she loved me. I smiled.

"Don't get smart with me, Egypt. My day was fine until I got woke up out of my sleep because somebody lost their keys again. I should smack the shit out of you for not spending any time with me or your son. I never had anybody cheat on me with the bar. Can I get a date?"

Sasha talked at me a mile a minute, looking sexy as hell, and all my dumb ass could do was smile. I didn't want to say too much because she would have kept talking, and all I wanted was a beer. So I continued to hold up the wall and smile. Blah Blah Blah, she said, and I nodded as if I were listening, just to make her happy.

"Don't stand there, E, like you're listening because I know you're drunk as hell. And don't think you're getting any pussy. You ain't nigga."

"No Mary J. Blige and no ass. That's a fucked-up ending to a fucked-up night."

"I don't want to hear about it because you always got some shit going on. Grow the fuck up, Egypt, and goodnight."

"But baby, I love you…."

That was the last thing I said, grabbing that beer out the ice box and falling into the couch. I plugged Mary J. Blige up to my ears and rocked out with my cock out. Sweet dreams…

CHAPTER ELEVEN

Locked in this room, I can still taste the sweet nectar of Sasha's passion some mornings even though she leaves a bitter taste in my mouth. But today, as I lay here in the midst of the chaos I chose for myself. I realize I was wrong for not meeting her demand—at least halfway. I just couldn't stop drinking...

The drugs they giving me up in here got me tripping off of shit I thought I'd gotten over years ago. And things I thought I worked through in my mind while I got high haunt me here; all my wrongdoing has come back to taunt me in my time of need.

I don't know how long I've been locked in this room. I've lost track of time, but the way I'm feeling right now, I know it's time to get high and dream a little dream.

This crazy-ass nigga ain't ever going to let me go. Most of the men walking through the door to claim their twenty-dollar prize are rather small. I could hear them approaching the room bragging about their instincts, but their fuck game wasn't about shit. Boo's ugly ass was the only one who was packing the whole nine inches with the tongue to match. And his nutty- ass sidekick General—his dick doesn't get hard enough to fuck me unless he rubs it between my ass cheeks or jams it down my throat as if my mouth is a piece of pussy. That man has some real women issues, and he hates the fact I won't call him daddy.

He's not any fucking daddy of mine. Niggas kill me, thinking they can turn me back to whatever it is they think. Shit! Bitches call my fine ass "daddy," ya dig? All his dumbass did was bring on a lovely new drug habit that I like, but straight I will never be. I wish they would serve me a dish of pussy in here so I could show them what to do with it.

Men can't take a lesbian woman like myself who takes on a domi-
nant male role. Me being a homosexual and a woman, I shouldn't be
inferior to him, a man. But the truth, is I can do what he does better
than he; that's why straight men be out to get at me. Lawd forbid you
getting more corner money than they no-hustle-talented ass, because
if so, you're every dike bitch in the book. And you better pray their
nasty-ass baby momma don't want any taste, because if she does, I
might get shot at.

But real niggas give respect where it's due. I got a few, and we
make it do what it do while paper chasing. The haters that evolved
from not making a dollar on the block need an exorcism for the evil
they possessed for me. I've been spit at, spit on, called a dike to a
carpet muncher. I've got drinks thrown at me and on me. Most of
the niggas I helped get a dollar in this vicious game are the ones to
slit my throat and do the evil that men do for the almighty dollar.
What thanks do I get for helping out thy fellow man? Becoming a gott-
damned fucking victim of circumstance.

Niggas done set me up to get robbed. They have robbed me, put
guns to my head and threaten to take my kid. Stole my cars to money
to coke to my girls, and they still couldn't stop me or break me.

The corner boys hated the fact that the more they took, the more
I earned. They got no status quo for the envy that flowed through
their veins, while my name rang bells from hood to hood that I was
a down-ass chick. Don't get me wrong—I had a lot of good times in
this lifestyle. But karma is a mean bitch, always out for vengeance.
The same shit I was selling to get rich is the same shit that has put me
in imprisonment. Can this be my fate? Will I live to see another day?
Will God bless me with one more chance? Or will I reap what I've
sown? Maybe, just maybe, I'll get one last chance to shine.

General sits on the edge of his bed staring down at his penis. It is
oozing with pus as he sits there holding his urine. Knowing he has to
go to the bathroom, he dreads the burning sensation that is getting

ready to take place. Squeezing the head of his dick, the yellow pus drips from it slow as he stands in front of the toilet sweating bullets.

"AAUUH!!" comes loud and sounds painful as the urine trickles out of him. Sticking his penis in any moistened hole that will allow and won't allow caught up with his dirty-dick ass. Having unprotected sex with up to four different people in a single day, General can't pinpoint the infection. He moves like that every day when it comes to his large appetite for sex with different partners.

"General, you cool in there, man?"

"Get the fuck away from the door, faggot-ass nigga!"

"I heard you scream, nigga. I was just making sure you were straight."

"I'm as straight as I'm gonna get, Boo, now get the fuck away from the door!"

After this nasty mutherfucker gets done pissing pus in the toilet, he comes straight for my naked ass. I'm about to sleep with half the niggas in the hood he done victimized and every girl under eighteen who fell for the bullshit he dished out.

"Boo, take ya bitch-ass in there and tie that hoe's eyes shut. I need to get my early morning nut off to release some stress," General screams down the hallway, and Boo jumps, hearing the roar of the beast. Hopping up off the couch from watching BET, he sets his blunt in the ashtray, taking a deep breath. He knows that one day this crazy-ass lunatic is going to tell him to kill me and he's going to have to do it or General will kill him. Why in the hell couldn't he just have fucked me and kicked my ass out back into the cold?

"Who was that screaming, ugly?" I already know the answer, but I can't pass up the opportunity to call Boo as I seen him and it was ugly. He was a ugly fuck!

"Shut up, bitch, I'm not in the mood. Put this on your eyes." Boo throws a black scarf at me.

"How come I can't see this nigga's face? I can see everybody else, but him. Do I know this mutherfucker or something? His voice can be real familiar to me in a weird-ass way."

"Girl, it's too early in the morning to be asking questions. I don't have any answers for you anyway, and I dare you to ask him yourself. But I will tell you this: the time will come when I will try to get you out of here since I'm the one who done this to you. So for now, just bite your tongue and do what he says. If he wants you to call him daddy, please just do it. Your bruises are healing up aiight and you don't want any more. No more heroin for you. I'll bring you a blunt to calm the craving, but I need you up and alert. I'm sorry for doing this to you, and I'm going to do everything in my power to get you out of here."

I wait for a moment to make sure he's finished talking.

"I know you're sorry, you sorry mutherfucker, and I want some shit bouncing around in my veins!" I yell at the top of my dope-sick lungs, blindfolded.

"You like the ride of the blue magic, don't you..."

My air supply cut off quickly from being choked out. General has his way with me, fucking every hole twice and hard. I want to see the man who is calling the shots. I swear I would yank the scarf off from around my eyes if he wouldn't kill me right here on the spot.

I need to plan my own move and not count on Boo's dumb ass. This crazy lunatic is going to kill me for sure. It could be a good thing he won't let me see his face. In the movies, it's a promising fact— when you see your attacker's face, you die. I think I will take Boo's advice and lay in the cut like a Band-Aid. I can feel the warmth of the drug taking over my body as I exhale in pleasure. I don't feel when he stops fucking me and I don't feel the pinch from the needle, but I feel the H take over my body. I mumble the words "I love you" as my mind escapes from the hell.

"I just introduced you into my fantasy of hell. You're once so pure in the eyes of men, now knocking on heaven's door to a God that doesn't answer. You can pray all you want, but nothing can save you from the wrath of me. When I'm ready for you to die, you will die bitch."

General is gone. He disappears, leaving me terrorized with his final analysis. I am only scared for a moment. The drug takes total control of my mental; it's mind-blowing.

My body is beat up and skinny from the massive blows of General and the drugs that consume me. My hair is falling out from not being combed, and if I was able to look at myself in the mirror, I wouldn't recognize the person who looks back. But do I care? No, I don't, as I float on cloud nine...

CHAPTER TWELVE

General thinks the Health Department will be empty on a Monday morning, looking around the waiting room to be seen. *The early bird always gets the worm and nobody is woke to tell*, he thinks, smiling. Ten minutes pass quickly, and a nurse appears from behind the glass window.

"The doctor can see you now, sir. Please follow me to the exam room." The slender white woman with puffy cheeks sizes General up as she speaks to him.

"Aiight. Is this shit going to take long? I don't want nobody to see me coming outta here."

"The doctor will be right in to see you after I check your temperature, blood pressure and weight. Can you tell me about the problem you're having today, sir?"

"No, bitch, I don't, and stop calling me sir. I'm not your pops," General responds sarcastically.

The slender white lady looks him up and down with a smile. Her skin is milky and her lips full with taunting grey eyes, surrounded by long, beautiful eyelashes.

"You don't have to be so mean, handsome," she replies, batting those eyelashes. "I've seen it all in here, and your secret is safe with me. Everybody slips up not protecting themselves, but you've got to be more careful."

General softens up a bit. His eyes says I'm sorry and his mouth fissures a smile. He leans back and takes a good look at the nurse. "Messing around with this young girl, I done got burnt, ma. My dick hurts every time I take a piss and pus is coming out the head of my best bud."

"I bet your best bud is mad at you right now for not covering him up. Why would you do your best bud like that?" The nurse speaks flirtatiously while taking General's blood pressure.

"Can you make him feel better or not? I got shit to do, Ms."

"No need for the Ms. My name is Danny. No, I can't make him feel better until after he sees the doctor. Afterwards you can come pick me up for dinner, and I can give you a follow-up appointment." The nurse rubs General's inner thigh, catching him by surprise.

"Aiight, Danny, drop me a number and I'll come through." What kind of dame picks up a nigga at the clinic? General chuckles, thinking how many niggas she had done this with. Cracking his neck, he put the number in his pocket while Danny leaves the room to get the doctor.

"Doctor Ortiz, your patient in room one is really nervous. I think it's another case of gonorrhea."

"Okay, I'm on the case as of now. Five more people have hit the waiting area, all women, so let's try to move quickly to get these people out of here. Mondays are always busy, and I already had one call off."

"I'm on it, doc. Don't worry. We will make it through lunch and then someone else will be in to help us."

The doctor and the nurse nod in agreement, going in route.

"I would ask you how you're doing this morning, but if you're sitting here looking at me, it's not good," the doctor speaks firmly. "I'm going to need you to give me a urine sample so I know what to do next. I will be back in a couple of minutes to check on you. Please put on the gown laying to the left of you when you return from the bathroom. It's located down the hallway to your right. You shouldn't have any problems finding it."

The doctor disappears from the room. There is no time for a question-and-answer period.

"Nurse, who do we have in exam room two?"

"A female by the name of Diane James. She comes in here about once a month."

"Yes, I know Ms. James. What's wrong with her this time?"

"I went ahead and pulled a urine sample from her to speed up the process. It's already in the lab. She wants an HIV test, also."

"Good job. I see you're up and at them this morning. It looks like we're going to have a busy day, just like I said. Every time we get a visit from Ms. James, the sick falls from the sky."

The doctor laughs and heads back to exam room one. The men who come through the free clinic are the hardest to get information from. They very rarely know the young women they were sleeping with and their reputations are always at stake.

"So, Mr. John Doe, I'm not going to ask you your name, but I am going to need to take a look at your family jewels."

"Doctor, my shit hurts," General says, showing his infection.

"Yeah, I know it hurts, and I can tell by the pus around the head it's gonorrhea. You're going to need a shot, and I'm going to have to clean all that pus out of that small hole, I'm sorry to say."

"Are you going to tell that nurse my business?"

"Don't worry, she took an oath of patient confidentiality. She would lose her job wishing to speak on this."

"I don't want anybody to lose their job, man. I'm just embarrassed about being here."

"That's understandable. Now, take a deep breath." Taking a shot in the ass wasn't that bad. Having the nurse in the room while the doctor scraped the pus from that tiny hole was another story. But General took it like the man he was and sucked up the tears.

"You should be okay after about a week. Until then, don't have sex with anyone."

Diane sits on the end of the examining table waiting for the doctor to come back with her written-out prescription for the chlamydia she has swimming between her legs.

As she tried to score two for fifteen yesterday morning, a random trick she got down with slapped the hell out of her. Leaving his car parked in the middle of the street, he whipped Diane's ass real good, like she was a man.

"Next time you fuck with me you better have a clean bill of health, trick-ass bitch..." came from the man's mouth, blasting her in the face one last time before returning to his vehicle.

"So I see your promiscuous ways have caught up with you, Ms. James."

"Don't worry about it, Doctor Ortiz. Just give me my prescription so I can get my medication please." Diane's head hangs low.

"You need help, Diane, before somebody kills you. If you keep playing with fire, you will get burnt sooner or later."

"Well, I hope it's not today. I'm trying to get high. Give me whatever it is I need so I can bounce. Mail my HIV test to my last given address."

"Diane, I really want you to think about going to rehab for your daughter's sake." The doctor wanted so badly to help Diane. She was a beautiful woman, even in her addiction. His day is too busy, though, so he gives up on her today. But he prays right there on the spot for her to be safe.

Diane snatches the filled-out prescription paper from the doctor's hand. Damn near knocking down the nurse as she leaves the room, General catches Diane's eye as she reaches the exit. Walking out the door, Diane can't help but think if the well-dressed man is holding.

"Excuse me, but do I know you from somewhere?" Diane asks, trying to break the ice.

General turns around, looking at the beaten-down female standing before him.

"What is it that you need?" General asks, already knowing the answer to his own question.

Diane wears her drug habit on her sleeve. She didn't know General from a can of paint.

"I got forty dollars, and if your shit is good, I got another hundred for you. Can you help me out?"

General looks around, giving a quick surveillance of the street. He never makes sales to anyone he doesn't know, but he feels some compassion for the broken-down spirit that's reaching out to him.

"Get in the car." General motions, disalarming his vehicle. General slides into the driver's seat as Diane gets comfortable in the plush passenger seat.

"Damn, who did that shit to your face?" he asks, seeing the black eyes up close and personal.

"Some nigga I beat for a hundred dollars."

"Oh, yeah? If it was me, I would have just tore the lining out of that pussy. I don't have time to be out in public beating on my money. You would have made it up to me."

Diane sat in her seat taking a liking to the statement General made.

"I'll give you an 8ball if you give me the whole buck forty. I don't sell anything but weight. I charge ten dollars more, but since you're having such a bad day, I'll hook you up."

Diane scopes out the chocolate man for a moment. His voice sounds so familiar.

"I think I do know you from somewhere, nigga. Where you from?" Diane looks directly into General's eyes.

"What, you don't know me from nowhere. And don't be asking me no questions! You police or something, bitch?" General snaps.

"Yeah, I know you. Your name is Trap. It's me, Diane, Egypt's aunt. I know you remember me. We had some fun nights together."

General looks beyond the black eyes and into the depth of her face. His eyes soften once again. That is a world-breaking record for the macho man.

"Get the fuck out of here. Is that really you, Diane? You can take a ride with me." General plays it cool, but reality was he was smoking, mad as hell.

"So where you been at? I haven't seen you since the cocaine days, Trap. You still off the hook?"

"You still talking shit, bitch? What the fuck was it you told Egypt about me back in the day?"

"I told her what I saw, nigga. What, I'm supposed to be scared now because you grew up? You didn't scare me then and you don't now."

"Well, you should be, bitch! I've matured in the game, and I owe you one, Ms. Diane."

CHAPTER THIRTEEN

Mornings turned into nights, which turned into days. The seasons changed, and I blew in whatever direction the wind carried me. Lovers came into my life and left. I had swore before God that I was done with bitches after what Sasha put me through. Well, I did play my part in the imperfections of our relationship. From best friends to lovers now hating each other as human beings, we killed whatever passion we once knew.

I had no family worth communicating with, so I sat at random bars looking for love in the bottom of empty drinking glasses. The alcoholism in itself tore me and Sasha apart. She couldn't understand why I wouldn't stop. How come her love wasn't good enough for me to give it up? The demons that laid eggs in my soul wouldn't allow me to do anything else more then to try to drink the pain away. Acrimony, resentment, betrayal, deceit and cruelty ran through my bloodline thick; I never knew anything else. The bottle comforted the craving for the mother I never had and the love I yearned for.

After the lust was gone between Sasha and me, and the thrill of something new turned into bad morning breath with burnt eggs served after weak make-up sex, it was a wrap between us. The endless arguments about me and her baby daddy didn't help any neither. Just as us females do, we say we can handle something, but the reality is, we never get over it and we can't handle the truth. The anger sits in the cut, causing cancer while it's asleep in the back of your brain. Everything I tried to do to show her that we were all we needed, her "bd" always got in the middle of things. From three-somes to lonesome I sit here in the bar in mid afternoon, playing Mary J. Blige.

"What up, Egypt? I see you're getting an early start on happy hour."

"Hey, girl, what's up with you? You just getting off work or something? You're all dressed to impress; your outfit is cute."

"Cute is for eight-year olds. I'm a grown-ass woman. Monica has a date tonight, and you're coming with me. So sip that last gin and juice and grab up a couple of six packs to go so I can dress you." My girl Monica laughed, calling the shots, doing what she does best—being the boss.

That's what I needed, sitting on this fucking bar stool feeling sorry for myself. I ordered two more drinks to listen to my line-up on the jukebox while Monica talked shit to some guy at the other end of the bar.

Monica and I got real cool the night Sasha put my black ass out for good. I met her sitting on this same bar stool seated two bar stools down from the jukebox. She had just broken up with her long-term boyfriend for having an abortion. She wasn't ready for the responsibility of having a nothing-ass "bd". She wanted kids, but when she was married. We sang and danced while we drank, having good conversation on fucked-up relationships. Monica became like a sister I never had, and I loved her from day one. She was so pretty with her redbone complexion. Built like a brick shithouse, men flocked to her like dogs in heat, wanting to take care of her every request. Yeah yup, Monica was most wanted by all men and the bitches envied her everywhere she rolled. You could say I became security because if I seen one bitch cut her eyes or act like she was one chromosome away from being retarded, I was handling that shit at the neck.

Tougher than leather and tight like glue, we was hanging hard, having a ball in the streets, tricking them lame-ass niggas. I didn't really tell Monica I was gay. Sasha turned into Stoney the night we met. A lesbian wasn't what I wanted to be at the time. Plus, how could I tell her that I was fucked up over a woman? Straight turn off. I just really needed a friend at the time, and I didn't want to lose her from one tiny flaw.

I never really felt out of place, but sometimes in the crowded rooms in the clubs, surrounded by many people, I felt all alone besides the comfort of my drink. It was the only thing that wouldn't let me down, ya dig?

Vibe played by R. Kelly and the Public Announcement as Monica and I sipped on the weak mixed drinks the bartender was serving up at the "O". Why is it everything I do revolves around liquor and bad judgment? One day I will be able to answer that question with a sober mind. Until then, I have to accept it and the cards I'm dealt from making bad choices.

"Monica, I know I didn't let you dress me up to hang out in the fucking Original's Hotdog Shop, lame-ass kiddie bar."

"It shouldn't matter what bar you sitting in as long as they got gin to serve your drunk ass. They ain't running out no time soon, so relax. I'm meeting some guy named Mario down here. He's bringing his boy along with him to meet you. His name is Shame."

"Shame? What kind of name is Shame?" I asked cross-eyed.

"I don't fucking know, Egypt. Ask him when he gets here."

"He ugly as hell, I bet you, with a name like that. You ever seen him before?"

"Naw, I ain't never seen him before, but he sounds sexy on the phone. Him and his boy, Mario."

"You haven't seen neither one of them in person! That's why you got me out here with you on this dummy mission. You know when they sound good on the phone they turn out to be butt-ass ugly." We both looked at each other and busted out laughing knowing the words I spoke was true to the game.

"Moe, I'm already feeling it. I don't got time for this shit. I done already drank all the beer I brought to your house while we got dressed.

I need something to eat before somebody's face turn my stomach." I rubbed my stomach playful as I made Monica laugh.

"I know, bitch. You should be drunk, drinking up all the beer like I wasn't thirsty, too."

"Anyway, how are we supposed to know what these niggas look like?"

"Don't worry. I told them when they get here to order a triple gin and juice. When the bartender yells out, 'Whose drink?", that's my cue to speak up. He will then know who I am. If he likes what he sees, and you know he will, he'll approach the scene to introduce himself in a proper manner."

"Proper manner... girl, you're tripping for real. You're so crazy. If they're ugly, I'm out of here." I sigh with boredom, resting my head on my hand.

"Whatever, Egypt, but you better make the nigga buy you something to eat with that drunk shit to soak up all that liquor. You know we can barely get a jitney now because your ass be throwing up chunks in every-body ride." Monica shook her head, finishing her drink. I seen her eyes comb over the bar and mine rolled in the back of my head. I was thinking about who was going to drink the triple gin once it was ordered.

"So, who's going to drink the drink? Are you, or can I have it?" I could see angry lines growing on Monica's forehead when I asked the question. I couldn't help but smile because it was funny as hell how I could get up under her skin.

"See, that's what the fuck I'm talking about. You need to go to some meetings wit your drunk ass!"

"Why should I go to AA? I tried, hoe, and when I left, I really needed a drink, in there listening to alcoholics' war stories for over an hour." Both of us busted out in laughter once more.

"You're sick in the head, Egypt, but that's why I love you. You keep it real all the time." We shared a moment briefly.

"Who order the triple gin and cranberry?" the bartender yelled out. I smiled because as soon as I heard what the gin was mixed with, I knew it was for me.

"That drink is down here for me," Monica shouted to the bartender, pointing at herself.

"That will be nine twenty-five."

"Oh, no, he didn't. It was supposed to be paid for, mister."

"All I did was pour it as the guy asked, and he said a female would pay for it when I finished it."

"Here goes a twenty spot for the lady's drink, and you can keep the change."

Me and Monica turned around to see who the voice was paying for the drinks. A well-dressed midget standing thigh high to every person in the bar stood down staring up at us with a smile.

"Let me guess, but I know that I'm right, you're Mario?" My sarcastic tone followed up behind the hysterical laughter brought tears to my eyes. While Mario and Monica stood there staring up and down at each other, I downed the drink.

"What's up, ladies? Yeah, I'm Mario and my boy Shame is downstairs getting himself a milkshake."

Bushwick Bill glared at me as I kept laughing at his small-fry ass. I couldn't believe it—he was a real, live midget.

"And your girl over here can stop all the fucking laughing because I don't see anything funny. I might be small, but my dick is only two inches from the floor." Mario was angry.

"I know that's right, little man." Putting the emphasis on the word 'little' made him even madder, and I laughed harder.

"Hi, Mario, my name is Monica and this drunk bitch here is my girl, Egypt. Don't pay her no mind; she got jokes!"

"That bitch must be drunk, disrespecting me like that. She don't know me from a can of paint," Mario snapped.

"Monica, hold the fuck up! Who is little mini-me over there talking to? I'll step on his ass and squash that big-ass head!"

"Girl, chill the fuck out. He my date, not yours," Monica whispered in my ear. "Let me talk to my homegirl for a minute, Mario and you go find your boy so we can get out of here. Is that cool with you, sexy?" Monica said, fake as hell.

"Yeah, it's cool. I'll be right back." Mario looked me up and down, hurting his neck, and I couldn't help but to laugh under my breath.

Mario went downstairs as Monica pulled me to the ladies' room. Pulling me by the arm as if she was my mother with an attitude didn't sit well with me, but I needed her help anyway because I was fucked up. It was the most fun I had in a long while, and who would have thought it would be at the lame-ass Original's?

"E, did you see that short baby thumper? What the hell was that?" Monica paced the small bathroom floor.

"I told you blind dates are fucked up, homie." By this time, I'm laughing hard as hell all over again. "But he is cute a little bit, Moe. Don't be mad. It's not his fault he's a small person."

"There's nothing cute about him, Egypt. Don't try to lie to make me feel better. He looks like Bushwick Bill from the Ghetto Boys group. Let's bounce girl. I don't want nobody to see me with him. I will not be caught dead with little micro *Boyz N the Hood*."

"Well, he did say his dick is two inches from the floor. Maybe you want to try it on for size." I kept laughing. I couldn't help it. I could see the anger lines creeping over Monica's forehead once again, so I decided to chill.

"You got jokes, Egypt, but I'm not feeling little man. I'm out!" Monica gave me the neck roll to let me know she wasn't playing any games with her hands on her hips.

"Hold up. Let's see what his homeboy look like first. When one is ugly, most times the other one is a cutie. It doesn't even matter at this point. I need a drink and his cute or ugly ass is buying. Plus, we all dressed up and we don't have shit to do. Let's just roll out with them to their side of town so we can get it in."

"That's a shame! All you can think about is drinking. I guess you're right. You're already on a roll and I'm not paying for your drinks to-night. Your ass can burn a hole in a bitch's pocket, so let's go and get this over with. Hurry up and do whatever it is you're planning to do so I can get home to my fuck buddy."

"You didn't tell me you were having company. What late-night stick is coming to see you?"

"Ain't nobody coming over my house! I'm talking about my vibra-tor, Teddy. He knows what to do to please me." Laughter bounced off the bathroom walls as we walked out.

We thought we would have a moment to clown before we met up with Mario, but by surprise, Mario and his friend were waiting a few feet away from the restroom. He spotted us as soon as we stepped out the door. This little dude is waving both his arms like he's trying to land a plane to get our attention. I shook my head in shame.

"Damn, Mario, you didn't have to flag us down like that. What, you thought we wouldn't see you?" Monica giggled under her breath at my comment as we approached both him and his friend.

"You don't have to be clowning my boy like that ladies cuz he's a little small. You know what they say—good things come in small packages."

"Yes they do..." My mouth fell open and my chin smacked the floor. "You must be Shame." I couldn't help but to lick my lips. Shame was fine as hell.

"Yes, my name is Shame, but I didn't catch yours," Shame replied with a smile. He had this sexy dimple in his left cheek that would cause you to say something funny every time you open your mouth. Quick, Egypt, think of something funny, bitch.

"I don't remember throwing it at you neither, but it's Egypt, play-boy. It's nice to meet you, Shame." I put my hand out for a proper meeting, as Monica called it. Shame bypassed my hand and went in for the kill. He gave me a warm embrace as if he known me for years.

It felt so good, it felt like I belonged in his arms. And the way my head laid up against his chest, you would have thought from the outside looking in that I was his woman.

"Did you need a hug, baby girl, because you haven't let go yet." Shame chuckled as I pulled away embarrassed. I hadn't realized I still had my arms around him.

"Let me buy you a drink," Shame offered, and I accepted with an empty glass. I was grinning from ear to ear.

"I'll take a gin and juice, please." I sobered up quickly. Monica and I look at each other, not knowing what to say. The catty conversation came to a halt. I could see in her eyes she wasn't feeling Shame paying me all of his attention. Mario was trying to hold it down the best way he knew how. He kept pulling out stacks of cash from different pockets.

"Can we get out of here when ya'll two finish ya drinks? Lawd knows Egypt doesn't need another one." Monica's voice was angry, and I could see the hate in my girl's eyes. She was really jealous.

"You know what, Monica?" Mario asked, fed up.

"What, wee man!" Monica said with upturned eyes.

"Fuck you, bitch! Make another comment about my size, and I'm going to shoot at you stink cock!" Mario had fire in his eyes as he yelled at Monica. Spit was flying as he tugged at his waist to pull his gun.

Pushing Monica to the side, Shame placed his index finger over her lips.

"Dawg, don't be like that. Calm down Mario, she just playing. Let's just go back to my crib and bust it up for a minute. We can play cards or something. We got plenty to drink and music, whatever you want to hear."

Shame was winning me over. I wanted to roll with him, but I see the neck roll back on Monica, and I knew the shit was about to hit the fan.

"Me and my homegirl don't know ya'll well enough to be going home witcha. Check ya self, Shame. It's not going down like that. As a matter of fact, Egypt finish that shit you're drinking with your drunk ass and let's go!"

I didn't get a chance to respond to Monica, but I was ready to smack the shit out of her.

"It's your girl's choice, Ms. Monica, if she wants to stay or go. I see what you're saying now, Mario. This bitch is rocking my nerve." Shame's smooth face wrinkled up. "You know what, Mario?"

"What, dawg?"

"Put her stuck up ass in a jitney. Fuck her…"

"No, fuck the both of you! I can get home on my own."

"I told you, Shame. Every time we do this blind date shit I get stuck with the stuck-up-ass broad."

"Hold the fuck up, Mario and Shame. Don't talk about my girl like that."

"I don't need your drunk ass to save me. I don't need you to take up for me never, Egypt!" Monica gave me the finger and took off down the steps and out the front door.

Mario ran behind Monica to see if she was alright. I wasn't feeling how she just fronted on me in front of a bar full of people, so I had to order me another drink. Sitting at the bar, me and Shame kicked up casual conversation, forgetting about everyone else in the room. I haven't been this turned on by a man since Trap.

Mario and Monica never came back to the bar, and I ended up going home with Shame as he planned all along. It was the best move I had made in a long time. His touch soothed my being. His kiss melted my heart and my middle spot splashed for the first time in a long time for a man to go deep. From top to bottom, he kissed every inch of my physique with his tongue to follow. I squealed in pleasure, moaning through our passion as I drank in every stroke he put on me. The lovemaking was magical, but I wasn't satisfied being in the comfort of a man at the end of the night. Shame held me in his arms as his head rested on my back. I lay there in silence, wanting the touch of a woman.

"It's morning and we slept the night away," I sang along to the old Shirley Murdock tune playing from downstairs, I think. I wiped my eyes clear from the sleep and the dried-up tears, looking for Shame. I could smell bacon and eggs cooking from the kitchen, and I could hear a female voice singing along with mine.

I looked around the room catching the athletic vibe that captivated the large space. There were pictures on the wall of Shame playing every sport you could imagine, even Polo. Trophies and accomplishments placed in various spots led me to believe Shame was more than a dope boy.

"You look so beautiful standing there naked. I'm getting a woody in my sweats just thinking about last night."

Turning around to face Shame, my eyes missed his zeroing right in on his woody standing at attention. My mouth watered for his manhood to bless me with a wake up.

"I'm guessing you want what I want, baby." Shame stood in the door shirtless. His caramel skin was enough to make me want to bite him. His six pack was talking to me in riddles while my middle spot heated up with warmth. He spoke, watching me stare a hole through his sweats.

"Good morning to you, too. I see someone or something is happy to see me, still without clothes on my body. But that will have to wait, Shame. I haven't brushed my teeth or washed yesterday's bar stink off of me yet. Can I freshen up a little and put something in my stomach?"

The answer was no. This nigga stuck his tongue down my throat, breath stinking and all. Turning me around, putting my ass on his dick, he had removed his sweat pants. Bending me over with force, my nipples got brick hard. Feet planted on the floor, he spreads my legs out and goes deep from behind. I could hear a sigh of relief as he entered me while I touched my toes. Thrusting in and out I touched myself, making my pussy throb more and more. Stroking me with excellence, sending me on an erotic high, I never wanted to come down off this feeling. This morning I didn't need the touch of a woman. I was satisfied.

As I came, my legs buckled from beneath me. Shame followed behind, me mumbling my name in a whisper, but I caught it. Breathing hot and heavy, I looked into his eyes and think I fell in love.

He led me to the bathroom where the towels hung from the ceiling. Everything matched from wall to wall. It was truly the work of a woman. I got into the shower and turned on the water full blast to let it beat on my back. I washed my body in slow strokes as I watched Shame watch me, and as he watched, me he stroked himself faster and harder. After making his body jerk, he simply washed and disappeared into the bedroom. I continued to wash slowly while my thoughts ran a mile in my mind. I took in the embrace of having a man look at me with lust-filled eyes. *Maybe I could make being with a man work*, I thought, when I was rudely interrupted by a screaming female voice.

"Girl, your name is Egypt? That shit sounds so exotic when you think about a man saying it when ya'll having sex. Anyway, I can't believe my brother brought you home. What you done did to the boy?"

"Who are you?" I asked, looking around the shower curtain annoyed.

"Oh, my fault girl. I'm Porsha, your new best friend and maybe sister-in-law the way my brother is downstairs talking about you. The nigga even sent me to the mall first thing this morning to make sure you was good when you woke up. So wash your ass girl and get out."

I smiled on the inside. I couldn't believe Shame had gone through so much trouble to make sure I was comfortable. I could get used to this. I hopped out the shower, dripping wet. Shame's sister sat on the toilet, taking in the sight of my body while I towel dried quickly. I think she even licked her lips at my flesh.

Bypassing her, I stepped in the bedroom to shopping bags from Foot Locker. I turned around to have Porsha staring me in my face with more shopping bags. The bitch wanted me to start popping tags off butt-ass naked.

"Can I have some privacy to put on some underwear, Porsha? You must don't get out much," I uttered under my breath.

She shook off my comment and reached down into a large bag, pulling out a smaller one. It was a Vickie's Secret bag filled with undergarments. She threw them on the bed, licked her lips and rolled to the left.

Truth be told, this will be the first time I ever tried on a thong. It was cool, but the string in my ass was going to take some getting used to. Even though Porsha had left the room, I still felt I was being watched from a distance. My stomach talked to me as I came across a pair of all- black Nike sweat pants and a tight, fitted shirt.

I found the downstairs kitchen again after I roamed Shame's house in amazement. It was flashy but homey, and I felt comfortable from the door. Shame sat at the table talking on the phone shirtless, looking damned good.

"Who are you talking to?" I asked, taking a seat next to him.

"It's your girl, Monica, " he answered with a blank stare on his face. "She's pretty upset with you right now."

"For what? Ain't nobody fighting with Monica spoiled ass today. My morning is going too good." I reach in for a kiss and Shame pulls back. Those wanting eyes of his searched mine for a millisecond, then he planted those soft-ass lips on mine.

"What, is she mad because I came home with you and didn't call her?" Shame's face was nonchalant as he stood from his seat. I was surprised his dick was still standing at attention. A smile crept across his face as he seen me staring at his dick once again while he passed me the phone. I watched him head toward the ice box. He wasn't going to leave me alone I figured out when he posted up on it and gave me the stare down. My face was cracked and on the ground. Monica went in on me as soon as she heard my voice. I didn't know how to approach the situation at hand. I couldn't deny it to Shame. My eyes told the story, and they couldn't lie as the passion of me loving a woman was all over my face. But how could I convince my friend Monica that whatever she heard wasn't true? I wanted to take the call in private, but I didn't want to seem guilty to the accusations Monica was throwing. So I put my boxing gloves on to block her punches.

"The way I threw that pussy on Shame last night and this morning, he can tell I'm no dike. Girl, who spoon feeding you those lies?" I laughed hysterically, putting on a front for Shame, who tried to act as if he wasn't listening. This nigga was real cute about it though. He was posted up against the ice box, reading *Jet* with a glass of orange juice in his hand.

"Oh, for real E, you ain't got to lie to kick it with me. Some bitch that goes with my cousin A.J., who claims to be your younger peeps, done put you on blast. She said you didn't fuck with no nigga named Stony, but a bitch named Sasha." Monica spit that shit to me as clear as day. The phone fell silent. This whole situation really showed me how small Pittsburgh was when you hung in the hood.

"My little cousin is a fucking lie, Monica!" I took a deep breath.

"So, do you also deny the fact that my cousin is your ex, and he's saying the same thing? Damn I thought I knew you, but I don't know shit."

"Whatever, Monica. A.J. is my ex, and my little cousin Chase—I smacked her in the bar over him—is spreading lies because she's a nasty little bitch out for revenge. She's doing all this because she thinks I still want him and I don't. I'm doing bigger and better things now, homegirl, so you can go run and tell them I said that. Let my name taste like ass when you speak it, bitch. Monica, there's a lot of shit you don't know about me or my family, so don't comment. As a matter of fact, this conversation is done until we are face to face."

I pushed the hang-up button quick, fast and in a hurry, hoping she didn't call back with A.J. on the line.

My head fell down into my chest. Shame came right to my rescue just as I planned a moment ago. Wrapping me in his arms, he didn't say a word.

"It's true, Shame. I did have a woman..."

"Hold up, Egypt. You don't owe me anything, baby. Everybody got a past, including me. If you want to tell me because you trust me, that's cool, but if you think you owe me something, you don't." Shame squeezed me tighter, and I felt damned good in his arms. It was time for me to put on an Oscar-winning performance of the somewhat truth.

"I can't front about me liking women, Shame. The shit is going to come out sooner or later, and I don't want you to get caught in the crossfire. It's a part of my life I want to forget. No good came from it." My head sank lower into my chest.

"You having a girlfriend is a turn-on to me, so you can lift up your head."

"You don't think it's nasty, Shame?" I asked surprisingly.

"I wish I was there to witness the action. I'm not here to judge you, woman. I'll leave that up to God. I just see something special in you. I also see that you've been hurt. I could tell by the conversations we had last night. You were really open with me." Shame cracked a smile. "I'll blame it on the alcohol. But can you trust me to love you past your pain?"

I went to answer his question, but he cut me off with that sexy little thing he did to Monica last night. He brushed my lips with his index finger.

"Don't worry about all that right now. We got all the time in the world to get to know each other." He winked his eye at me, reading my thoughts and it turned me on. "Just say yes, Egypt. Take a chance with me. I just might be your fairy tale ending."

I shook my head yes and kissed those sexy, thick lips. My heart pounded, the knots in my stomach untangled, and I fell in love on the spot.

I finally got some breakfast in my stomach. Shame got into his life detail by detail while we ate. His parents died in a car crash when he was in high school leaving one of his basketball games. Going to an after-party saved his life. His sister didn't like basketball, so she sat at home waiting for her parents to return, and they never did. Shame explained to me how his father taught him how to respect women as if they were his mother and how family always came first, no matter what. Playing college ball for two years on a scholarship at Pitt, he got a degree in accounting to make it in the real world. He had to take care of him and his little sister. After he got his degree, basketball didn't mean anything to him anymore. He felt as if his parents' death was his fault. If he didn't play ball, it might not have ever happened. *But that was a big might*, I thought. Landing a job at First National Bank in charge of the accounting department, he made a name for himself in six months. When the bank hired Mario to process checks, Shame caught on real fast that there was a big difference between the bank paychecks he was getting and Mario. Mario kept the freshest suits to a brand new car every six months. At first Shame thought he was stealing until he was introduced to the American dream—hustling. Him and Mario became the best of friends riding dirty.

Shame kept going on and on about his ups and downs and how his sister was leading a double life. He thought she needed a woman around to talk to, maybe someone who could guide her decisions. By his boyish looks, I wouldn't have guessed that he was thirty-one. He didn't look a day over eighteen. I don't know how I'll be able to guide her decisions; the bitch is older than me by two years.

From that moment on, me and Shame were inseparable. We told each other every thought that crossed our minds. Porsha was never around and when she was, she followed me around like a lost puppy needing love and affection. Me and Monica didn't get the chance to have that face to face visit, and after a while, I didn't miss her mean ass as much. Mario always tried to convince me and Shame that he fucked Monica the night he took her home, but I knew his ass got dropped off around the corner. Monica never let a stranger know where she lived at. We both knew he was lying, but the story he told on how shit went down was always funny to hear.

Over the course of six months, my life changed for the better. I moved in the house with Shame, and Mario followed behind, putting handcuffs on Porsha. I knew that she was fucking Mario, but it wasn't my place to tell Shame. Shame should have figured it out, though, when Mario brought her a brand new car. Don't know brother do shit like that if he ain't getting no ass, ya dig? But when the cat was let out the bag Shame got over the fact that his best friend was fucking his little sister, he got on board because Mario had her ass in check. She wasn't pulling anymore disappearing acts. That made all of us happy. We all became a happy little family…

From the block to the business suits, Shame and Mario stuck together. Porsha and I started seeing less and less of them when the money grew larger and larger. The passionate fucks turned into early morning quickies, but the stacks of cash made up for the wet ass. All in all, there wasn't any disrespect.

CHAPTER FOURTEEN

"Egypt, is *Party of Five* coming on tonight?" Porsha yelled from the kitchen into the living room.

"I don't know. What's today?" I roll my eyes in the back of my head. I can't watch another stupid-ass show on white people and how they fix their problems. I got my own problems.

"Shit, I've been stuck in this house with you for so long smoking this weed I couldn't tell you what day it is. But I do think it's Thursday."

"Well, if it's Thursday, it's coming on at eight like it always do." I know she could hear the sarcastic tone in my voice, but did it stop her from talking to me? Hell, no…

"I want you to watch it with me. Some chick is supposed to come out and tell Julia she's gay. I've been waiting to see this episode all week." Porsha ran in the living room and jumped on the couch right next to me.

"What you know about that, Porsha?"

"You don't know everything about me, Egypt. I've had a girlfriend before when I worked at this strip club. You better not tell my brother neither." Porsha giggled, telling her secret.

My eyes opened wide and my ears started to burn to hear the secret tale about Porsha fucking with a girl and working in a strip club. "When was you doing all this? Please, let it be known. We can have our own episode of *Party of Five* right here on the couch."

"Damn, Egypt, you want to talk to me now. Just a minute ago I had to pull fucking teeth for you to talk to me." Porsha crossed her legs into Indian style.

"So what happened? Spill the beans, bitch!"

"Aiight, aiight, aiight, you thirsty as hell to hear the dirt. She wasn't my girlfriend, but she did put me on to some game. Her name was Stardust, and she was the baddest bitch working at the club called the Pinky Ring." Porsha took a deep breath. "You know what club I'm talking about?"

"Yeah! Now finish the damned story before *Party of Five* come on." My emotions jumped around in my skin. I was happy that it wasn't just me that had an experience with a woman.

"Stardust had made five grand off these rich-ass businessmen from out of town. She sat backstage of the club like she was the head bitch in charge, smoking on a blunt and sniffing coke. My ass comes from the rear, oiled up like an engine part for a car, damned near in tears. I had only made three hundred dollars, and I got screwed out of two hundred dollars doing a private dance, a favor for my boss. I had did the private dance for my boss, right, when the nigga I'm dancing for pulls his dick out and bust a nut all over me and then leaves the scene without paying me. He gave the money to my boss, he said, and my boss said he didn't give him shit. I just got beat. So anyway, I'm standing in the back crying and shit about the little bit of money I made when Stardust swipes a stack of money in my ass crack. She tells me to ask her what do I have to do to get it? I asked her what do I have to do? She says, 'I want you to sniff this,' handing me a bag of coke, and then she says, 'I want to lick your pussy.' 'WHAT!!' I scream, laughing loud as hell. She stands there looking good as hell with a serious look on her face. And I say yes with the next blink of an eye. I take the money, sniff the bag and spread my legs right there in the open. I laid on the floor, heart racing, my pussy throbbing as she sucked harder and harder. I thought it might have been the coke making it feel so good, but when we rendezvous on many other occasions, I found out it wasn't. Every time I hooked up with her after that, the sex just got better and better, and no she didn't continue to pay me. I liked her. I still see her when I can get away from Mario and hide out from you. But since you know now, I hope I can be me."

I sat there in awe, pussy wet. I couldn't believe it. I really couldn't believe she told me that. I didn't know what to say. I was in shock.

"Damn, Porsha, that's deep. Are you still seeing her for real?"

"Yeah yup, as you say, Egypt." Porsha sparked up a blunt and took a long drag.

"You love her?"

"You love my brother?"

"Yes I do, but why you ask me that?"

"When the last time ya'll fucked, let alone have a conversation without fighting? Yeah, I love her."

I went to answer Porsha's question when vomit rolled up my throat. I ran to the kitchen sink and threw up. It was my third time today. Porsha followed behind me, screaming she was going to be an auntie.

"Not to change the subject or anything, but I hope you do love my brother because you're carrying his baby. I don't know when ya'll had a chance to make it, but I won't take you on *Maury* until it gets here."

'I'm not pregnant, Porsha, and that shit ain't funny. I'm just sick with the flu or something. Don't be burning bread on me, sis. I don't know what to do with no baby." Just the thought of me being pregnant made me sicker. I went to the bathroom to rinse my mouth out and looked in the mirror. Face flushed, I knew I was pregnant and I knew it was a boy. I don't know how I knew, but I knew. With Porsha right there on my heels, I decided to change the conversation and put the attention back on her.

"Anyway, Porsha, do you see yourself leaving Mario to be with a woman?" I sat down on the side of the tub and fought with Porsha to get the blunt out of her hand.

"Yeah, I could see myself with a woman if she was pulling in the money Mario was. But don't try to flip that shit back on me. What are you going to do about the baby you're carrying? Are you going to tell my brother?" I sucked in the brown smoke from the blunt. I inhaled it deeply and held it in my lungs for as long as I could take it.

"I don't know what I'm going to do, but this is the best episode of *Party of Five* I've ever seen."

We both laughed as my face saddened. I rubbed my belly in guilt.

"Fuck *Party of Five*. We going to the CVS around the corner to get a pregnancy test,," Porsha said with a smirk.

I put my head down. That would be the moment of truth when the pregnancy test reads positive. I would have a lot of explaining to do when I revealed I don't want any children. Better now than later.

"Let's walk," I added brazenly.

"Why walk when we have two cars?"

"Because I want to walk to clear my mind, lazy ass. I don't want no kids, Porsha."

"Be happy you can carry a child. What you mean you don't want no kids, girl? We women, we supposed to bare children for our men."

I could see the attitude forming all over Porsha's aura. But nobody knew my struggle, and it wasn't nobody's choice but my own when it came to bringing another life into this fucked-up world. Better now than later, I might as well tell her I don't know how to love somebody else.

"If I'm carrying something in my stomach, Porsha, I don't know how to love it, and I don't want to take care of it. I don't know how; my mother wasn't there to show me." I looked Porsha directly in the eyes and spoke the truth. I didn't care if she told her brother.

The room fell into a sudden calm. Porsha glared back at me. I watched her whole face transform, as if the words I spoke cut her like a knife.

"Let's be the fuck out. I need some blunts messing around with your nut ass." Porsha rolled her eyes and kept it moving.

We both didn't say a word as we stepped outside on the curb. The leaves were changing colors as the existing summer came to an end. My twenty-first birthday came and went as my happiness faded to black. I wasn't sad, but I was missing something special in my inner being. I needed to do some soul searching, I guess. I found myself looking at my boyfriend's little sister as if she was some sort of consolation prize to be won. I was thirsty for the touch of a woman. I was pregnant by a man I never seen, and I had nobody to talk to. It was going to be much harder to control my eyes now since I've heard the tale of Porsha sleeping with another woman. I'm dying inside right now; I can feel the heartbeat in between my thighs. I try to walk with a limp to keep from moaning, and in the back of my mind I'm so anxious to fall victim to her touch.

"Why so quiet, Porsha? You all in your head? Spark something for the walk. I need to get high and laugh at some shit."

"I don't feel like laughing, punk." Porsha smiled and put her arm around my neck. She kicked off an old-school jam, lighting up a blunt. We skipped the rest of the way to the CVS, rapping my favorite song, *My Buddy* by De La Soul.

We rolled in the store and bought five of the most expensive pregnancy tests with two boxes of blunts. The walk back home started off quiet once again. There was something wrong with Porsha. I can never get her to shut up; she always got something to say even in her sleep. She was just too quiet for me. On our way back home, I thought maybe it was what I said about the baby if I was pregnant. The mood did shift from that moment.

"How long do we got to wait for the sign to pop up? I'm scared as hell right now." I sat rocking back and forth on my bed while Porsha checked the last test.

My legs shook and my heart raced as Porsha walked back into the bedroom to read me the verdict. She looked at me and shook her head at me without eye contact.

"Egypt, you're straight tripping if you think you're killing my niece or nephew. This test is reading the same result as the other four—you're having a baby, mami. Every one you've taken has come back positive. You're knocked up. You're going to have to face it, boo."

The tears didn't waste any time falling down my face. I sobbed very loud, falling down to my knees. I couldn't believe that I didn't protect myself from this. Now I was about to kill a baby, crush my man's dreams of having a family and have to fight Porsha for the decision I was about to make.

"Don't cry, Egypt, I'm going to be here for you, and my brother will always take care of you and the baby. On the real, I wish I was you, baby girl." Porsha wrapped me in her arms.

Sympathetic tears came to follow mine. "I wish I could feel another human being's heartbeat inside of me. You can do something I'll never be able to do and that's have children."

I couldn't believe it when I heard Porsha tell me that. I was being so selfish, but her reality wasn't my cross to bear. The tears from us both consoled each other. I wanted to be her and she wanted to be me. We felt each other's pain.

"The reason why I got quiet earlier was I always wanted a child to love and to love me back unconditionally. I've been trying since I was about nineteen to have a baby. I keep trying, hoping God maybe bless me. My ex-boyfriend left me behind this. He wanted a child and I couldn't give him one. We made a cute couple. Tyler and I was together since the eighth grade. I still remember him as if we met yesterday, his face, his touch... damn I loved him. I had the ring, the right man and a hyperthyroidism that kept me from getting pregnant. We were supposed to get married on my eighteenth birthday and Tyler wanted me pregnant walking down the aisle. When the doctors told us I wouldn't get pregnant and if I did, I wouldn't carry full term, he left me. Tyler, the love of my life, left me for some white bitch he only knew for two weeks and married her. I wished death on them, but they're still together to this day. We was together for all those years, and he just up and left me. I still can't believe it, Egypt. I haven't been right since. I didn't have to strip to get money, I didn't have to do a lot of dumb shit I've done in my life, but hurt people do hurt things, and I still do struggle with this shit. I know our child would have been beautiful no matter if it was a girl or a boy. I knew it wasn't God's fault, but I blamed Him anyway for a long time. Who else could I blame? But I got past that real quick. I know God is real and God is love. My parents have to be somewhere."

I laid my head on Porsha's chest, crying while she told me another part of her life. Shame was right—the girl was leading a double life and been through some shit. I felt obligated to open up to Porsha, but I couldn't do it. I just attacked the subject I knew.

"Where the fuck is the love, Porsha? What God are you talking about? I've cried so many days and nights to God and look at me! I'm a drunk-ass bitch with a man I don't even know. I ain't got no family, my mom left me and never came back, my aunt fucked the only man I really loved and God took the only person in my life away from me that cared, my grandmother. I'm alone out here in these streets and ain't no God out here protecting me. Nobody cares about me. There ain't no God, Porsha," I spat, snapping out. All the tears I had hidden inside poured out of me like a waterfall. As I let it out, Porsha tried to calm me down. Grabbing me by the arms, she pulled me into her character and embraced my lips with hers. The warmth of her hands cradled my face. I couldn't deny her kiss, and I didn't resist her caress, feeling our connection.

The touch she put on me stimulated my mind, body and soul, shaking the core of my deepest thoughts of having Porsha to myself. Tasting her sweetest nectar, the subliminal message was clear to the naked eye of the naked truth as our naked bodies collapsed in each other's naked arms.

CHAPTER FIFTEEN

"The deal should be going down in three days, Shame. You better be ready to do this, nigga!" Mario paced the floor back and forth strenuously. "If we make one false move, the breath we breathe can be snatched from the both of us. We don't have no crew to hold court in the streets for us, dawg. We got to handle this shit up close and personal with no mistakes. This punk-ass muthafucker done killed my cousin and he's dangerous. He blew up his asshole... who does shit like that? So you got to be ready, Shame. We fucking with a sick bastard."

Mario couldn't stress enough about making no mistakes. He hadn't sat his ass down in the last hour. Back and forth and back and forth he went, pacing the floor.

"Nigga, please, you don't have to keep telling me what to do about this here. I know I've never killed a man before, but there's a first time for everything. Dawg, you've been carrying me through ever since we started this business and now it's time for me to put in work."

Mario looked at Shame and his eyes read WHATEVER, MAN. He ran his tongue over the top of his teeth and flipped his toothpick to the other side of his mouth.

"I'm gonna kill the dude if my life depends on it, Mario. I'm for real about it, too, nigga! And after I kill him, I'm going to take over his side of town, fuck his main bitch in the mouth and stick a homemade bomb up her ass and set it off." Shame spoke smokescreens, but deep down he wanted to be that killer. He said whatever it was Mario wanted to hear because he couldn't take that look that he gave off. The not-a-real man look.

"That's what the fuck I'm talking about, nigga. You starting to think like a soldier, a muthafucking menace! We niggas at war out here on these streets, and it's time we decipher the code and change the hood politics. Two niggas on the rise and one bitch nigga DEAD!" Mario shouted in a rage all into himself. He was pre-hype, feeling like Superman from all the candy he had put in his nose. There was no calming him down, and Shame just amped him up to pace the floor for another hour.

"Baby, can you please calm down. All that screaming ain't necessary. You are wired up. Let me roll you a blunt so you can chill the hell out. Get your homeboy ,Shame, please..."

"Don't ever tell somebody to get me, Keya. This is me. This is me, all day, every day, you hear me! Now roll the weed, bitch!"

"Who are you talking to, Mario? You're in my house, boy. I'ma let you slide, but you got one more time and your ass is out. Get your boy, Shame. This is the last time I'm going to tell you..."

SMACK! Mario smacked Keya with an open hand. He couldn't stand to be called a boy, being that he was so short. Wired off the coke, he couldn't control himself doing the unthinkable.

"Mario, what the fuck are you doing?" Shame gripped him up, slamming him up against the wall in Keya's kitchen. "That's a female, nigga. I better not never catch you doing that shit again! Keep your muthafucking hands to yourself," Shame yelled, going to Keya's rescue. He helped her up from the floor.

"You're done, dawg. It's time to get the fuck up and out," Shame said, looking at the rising knot on Keya's left eye.

"That's the fuck right, nigga. Go home and beat your bitch! Get him the fuck out of here, Shame, before I shoot his ass."

Shame cut his eyes at Keya, giving off a cold look.

"I know you're mad, but watch your mouth. You're talking about my sister. And you, nigga, get ya shit and let's go."

"I'm sorry, Shame, but your man just got me hyped. Look at my face, all because he can't control his high. Y'all can roll back through after he handles his business with that nigga who killed his cousin." Keya said with hurting eyes. She didn't mean to disrespect Shame's sister.

Mario wouldn't shut the hell up. Shame had to fight him out the door and into the car. Shame didn't want to knock him the hell out, but he had no other choice.

Mario had started doing coke just to chill after a hard day at work on the block and maybe once in a while to loosen up in the clubs. But it had turned into an everyday thing after his cousin passed. He got hooked pretty fast and out of control with it. He can't hide his addiction that well, and Shame is hiding his secret, not wanting to answer questions at home. That's what best friends are supposed to do for each other, and Shame sold his sister short to protect him.

Shame had thought once he killed the man who killed his cousin, he could get his best friend to clean up his act. That was the only plan he had, so it would have to work. He needed his best friend back clean and sober because the streets were beginning to talk.

Killing another human being never crossed Shame's mind when he got into the dope game until this point. But he knew he had to maintain his focus to do the unspeakable—to take the soul of another human being. Mario slept in the passenger seat as the mellow sounds of Sade poured from the speakers in the truck. Egypt was going to be happy to see her new Range Rover, and Shame thought it was a perfect peace offering for not being home in over a month. Thinking to himself about the argument he was getting ready to face with Egypt, Shame did something for the first time. He fumbled through the ashtray, found a half a blunt Mario had smoked and put fire to it. Pulling on the blunt a little too hard, he coughed up a lung on his first hit. Hitting it again, though, Shame took his time and deep-throated the smoke. *No Ordinary Love* had never sounded so good to his ears as he exhaled the weed, switching lanes on the parkway, doing sixty-five in a forty-five-mile zone.

By the fourth hit, the smoke took over, leaving Shame more relaxed than he had been in months. All he could think about was spending the next couple days with the woman he loved until it was time to do the deal and handle the deed.

"I should have been smoking weed," Shame said to himself, looking over his face in the rearview mirror. He liked how it made his eyes look glassy. He thought it was sexy.

"Come on, nigga, get up. We home," Shame said to Mario, punching him in the arm.

"Come on, man, don't do that shit. You never know, I could wake up swinging. Damn, we got home fast. Now I got to hear your sister's mouth." Mario fumbled around the ashtray as he spoke.

Mario wiped his eyes, checking the ashtray for the blunt he had left. He looked over at Shame crossed-eyed, investigating him as if he stole something.

"Yo, you smoke my weed I had in this ashtray?"

Shame turned to face Mario and his face was self-explanatory. He had a I-don't-give-a-fuck attitude written all over his it.

"Yeah, dawg, there's a first time for everything. I needed something to ease my mind. You was bugging out at Keya's house. I'm sorry for smoking your weed and hitting you, but I\ needed to relax." At ease, Shame spoke, rocking his head to the music.

Mario fished around in his pockets until he found a blunt. He was happy because it was already rolled and ready to smoke.

"You know what, Shame? It's Friday today, and you ain't got no job, so I'm gonna get you higher than a mutherfucka."

Both Mario and Shame laughed as Mario put fire to the blunt.

"You hit me hard, too, bitch. I remember now..." Mario felt his busted lip when the open cut stuck to the blunt.

"I'm all bleeding and shit. You was showing off for that hoe wasn't you?"

Shame began to laugh again, highed up. Mario followed suit,

passing him the blunt. It was the first time in a long time they enjoyed each other's company, and it felt good to the both of them.

"You should have been smoking weed with ya uptight ass."

Standing at the bedroom door, Shame gazed upon his only piece of mind. He wished things could be different between him and me. The man he once was was lost and without direction. The sun crept through the vertical blinds shedding a dim light across the bed as his conscience reflected back on the family values his father installed in him. He wasn't raised to treat women this way, and some days his thoughts made him feel bad.

Shame knew nothing about the depression that overwhelmed me in the past month. He only thought about the reason why I hadn't been on his heels about not coming home. He brushed the hair from my face as he sat down next to me. Maybe the love we once shared was gone. The aromatic scent of lavender caressed Shame's skin as he laid between the sheets. Coming up from behind to hold me, he stroked my skin softly, causing him to rise. Putting the nasty thought out of his mind, he wrapped his loving arms around me, creating a comfort zone for his restless mind. Our heartbeat was one with each other as every breath we took moved in sequence.

Shame didn't know the truth of the situation—I wasn't sure I was happy he was home.

Mary J. Blige's *My Life* played softly through the basement. Mario approached the steps to find a place to hide to do his dirty laundry. Stepping downstairs into the newly remodeled bedroom, dolla signs flashed before his eyes. He wasn't aware of the plans the girls decided to do to the basement, but it had gave them something to do besides christening every room in the house with the essence of sex. Belching out every note with Mary J. Blige in tune, Porsha hadn't realized she had an audience as she escaped through the music. Hidden in the cut, Mario watched as she sang out the words with such empathy. The words might as well have been her own as the song stroked and calmed the fibers in her backbone calm. Sitting at the black marble bar sipping on a cocktail, Porsha scraped a mirror to finish off her last line of coke. In the shadows, Mario took in an eyeful with a devilish grin on his face. The whole time he was trying to conceal his habit from his woman, she did the same thing behind his back. He could have been at home getting his freak on while treating his nose to the candy if only they were being honest with each other.

"Damn, Porsha, I didn't know you could sing like that. You down here drinking and singing early in the morning. You do know the coke clears the throat, don't you?" Mario let it be known right there on the spot that he saw her.

He couldn't keep quiet in the shadows for no longer, and he couldn't take learning another secret from standing in the cut. Evil lurks in the dark and in your most comfortable being, showing its horns in the light and taking on a fleshy form. You can never hear it or taste it as you're blind to the unclad eye, and what your mind seeks as reality are disastrous attempts at grasping the nature of evil. Evoking the spirit, Mario laid his stash on the bar in front of Porsha.

"Why don't you go 'head and bust that down?" Mario raised a brow. Porsha twisted her lips. Looking at the coke, she sucked her teeth. She knew she was busted, but she didn't care. And now that he knew, she could finally stop stealing it from him and fucking Stardust on the side to get by.

"Where you been at, boy?" Porsha spoke nonchalantly, taking a drag off of her squed. "I haven't seen you in weeks, big head-little body. How much money you plan on leaving here for me because since you said I sound so good singing, I just might want a mini studio to chirp in."

"Whatever, I've been around. You know shit has been thick in the streets since my cousin died. Me and Shame are out there all alone and the streets are watching us. Ain't nobody trying to bury no one else, so we trying to stay as far away from the crib as possible until we take care of business. But what you been up to with your sneaky ass?"

Porsha shook her head. The look on her face read "YOU LYING MUTHAFUCKER" clear as day. She busted open the blow and stuck her nose in it.

"Egypt getting high, too?" Mario asked, taking a seat next to Porsha. He sipped her drink, grabbing his chest from how strong it was.

"Nope. I think she knows I get it in, but she leaves me be. We in this fucking house together all the time. If she doesn't know, she'll figure it out sooner or later. I just don't want to hear Shame's mouth about the whole ordeal."

"Yeah, I don't think he could handle any more bad news. Your secret is safe with me. I done put him through enough shit with my dumb ass." Mario made his comment, rubbing the bulge in his pants. He took a hit of the coke in the privacy of his own home and with the woman he grew to love.

"Don't give me that look like you about to come up in here and fuck me. I don't know what rock your poisonous ass done crawled from up under, but your butter is the bomb. Beat your dick." Porsha busted out laughing. Mario turned red in the face.

"Why you got to be like that? You fucking somebody else, woman? Don't make me fuck you up!" Mario gripped Porsha up by the neck.

The blow was starting to take effect on the both of them. The astounded look on Porsha's face made Mario thirsty to touch her on the inside. Porsha tried hard to get the thought of me out of her head and answer "no" to Mario's question. She was scared he could see right through her.

"Don't you know I can easily get the bitch down the street to suck me off!" Mario tried to keep his voice down so Shame wouldn't hear him, but he wanted to get his point across. But why in the hell did he say that?

Porsha's demeanor turned crazy, sexy and cool. Smacking Mario upside the head, he unhanded her quick.

"How dare you come up in my house and disrespect me like that? You could have come home to another nigga up in me since the last time we had sex was back in the day, but I would never. Fuck you, Mario and the boat you floated in on." Porsha produced some fake-ass tears to go along with the bullshit she was spitting. If only he knew, she thought to herself, that his best friend's girl was doing his woman on the regular. There wasn't no need for the risk to bring in an out-sider; she knew I could hold my own.

"I'm sorry, Porsha, please don't cry. I wouldn't never do anything like that. Your mouth is just so damned smart, and I'm so damned horny. I miss you, baby. Don't you miss me?" Mario kissed the back of Porsha's neck. He went in straight for the kill, going after her hot spot.

Porsha began to tingle down below. She hadn't had anything hard up against her in a minute. She wanted to give in, but decided to play. She pushed Mario to the side and pushed her nose in the coke. She got up on the bar and began to strip down to nothing.

"If you want it, come get it," Porsha said seductively.

The house of romance only lasted five minutes. Mario was too high to get it up again. Porsha rolled her eyes to the left in deep thought about what the hell I was doing upstairs if she was downstairs with a wet ass.

"I'm glad the blow brought us back together. I thought I was go-ing to lose you behind this, but we on the same page. I don't want to know any details on how you got started and don't ask me any questions neither." Mario pulled his pants up. He picked up the blow from the other end of the bar and went upstairs. But before he left, he imprisoned Porsha.

"Your habit isn't mine, baby girl. You will trick to get this." Mario laughed the last laugh, leaving Porsha looking stupid as hell.

CHAPTER SIXTEEN

Meanwhile, back at Keya's...

"How much longer do I have to put up with his lame ass? You know he hit me today, highed the fuck up off that shit," Keya yelled into the phone, holding an ice pack to her face.

Keya had a direct order to keep Mario and Shame in eye contact. They were coming up in the drug trade, stepping on the man in charge of running the most major parts of the inner city. The block money was good, but the long money was fading and the man noticed he wasn't making his cut.

"All I need you to do is do what you're told and everything else will fall into place. Don't forget you work for me, bitch. You will put up with them until I decide you don't have to no more." The phone went straight to dial tone. There wasn't an opportunity for Keya to respond for getting banged on.

A month before...

The 412 was crawling with swagger as the top ballers came through the all-white party fresh to death. Even the hoodrats were on their grown and sexy for the event. If you were anybody, you were there representing your bank account in the masquerade setting.

The VIP room was decorated in seduction and every man had lust in his eyes wanting a piece of something sexy. The soldiers held down this room with confidence, looking down on the next man like they weren't shit. Introducing havoc to the room, all eyes fell upon the coldest bitch who hit the VIP section. She knew she was fine, too, by the way she walked. The tall, thick redbone with jet-black radiant hair falling all over her neckline was beautiful. *That bitch is so fine, something has to be wrong with her*, Shame thought as she walked past him slowly. He felt his pants getting bigger when he caught just a faint smell of her perfume. You could feel the heat rise in the room to scorching hot. Her sultry walk had the attention of every man in the room. Nothing but pure beauty poured from her being, and she only has eyes for one man.

Knowing that the women in the club couldn't hold a candle to her flame, she stole the scene once more by ordering a six hundred dollar bottle of champagne. And to top it off, she paid three hundred dollars for her own exclusive booth. With the tip, the bitch dropped a grand in five minutes. She made the VIP room elite and quiet as she peeled off them hundreds. Standing next to Shame, paying the bartender, it was the first time he had the thought to cheat on me. She was everything I wasn't. I was sexy but in a tomboy way, and there wasn't anything boyish about her. Her walk was mean as hell, her scent marvelous and yes, she was sweet on the eye. Trying to speak, the words choked up in Shame's throat as he memorized every feature of her to play back in the company of himself.

His conspicuous characteristics caught the corner of her eye as she walked away giving him a glance-over. As their eyes locked, she gave him a signal to follow her. He tried to play it cool, but tripped up and fell into the barstool next to him. Shame slowed his roll and ordered a bottle of the most expensive champagne. He wiped a tiny bead of sweat that had formed above his eyebrow and took a deep breath.

The ballers flocked to her table, trying to strike up small conversation, but she gave a devilish grin and dismissed her predators with kindness. She turned them down with such style and grace, a nigga couldn't get mad, he could only quote the word "DAMN" and keep it moving.

"Yo, what up, dawg? I see you eyeing my candy over there." Mario came up on the left side of Shame, talking shit. He was grinning from ear to ear.

"Dat's you, dawg? I can't believe it! This must be a joke or something. Where the hidden cameras at?" Shame shot back, grieving with envy.

"Any other time I would get mad at the shit you just said, but shit, I would be hating on you, too, if I had a woman that fine waiting for me in the booth. And guess what else, dawg? She paid for all that shit herself."

Mario walked over to the table after picking up the bottle of champagne Shame bought at the bar. He slid next to the perfect woman in the eyes of Shame and planted a soft wet kiss on her lips. Placing his lips on hers, Mario could feel the hater in every man rise to the occasion.

Mario signaled for Shame to join them. He approached the scene, putting all his jealous thoughts on the back burner, giving his man his just do. Shame sucked his teeth and poked his chest out. He walked to the booth, pulling down his shades that rested on top of his head.

"This here is, my dawg, my right hand man. I don't make no moves without him, baby. Keya, this is Shame." Mario was cool, calm and collected, resting his arm across the booth.

"It's nice to meet you," Keya said, extending her arm.

"It's nice to meet you, too," Shame replied, kissing the back of her hand as their eyes deadlocked.

Shame's stomach was knotted up with butterflies. He wanted to scream out loud from the frustration building up from his pit. He clearly knew he wanted Keya for himself. Shame felt guilty for only a second. He had never cheated on me until the moment he mindfucked her right there on the spot, wanting his face all between her legs as she straddled his tongue. It made him sick to the stomach to watch Mario throw his tongue down her throat repulsively. As he watched Mario touch her skin, he tried to think fast on how he could remove himself from the situation.

Raising up from the table, Mario stopped Shame from leaving. He requested that Shame keep an eye on Keya while he went to the bathroom to handle business. Shame jumped at the demand, wanting to be alone with Keya. He felt there was a connection between the two of them when they met at the bar and wanted to explore the options.

"So why did you buy a bottle of the most expensive champagne in the club if you don't drink?" Keya asked before Mario was two feet from the table.

"I don't know really, but I think it had something to do with you. And who said I didn't drink?" Shame replied, licking his lips in mac mode.

"I haven't seen you drink anything since you've been at the club. Plus, you don't look like you're into the whole drinking to get drunk thing."

Shame thought for a minute. His heart started to race from her comment. *Was she checking me out?* He thought to himself...

"Are you fucking my boy?" Shame couldn't hold his tongue. He couldn't believe it when the words came out of his mouth so bluntly.

"Stupid..." he whispered under his breath, wishing he could turn back the hands of time.

Keya cooed over the question. "Yes I did, and I want to fuck you also. That is where you were going with this, right? Do you mind if I do? That's fuck you I mean, the two of you."

The devilish grin appeared again as Keya moved closer to Shame. She rubbed up his thigh and stopped at the bulge. Placing her hand inside of his pants and on his muscle, she could feel a heartbeat in it as it stood hard at attention.

"I tend to have that effect on men," Keya whispered in his ear, stroking him up and down, faster and harder.

Shame grabbed the table as he pumped for dear life, and Keya picked up a napkin knowing his look way too well. Ten seconds later Shame's head fell back against the booth out of breath. Keya saw Mario heading back to the booth, and she broke out in laughter, wiping the beads of sweat from Shame's forehead.

"Damn, dawg, you look like you just seen a ghost. Did Egypt and Porsha just walk up in here?" Mario clowned, taking his seat.

"I hope not. This event been played on every radio station and been spoke on by all the lips in the hair salon, so it could be bound to happen. On that note, let me go check it out and give you and your girl some time alone." Shame excused himself from the booth. Shame and Keya's eyes told a story as he walked away.

"Oh, yeah, don't disappear tonight. I got a surprise for you, my nigga. We came together and we're leaving together. So check back in at a quarter to two." Mario leaned back in the booth all smiles, waving off Shame.

The deed was done.

The early morning dew drops fell from the sky on the top of the freshly cut grass. A thick fog covered the street as the sun peeked over the horizon. There were so many nights Shame had spent having a threesome love affair with Keya, it put a bigger gap between him and me. Mario was so busy being a coke star he never realized his boy, his brother, his dawg, had fallen in love with a trick. His trick.

Shame and Keya both played their positions right always. And Keya always made sure she kept it sexual without being jaded by emotions. *Don't go looking for love; go out looking for respect because love can't pay the bills*, her mother taught.

Truth be told, Keya did love Shame, but she loved money a lot more. Her loyalty to the game would never be slowed down by an emotion that didn't have any loyalty. Love was unkind, and even though she was as beautiful as they came, her heart had got broken too many times before.

The second part of the plan was in motion and was already playing out perfectly. To destroy the allegiance Shame and Mario had would be easy since Keya had known for a fact Shame was in love. The friction was soon to come between them both.

What's the best way of doing that? Keya's boss thought to himself when he set out on this journey. And the answer he came up with when he paid Keya ten thousand dollars plus expenses was cool. Her direct order was to use sex as a weapon.

Playing her part, it wasn't hard with loose-lip Mario to find out all the information she needed to report. Within three weeks, she had learned most of the stash spots, the pick-up crew, and the out-of-town connection to the dope. Weak-minded to the pussy, whatever Mario didn't brag about high, Shame told between the sheets.

The call back...

"Why you keep hanging up on me, nigga?! I know I got enough info for you to end this shit. I do believe that they're going to kill somebody, and that somebody is you. I didn't hear your name for sure, and Mario ain't giving it up. I tried, I swear I did, and what Mario won't say, neither will Shame. They're keeping a tight lid on it. I want you to be careful because it supposed to go down in three days."

"Good work, baby. I'll see you in the morning."

CHAPTER SEVENTEEN

"**Y**ou don't have the right to be in my bed, mutherfucker. Get up and get out!!" I exploded, finding Shame in the same bed as me.

Yeah yup, I wanted it to be his sister. And I pushed his dirty dick ass to the floor.

"Where you been at this time? Come on and hit me with the lies now. You out there fucking some other hood bitch while I'm carrying your seed." I pause, letting the cat out the bag.

"What did you say, E? Did you say you're pregnant by me?" Shame raised up off the floor. He had a crooked smile with tears in his eyes.

"Whatever, man! Don't act like you care about me. If you did, you would be here more with your selfish ass. I ain't carrying shit, nigga. I just wanted to see your face if I was." I tried to lie, but I knew Shame wasn't going for it. My eyes never left the floor.

Shame knew there was some truth behind the lie. He sat back on the bed and pulled me to him.

"Please don't start crying now, Shame! I'm not for your shit!" I pulled away from him and smacked his face. "Oh, you feel bad? Well, guess what, nigga? I'm carrying your seed, that's the truth. I'm two-and-a-half months, and I've been trying to tell you, but you're never here. I haven't seen you in days. I don't see how this happened. We have to fuck to get pregnant and the only action I get is from a Play-mate toy." I got up from the bed and tried to walk away.

That's what I tried to do. Shame grabbed me up by the neck from behind. "You belong to me!" He roared as he threw my tiny frame back onto the bed.

"Oh, you jealous, nigga, of my vibrator? Well, you should have been here last night. I do things to these plastic dildos I should be ashamed of. I hope I'm not carrying a Cabbage Patch doll inside of me." I smile on the inside, thinking of my ex for just a moment.

"So it's true... you're carrying my baby. You got my child in there." I saw his eyes soften by the news. He touched my stomach self-satisfied. "I always wanted to have a child..."

"I don't think it's a good idea for us to have a baby." I just put the shit out there. There wasn't no reason to beat around the bush. "I don't think we're going to be together that much longer anyway, Shame. I don't want no kids, neither. I don't know what to do with one."

The excitement written all over Shame's face came to a screeching halt. His eyes turned angry as his eyebrows came together by the wrinkles on his forehead.

"Do you think you're going to kill my child, Egypt?" Shame asked calmly.

"Shame, real shit, just give me the money to handle this so I can go on with my daily activities!" I spat.

"For what?" Shame said indignantly. "Your day-to-day is spending my money and drinking yourself under the fucking table. We need to talk about this before you do something stupid and really piss me off."

"Shame, there's nothing to talk about. It's my body, and I do what I want to with it, and I'm not ready to have a baby with you."

I seen horns grow from the top of Shame's head right before my eyes. Digging down in his pockets of his pants he pulled out a rubber band full of money.

"You right, drunk ass! You're not worthy to carry my child. Go ahead and get rid of it!"

Shame threw the money at my face and walked out of our bedroom in a fit of a rage.

"That's what you do, Shame? You think you're going to walk out on me and leave this house. I swear I'll pull a *Waiting to Exhale* in here." I ran behind him heartless.

Shame continued to walk and picked up a slow jog when he heard my voice following behind him. Damned near knocking over Porsha in the scheme of things, he didn't even stop.

"Shame, you can't speak to your sister?" Porsha yelled after him.

"I don't got nothing to say! But you better get that bitch before I kill her!" Shame yelled back, slamming the door so hard it made the whole house shake.

"I see you telling my brother you wasn't keeping the baby didn't go over so well," Porsha said, walking into my bedroom, shaking her head. "Are you okay, Egypt?"

I couldn't even think about Shame; my heart was somewhere else. I didn't care about how he felt. He didn't care about me, so we were even. I only had one thing on my mind and one thing only: "Did you fuck Mario, Porsha?"

"What?" she asked, as if she didn't understand my question.

"I said did you fuck Mario? You heard me the first time!" I walked over to my bedroom door and shut it. I put the lock on to let her know she wasn't walking out on me, too. Porsha bit her bottom lip nervously and then shrugged her shoulders. She pushed me to the bed, speaking volumes with her actions. Climbing on top of me, she placed sweet and soft kisses on the dried-up tear stains. Grinding on me slow, Porsha took away every thought I had about her and Mario.

As quick as we started, the heat ended in rapid breathing, but the question remained in the air.

"Did you think just because you made me cum with Shame and Mario in the house that I still wouldn't want to know what happened between the two of you?"

Lying next to me, I saw Porsha roll her eyes in the back of her head.

"Didn't anybody ever teach you to never ask questions you really didn't want to know the answers to?"

"Nope! Now answer me, dammit."

"He's my man, Egypt, and I do love him. And I'm not going to apologize for wanting to be touched by my man."

"Do you love me, Porsha?"

"Please, Egypt, don't start with me. I love you both, and I can't just up and leave him. What about my brother, girl? He'll kill us. And before you ask, I can't leave you alone neither."

"So you fucked him!" I shot back with my one-track mind.

"Don't worry about me fucking Mario. You better worry about fixing shit with my brother a.s.a.p."

"I got that nigga. He gonna hate me 'cause I'm taking my drunk ass to the clinic."

"What the fuck is wrong with you? Why would you want to do that? It's not because of the money. I know for a fact we got plenty stashed away."

The unexpected banging on the door caught the both of us by surprise. Startled, we both jumped to our feet, forgetting we had house guests. We pulled ourselves together quickly, kissing each for good luck—and I needed it. Porsha opened up the door and breezed past Shame. She didn't have the heart to look him in the eye. And Shame slammed the door behind her when she left.

Remembering what Porsha said, I knew I had to fix things between me and Shame quickly because I didn't have nowhere to go. And I couldn't risk being kicked out the house 'cause I had to be close to Porsha. I throw myself into Shame's arms.

"Make love to me baby, please. Take all this hurt away I feel from you not being here." I wrapped my arms around my man, begging for sympathy.

I was jealous for real that Porsha fucked Mario, and I thought if I did the same, it would take the sting out of my heart. What I thought I had with Shame was no more; I was in love with his sister.

So what do you do in a situation like this? I put on an Oscar-winning performance for Shame and his back-stabbing-ass sister. From start to finish, there was non-stop moaning for forty-five minutes straight. Shame could feel that I was putting on a show for him, but he never figured out for what or for who.

Maybe it wasn't my touch he was used to anymore. Maybe it wasn't my moan he was used to neither. I don't know...

Shame was a million miles away. It could have been from the fact I just threatened to kill his child. It was the first time he ever faked having an orgasm with me. Maybe it was the touch he wasn't used to. The way I moaned his name had no finesse or feeling. Maybe, just maybe, it was himself putting on the front. But why, and for who?

CHAPTER EIGHTEEN

"Come open up the door, baby. I need to holla at you for a minute." Shame sat outside in front of Keya's house for over an hour waiting to get through on the line.

"I'm guessing you're by yourself, sexy. You sound very intense over the phone. Give me five minutes to freshen up and come through the back."

"You got it, babe. I'll come around the back in about ten minutes when I'm done smoking this blunt."

"You smoke weed, now?" Keya asked, shocked.

"You ain't never too old to learn a new trick." Shame hung up the phone. He smoked his weed and jerked off in the front seat so he would last a little bit longer when he got in the house.

He learned early in the game to never walk in on some good pussy fully loaded. The sexy tone in her voice set Shame off every time, sending him into a frenzy that he couldn't control. The things she did made him feel as if he were a king and untouchable.

"What are you going to do with him?"

"You don't have to worry your pretty little head about that. You just make sure Mario's lame ass ends up over here also."

"Please don't hurt Shame. It's Mario that wants you dead."

"Don't get soft on me now, Keya! You knew what the deal was from the door. I can't just let the nigga run loose after I kill his best friend. That's why I'm getting hunted now, right? I let him live, and it will come back to haunt me. I don't care how much you say he ain't no killer, he ain't going to live so I can find out. You know what happens when you don't catch the cancer in time?"

"No I don't, but I'm sure you'll tell me."

"It spreads, baby girl, then eventually it kills you."

Lighting fresh candles around the room for Shame, Keya could smell the stench of death in the air. There was no way she could stop it. The aroma from the candles should erase any trace of the man who just left as Keya hopped in the tub to wash her ass. Shame should be walking in the door any minute. As Shame entered the back, another man walked out the front door.

"Baby, is that you?" Keya cried out from the tub filled with hot water.

"Yeah, it's me. Where you at girl?"

"I'm in the tub. I'll be out in a minute. Take your clothes off and relax. I'll be in there to tame that ass in a second."

"My woman is at home carrying my baby, and I'm at my best friend's hoe-house getting ready to fuck his girl. How could I let a man treat my sister like this? This bitch is fucking up my head." Shame sat on the edge of Keya's bed, talking shit to himself.

"Lawd, save me from myself." Looking over the room, sadness overwhelmed Shame, but he couldn't will himself to leave. Kicking off his shoes, he sparked the bullseye of the blunt. Lying back on the sheets, something just didn't feel right to him. *My cheating ways are catching up to me,* he thought to himself, hitting the blunt for the fourth time. Keya came into the room shortly after.

"First off, when you start smoking weed, baby?" she asked, rubbing lotion on her legs.

"Stress made me do it. I was so mad Mario hit you, I wanted to rip his neck off and shit down his throat. I needed something to calm my nerves. I like it, too. I should have been smoking weed. Everything is about to change in my life, Keya. Egypt is pregnant with my baby, and she wants to kill it. I'm never home, chasing after money and lusting after you. Look at me, Keya. I'm laid up in your bed that smells like another man, and I don't even care, I'm so gone off of you. Mario wants to kill some nigga about his cousin tomorrow, and I'm not even built like that, for real. I never want to go home, but I still got love for Egypt. So why not get high, ya dig?"

Keya laid her head on Shame's chest to listen to his heartbeat for the last time. Right then and there Keya knew Shame was going to die.

"I hear you, baby, but I'm not equipped to handle emotions. I can't do anything but give you a good fuck. I aim to please, but I don't handle problems. So what do you want me to do?"

"That's cold as hell. That's how you see yourself?"

"Look, Shame, money can't ever disappoint you, only people do. You're nothing more or nothing less to me than a fuck."

Shame pushed Keya off of him. He climbed on top of her, forcing himself inside of her. There wasn't anything pleasant about their lovemaking. Every thrust was out of anger and frustration as Shame choked the life out of Keya. He made a vow to himself that he wouldn't touch the succubus ever again. Nothing good would ever come out of the love affair, and it had to stop, but only he could end it.

The water ran down Shame's broad shoulders as he stood in the shower praying for strength. He felt Keya had some sort of voodoo shit on him, and the only way he could escape it was to kill her. Wiping the thought out of his mind, he towel dried slowly, thinking about what he would say to Keya.

"Why you getting dressed? You going to leave me since I told you the truth about me?" Keya asked, walking into the bathroom.

Shame didn't say a word. He continued to get dressed all the way down to his shoelaces.

"Why are you leaving, Shame?"

"I can't fuck wit you no more, Keya. We done. I don't care what you and Mario do from now on. As a matter of fact, my nigga ain't coming through here no more neither. This shit here is dead."

Panic started to set in. Keya didn't know what to do, but she knew she couldn't let Shame leave. She had to find a way to get Mario over to her house.

"Wait a minute, Shame. At least let me see Mario again before you break us up. Please, I need to feel you and him inside of me one more time. Please call him. Give me one more night."

"I never heard please come out of your mouth before, woman! It's beneath you. Don't beg. You don't have any emotions, right? So you don't care about my dick or his, and that's why I'm the fuck out, Keya. Something ain't right with this picture."

Shame walked down the steps and Keya descended behind him. She was tripping, trying to find a way to get Shame to stay and call Mario.

"So you think you can stay away from me?" Keya asked methodically. She grabbed Shame by the crotch from behind.

"I'm done with you, Keya, and I won't say it again. You're right, baby, you're not equipped to handle a man like me, and the only one who is sits at home waiting for me alone. But she don't have to be alone no more. Tonight, I'm getting my life back, and I'm changing all the wrongs to right. I got to start somewhere, baby, and it's you. I'm DONE!"

Throwing a stack of twenties on the floor, Shame thanked Keya for a wonderful many evenings and walked out her front door. Keya was at a loss for words as she dead bolted her door. Diving straight for the floor, she kept her fingers crossed so her scandalous ass didn't get hit by a stray bullet.

A few moments later, Keya heard a loud voice coming from outside. She got up from the floor and peeked out the window to see Shame on his cell phone. From the window it looked like both of his front tires were slashed. The streetlights flickered on and off, creating shadows of the cars on the ground as Shame blew a fuse into the phone. A sly smirk played on Keya's lips as she figured out who slashed his tires. She ran to the door and unlocked it.

"Shame, what's the matter with you? I do have neighbors, boy, and they will call the cops if you keep standing out there yelling like a mad man." Keya spat from the cracked door.

"Listen to yourself. You're out here screaming, too, bitch! And why do I feel you have something to do with my tires getting slashed?" Shame shouted as he walked back towards Keya's front door.

"That sounds like a job for a baby momma, nigga. I don't get down like that! You better call, Egypt," Keya hissed.

Shame ran up on Keya and dotted her eye. Next his hands went around her throat as he pushed her back in the house.

"Keep your mouth shut!" he instructed, oblivious to the facts. "I'm just staying here until Mario comes and get me. I told him I came over to stash some blow because the stash house was hot. And you better not open your mouth about anything because if you do, I swear I'll come back to haunt you."

The look in Shame's eyes made Keya frightened by his touch. She was ready for whatever, but at that moment she feared for her life. She no longer smelled the stench of death in the air—she felt it creeping from around the corner.

BANG!! BANG!! BANG!!

The door shook from the powerful fist that hit it hard. Shame pulled his piece, the uncertainty of who was at the door set in.

"Damn, Mario got here too fast for me. Are you expecting somebody?" Shame asked, feeling suspect.

"You need to check that shit out, homegirl, right now."

Keya raised up from the couch. She didn't want to answer the door, but she didn't want to fight Shame neither. She put her eye to the peephole and from the outside it was covered. Keya's heartbeat picked up by fear.

"What's wrong with you? Who is it, bitch?" Shame asked, gripping his piece.

Keya looked in the peephole once more to see a flash of lighting. Shame watched her lifeless body hit the ground. She never had a chance. The next thirty seconds hit Shame in slow motion. The door got kicked in and his piece was on safety when he tried to fire. A blow to the face with the butt of a shotgun made him realize early in the game he was going to die. Shame only got to blink once before he died execution style. As quick as they came, the intruders disappeared into the still of the night, leaving their work as an unspoken warning.

CHAPTER NINETEEN

eanwhile, back at the crib...

"Egypt, turn that shit down. As a matter of fact, turn Mary J. Blige off period, point blank. You or Porsha don't let the girl's CD breathe. I don't know why ya'll always listening to her ass. She ain't happy," Mario bitched, turning off the stereo.

"Stop playing around, Mario..." Porsha and I yelled in unison. We rushed over from the kitchen to the living room to see why he would touch our Mary J.

"You want to know why we listen to Mary J. heavy like that, for real?" Porsha asked, pointing her fingers in Mario's face.

"You take this question, Egypt. You know Mary better than anybody." Porsha flopped down on the couch to watch her girl in action.

Egypt walked over to the stereo and started the track *I'm Not Going to Cry.* Mario rolled his eyes in the back of his head, flopping down on the couch next to Porsha, awaiting an answer.

All the time that I was loving you, you were busy loving yourself, I would have stopped breathing if you told me to, now you're busy loving someone else.

Drink in hand, I kicked off the perfect song to explain to Mario what exactly Mary J. does for the hurting soul. I didn't miss a beat with tears in my eyes.

Eleven years, out of my life, besides the kids I have nothing to show, wasted my years, a fool of a wife, I should've left your ass a long time ago. By the time I got to the chorus, Porsha had joined in. And we sounded damned good singing with Mary.

And I'm not going to cry, I'm not going to cry, I'm not going to shed no tears...

"Do ya'll see this shit! Ya'll crying and shit, fucking up all ya'll pretty little makeup and for what? Ya'll ain't going through this shit!" Mario jumped up from the couch, fed up with the answer he didn't get and the antics I used to call him and his boy cheaters.

"You just don't get it, Mario. We sing this shit word for word for one because Mary is the shit, and for two, because we feel this way every day. But you know why you don't see it, Mario? It's because you and your brother are selfish. Ya'll muthafuckers run the streets, sucking and fucking, making her truth our reality. Then ya'll come home and throw some cash around, thinking that's going to mend a broken heart."

Mario stood on the sidelines, looking down at his watch, feeling it was better to give no eye contact. Speechless, he cleared his throat.

"You see this nigga, Porsha? I see you checking your watch. You gotta go, right, Mario? Who's pussy you about to go run up in?" I stood firmly in Mario's face as he stared beyond my thighs. It looked like he was in deep search for a lie.

"Egypt, you need to chill out with that shit. Ain't nobody doing shit. We just getting money. I'll call him right now and put it on speaker phone. He got a flat somewhere, and he needs me to come pick him up. We coming straight back home after we get the truck towed."

"Thanks, but no thanks, Mario. You don't have to do me any favors. I know Shame ain't shit. He can do him 'cause I'm doing me from now on."

"You got a real smartass mouth, Egypt! Porsha, get your girl before I smack her face! She's a real disrespectful cunt!"

As soon as the words left Mario's mouth, Porsha jumped up and put up a gag order over my mouth. From behind, she whispered in my ear, "You better not say I'm your woman, Egypt. Don't blow up the spot. We don't have nowhere to go, girl."

"What the fuck is that, Porsha? Why it look like you just licked that bitch's ear."

"Mario!" Porsha yelled "Boy, go and get Shame and stop this bullshit right now. I'm not a dike. You better go somewhere and get that shit out of your head now! You out of pocket!"

"What the fuck ever!" Mario shouted, leaving out the door. He didn't look back as Porsha yelled out to him.

"Is it done?"

"We only got one of them, boss. The girl is dead too."

"God dammit. I flatten the tires myself knowing that my plan would work. Ya'll stupid asses jumped the gun. I told both of you dummies if you messed this up you would get fucked, didn't I?"

"But boss, it's not our fault. Well, it's not mine. I told Killer to wait, but he made me go to the house with him anyway."

"That's such a sad fucking story. Where the hell are your violins at? Better yet, you need some theme music for the dramatic effect. It's not your fault, little nigga, but it's mines for sending a boy to do a soldier's job. Dump your phones, clean ya self up and report a.s.a.p."

The young boys sped off into the night, hearing the police sirens following behind. They didn't have the option to fight for their lives. They were already dead as they opted to skip town.

"Why in the hell this nigga ain't answering his phone?" Mario uttered his words, afraid for his boy's life. Thoughts ran back and forth over his brain about Shame fucking Keya on the low. He had a funny feeling the shit was about to come out. Why in the hell else the both of them aren't answering their phones. *Maybe they're both waiting on me for a threesome*, Mario thought, slapping the steering wheel with a smirk.

Two blocks away from Keya's house, Mario could see the flashing light activities. As he got closer, the action became clearer.

"What the hell done happened around here?" Mario said jumping out his stalled car in the middle of the street.

Taking no chances, Mario hopped back in his car and made a U-turn in case this was a set-up. Heart in his throat, he regretted wasting time fighting with stupid Egypt. Parking his car around the corner, Mario made sure he wasn't dirty. He began to walk on foot back to Keya's house. By this time, the townspeople were already making their assumptions as he passed by, and none of them sounded nice.

The yellow tape surrounding Keya's house read crime scene. As Mario approached her house, words couldn't express the hurt he felt. He knew his best friend was dead. The tears stung his eyes, and his heart weighed heavy. He looked to the east, and there wasn't a cop; he looked to the west and again no cop. Mario broke through the tape and made a run for Keya's front door.

Running up to the front door, he slipped and fell, catching a glimpse of the blood and bone fragments right there on the walls as he entered her house. Quickly he remembered the last time he hugged his brother. Crawling back to the sight, Mario drank in every detail of the room.

"Somebody do their damned job and get that thug away from my crime scene before contamination sets in," a detective screamed from afar.

"This is my girl's house. What mutherfucker did this shit? If you out there in the crowd, mutherfucker, you dead. I put it on my life, YOU DEAD!!" Mario screamed at the top of his lungs as a policeman picked him up from the ground.

"Take the young thug to the station so I can question him when I'm through here. These young thugs got my city in ruin, and I'm going to get to the bottom of this." The detective nodded his head, indicating he was through. The policeman put Mario in back of the squad car, where he sat enraged.

Sitting in the police station under the hot lights, beads of sweat ran down Mario's forehead and the tears fell from his eyes. He didn't hear anything the detectives had to say; he didn't answer one single question in the moment of disorder. Leaving out the police station hours later, the sun was bright, but not bright enough to bring back Shame. Mario pinched his hand to see if it was all a dream. In a blank state of mind, Mario walked back to his car. He was all cried out, ready to be strong to drop the bombshell on the girls.

He knew the bullet that Shame took was meant for him, and he knew the person that pulled the trigger was the same person that killed his cousin. Mario made a promise right then and there to take care of Egypt and her baby, along with his sister, forever and a day.

Pulling up to the crib, Mario got real nervous. He didn't give a fuck about who knew he sniffed; it was time to get high. Walking through the door, he tip-toed slow to the basement.

"Did you hear someone come in the house?" Porsha asked half sleep.

"Them niggas ain't coming home no time soon, baby. They were in the house for two days. That's a world record for them, and now we won't see them for another month."

"You're right, but I swore I heard something." Porsha yawned and stretched her arms out around Egypt. Putting no more thought into it, she fell back to sleep with no worries, comfortable in her surroundings.

Snorting a quarter ounce up his nose in less than an hour, Mario numbed the pain. He poured himself a drink and felt the need to go to Shame's room and talk to Egypt. And then he changed his mind, giving it a second thought. He could tell Porsha first, and she could help him unload the bad news. Staggering up the steps, Mario began to cry again. He stood in front of Shame's door wired off the coke. Vision hazy, he opened the door and the delivery on sight was just as he thought. A perfect ending to a fucked-up day. Not disturbing the peace, Mario sat on the edge of the king-sized bed and watched the woman that he loved stark naked in the arms of his best friend's baby momma. She laid in the arms of her lover... the last kiss...

CHAPTER TWENTY

"*Another woman has been found dead in the Northview Housing Project over the weekend. There were no witnesses to the crime that took place in the woods behind these residents' backyards. Two children from the housing project community found her body just thirty feet from their backyard, on the edge the woods. Residents have been complaining about the woods beings dangerous to city officials and demanding that they do something about the area since this is the fourth body that's been found in recent days. Residents who live here say they are afraid for their lives and the lives of their children. Stay tuned to Channel 11 News for more updates on this story.*"

Changing the channel, Boo looks at General sleeping in the chair on the far side of the room. He know General had a hand in anything that went down in the Northview project. Boo glares at a gun sitting on the floor next to General. If only he had the courage to end the mayhem.

Today could be the day I man the fuck up and get payback for everybody my brother did dirty. Pondering on the thought a little too long, General awakens, gripping up the pistol that rests next to his chair. Wiping the thought clear from Boo's mind, General jockeys him, waving his pistol back and forth.

"One, two, General comes for you; three, four, you better lock your doors; five, six, you better do as I say; seven, eight, you can't escape; nine, ten, my ultimate wrath that oversees all." A sinister laugh erupts from the beast.

Boo just looks at his brother like he lost his motherfucking mind. General appeases him, looking back, squinting his eye, trying to read Boo's mind.

"What the hell was that you were singing? And by the way, nigga, you can't sing. I think somebody has been watching too much TV."

"You like that shit? Don't front," General says, chuckling. "I thought I would take Freddy's lullaby and put some stank on it. I love the way he kills niggas in their sleep. When I die, that's how I'm coming back. I'm coming back in niggas dreams to get them."

"Whatever the hell you were smoking before you fell asleep, I want some. You're on something crazy as hell, for real. It would be nice to be reincarnated into a man who can control people's fate throughout dreamland, but it just ain't real, man. You know that, right?" As soon as Boo finishes speaking, he finds out he should have just kept his mouth shut. A quick elbow to the face lays Boo out on the dirty carpet. General towers over his body, pointing his gun to Boo's head.

"So you trying to tell me niggas don't run from me in their sleep? You do all the time, baby bro. I watch you while you sleep. You cry out loud for me to stop, for me to get away from you. I think you try to kill me, but I always get you first. Don't get mad, baby bro, that's what I do—install fear." General bent down and got closer to Boo's ear in a whisper. "You're not the only one, nigga. These so-called gangsters whose manhood I've taken dream of me every night, waking up in cold sweats. Remember little Jimmy from around the way?" Boo shook his head yes and gasped for air, scared for his life. "I'm the one who made him kill himself. He hung himself 'cause he couldn't escape the dreams of me stealing his manhood. I raped him whenever I damned well pleased. Let me tell you another little secret, Boo… I don't think I'm human, nigga. I'm too evil to be a human being. I will always wreak havoc on this here earth and in spirit. This is my realm, my reality, and I will seek revenge in niggas hearts and thoughts long after I'm gone."

General never breaks eye contact with Boo. As he reaches out his hand to help Boo get up off the floor, he flinches with fear.

"That's just the way I like it, baby bro. I can smell the fear coming off your body."

RING! RING! RING!

"Now excuse me, Boo, I have to take this call." General pulls his cell phone from the clip, reading the number back to himself. "Oh shit!! He must have that info I need."

"You need me for anything?" Boo asks, helpless.

"I just told you to raise the fuck up nigga! That's it and that's all! Go check on the bitch or something!" General shoos Boo away with his hand.

"Holla at cha boy!" General yells into his cell phone, sliding back down into his comfortable chair.

"I love you, Porsha… I love you…" I toss and turn, stuck in my own bad dreams. I can't even remember the last time I thought about the death of my son's father. Could it be because I wifed his lil' sister or because I don't give a damn about nobody but myself? I deserve to be right where I'm at. This here is my death sentence for all the wrong choices I've made in my life.

"Wake the hell up, girl!" Boo smacks me upside the head, bringing me back to reality. "You dreaming because ain't no Porsha here."

I lay there, limp to this touch. Stained from the inside out, completely drained of strength, I open my eyes as they flutter to adjust to the light.

"I'm sick as hell, Boo." I speak in syllables reborn into the addiction of heroin. I scratch at my veins in pain.

"I'm going to give you this because I need you to hear me." Boo ties up my arm, slaps my vein and injects the deadly fluid that made my body come alive. I exhale into a deep dope-fiend nod.

Boo leaves out the room. He creeps down the hallway, trying to make it to the small kitchen unseen. Coming up on the living room, Boo hears General's conversation.

"Yeah, I know they call her dike-ass Nikko, but what I didn't know was that she was making power moves right under my nose in my own spot. I didn't have a clue about the bitch being my ex until she told me her name. She didn't look shit like no boy back in the day, I can tell you that." There was a moment of silence.

"And about the kid? I want you to find him a.s.a.p. I want to see him for myself. Who the fuck would knock her up, looking like a dude? She had to get knocked up by me. I bet you little man is my creation. Handle business as usual and get at me when you hear something."

General hangs up his cell phone as Boo tries to make the sharp left into the kitchen.

"Why you creeping, nigga? What you up to with your sneaky ass?"

"I'm just getting the girl something to eat, General. Can I do that, man?"

"I don't give a fuck what you do when it comes to her! You need to starve her ass to death 'cause you don't have the heart to kill her, and we're not letting her go! So what you gonna do?"

"Don't worry about it, nigga, I'm gonna handle it."

"Well handle it then, muthafucker! Better yet, why don't you wife the bitch? She should be like a born-again virgin; you just might make her straight again. You like hoe's and tricks so much you kidnap them. You better finish what you've started, nigga. And if you don't, she will die a horrible death messing around with a nigga like me."

"*We interrupt your daytime viewing to give you an update on the body found in the Northview Housing Projects.*"

General and Boo both look at each other, taking a pause. Taking a seat, they both watch the television, turning up the volume.

"*The woman found this morning has been identified as Diane James. Police believe she wasn't murdered at the scene of the crime, but was placed there some time later. Residents of the housing project are demanding answers from the police. We here at Channel 11 News will keep you posted on any new information as soon as we get it. Please stay tuned for details as they unfold.*"

General's face is sculptured in fury. Ill-tempered, he stands up and knocks his chair to the floor. Removing his cell phone from his clip, he heads toward the bathroom. Kicking the bathroom door straight off the hinges, he curses at the top of his lungs.

Boo takes it as a sign that somebody fucked up bad. By the look of things, General isn't happy about that body being found. Picking up a box of takeout chicken from off top of the stove, Boo doesn't ask any questions. He heads back to the room to remove himself from the hot-ass flame.

"Tell Craze I want to see him now! He better make it his business to get at me!" General slams his flip phone so hard it cracked the screen. "DAMMIT!" yells out, kicking another hole in the wall. "The main objective was to burn the bitch up. Craze trying to set me up for real. That's why that nigga been back on my dick rock hard. SON OF A BITCH!! I'm going to kill him." General paces back and forth, ranting and raving about the mistakes made. And he has to do something fast because his prints are all over Diane's body.

Placing a call to an old cop buddy who's been on his payroll for a while, General puts the word out to get the autopsy on Diane destroyed. Putting up a twenty thousand dollar reward for the person that can make it disappear, General knows it will vanish into thin air. *Money talks and bullshit runs the marathon* General thinks with a devilish grin, closing his cell phone a little softer this time around.

Still worried, General sits on the toilet and fires up a blunt. He feels he was slipping with this whole ordeal. He is making a past vendetta personal to the present, trying to settle a score long overdue.

Opportunity knocked when Egypt fell into his possession and her aunt was only a prize mercenary, a slave to the rhythm and a pawn in General's own sick dominion. The skies turned from blue to gray, as no one could find the quiet in the midst of the thunderstorm.

"Come on, girl, and eat this food. I need to talk to you." Boo breaks the beautiful silence surrounding the room, whispering in my ear.

"What kind of food do you have for me? I'm hungry as hell." As I speak in a slur, slobber falls from the corners of my mouth. The dope is greeeeeeeat. It takes everything in me to focus on the chicken Boo sets in front of me.

"You're going to eat that shit if I have to push it down your throat. You're going to need it for strength. Just please eat it."

I push a piece of chicken in my mouth so I won't get assaulted by it. I focus enough to see ugly-ass Boo in a cold sweat, staring at me.

"How do you know my brother?" Boo asks brazenly.

"What are you talking about, Boo? I didn't even know you had a brother, and I've known you for a minute. I thought I knew you well, but I don't know shit. I still can't believe you done this to me. I never thought in a million years you would play me like this."

"I know, I know, and I would have been let you go, but my so-called brother won't allow it. He's going to kill you if I don't find a way to get you out of here."

"Who in the hell is your brother, and why does he want to kill me?" The dope no longer has me subdued. I'm wide awake and alert.

"He's the fucking boss, girl. He's the General."

"Who... and he's the what?"

"His name is General, and he claims to be your ex. I just over-heard him talking about you."

"You're lying, Boo. I don't know General, but I've heard stories about the dude and he's off the hook. You know what, I'm not wor-ried about it, Boo. If it's my time to go, it's my time. Now spark some get-high in this mutha."

"I'm sitting here telling you a nigga wants to take your life and all you can think about is getting high." Boo shakes his head in disbelief. He threw a spliff at me, and I sparked it up.

"What am I supposed to do?" I really don't believe a word Boo is saying. He is too much of a bitch to have a brother who is top dawg in the street.

"You think this is a fucking game? I'm for real about General, and you fucked him. Ya'll had something together back in the day, and now he's looking for your son."

My throat instantly chokes up. I drop the spliff to the floor. "My son! What does my son have to do with this?"

Boo takes a deep breath, letting out a long sigh ending in his brother's name. "Trap Burrow is his name, and mine is Trace Burrow."

I can't believe what I'm hearing. It's unbelievable. I can't believe Trap wants to kill me.

"I want you to stop playing with me. Trap is not running 'burgh, he's not your brother and he wouldn't do this to me. I fucked with Trap for over a year. I never once seen you with him, in his crib, in a picture or nothing. He don't got no family. It's only him, and I haven't seen him for years. I was a teenager when we met. I still don't understand why he wants to kill me. I don't understand what the hell I did to piss him off. If he's the one holding me hostage, I should want to kill him. Hold up, hold up..." I recount my last moment with Trap. "Could it be because I seen him shoot up a porch full of niggas back in the day. What? Do he think I told on him about something? That shit turned me on to the point I gave him a show. I fucked my best friend in front of him that night. That night was crazy but fun, and after, that I don't think I seen Trap again."

"Oh, my, God... it's you!" Boo whispers aloud.

"What are you talking about, nigga?" This nigga, Boo, is spinning me for another loop. I pick the spliff from up off the floor and put some flame to it. Boo looks at me with death written all over his face.

"He hated you for embarrassing him. He hated you for being you and not being afraid of walking your own path. He couldn't figure out why you didn't want him. Shit wasn't the same with him and women after you. Now I know why he's been acting so different when it comes to you. He hates you for leaving him for a woman."

"Boo, hold up. Trap knew I couldn't be with him. He slept with my aunt on more than one occasion." I put the spliff out, blowing a cloud of smoke. I shake my head, having sympathy for one's self. "So he's going to decide my fate with life or death because I couldn't love him after he cheated on me with my aunt?"

Boo sits quietly, knowing the door he just opened is going to send him to an early grave if General ever finds out what he told. Shaking in his boots, Boo rubs the beads of sweat from his forehead.

"He's never going to let you go, girl. I'm sorry, and there's nothing I can do about it. If I try to interfere with his plans, he'll kill me, too. I don't want to know, and I can't even imagine, what he has in store for you. He's been playing me the whole time about killing you. He was going to do it himself all along." Boo begins to pace the floor once again.

Too many unspoken words come into play in one scenario by the making of so many bad choices. My life itself is nothing but a twist of fate, a mere challenge of one's actions, and death is seeping right through my pores. In a panic, Boo knows he told too much too fast, and I know I have one step up on him because of that.

Speak no evil, see no evil, hear no evil, but the evil is there stirring about and constantly absorbing energy. No matter where you turn, the evil lurks. No matter what I do, I'm destined for death.

CHAPTER TWENTY-ONE

"**D**on't worry about Craze, nigga. I want my face to be the last he sees before he dies. You just make sure I see him tonight in the shadows." General hangs up his cell phone without a worry in the world.

Getting the feedback on Craze didn't break a sweat gland out on General. Even though he has heard he was running his mouth to 5-0 making a name for himself. In return for snitching, the crooked police let Craze sling dope up and over Perrysville Ave. without a problem. In the making, he was setting up General's runners, getting them off the streets so he could gain control. He had stopped running the base for General, taking what he saved up and started a new and promising future in selling dope. Craze did this deciding his fate with death, but didn't mind. He had made a vow to himself that he wouldn't fall victim to General's gun or dick again. He would die first or go out trying.

Craze knew he couldn't run or hide, so he founded more troops in General's camp to ride dirty for his cause. He created his own team of warriors ready to go to war. Craze worked hypersonically within the game because General monopolized the streets to the point he knew what niggas was thinking before they thought it. He had seen the news right along with everybody else who ever served in General's camp still following the code of death, the fifteen minutes of fame. Everyone in General's camp was always instructed to watch for any fallen soldiers by the gun that came up floating, or any rival who came up smoking. Fire and water were the best ways to get rid of the evidence keeping most of the murders unsolved mysteries.

Craze worked on a one-way street to protect himself from

outsiders. Only one way in and one way out, only having to look one way when General's troops came, making it easier for him to get money. He had the whole street booby trapped to his liking for his protection and safety for knowing how sick in the head General really was. Craze made it impossible for anybody to infiltrate his spot, for General would have to come after him himself. And when he did, Craze was ready for the BOOM. If you live by the gun, you die by the gun.

"How long I been here, Boo?"

"For about a month I think. I'm not sure though. Why? Ain't anybody looking for you, so kill that noise."

"I don't give a fuck about nobody looking for me. I want some dope, pleeeeease. I'm begging you to pleeeeeeeaaaaaase smack my vein."

"NO!! You don't need that shit right now. Stay somewhat sober so you can have the chance to run if it happens. You ain't running nowhere doped the fuck up."

"Where am I going to run to, Boo? I've exhausted every possible good thing in my life to the fullest. Look at me; I'm a junkie." I cry tears of sorrow for myself. I want him to have sympathy on me and my cry for the dope. "You just remember my blood is on your hands, and don't let my son fall victim to your brother's hand." My eyes are stinging from the fake tears as Boo shakes his head no. "Give me the dope, mutherfucker! Look, Boo, I don't want to escape. I want to get high. And what happens if I do? This crazy-ass nigga is going to kill me and whatever family I got just for the fun of it? This is my fate; it's my time to die and this is my life."

"Yeah, this is your life, but don't you want to try and see your seed again? That's so fucking selfish of you. How could you be a mother...."

Boo's words sliced across my wrists, but I bleed out nothing. "Just give me a shot, shoot and kill me! Shoot the shit right into my heart! I'm asking you to kill me, Boo, pleeeeeease kill me." I cry out for the drug to bless me one last time and take my life. I want it oh, so bad.

Boo pulls the works from his pockets. He prepares a dose that will be my last. He thinks to himself, *Who was the girl I often spoke about in my dreams?*

"Who's Porsha?" Boo asks, putting the flame to the dope. This is my chance to put my shit on thick.

"She's just a girl that I will never see again because of you!"

"Damn, I'm sorry!" Boo puts it mildly.

"Sorry didn't play a part in this, Boo, but if you must know, she is the reason why my son was born."

"Where is his dad at?"

"Why, Boo, he died. There's nobody coming to avenge my death. He died over some bitch house he was cheating on me with. They both were shot in the head at point-blank range."

General is outside the door taking mental notes. He knows Boo has a bleeding heart. He was banking his last dollar on him selling me a get out of jail free card.

"I think I seen that shit on the news a couple of years back. Where it happen at?"

"Somewhere on the west side, but I can't remember, though."

"Your brain that fried you can't remember where your baby daddy got shot? It was in Turtle Creek, out there in the white folk area."

"You got a good memory. How did you know that?"

"It's just a rule I have to follow, and that's not the west side, that's the east side of Pittsburgh."

"Well, thank you for correcting me, nigga."

When General hears that, his head falls into the door, remembering the shooting his self, because he was the one who ordered the hit.

"You hear that, Boo? It came from over there by the door."

"Nope, I didn't hear shit but this flame crackling under this spoon.

You just tweaking to get high, and I'm going to put you out of your misery."

"You can be funny all you want, but I heard something, nigga. Where that crazy-ass brother of yours, slash ex-boyfriend."

Boo turns around to give me a glare as to shut the fuck up. He sits the works down on the table, rushing towards my small frame. He mugs me with his hand hard. When my body bounces up from the bed, he grabs me by the throat.

"Don't you ever repeat anything I've told you in here. You will get us both killed, for sure. You never let that shit off again about us being brothers. I could get killed by another nigga in the street behind some dumb shit he done did to somebody. And he must never know I told you that. I'm nothing to him, and he's nothing to me. You got me, girl?"

The question isn't meant to be answered. Boo walks back over to the table knowing he has to shut me up for good. He fills the hypodermic needle to the top. It can't fit another drop of dope in it. I put out my left arm with a fresh vein popping, ready to receive one last dream. My mouth waters while Boo takes every step closer to my body. Feeling the pinch, my eyes go cold as my limp body sinks into the soiled sheets. You're nobody until somebody kills you, fifteen minutes of fame...

CHAPTER TWENTY-TWO

Who is always in trouble? Who argues and fights? Who has cuts and bruises? Whose eyes are red? Everyone who stays up late, having just one more drink. Don't even look at that colorful stuff bubbling up in the glass! It goes down so easily, but later it bites like a poisonous snake. You will see weird things, and your mind will play tricks on you. You will feel tossed about like someone trying to sleep on a ship in a storm. You will be bruised all over without even remembering how it all happened. And you will lie awake asking, "When will morning come, so I can drink some more?"

PROVERBS 23:29/35

"I can't believe you left him in the house by himself all day long. Don't you know the people in the building could have called Child Youth Services on your dumb ass! Do you even give a fuck? Do you care about anybody else but yourself? Look at you standing there like you the man. You all high and drunk while your own son lies there in his playpen with the same Pamper he had on all day. You couldn't leave that tramp bitch up the hill that don't give a fuck about you for one second, could you, stupid?!" Porsha stood there holding our year-old son in her arms, hating everything I became.

Porsha had left me and come back once too many times, breaking the little bit of heart I had left. Her excuse was she was teaching me a lesson, but that was one lesson that went over my head. I stood against the wall nonchalant, with my hands in my pants, looking down on her. Picture that, talking to me as if her shit don't stink. The thought of her teaching me a lesson made me sick as it backfired on her, making me a product of a bad relationship.

I threw myself into the drug game, coming across the perfect connect and meeting the perfect person to put me on to some game. I wondered if Porsha knew she created this monster standing here in front of her. Coming back from time to time, throwing other niggas and bitches in my face who already had the hustle on lock made me go hard after the American dream. I laid alone many nights swallowing my pride and sucking up the tears while Porsha slept in the next room with the next bitch. I allowed it, I let it go down just to have her close to me. What the fuck does that make me? STUPID!!

"Why do you stand there like you don't care about us?" Porsha switched our son from hip to hip, looking at me with those soft, wet eyes. "What happened to us, baby?"

I stood there with a blank expression on my face as nothing came across the brain. I didn't give a fuck. She was right, so I did what I was taught. I blew Porsha a kiss and walked back out the door, turning my back on her and my own child and looked for love in the streets. I opened the door to the only thing I had left of Shame's gifts and sat pretty in the front seat of the Range Rover. I sped off into the night to handle business like nothing never happened. Bumping Jay-Z's *underground music* as loud as the stereo system could go, I thought to myself about the situation. And you know what I came up with? She wanted the bastard child, not I, so deal with it.

Mario didn't let on for months that he knew about our love affair. I'm guessing Shame's death was just too much for him. But when he finally let the cat out of the bag, we were in for a rude awakening. Mario had sent us on an all-expense paid trip to Jamaica for two weeks. Porsha, Shame Jr. and I soaked up the beautiful sun, hitting up every extravaganza on the to-do list only to come home and fine a for sale sign on our lawn. The house that we knew as our home was gone. The windows were bare and the rooms were empty. There was only an envelope taped to the door with both of our names on it. In a nutshell, the letter read the truth in his eyes.

Explaining his actions, my jaw hit the ground. The note told us he seen us naked in the bed together the morning after his best friend, my baby daddy and Porsha's brother, died. He called us two nasty bitches, saying no good would ever come of our relationship. We tried to play the game, but got played out as he got revenge for him and his best friend both. Signing off don't bite the hand that feeds you. His bitch-ass sealed it with a kiss and a sold sign.

Months later, Porsha and I, with the baby, set up shop in a tiny apartment. Watching the news one evening, we heard Mario was found dead in a car crash. He died behind the wheel of the car while in motion from a drug overdose of cocaine. It took a lot out of Porsha to bury her brother without no family, then to have to watch Mario, the man she truly loved, go six feet deep, drove her crazy. Lashing out on the closest person to her, she took all of her hurt out on me. That's when everything started to change. That was the excuse popping up every time she did something wrong. So why not do the same and find my own escape? Two wrongs don't make a right, it makes it worse, but I never figured that saying out. There was nothing neither one of us could do once the hurt consumed our hearts, but continue to hurt one another again and again.

"Ching-ching, I'm getting paid over here!" The hood bar was packed and popping as I moved through the crowd. I shouted out my slang, slapping a twenty dollar bill on the bar. The superstar came out of me so magnificent, painting my life picture perfect from the out-side looking in. You would have never thought I just walked out on my wifey and child. The crowd always loved to see me coming, knowing I was getting ready to set the party off. The cluckers was thirsty for a hit and every drunken ghost who craved one more last drink without a nickel in their pocket was happy to see the kid.

"Give a round to my thirsty drinking partners who ain't got a dollar to spend, but the best advice in the world to give. Make sure you take a drink for yourself, Ray-Ray." I slapped another twenty dollar bill down on the bar to handle the low-budget tab. "Ya'll shiftless Negroes need to give a round of applause to this man. He keeps our throats from being dry, and he never makes me wait for a drink." The front end of the bar put their hands together for the bartender, my man Ray-Ray, and it made me feel good.

Terror, traps and pits are waiting for everyone. If you are terrified and run, you will fall into a pit; if you crawl out the pit, you will get caught in a trap. The trap was set for me—money and power was its name, and I had fallen into the pit, oh, what a shame.

"Your mother will never change. When will she see she is doing the same thing to you her own mother done to her, Shame. What am I going to do? I can't take much more of her or this situation. I can't sit here and watch her self-destructing ways anymore. Legally you are not as you lay in my arms, but you're the only family I got left. I can't even imagine my life without you. I love you, baby boy." Porsha rocked Shame Jr. to sleep in her arms in dire need to right all of her wrongs. She cried out, her body ached for love, affection and answers for herself and her son-slash-nephew, who would never know his father.

Running a hot tub full of water, she hit my pager, leaving the song *G.H.E.T.T.O.U.T* by Changing Faces until the voicemail was full. It was impossible to love her. With mind made up, Porsha was ready to walk away.

Sunday morning came about quickly with the gospel of Trinity Baptist Choir singing through the hills of Homestead. Porsha wiped the sleep out of her eyes, awakened by the loud pounding on the living room window. Taking blow from Egypt when she was out cold helped Porsha to get on. Never a stranger to the game, she took on some of her own clientele, making moves of her own so she could feed Egypt's son when she disappeared for weeks at a time.

"I'm sorry for waking you up, but I got three-hundred dollars for you. I need all dimes if it ain't too much to ask." The toothless young woman smiled without shame, handing over the money.

"I got you," Porsha replied, taking the money.

"I'm so glad you answered the knock at the window, because, yo, your girlfriend was blasted last night. I knew she wasn't going to be up this early."

"Did you page her?"

"Yeah I did, and some female answered the page telling me that she was asleep. I figured it was you, so I called you by name and the bitch on the other end of the phone got real offensive. Anyway, girl, don't sweat it. Whenever you ready to beat that hoe down, make sure you let me know. I'll beat her ass like she stole my crack!"

Porsha grinned, handing the young smoker her bundle and giving a nod of approval on the suggestion.

"You keep your head up, boo. They only act like assholes for the moment. It's only the money making her smell her own ass. She will realize one day that everything she's looking for out here in these streets is right here with you at home."

"I hope you right, 'cause I can do bad all by myself, you feel me?"

"Don't worry about it, pretty Porsha, I know these things and she will be back." The smoker counted through the bunch quickly. Porsha shut the window, sat down on the couch and glared at the phone. In the next breath, she was holding the phone to her ear, paging me one last time to see if I was bold enough to call her back. Pacing the floor, she gathered her thoughts on how to handle the upcoming conversation. Two minutes later, the phone rang once, twice and then three times. Porsha stood there looking at it like it was cursed. The phone rang for the fourth time when she decided to pick it up and answer with an early morning moan. Sounding seductive, she cleared her throat. "Helllllo."

"Did someone page this number?" the unfamiliar female voice asked.

"Don't play no games with me, miss, you know who the fuck it be. It's the number one bitch, you know, the one you want to be." Cool and laid back, Porsha relaxed, sitting back down on the couch.

"Baby, it's not hard to fill your shoes. I'm not calling for my woman, but you are." The phone became extremely quiet. "So what's up? Egypt is sleeping right here next to me. Do you want me to tell her to call you when she gets up or should I tell her to give you a minute ,because you're playing with your toys."

Porsha sat quiet, caught off guard. Thinking about what the hell the bitch just said, she caught on quickly to her sarcasm. "Nah baby girl, ain't no toys here. Just your baby daddy, you know, an eye for an eye. So when he comes back to you it will be my pussy you will be tasting on his lips."

"That line is so third grade, Porsha. Porsha, that's your name, right?"

"Yeah."

"I don't want to fight with you about a female neither one of us have. She's feeling herself right now, fucking and sucking her way to the top. If you want her drunk ass, you can have her, but today she wants me. I bet you want to know my name, but only God knows why, and I'm going to let it be known——Lexus. You happy now? You know just as much about me as I know about you." There was no punchline coming back from Porsha. The bitch on the other end of the phone had her beat.

"Why the fuck you so quiet, miss? You paged your woman, wanting me to call you back. As a matter of fact, let me school you just one more time. Egypt can't do nothing for me but make me bust a nut and give me a couple of dollars. I love dick too much to be a dike. Us bitches up the top of the hill get her and send that ass home broke to you. You the talk of the hood, girl. You stupid. You's real stupid for trying to wife her. You need to just get her like everybody else." The dial tone never sounded so good. Porsha couldn't believe what she was hearing. She didn't want to hear it, but couldn't hang up the phone herself. The dial tone turned into a busy signal as Porsha stared into space.

Pondering the conversation that just took place, she sat on the couch as her heart bled out from the daggers thrown by Lexus. She couldn't believe how she talked about me—her woman—like that. Stupid and played was how Porsha felt, and she had to do something. She did not want to give up on me, but she knew the girl was right. It was a neverending battle between the both of us with little man caught in the middle. She was ready to slice her own wrist about a bitch who cared nothing about her.

Porsha picked up the phone once again. This time she dialed information for a list of rehab centers that would take a child. The first thing she had to do for herself and her baby was get clean from the major coke habit she had picked up from over the years. She didn't have a plan or the strength to leave her addiction, but she knew she had enough.

CHAPTER TWENTY-THREE

"**E**gypt, get up! Get up right the fuck now!" Monica yelled directly into my ear, but I didn't know it was her at that present moment. "Come on girl and get up before my man gets here!" She continued yelling in my ear while kicking my foot.

I started to show signs of life when I felt a gust of wind hit my asshole, chilly.

"Egypt, GET YOUR NAKED ASS UP!!!"

"My name is Nikko to you." A drunken slur, my words spill out, breath stinking to all is damned. I thought it was Porsha yelling at me until it registered that a man was on their way. I opened my eyes, checking my surroundings, and I don't know where the hell I'm at.

"Who be calling you that funny-ass shit, Egypt?" Monica replied with laughter.

I caught on to that laugh almost in an instant. It finally sank in as my eyes focused. "Is that you, Moe?"

"Please get up and put some clothes on. I see some things just ain't never going to change. You still out there drinking like a fish and can't hold your liquor to save your life."

"Why am I naked? Did we fuck?" I was a little bit confused, but I was hoping we did get down. Monica was looking good as hell.

"You don't have the right equipment to fuck me, and you know you're wrong for coming at me like that. Hell no, we didn't do nothing! I told you, my man was on his way. You don't remember anything from last night, do you, drunk ass?" Monica posed with her hands on her hips. It had been long overdue since we last saw each other, but she hadn't changed in looks one bit. For real, she looked better than ever.

"No, but how have you been? I haven't seen you in a long time. But

I don't think it's been long enough." I cracked a smile as she stood there judging me like always. "Just tell me how I ended up on your floor, Moe."

"Put your clothes on and go brush your mouth, and I'll enlighten you on the matter." Monica walked toward the kitchen. I knew what that meant——she was getting ready to hook up some breakfast just like she used to for my drunk ass back in the day.

I picked up my clothes and hit the bathroom and never once did I feel embarrassed as I found a new toothbrush in the cabinet. She hadn't changed a bit.

Monica started to cook, hoping the food could be a good ice breaker for her to talk to me and introduce her boyfriend. Monica knew she had to find a way to make the only real friend she ever had listen to her before she ended up dead. Just another memory on the Channel 11 News. She always had questions on my moves that caused them to repel. Monica had heard many stories from my little cousin on how they grew up and a lot of my ways came to light, making Monica understand some of my destructive patterns. She thanked God often for having a mother and a father who loved her.

There was a lot of resentment on Monica's part when it came to light about me being a dike, but after the excitement wore off, she loved me even more. She wanted to be the friend I needed and wanted and never experienced having. It was only fate walking into the bar and finding a long lost friend buying out the bar baller style.

"You still keep them dollar packs of toothbrushes in the medicine cabinet, I see. It smells good in here. What you cooking?"

I walked up on Moe from behind. As she walked to the left, she slowly answered, "Some bacon and eggs, your favorite."

I smiled. "You remember that?"

"Yeah, I do. You were a lush, but always my partner in crime." Her face went from sweet to sour. "And I see you still shutting down bars like you eighteen without any responsibilities. When are you going to grow up, home girl?"

I put both hands up and covered up my ears. I didn't need a sermon from anybody.

"See what I mean, Egypt? Grow the fuck up!"

"You're burning the eggs like you always do. You know you can't talk and cook at the same time, so chill with the preaching." We looked each other in the face for a second, giving up a smile as I changed the subject. I knew she meant well, but damn. What gives her the right to pass judgment on me after walking out of my life for being gay?

"So, who's your new man I keep hearing about?" I really did want to know. Monica was the only friend I had left in this game called life. And even though I was mad at her back in the day, I'm glad she found me and I found her.

"You met him last night, but I knew you wouldn't remember." Moe laughed, pointing the finger. "He drove your truck here and carried your drunk ass up the steps and into my crib. By the way, nice-ass truck, too."

"Are you for real? I don't remember none of that shit."

"You didn't even know who I was. And guess what?"

"What?"

"You didn't throw up, woman. There's a first for everything, and I'm happy you learned how to handle your liquor. The E I remember would have gave it up ten minutes into the ride. It was shocking to me how cool you played it off until you passed out. Is this enough eggs for you?" Moe hooked my plate up while I sat in awe. I didn't know anything that had happened. It wasn't a good look.

"Yeah, that's cool, but where's the beef?" I fingered like five pieces of bacon quick. "Why you keep staring at me?" The look she gave off was confusing, and I didn't have a clue what the answer was going to be.

"You look so different, that's all. I noticed you by voice, not by appearance."

"Is that good or bad?"

"It's good, I guess. You look like a pretty boy with your corn rows to the back with your wife beater on."

"I know, I know, I'm sexy as hell, ain't I?" Conceit poured out willingly once she gave out the compliment.

"I wouldn't say all that, big head, but you're cool!"

"I'm pretty goddamned cool. Your man better hurry up before I turn you out." I licked my lips playfully, but I meant every word I said.

"On that note, let me page Tre right now. And please, don't play with me, Egypt. I'm a stickler for dick and balls. But anyway, cutie, you're going to love his baldheaded ass. That's my baby. I love me some Tre." Moe shook her hips in every direction while she spoke. I swear she was flirting with me, but I let it go.

"Speaking of pagers, did you see mine or better yet, did you hear it? I know my woman is going crazy wondering why I'm not calling back." While Moe paged her man I got up from the table to look for my pager. I fucked her food up, got caught up on old times and now it was time to go. I had business to tend to.

I checked through the stuff Moe had in the cut folded up and found nothing. I checked both of her couches and the floor but still found nothing.

"When you hang up, Moe, pass me the phone." My temp was rising high.

"Here you go, Ms. Important." She danced the phone into my hand. Those little ass booty shorts kept rising also, straight up in her crotch. She was flirting, Ray Charles is blind, but she was so blunt he could see it. I paged myself a couple of times, putting in Monica's phone number. Afterwards I went to check the truck outside the apartment.

RING! RING! RING!

"Tre, where you at, bighead boy?"

"This ain't no muthafucking, Tre. Did you page Nikko, my bitch, bitch!"

Monica almost dropped the phone from the disrespect blasting her eardrum. Her neck snapped back hard; you know how females get down. Monica thought she should blast the smart mouth heifer from the gate, but decided to chill, not knowing the shit I had put the girl through.

"Yeah, I paged Nikko, and who the hell are you?" Monica played with the female's emotions on the other end of the phone, hoping one day she would meet my girlfriend and they would laugh about the whole ordeal over drinks.

"Don't ask me no questions, whoever the hell you are. I got enough of those this morning. Anyway, I know this is you, Porsha, playing on my woman's pager from different phones."

"This ain't no Porsha on the other end of this phone. Don't know her, but you can give my girl back her pager, and by the way, my name is Moe, hoe."

"Your girl an everybody the fuck else's! Here we go with the bullshit all over again. You know what? Tell Egypt I said to call Lexus back when she gets out of your pussy while I think about giving her her pager back." At the same, time both girls banged the phone down on each other. Monica laughed aloud in shock. She couldn't believe what just had happened. No, she didn't just get done arguing with a female about another female who she wasn't fucking. It reminded her of a man getting caught up in his lies.

"What the hell are you doing out there in them streets?" That was the first question from Monica's lips when I walked back through the door.

"I'm getting a lot of everything on the lines of money, power and respect out there in them streets, ya dig?" I cock my head to the side with finesse and throw my hands inside my pants.

"Some bitch just called my house. She got your pager. She said her name was Lexus, and if Porsha is your girlfriend, she done talked to her also."

My face was cracked and on the ground. "Are you for real?"

"Dumb question, player! How the hell else would I know their names? You sure didn't tell me." Monica posed with her hands on her hips, awaiting an explanation like she was my woman.

"SHIT, SHIT, SHIT AND MORE SHIT!!! I'm going to kill her."

"So who is Lexus?" Monica asked, needing details.

"You all in mine, Moe! Damn, we ain't fucking!" Monica's face frowned in disgust as I threw the look right back at her.

"Ugh, bitch, you sound like a nigga. Keep it the fuck up and you're going to make me act out. You really can't do anything with me, Egypt. So you better rest ya neck and check the tone in your voice. I'm not one of your little hoe's you got out there in your hood. I'm trying to be your friend."

"So now you want to be my friend?"

"I never said I didn't. You got caught up and I pulled your card to a nigga you didn't even know. Instead of you telling me the truth, you cut me the fuck off. You stopped being my friend, not wanting to face me. You was all up in my face, sleeping in my bed with me, watching me get dressed and shit! You even saw me naked, bitch. You robbed me of my choice of being your friend or not. You leaving me in the dark about you being gay, bi-sexual or whatever the fuck you are because I know for a fact you like dick, bitch. Now you tell me who wasn't keeping it real on the friendship-type shit."

I stood there dumbfounded, scratching my ass literally. She had me at that point, and there wasn't a comeback line in sight. I didn't know the truth until she spoke it.

"I swear, Egypt, don't stand there like you don't know what I'm talking about. Just chalk it up as a loss and apologize. It will make you feel better. I done already forgiven you, homie; if I wouldn't have, you would have killed yourself trying to get home last night."

"Yeah, you know," I replied looking to the left. "Moe, I done fucked up so bad within these last few years. Even if I tried to explain what went down, I wouldn't know where to start. But one thing is for sure—I missed you and yes, I'm sorry for keeping you in the dark and not trusting you as a friend with my dirty little secret. I just didn't know how you would take me liking females." My head hung low, embarrassed by my actions. The silence surrounding the room made me feel uneasy, and I tried hard to avoid eye contact with Monica.

In the midst of the silence, I picked up the phone to check my voicemail. Monica departed to the kitchen to clear the table. My voicemail was full as I checked through every message and every last one of them was from Porsha. Porsha was pouring her heart and soul out into every message, playing songs that matched her pain, getting her point across. My eyes grew weary from trying to hold back the tears as a simple knock at the door brought me back to reality.

"That's Tre, I bet. Open up the door, Egypt," Monica yelled from the kitchen. It was cool— I needed a break from the messages Porsha left anyway. I wiped my eyes, put a smile on my face and opened the door with welcoming arms. Opening up the door, I was stopped dead in my tracks with a blow to the face. Pandemonium struck fast and hard in the middle of Monica's living room as I exchanged blow for blow with Lexus without a word. It was the quiet before the thunder came crashing, breaking the window from the pager leaving the palm of Lexus' hand. The altercation grew out of control when Monica heard the impact of sound waves coming from the living room. Moe ran in and picked up the phone. I thought to myself who the fuck could she be calling at a time like this. But I should have known she was up to no good. She smacked the hell out of Lexus with the phone and didn't stop neither. Biting off more than she could chew, Lexus came from up under the blows of the both of us, pulling a gun to make the fight fair once again.

"Back up off me, bitches!" Bloody as hell, Lexus waved the punk deuce at us, scared.

"Egypt, get your girl right now before she makes a big mistake."

Moe spoke softly, backing up behind me. I didn't know what to do, but when I looked into Lexus' eyes, I knew the fight was over. The girl was fucked up in the head and hurt by my bullshit, too.

"What the hell is wrong with you, baby? This is not what it looks like. This girl standing behind me is my best friend. You know I love you, right? Why would you want to hurt me or my family? Come on, Lex, please put the gun down." Coming up from the rear I seen a knight in shining armor as Moe gave me the heads up by a tap on the back of my foot. Creeping up from behind Lexus, Tre finally decided to join the party. Walking into a situation confused, he sensed danger from the door. Tre grabbed Lexus from behind, knocking the gun loose from her hand. Moe stepped from behind me and kicked the gun across the floor, coming back with a strong uppercut, putting Lexus to sleep.

Tre dropped her limp body to the floor and looked directly at me as he asked, "What the hell is all this, Monica? She only been here a couple of hours and look what the fuck done went down. I told you last night her drunk ass ain't nothing but trouble."

"Tre, you don't know what happened." Monica tried to come to my defense.

"What the hell happened then?" Tre replied harshly.

They both looked at me for answers I couldn't give them. Moe was trying to pull me out the fire, but she didn't know what the hell started it. I focused my attention on Lexus, trying to wake her up. On the real, I was trying to find an answer on what had just happened.

"What are you going to do with that bitch, Egypt? I know somebody in my building done called the cops by now and personally, I want the bitch to go to jail. Plus, somebody gots to pay for my window."

"Please don't put her in jail, Moe. We handle court in the streets, baby, by all means. I'm going to take care of everything and give you a couple of dollars for the trouble." I drop a knot of cash on the floor and kick it over to her. I gave direct eye contact with Moe's man Tre when I did so just to catch that hater expression. The muthafucker didn't even know me and didn't like me already. It turned me on to know Moe went against her man to look out for me.

"See, what did I tell you? It was her; it all had to do with her! She's nothing but trouble, Monica. Please listen to your man on this one." Tre grabbed a hold of Moe by the arms with a profound look on his face. He wanted her to choose right then and there if it was going to be me or him. I knew this, being placed in this situation so many times before.

"You right, homeboy, it was me that she was after. She must have followed us from the bar last night. But you don't know nothing about me so you should watch your mouth. Let's go, bitch!" I slap Lexus in the face, pushing her out the door. I look ol' boy up and down and excuse myself from the situation for a moment.

"Are you outta your fucking mind, Lexus?!" I couldn't believe how shit went down twenty minutes ago. My heart still in my throat, I slapped the shit out of her once more, flexing my muscle. I spoiled her with the tongue and now she just sprung.

"You can't hurt me, baby… I like that shit. You can hit me all you want, but I will never leave you alone." A sinister grin overwhelmed Lexus' face, followed by an inauspicious laugh. "I promise you, Nikko, you will see me again. You haven't seen the last of me yet."

Lexus shook off the wounds and descended down the steps. Without a trace, she was gone as I heard the police coming up the steps seconds later. The police had arrived just in time. I stepped back into the crib to warn Monica just above a whisper. The knock was expected, but it still shook all of us as we played the not home game on them boys. The tension in the room was thick; I felt all eyes on me. I could feel the hate, transmitting rays toward me from both sides of the room as Mo, Tre and I posted up quiet as church mice. It was obvious Monica's man and I would never get along. If he knew what I knew, I wouldn't want my own woman around my smug ass.

But truth be told, Tre was schooled to the game early in life. He never had the chance to see his mother with a man because she was always a lesbian. She was a lesbian, but a butch one with a reckless life style. She groomed him to never be a fool and observe because knowledge is power. The unbalanced chemical makes women unstable creatures, give them the mastery of being cunning. Being loving and passionate are geared in mostly every woman with supportive tactics, but tremendous distrust comes along with it in love. Love is a word of so much emotion, selfish and often the cause of a lot of commotion. Love is always mistaken for lust and love is a word often misused. Love, a four letter word, with unlimited power, precious as a diamond and as soft as a flower. Everyone wants it, needs it and craves it, and often go too far and fake it. Momma said there would be a day like this and to be alert when the day came to light. If not on point, the one you love can fall astray. You have to protect their trust just as well as your own or fall victim to hurt. Tre wanted Moe to be his wife. He wanted a lot of children, and his wish wouldn't fall to the back of the wish list being naïve about the next woman. His wish would come true if it was the last thing he had to do in life. Words to the wise, a mothers' wisdom——never trust a dike around the woman you love. She's worse than a man and more conniving than the devil.

Everything had calmed down for the moment. I didn't have the heart to call Porsha back, and I couldn't leave until the glass cutters came to fix the window. Tre watched me like a hawk, while I watched Moe watch him.

"I need to talk to Egypt in private baby, okay?" Monica spoke to Tre under her breath. I have to admit, Tre was fine as hell from head to toe, but his dress game was fucked up.

"Whatever. Do what you got to do, but I'm not leaving you in this crib with her alone." Tre licked his lips, sat back on the couch and crossed his arms over his chest.

Moe pulled me by the arm into her bedroom. Shutting the door behind her, she jumped dead into my arms. We fell onto her bed, lips locked together.

"I've been dying to kiss you since all this shit went down. I've never been this turned on before in my life. I thought that bitch was going to shoot me and you." Moe continued to kiss me softly, as if her man wasn't sitting outside in the living room. "Your head game must be official if you got bitches tripping off of you like that."

I flip her on her back and head straight for the thongs. Skin so soft, hot and tempting, we play fight for the draws to come off. Tenaciously, she doesn't give in. She just taunts me by saying my name over and over again.

"Egypt..."

"Egypt, can you hear me..."

"What the fuck, Egypt? I know you can hear me!"

I can feel my middle spot heating up as I crave her touch. It's too much for me to handle; her touch drives me crazy.

"The window is going to cost a buck fifty, girl! Can you hear me talking to you!?" I was awakened out of my fantasy with a slap to the back of the head.

"Ouch, punk! What did you do that for?" I damned sure knew why she hit my nasty ass.

I'm allowed to daydream, ain't I?

"You didn't hear shit I said to you, and I know you didn't! Pay the man his money for my window and get your ghetto-ass head out of cloud nine. You got me?"

"I got you!" I reached down in my pockets to pull out the money.

"You didn't answer my question neither, Egypt."

"And what question was that?" I answered her with the same sarcastic tone she gave me.

"Why are you calling yourself Nikko? Where in the hell did you come up with that handle?"

I paid the man his money while Tre watched me out the corner of his eye. I played along with a wide-ranged pimp with a switch dip in my walk, so narcissistic I couldn't stand myself. I checked him rolling back to the room where his woman laid down the law and shut the door. There she waits for an answer, laying on her stomach with her chin resting in the palms of her hands and her legs crossed.

"Long story short, Moe, I got the name from an old Steven Segal movie called *Above the Law*. After I watched Steven Segal as Nikko kill all the bad guys, I went in the bathroom to look in the mirror. I tried the name on for size. It's sexy I had thought to myself, staring back at my reflection, and Nikko was born."

"You know you're sick right? That's crazy girl. What are you trying to do, reinvent yourself?"

"Maybe I did, but that doesn't make me sick in the head. This is just the new me, Moe." I put my head down. "I didn't like the old me that much anymore."

"Well, I'm not going to lie to you, Nikko. Being around you for the most part of the day, I miss the old you, but I will respect you at the end of the day, okay? Is we cool?"

"Yeah, we cool." I was happy Moe didn't try and judge me about my choice. "You know, you're much daintier then you used to be. Yes, home girl, you've changed also," I said, cracking a smile at Moe.

"So when are you going to tell me your baby's name?" Moe caught me off guard, and she knew it by the drop-dead expression I had on my face. I took a deep breath. "I know I'm the godmother, right?" I didn't know how she knew, but I couldn't deny my child, even though I wanted to.

"His name is Shame. He was named after his father. How did you know about all that, because he's not mine, he's my girlfriend's baby."

"What the hell are you talking about, and what do you mean he's not yours? Did you or did you not carry him for nine months?"

"How do you know all this?" I asked, puzzled.

"I spotted you in the grocery store one day on my way out the door. I didn't have time to stop and speak because I wasn't ready for a reaction from you at that time. So tell me, what's up, Egypt... I mean Nikko. What do the daddy have to say about all this? You running around with females and all."

In an instant, I began to cry. Moe was asking questions I could not answer without wet eyes. I took a long pause, sobbing. I tried to find an easy answer, but when I opened my mouth nothing came out and more tears fell.

"What's wrong, homegirl? You can talk to me, E. I'm here to help with anything you need to do."

I could see Moe was being for real about the situation, but I knew deep down she wasn't ready to hear the whole truth and nothing but the truth so help me God.

"Awe, you need a hug, boo boo?" Moe asked while pulling me into her embrace. I continued to cry harder, laying my head on her heartbeat. Crying became so natural to me at that moment, I just let go.

Next thing I know, Tre was busting up in the room unannounced feeling not welcomed to the party. Me all laid up on his girlfriends' breast didn't help the situation none. "I need to holla at you right the fuck now, Monica!" The bass in her mans' voice shook my insides. I pulled back from Moe and wiped my wet, red eyes. I gave him the up and down effect of my puffy eyes walking out the bedroom. I felt the wind behind me a second later after I walked out the room from the door slammed shut so hard the walls shook. I smirk wisely.

"I want that bitch out of here now, Monica, and I'm not playing with you neither, girl!"

"What! You tripping hard Tre for no fucking reason!"

"You the fuck heard me, woman! You already getting caught up in her hype, paying me no attention. You was supposed to cook me breakfast, and I never seen a plate. But I saw that you and mister ate together this morning. I came to that conclusion seeing the two dirty plates in the sink when I was getting me some water. You said befriending her wouldn't come between us, but baby, I feel that it will and you should listen to your man. Be a friend from a distance, dammit, and trust her not at all."

"First and foremost, I want you to lower your voice. Second, you're so sexy right now with the jealous look all over your face. I've never seen you act like this about no nigga, so why about a woman, my best friend at that?"

"Monica, you know my mother—she taught me well. I've witnessed firsthand the power aggressive dikes have over women." Tre put on the meanest face possible, sticking his hands in his pants pockets like a little-ass kid. Monica laughed to herself for a moment. She placed her hands on Tre's arms, pulling them out of his pockets. She took his hands and placed them over her heart.

"Do you feel that?"

"Feel what?"

"My heartbeat, stupid. It's beating for you, baby. I love you and nothing can come between that. I only have eyes for you, Tre. Believe me when I say we are meant to be." Sincerely, Monica placed a kiss on the top of Tre's forehead.

"My mom told me trust my loved ones, but not love; love is a loveless emotion. So, on that note, I will always play you close. Believe me when I say, yes, we are meant to be, Monica. But don't think for one minute I won't punch that dike bitch in her face, best friend and all. She will get dropped like a bad cold if she ever step over the line with you."

I could hear the passionate lip lock from behind the closed door. It made me miss Shame and the strength of a man for only a second. Then I realized I was the man, and I had too many bitches on my team to be getting all sentimental and shit.

CHAPTER TWENTY-FOUR

R ING… RING… RING…
"Hello."

"Your girl is dead when I see the cunt! Let her know she better lay low."

"Stop playing on my phone, you stupid bitch." Porsha relaxed in the tub filled with hot water. Wine sipping, she was putting together this morning's events.

She had come to the conclusion that Lexus was young as hell or just didn't have no life. On the phone for the most part of the afternoon, she also found out about an outpatient rehab to work on that little cocaine problem of hers. And the place even had a daycare spot to help out with Shame Jr. The hill house was perfect for them both Porsha thought, sipping slow.

Stepping out the tub of water, an uneasy feeling came over her. For some reason, she needed something but couldn't quite put her finger on it. The coke sat on the entertainment system with Mary J. Blige on pause, and her body was so tempted to grab the plate, but she moved on. Nose running from the eighth she just put up it, she downed the rest of the wine. Porsha looked at herself in the mirror and didn't notice the person who looked back. Minutes later she fled from the apartment after getting dressed to the old lady who lived upstairs. Before she could knock, the old lady who kept an eye on Shame from time to time, opened the door.

"I already know, chile. Bring the baby up here and take some time out for yourself."

"Thank you so much, Mrs. M. I really do need to handle something important. Here goes twenty dollars for now. if I'm too long, I'll throw you forty more and a bag of weed, okay?"

Deal made, Porsha changed her clothes and got Shame Jr. ready. Paging Egypt one last time, she felt it was a mistake and left out of the crib without waiting for a no call back. Kissing Shame Jr. goodbye, tears fell softly as if this was the last time she would see him.

"Do you trust me, Tre?" Monica asked in a whisper.

"Yes I do, baby."

"Well, let me do this please. I love Egypt, and she needs me."

"What is it you want me to do?"

"Just give us some time to talk, and I'll call you later, baby, I promise."

"You promise, sexy?"

"I promise, and I'll cook you a bomb-ass dinner to go with this little red cute teddy I bought." Planting soft wet kisses on Tre's lips, he couldn't deny his woman. He let his guard down and simply said, "Yes." I ran away from the closed door like a little-ass kid would do when they know their parents were coming. I picked up the newspaper from off the couch and turned to the sports section quick. Moe came out the room shaking those baby-making hips from the left to the right as Tre followed behind. They kissed one more time and Tre disappeared from the apartment.

"Okay, smartass, you can put the newspaper down. We both know you was eavesdropping on my conversation with my man. That's what best friends do, bitch. I ain't slow."

I dropped the newspaper that I just noticed I had upside down from in front of my face.

There she stood in front of me with her hands on her hips, sassy as hell. I couldn't do anything but smile.

"I got something to drink if you want to chill with me for a minute and just talk. We can catch up on old times, you know." Moe walked to the ice box and pulled out a bottle of chilled gin. I could work with that.

"We done did enough of catching up on my side, but I will take you up on that drink. I got a bad day to look forward to. Please and thank you for the drink you're about to pour. Gin always makes the morning go more smooth. I got to figure out what the hell I'm going to tell my woman. She'll never believe me when I tell her that I wasn't with Lexus." Moe shot me a look as to say, *as if.*

"Just tell her I said whenever she ready to beat that hoe down to call me. I got her back and your back on that one." Getting hyped by the thought, I watched Moe pour the drinks while she pointed her index finger, acting like she was in demand to whoop somebody ass. "I feel like I've been sleep since we stopped hanging out, Egypt."

"Call me Nikko...."

"My fault, Nikko. But anyway, I haven't been in a hood bar or a club since I've became the ideal woman for my man."

"Maybe this one you can have your first child with. How did ya'll meet, because he's cute as hell in the face, but he doesn't fit into your thuggish, ruggish playboy style you always go for?"

Moe went on to explain how she and Tre hooked up as I checked that bottle of gin shot for shot like I was a fucking bartender. Tre had saved her life, she went on to tell. Almost being raped leaving a party with a cutie, who had a Hummer, she put her head in the books and stepped away from the fast track that led her to the ordeal. Attending college courses in business management at CCAC, a community college on the lower part of the North Side is where she met prince charming. Moe ran right into Tre, knocking all of his books out of his hands. Starting a high-school crush in college, the more they tried to avoid each other, the more they bumped heads. Tre thought Moe was just another around-the-way girl from the hood taking classes to keep her food stamps. And Tre just wasn't hood enough for her in looks or dress code. His crisp JC Penney shirts down to his Docker pleated pants wasn't the worst of it neither. The man wore white tube socks with Stacy Adams shoes. I busted out laughing trying to picture the look on Moe's face when she first saw him dressed like that.

Stylish to perfection, dressing to impress, always the center of attention of course, my girl kept her classmates on their toes. From the expensive diamond earrings and necklace to match all the way down to the different pairs of tennis shoes she rocked everyday of the week to keep all eyes on her. Us hood bitches need that shit, ya dig? Long story short, Moe and Tre couldn't stand each other until fate stepped in and decided different. Moe was failing calculus and Tre was failing theoretical business when the teacher brought the two together. The both of them was the bomb in the other subject, so why not help each other out the teacher thought, assigning them to tutor each other. Both of them had too much potential to fail out of class over personal conflict. Study partners they became, enjoying each other's company. After a while, more time was in demand to see each other, and after Moe got that man to take off them socks with them dress shoes, it was all good. Judging a book by its cover was a well- learned lesson between the two as their styles clashed, painting beauty as one.

"Damn, so my girl is going to be running some big bank and she most definitely is going to marry Mr. Brooks Brothers. I do believe that you're going to get everything you want out of life. I know you and Tre are going to be for a long time, if not forever, too, girl." I sip my drink slow as the buzz starts to catch up with me.

"You should believe in yourself, too, homie. Stand up and be the woman you need to be. Be a mother to your child you don't want to talk about to me. You need to leave all this foolishness you're wrapped up in behind. You do know the path you're walking will only leave you dead or in jail?" I took the words Moe said to the heart and believed them for a moment, and then reality hit hard and fast.

"This is me, Moe, for real, I'm a diamond in the rough. I don't want to be nothing but what the fuck I am. Your thing is books; my thing is the corners. I get mad love on them corners. I'm needed to each and every addict. You feel me, Moe? I'm important on them corners and the people rely on me to give them what they want. Shit, I'm one hell of a sales slash businessman myself. You might as well face it, Moe—I already have money, power and respect. It's all a hood bitch like me needs. Shit, that's all I want."

"If that's all you want, then it's not much. But a bitch like me can't knock your hustle, so do you." Moe sat there and let me continue to talk about nothing important with sorrow in her eyes.

Moe felt that I was lost, and it was her duty to help me find my way back. She wouldn't give up if it was the last thing she had to do every other day of the week. Her life as she knew it was spared for a reason when that nigga tried to rape her, and Moe felt that it was fate that brought us back together. Deep down in her inner being, the feeling was too strong. One life was spared to save another.

CHAPTER TWENTY-FIVE

There was no need to read in between the lines. I noticed a change in my woman and a pretty goddamned big one. My packages weren't as light as they used to be, and she didn't hang out in the bathroom as much as she used to neither. I didn't see much of Shame Jr. or her, as they always had something else better to do with their time.

I invaded Porsha's space every chance I could get, trying to find clues of disloyalty. But doing so, I never found anything pressuring me to think that she was cheating. Only discovering small packets of information on Narcotics Anonymous amongst other things of that nature, my lead detective days were outlawed.

My days were numbered anyway as I picked up the nasty habit of mixing coke in my weed as I smoked problem free. I can't really remember what day I started, but I do remember yearning for the feeling of what people hunted me down for all day. I grabbed a cold beer from the fridge and took a seat on the couch. I put the flickering flame up to the spliff and exposed myself to a chase I would be running from for the rest of my life. When it rains it pours, coming down extremely hard, blinding the vision of the eyes. And I couldn't see a damned thing as I inhaled the smoke and trapped it in my lungs.

This is the part of the drug game nobody tells you about. As you fall so deep in love with your own pain, you see nothing or no way out. You no longer enjoy the high of profitability off of other peoples' misery, and you no longer get the rush from holding stacks of cash in your hands.

You're powerless over your own addiction, and the addiction is your mind on the chase for something to replace the high of the lifestyle. Covering up the pain—so you think—you seek, search and destroy, aware of the damage you generate but can't stop.

Wanting to feel no pain for once in my life, I sat and talked to the get-high as it spoke back to me. In the cloud of smoke, sleeplessness bit at my ankles as my eyes beamed, focused on one spot. I was all fucked up, nose wide open with a racing heart and muscles tense, rolling blunt after blunt. I smoked a quarter ounce of weed and three hundred dollars worth of product. I didn't give a fuck. I sat on the couch in a moment's bliss, craving just another puff as a single tear fell from my left eye. I shed a tear knowing at that moment I was lost. I had lost my identity, never feeling so damned good. I knew it wasn't right; I knew it was against every hustler's law—don't get high off your own supply. Even though I knew it wasn't right, I was willing and able to take that flight on the path of the new demon I was lighting up. I went afloat, escaping the past, making the present content and the future tainted. How did it come to this in just a single moment...

Spending a night in jail, the good times of standing on the corners was coming to an end. Lexus wouldn't give up her malicious antics and niggas was popping up all over the scene, slinging hard. I thought I was going to end up in jail for possession of a controlled substance, but no... I spent the night in jail for aggravated assault. One night of passion was causing me a lifetime of pain. The little young bitch wouldn't stop until she got sliced and diced, landing herself in the emergency room. I tried so many times to turn the other cheek to her countless unthinkable acts, but when the actuality set in that she wouldn't stop, I had no choice but to retaliate.

With the vicious lies she spread came horrible rumors which destroyed any trust Porsha had left for me. Lexus just couldn't take or understand that no matter what, she couldn't be queen bitch, even though she tried just about everything. So it was written in stone and on many drunk late nights it was told that she wasn't wifey material, just the back-burner hoe, the chick on the low, counting the dollars and storing the blow. But Lexus was going to fight to the death about me. She just wouldn't let it go, popping up once again in the middle of downtown. The crazy bitch was following Moe and me while we shopped for new clothes. This time when she jumped out on us, I gave her an ass whipping she wouldn't forget. White people called the cops quick, being witnesses to so much blood. You damned straight! I cracked that bitch's nose with the first punch, and the police sprang my wrist, arresting my black ass for causing a riot in downtown Pittsburgh. It didn't sit well with Porsha, neither that I called her three in the morning for bail money. "Why?" she asked me. I knew her from top to bottom. That's why I told the truth, and that didn't smooth over too well. There isn't that many ways to tell your woman you're locked up because some bitch you was fucking done went crazy on your ass. No matter how much I told her Lexus and I was not together, the harder Lexus went and Porsha didn't believe me. That little bitch had her brainwashed. And when Moe opted out of nowhere and we were thick as thieves, Porsha damned near had a stroke. Fed up and all, she didn't leave me like she used to do—she did something different and that was pray. Leaving her vengeance up to him, she stayed loyal to me. She owed it to her big brother that rest in peace, to his son and to us, so she said.

Watching my life spiral downward, she tried to give me testimony to the new peace she had found in her life, but I couldn't hear a word. Porsha told me time and time again—one day your ears aren't going to be deaf to me and you're going to hear everything I'm saying, but you know what, it's going to be too late for you to answer me. I couldn't figure out what she meant at that time, but you know what, I get it now. I can hear her, but she can't hear me as I'm locked up in hell...

CHAPTER TWENTY-SIX

*A*nother day, I thought as I stretched my breakfast. Finding a note attached to my box of blunts, the sight of Porsha's handwriting sickens me to the point my stomach turns. Snatching the note from the box of blunts, I balls it up and shoot a free throw with it.

My appetite had picked up for the drug I consumed daily, making one blunt just an appetizer. Not hiding the lust for the temptation made me invincible and very dangerous to the eyes and ears on the corners. My status quo had risen from the recent incident of the precise incisions I made to Lexus's facial structure, blow for blow. My pussy stampede was flowing like a beer tap as the jail rep made me extremely sexy. I rang bells throughout the streets of the borough, and my name was spoken off of many lips.

The streets had to give credit where credit was due. I was the first female to push some major weight this far. I could do what any hood-politicking male figure could do and better. I was only pushing a half a key of coke on the streets, but from the outside looking in, I was doing big things. I might as well been pushing keys from the one-hundred thousand dollar truck I was racing and the 24-karat gold I rocked hard around my neck, wrist, and fingers. Always having Porsha plushed out was a bonus.

But behind closed doors, my dream of becoming the first female Nino Brown was being flushed down the toilet as I lit up my blunt.

"My name is Porsha, and I'm an addict..."
"Hi Porsha, we welcome you..."
Porsha looked over the crowded room of drug addicts and

alcoholics. The crowd fell silent to hear her testimony. She felt like every set of eyes in the audience was giving her direct eye contact. Clearing her throat, she took a deep breath.

"This is my first time sharing, so please be patient as I find the right words to say." Porsha wiped the little bead of sweat from her brow with the tip of her fingernail.

"Just speak from the heart, sister!" a supportive group member shouted, trying to loosen Porsha up a little.

Porsha scanned the faces in the room that she had grown to love. Shame Jr. was being held in the arms of the program director who had been a great friend and mentor in her time of need. Looking into his big brown eyes, tears began to form. Choked up, Porsha wiped them away, taking another deep breath, she exhaled to release the tension and started her journey.

"In these past couple of years, I've grown to love and hate cocaine. I first got started in this rundown club. I got high for some money, and I let a female take advantage of me to satisfy her own sick fantasies. My life was a mess, and I felt it didn't have any value. I had just let a man moments before shit on me like I was a toilet for five hundred dollars I never saw. I mean it when I say I was in a dark place. I was in a place so dark I couldn't see the light. Ya'll know what I mean?"

"Yessss, sister! I know exactly what you mean!" A lady shouted from left field as if the words Porsha spoke told her story.

"My mother and father were dead and gone," Porsha continued. "They took onto a higher power, leaving me to defend myself against the harsh realities of the world. I did have a brother that tried his best to raise me into a respectable young woman, but ya'll women know how head strong we can be. I wouldn't listen to a damned thing. My brother dead and gone now, too, but there sits his son over there." Porsha pointed to the program director.

"Ya'll all know him as Shame Jr." Porsha shook her head feeling that she was rambling on. She took another deep breath and pulled the story back to the start.

"In that club I thought I had it all under control. We done all said that at one time or another, now haven't we?" The crowd chuckled at the comment. Knowing that her expression was true, the crowd nodded in agreement as Porsha continued. "I would only do it before I performed on stage to get me in rare form. But before I knew it, I was hanging out in the bathrooms everywhere and anywhere way too often. The coke made me feel like everything I was doing wrong was right. But yet I still felt in control. I even slept with my brothers' best friend and his woman. The guilt and shame I endured was overwhelming all the time I tried to play sober. I couldn't stay away from her, the coke, or the woman I cheated on her with to supply my habit. I just told myself that everything was going to work itself out. Then the only family I have left is shot and killed. He was found dead at his creep's crib cheating on his girlfriend that was cheating on him with me. The bullet was meant for his best friend and my boy toy at the time. I wasn't serious about nobody or nothing but the get-high and the party-popping bubbly. My boy toy ran the fast life. Everybody in here knows what I mean! He was a drug dealer on the streets and a star to the addict, which was me. My baby forever and always." Porsha got choked up once again. "Mario," she said as she wept, "you rest in peace also… Lord rest his soul. He died, too, ya'll. The cravings surpassed anything I ever could imagine after losing so many people to me. And the only person left to love me… I wasn't so sure if I loved her. I loved her when we was doing wrong, I do know this, but that was the whole turn on, ya dig? Shame Jr.'s mother didn't judge me, but she didn't stop me from getting high neither. She was in her own addiction, I know that now. Two sick people can't help one another; it's like the blind leading the blind."

"I felt cursed by God! He was taking everything from me. So I did what hurt people do—I pushed my woman and the only real friend

I had away, because she wouldn't get high with me. The goddamned bitch was too much of a fucking drunk." Porsha shook her head in shame, but as she spoke, she felt the burden being lifted from her heart. It was a story dying to be told to save someone else's' life.

"She couldn't get high anyway. I really didn't want to share with my greedy ass. I wanted her to leave me... I wanted Egypt to walk away from me because I didn't have the strength to do so. I couldn't control the drugs anymore—they were controlling me, and I was out of control. I thought God was going to take her from me, so I was afraid to put my guard down to honestly love her. I know I shouldn't be up here saying all this shit... but dammit, ya'll, I need help! My life right now is still out of control! I want control back over my life!" Porsha screamed in tears. She wanted someone to stop her now, but wouldn't nobody move. The crowd wouldn't be a crutch. A dramatic pause took place for sixty seconds as Porsha tried to control her meltdown.

"So many feelings are awake now since I've been clean for thirty days." The crowd applauded. "I don't want to deal with them without getting high is what I would have said yesterday, but today I got to do it for me, my baby Shame Jr., and my girl Egypt, who's out there smoking spliffs from dusk to dawn. I feel like it's my fault where she at right now in her life. All she wanted was somebody to love her and I couldn't do that. I loved the drugs more than I loved myself at the time. I didn't have the love to give, but now I do. She can't hear me right now. Her ears are deaf to me, and now since I'm changing my life, I don't think she ever will." The tears began to fall again. Each time she started to cry, the rivers became deeper. The crowd stood to their feet and clapped vigorously. A couple of guys even whistled, giving her a thumbs up. Nobody really could believe that young woman stood in front of a room full of people and told that story. The program director that strongly suggested Porsha should share was in tears, never hearing a story quite like hers.

Porsha fell to her knees, grief stricken. The program director handed Shame Jr. to her assistant as she knew Porsha needed her. Rushing to Porsha's aid, she said a quick prayer to the man up above.

"I got three for fifty and seven for a hundred. It's the first of the month, and the money is talking." I stood on the corner dressed in all black with a skully hat to match. Profiling and styling, I politicked the product I had in my pockets. The police knew what I was about, but couldn't do too much damage control on any female who got at a dollar on the streets. It was all due to a rookie cop that wanted to make detective in a year. He fucked up so bad a new law was placed in order.

The rookie made the mistake of walking up on a drug deal going south. The hand-and-hand exchange had been made without being seen, but the cop knew what went down. Mad that he couldn't do anything about it, scared to approach the big black buck, he attacked a random female going into a project building. Standing up for the law in one of the roughest projects had to be hard, but he swore to himself it had to be done. Checking her for drug paraphernalia and drugs, he made the underage girl take her clothes off in a hallway filled with piss and knotted baggie corners that once upon a time possessed crack. He just should have stopped when he checked her pockets, but he couldn't. Making her strip down to her underwear, the young woman's private space was invaded while she was enduring her menstrual cycle. It would have been great for the rookie to find some drugs in that bloody pad, but he didn't.

Black folks took to that shit and ran with it all the way to the top. News crews everywhere reported on the story until justice was served and a new law was passed. The city officials gave the women in the drug game a step up. They were not allowed to be searched by any male cops without a female officer being present to do the search. It was something that had to be done since the young woman that was dramatized by the rookie walked away a millionaire from off the state of Pennsylvania.

The women had power because there wasn't any female cops, and the city couldn't afford to hire any. The ladies stepped up into the American dream, making moves as leaders and not followers. And I took the dream and ran with it, just like black people do. All hail to the almighty dolla.

It was time for me to put a team together. Taking applications, I comb the streets of the hood looking for the motherfucker who was more greedy than myself. It was the first of the month, LET'S GET IT…

"It's three o'clock in the morning and you still here at this bus stop?"

"Yeah yup, I'm still riding this bench waiting on the bus. "

"You and I both know that the bus ain't coming. If you knew better you would call it a night."

"But you see, sir, I don't know any better." I make shifty eyes at punk-ass officer D. Ho-Mo as he rolls up the window to the squad car. It was his fifth time riding by the bus stop, and it was his last for his shift. I didn't give a fuck about him or his observations. I was going to do me until I seen a female cop walking the beat. There was no way I was leaving the Ave. The big money was getting ready to walk the streets until the break of dawn. There's only so many hours in a day and crime never sleeps, but the police do. Officer D. Ho-Mo called it the night, ending his shift, leaving opportunity knocking for the criminal minded. And twenty minutes past three, the rush came from the north and the south, flooding the Ave. It was just me and the 24- hour store that was across the street from the bus stop. The store picked up just as much business as me and more, as I used the store as a front, too, when I got tired of sitting on the bench. I made sure they bought off of me and out of the store. Therefore the owner had no problem with the drug activity as long as there wasn't any disrespect.

There couldn't be any disrespect to the employees, vandalism out and in the store was a no-no, and no dropping drug paraphernalia in or outside of the property. Black-owned with black firepower, all hustlers abided by the rules, showing their respect. If you had a beef with anybody in front of the store, you would be banned from the store. Ya best bet is to take that shit across the street or around the corner because Joe Crack didn't play.

Joe Crack had the best surveillance cameras that money could buy surrounding his place, and I knew for a fact he watched them on the regular basis. We hustlers that thought nobody was watching did a lot of things in the alley behind his store. What happened in the dark came to the light one day when Joe Crack snatched my ass up. Why me? I didn't know at the time, but he pulled me off the corner into his store office. He gave me a glance-over from head to toe, looking over his reading glasses as I stood in front of him. He shook his head at me, pressing this button from somewhere up under his desk, revealing all these televisions on a wall behind him. My eyes glistened at the high-tech surveillance screens as the Ave. made prime time. Joe Crack turned toward the televisions, pressing a button on a remote control he now possessed.

"Take a look at the far left top television," Joe Crack said, pointing to the TV with his index finger. It was the corner TV in a row of five televisions. He pressed play. The screen went into a split left and right halves. The right was the alley way behind the store where the employees put the trash. Then there was me in the midst of the dumpster and the shadows getting high off my own supply. I watched the split screen, stunned by what I saw. I looked like a straight fiend myself as I put the fire to the spliff with my cheeks sucked in like a damn fish. I wasn't so embarrassed about shit because the high was a part of me, but I did feel stupid for not obeying the ten crack commandments.

"Damn, Joe! You on some nut-ass shit up in here." I couldn't help but to be angry, though—I felt like my privacy was invaded. I didn't care if I was on his property or not.

"I'm not on no nut-ass shit. I'm up on the game." Joe then hit the button on the remote control again. I got to see a lot more than me sitting In the cut getting high on them outside hidden cameras I had never seen out there.

Transaction after transaction, the cheap chick and faggot-ass tricks sucking dick for crumbs, police making deals with dealers to get high… and I thought their jobs were to protect and serve.

We all were playing a part in Joe Crack's home-video collection he was putting together. He had enough dirt on everybody that did dirt by his store to extort money from them. Then I put two and two together. He wanted me to pay him for keeping my secret.

I ask him why he's showing me all of this shit. And Joe just turned around and ignored the question. I then took a seat and watched me some television. I ended up peeping every video he had on the hood soap opera from last week as I didn't have a chance to make a decision. The door was locked. He made me watch, giving me a lesson that I would never forget: what happens in the dark will come to the light.

Joe told me to take the information and use it the best way I could. But I better leave his name out of it. Sharing with me a little bit of his past, I found out why I was locked up in his office. I had reminded him of his daughter who had died from a terrible accident that was really his fault, so he wept. Her name was Cheris and she fell 27 stories down an elevator shaft in a project somewhere in New York. He said it was nothing but fate that brought us together as he watched me on his tapes. For a moment he really thought I was her. A thoroughbred to the game, he said I was. I somewhat kept it pure, holding down the corners, but as I walked in the alley with the shadows of death following behind me, I would soon be dead if somebody didn't put me on to the game. The key was to understand that I would never win as long as

I didn't do right by the man upstairs. That was bullshit to me because I didn't believe in God. One day I would understand what the fuck he was rambling on about, but until then I would remain lost in the eyes of the beholder. Joe Crack was most definitely a deep dude surrounding himself with knowledge. He said his daughter sent him a message the night he came across me getting high on his tapes. He fell in love with the person of his daughter, which was me.

"Knowledge is power," was the last thing he said to me before he kicked my dumb ass out of his office. But just before I stepped out, he also informed me that I would return to his office very soon for reasons of my own.

I didn't tell anybody about the hidden cameras surrounding the store, and I kept my ass away from the alley behind it. I didn't want to get caught up on his tapes again.

"Can I get a double up off ya, Nikko?"

"Why me? You don't know a bitch from nowhere."

"It's four o'clock in the morning. You the only one out here holding, and we the only ones out here trying to make some money. Everybody else is sleeping or fucking up some headboards. And the fiends are looking for you. I'll help you get the rest of your PK off if you hook me up."

I stood there looking at the nigga that was before me. He was dusty as hell, but he had determination in his eyes. I checked the time and he was right, it was five minutes past four a.m., and the nigga was out on the block willing to work with the scraps he was given. "How do you know my name, playboy?"

"Who don't know you, SHIT? Who hasn't heard of you on this side of town?" I didn't know niggas was talking shit like that for real, and the dusty-ass nigga was really stroking my alter ego.

"You the female out here getting that money to blow, pushing trucks and shit. You keep a fly-ass, busy body, even stealing my nigga's baby momma right from right up under his nose. I would watch my back around that nigga, but besides that, everybody got mad love and respect for you. So, the question is, who don't know you?" I couldn't front; I was impressed with his answer. I like the fact he was willing to kiss my ass to get what he wanted.

"How come I haven't seen you around here before? Homestead isn't that big, and I swore I knew everybody. You an undercover?" The words that Officer D. Ho-Mo said replayed in my mind. "If you knew any better, you would call it a night..."

"You know if I ask you if your punk ass is the police and you lie to me, that's entrapment."

"Man, I ain't no police, and that's some bullshit you just said." The little dirty motherfucker had the nerve to suck his teeth. "My name is Raw, and I just got out of jail. I'm just trying to get some of the late-night money. Shit, I'm out here selling burner." His last comment didn't sit well with me, but I had to admit it—the nigga was trying to get at a dollar. He was hungry, and I was going to be the one to feed him. It's all in a day's work.

"What time you trying to go in the crib?"

I asked this question, looking for a specific type of answer. His answer would determine if this nigga Raw would work for me. I looked him dead in the eyes, awaiting an answer. Cocky as hell, he spoke. "I ain't going nowhere until you out of work." It was a wrap from there on out. The little dirt had gotten under my skin.

"You work the corner on the north by the bar, 8th Ave. and Amitty, and I'll stay right here on this corner by the 24-hour store. Take these ten dimes for fifty and come back when you're done."

The one-man show turned into a dynamic duo in a matter of a couple hours. The boy Raw was on point with his salesmanship. He sold off about three hundred dollars worth of dimes in less than an hour. I couldn't keep up with him, and I liked that. He kept me focused, and I didn't get the chance to think about getting high. Raw wasn't letting anybody past his post without them copping off of him.

By six o'clock in the a.m., 200 dimes were sold, bringing in about seventeen-five. I was cool with the help.

"The same time tomorrow, boss?" Raw asked when I broke him off his cut.

"Yessirr, baby boy," I answered quickly as I recounted my cash on hand. "Where you crashing at? I hope somewhere close by."

"I'm close. I just hope my aunt up there on 16th lets my black ass in. She be tripping. She lives next to that chick who's face you created a masterpiece on."

"Don't even bring that shit up. Lexus' ass was asking for it. You just got out of jail, but I might be on my way in for that lil' stunt I pulled in the middle of Downtown."

Dapping Raw up, we called it a night, making promises to hook up later.

CHAPTER TWENTY-SEVEN

"I just want to thank you once again for letting me and Shame Jr. crash at your place. I know if I would have went back to my house, well, my tiny apartment with all the good/bad memories, I would have relapsed." Porsha talked to the program director Mrs. Bloom, trusting her fully.

"Why don't you just move out and move on, baby?" Ms. Bloom asked, cupping Porsha's hand.

"I can't afford to move out on my own. Egypt has been taking any money I have coming in to keep her business afloat. I owe it to her anyway for using up all her product once upon a time. At one point in time, I was up on my game, making more money than I used. Then I woke up one morning knee deep in the shit. Excuse my language," Porsha said, covering up her mouth in shame. "On this unforgettable morning, I woke up naked on my bathroom floor. I had a big knot on the side of my head and I smelled of urine. I couldn't remember when I had shut my eyes, let alone why I was in pain and why I was stinking. Nothing but beer bottles and filth laid around me as I started to come to. My body weighed a ton as I tried to stand to my feet, and I only weigh a buck-o-five soaking wet. Once I was able to stand and face myself in the mirror, I damned near fell back out as my reflection scared the hell out of me. My face was so skinny and my nose was so big with dried-up blood and cocaine residue surrounding my nostrils. Then my hearing tapped in as I heard Shame Jr. screaming in the distance. I had no sense of time whatsoever. When it all came back in at a warp speed, remembering that I bet myself to do a whole 28 grams. I was trying to kill myself, Mrs. Bloom. Shoving an ounce of cocaine up my nose set Egypt back about eighteen hundred dollars.

She'll never let me go, and maybe I don't want her to. That's how I knew, Mrs. Bloom. I felt another one of those nights coming on, standing there confronting all those demons in front of an audience. I felt so damned stupid, the pain came from all angles and my spirit engulfed every bit of hate down to the last drop. I had no other choice but to break down and ask for help because getting high was what I wanted to do. I wanted to take the easy way out, but then I thought about Shame Jr. and not myself."

Porsha was crying, coming to the end of her story, and Mrs. Bloom showered her with the tender loving care she needed. Mrs. Bloom took a firm grip upon Porsha's hand and stroked it gently.

"Look at me, darling" she said, placing her index finger up under Porsha's chin, bringing her eyes up to meet hers. "You done won half the battle. You seen the trigger and put the gun down; you didn't pull it. There's people who have been working the program for months and still don't know their triggers. You are soooo brave, Porsha. You're brave for getting up out of a bad situation; you're brave because you made a way for you and your baby as you get up and carry him with you everywhere you go. You even brought him with you as you were seeking help in your recovery. Only a brave and strong person could do that, so hold your head up. You are brave enough to say enough is enough, but it's all up to you and the choices you make. And guess what? You're making the right choices. You will be an addict for the rest of your life, but it's up to you to choose what kinda addict you want to be. A young woman said to me when I was working in the prison ministry upstate at a all women's prison called Muncy was this: she was an addict and to pray for her. She said she was 'a sober addict, not a righteous one.' I wish I could have asked that woman what her name was. I wish I could have heard her story about the made-up phrase. But today I know it's your story, and everybody else's story I've heard."

"What does it all mean, though, Mrs. Bloom?" Porsha asked perplexed.

Mrs. Bloom let go of Porsha's hand and walked over to a wall that held a bookcase, picking one book out of many. She walked back over to where they were seated and handed Porsha a dictionary.

"I want you to look up the word addict in there and read me back the definition."

Porsha found the word quickly, thumbing through the first couple of pages. A smile appeared brightly on her face as she read, "To surrender (oneself) habitually or compulsively to something, as caffeine, alcohol or narcotics." Porsha paused when she was finished, looking up at her teacher.

"Now, I want you to look up righteous and tell me what it means."

Porsha put her head right back into the dictionary, skipping past the pages until she reached the letter R. "Right, right angle, right away, righteous. Okay, here we go. Righteous means meeting the standards of what is right and just."

Mrs. Bloom sat back down on the chair beside Porsha and looked her dead in the eyes, trying to come up with the best answer that fit Porsha's situation. Cupping her hands once again, she began to speak. "Now take the two meanings and make them an equation using your life experiences as the answers. Everyone has a choice to make about something, even if it's dinner, but today your choice is to stay strong or give in to your addiction. Take one day at a time, baby. You can be sober, but you will not always go about it right. You will forever and a day have to make that choice to stay clean. And don't never get too comfortable with your sobriety. Because when you do, the sneaky, slithering, conniving snake will be there with temptation in its eyes. The meaning of the quote changes with each individual, so study the quote like your life depended on it. I'm still studying the quote to the point I say it every day in the morning aloud." Mrs. Bloom and Porsha both held tears in their eyes.

"I kinda understand what you're saying, Mrs. Bloom. I have to explore all the possibilities to stay sober and exhaust the negativity to start my journey towards righteousness. But how do I get there?"

Mrs. Bloom wiped the imaginary sweat from her brow. She gave Porsha a facial expression that told her she was on the right path. Mrs. Bloom was pleased with Porsha's enthusiasm, because she was in dire need to have all the answers in one day. This was something new for the boss lady. Not the questions, but bringing her work home with her. There was something about Porsha's story Mrs. Bloom just couldn't let go. She felt bad for Porsha, but was happy to see the young woman didn't want to be a victim anymore. One thing is for sure— you can't choose your parents or the path you shall walk, but if you're dealt a good hand, take it and run. Just realize what's at stake. Good isn't always great, and vice versa goes for the bad.

CHAPTER TWENTY-EIGHT

The preacher ran across the elevated platform from the left to the right, throwing his hands up in glory.

The light beamed down on the passionate speaker, making him a miraculous view. Porsha sat next to Mrs. Bloom excited, holding Shame Jr. close to her being.

With all the shouting and organ playing, he laid asleep in her arms at peace with a smile on his face. He didn't have a care in the world.

"You got to pray about it!" the preacher shouted. "You got to talk to the Lord and tell him the good and the bad. If you hear me, let me get a amen!" The preacher's voice carried over the whole congregation as they shouted back with joy, "AMEN!"

"Church, if you feel me... hold up." The preacher took a sip of water, "LET ME BREAK IT DOWN LIKE THE YOUNG FOLK!" he shouted. "CHURCH, IF YOU FEEL ME, SAY GOD IS LOVE!" As the preacher made his point, the organ player came right behind him, enhancing every word he spoke with the right stroke of the organ keys. The congregation went wild, overdosing off the vibe within the church. The preacher kept going as he stomped his feet hard on the pulpit. Porsha couldn't keep her butt in the pew no longer. Raising to her feet to praise God, she scared the hell out of Shame Jr. He began to whimper, slowly opening up his eyes. Ms. Bloom took notice to the baby about to have a fit as he was broke out of his sleep. Gently she removed Shame Jr. from Porsha's arms, giving her the okay to enjoy herself in the name of the Lord. Mrs. Bloom retired to the back of the church into a room overlooking the church. It had a two-way piece of glass. You could see out, but nobody could see in, unless you turned the light on. On the ceiling was a speaker that you could control to hear the sermon. Mrs. Bloom turned it up just enough to hear. She sat from afar and watched Porsha shed tears of joy as she worshipped the man upstairs.

A great feeling overwhelmed Mrs. Bloom as she witnessed a soul being saved. Porsha was getting stronger day by day, taking her sobriety seriously. She didn't miss a Monday night meeting, and she attended church on her own. The bible studies on Wednesday and prayer meetings on Friday put the icing on the cake. Porsha used her pain to bring her closer to the Lord, trying to find herself so she could find me.

Mrs. Bloom felt her mission was almost complete, getting the young woman to step foot in a church. To get her faith to the point to believe in a higher power. This would be the best gift Mrs. Bloom could give her—eternal life...

CHAPTER TWENTY-NINE

"**N**ikko, why in the hell is your ass getting high so early in the morning?! You know damned well we got to make up this money!"

"Don't worry about it, Raw. I'ma be aiight once I take a shower. I'm just going through some shit right now. I ain't seen my girl or my son in days, and I'm really fucked up about this."

Raw cut an evil eye at me. "Why?" he asked irate. "You don't care about that shit! You don't speak to her or the baby when they around. You be fucked up." Raw shook his head in disgust. "I pay more attention to them than you, homie. She went to church with that lady she always hanging around with. Now, can we get back to business please?" Raw was fed up and downright mad at how the situation with me and Porsha was getting high spun out of control. He wasn't no babysitter; he was trying to get at a dollar. My lifestyle was extra bullshit not needed.

"Church?" I asked puzzled. I looked around the messy apartment, catching a faint smell of Porsha's favorite perfume.

"God can't help her ass. He don't hear people like us. I don't believe in God."

"You're tripping for real, Nikko. How don't you believe in God? You a dumbass. How you think your boyish ass got here on earth?"

"Shut the fuck up, nigga! You don't know shit about no God. You know what, nigga? I'm going to prove it to you! None of that shit in the bible is true!" I walk over to the entertainment center to turn Jay-Z on. The Holy Bible sat right there on the stand in its leather jacket.

"How the fuck Porsha go to church without her precious book? I told you, Raw, she was a no good bitch!" My anger was at its boiling point, the drug taking its own form on my soul. My every thought was distorted.

"What are you talking about, Nikko? You need to stop putting that shit in your weed. The girl writes you love letters every day, and what your dumb ass do?" By this time Raw is up close and personal in my space. I can feel his hot breath on my skin as he spat.

"Let me tell you what ya dumb ass do. You ball them up and throw them in the trash. You don't even read the shit, and it's a damned shame. But I have read a few a time or two. It was enough to make this grown man cry. Even if she is stepping out on you, what the fuck is she supposed to do? Even when you're here, you're not here! Step yo' game up!"

I stood there in awe. Looking around with a dumb-ass facial expression on my face, I didn't know one word. I cracked my jaw and did what I knew best. Picking up the bible, I unzipped the jacket, pulling it out slowly as if it was a deadly weapon. I sat it on the entertainment stand next to the naked weed and coke. Mixing the coke and weed together, I looked upon the book with disgust while Raw stood at ease in the rear watching me move. Nauseated to the touch, I ripped out the first page in the book of Genesis and read from it. "In the beginning God created the heavens and the earth. The earth was barren with no form of life."

"What's wrong with you, homie? Why would you rip the page out of the good book, nigga? Have you lost your mind!? I'm about to bounce because God getting ready to strike your ass down."

"I don't need no interruptions, motherfucker!" I bit my lip as I spoke. I was in rare form.

"God ain't gonna do shit to me!" I spoke very harsh as I meant every word I said. "Watch this…"

Taking the page I just ripped out the Bible and read from, I clothed my mixture of get-high. Raw sat on the other side of the room with his mouth wide open. He couldn't believe I did that shit. I rolled it, licked it, and put fire to the long-ass joint. I puffed, waiting for the Lord himself to strike me down.

"Homie, you're going to HELL with gasoline draws on." Raw stood to his feet, shaking his head, disgusted once again. I inhaled the smoke, turning Jay-Z up a couple of notches.

"If I go to hell today, I'm going high as a kite, nigga. But I don't think the good ol' Lord has time to strike people down today. He doesn't have time in his busy schedule to punish me because THERE IS NO GOD!" Now it's my turn to hover over Raw, poking him in the head with my finger as I made him take a fucking seat.

"YOOOOO, Nikko, I'll fuck your wannabe-boy ass up! Don't touch me or my body again. You being real disrespectful right now! You need to check yo'self. For the last time, somebody is going to fuck you up. I put that on God! I'm the fuck out! Call me later..."

"What, Raw? You leaving 'cause a nigga got in ya face? You talk a lot of shit, but you bitch made, nigga. You need me! You ain't going nowhere without no work. You do want to get at a dollar today, don't you?"

Raw looked at me with nothing but disgust. This was the female that put him on when nobody else would. His heart softened for her at that moment.

"Give me the P.K. and I'll handle everything while you get yourself together. I'll bring you your cut later."

"Naw, nigga! You bring me all the money, and I'll pay you back after I flip the P.K. I spent too much cash this week."

"You mean you smoked up too much product, bitch," Raw said discreetly, under his breath. "Whatever, you got it Nikko, just give me the shit." Raw spoke this time so I could hear him. He replied staring at the person he used to look up to and admired for being a gay woman that could get at a dollar. A shot caller, a hood baller, but now just a fiend with a couple of dollars. As quick as I came up was just how quick I fell.

"Look at my baby boy. He's getting so big and strong. Isn't he, Mrs. Bloom?" Porsha tied a bib around Shame Jr., tickling his chin while doing so.

Porsha sat among Mrs. Bloom and a few of her church buddies at the Eat-N-Park right outside of Squirrel Hill. She was getting to know everybody very well through the bible studies and the prayer meetings. Mrs. Bloom invited her to go to lunch after church with her and the ladies.

"Yes, he is Porsha. You're doing such a good job raising him, coming from where you were coming from. He's so handsome," Mrs. Bloom replied, rubbing Shame Jr.'s chubby cheeks. "I wanted to hold this luncheon for you and your son. Us ladies wanted to congratulate you on your progress." Mrs. Bloom continued to talk, giving the ladies the okay to join in when needed. She wanted to enlighten Porsha with the testimony of other women.

Porsha sat with her eyes and ears tuned in and her heart open. She was hanging on to each word they spoke as if her life depended on it. Hearing their life experiences and the different struggles they had in their lives gave Porsha the confidence that she needed to get through her own trials. It also made her feel a little more at ease around them. Porsha thought all church people were uppity and that they didn't endure the cries of hunger pains. She thought everything was well in their lives before and after finding a higher power.

But the ladies took her by surprise with their issues and their problematic children stories, the vulnerability made them the same as herself—human. She learned that even though the ladies gave a lot to the Lord, their faith wasn't always strong. But they all had one thing in common—the faith they had in a spirit they couldn't see, hear or touch.

"Give your heart to Jesus. He can do and will do all things. He can open any door, but on his terms, not yours. We think we can con God, make bargains, but we can't. He is the one in control. When we trust Him, he gives us what we need." As Mrs. Bloom closed out the conversation with a little sermon of her own, she smiled abundantly with joy.

The women continued to talk about their lives and how Porsha had grown but had a whole lot more growing to do. They socialized over the baked chicken they all had ordered with glowing smiles. Porsha's legs felt stronger than they ever had before, and she was feeling ready to stand on her own two feet. She felt it was time to move on with their lives, her and Shame Jr. She dreaded the fact that she had to go back to her biggest triggers—her home and her woman. The smiles faded and the hugs began to go around the table as the waiter dropped off the check.

"Since I invited everyone here, I'll have no problem with picking up the tab," Mrs. Bloom said with an attitude in disguise as the other women ignored the check sitting on the table.

Now that's church folks for you.

"Mrs. Bloom, don't worry about the tip, I'll take care of it. It's the least I can do since you've been so good to me."

Mrs. Bloom looked up from her handbag with graciousness written all over her face. "Do you have it to spare, baby?"

"If I don't, I'm not going to worry about it right now. God will make a way, and I know He won't let me go hungry for too long." Mrs. Bloom and Porsha both returned eyes pleased with the given answer.

"I know that's right! Praise the Lord..." Mrs. Bloom replied, giving Porsha a warm hug. Cutting her eyes at the other church members, she gave her approval of Porsha.

The dinner went well, and as planned, Mrs. Bloom was ready to put phase two of her plan into motion.

CHAPTER THIRTY

Moe stood in front of my apartment building banging on the main entrance door and on my windows for over a half hour. Moe had to come see for herself if the rumors were true that she was hearing through the street wire. Word had it that I was doing more drugs than I sold and was getting in major debt with big ballplayer-type people. They were killers first, asking no questions. Moe was convinced that her best friend needed help before she killed herself. She had sat back for a long time watching her friend kill herself slowly and couldn't do it any longer. Moe could see how easy it was for me to get sucked into the life of drugs since I was already an unloved drunk.

Both cars were parked in the mini driveway and the truck was parked at the curb right next to the apartment building. *Street Symphony* by Monica poured from the bottom-floor windows, making it clear that someone was in there.

"Egypt, I know your ass is in there. I know you can hear my big mouth yelling out here like a fool. Open the damned door, crazy ass!"

I stood in the middle of the living room floor smoking heavy. I filled my lungs with intoxication, paranoid to open up the door. There wasn't a way to cover up the drugs polluting the air, and there wasn't a way for me not to appear high out of my mind. There wasn't a lie that could cover up my addiction. I didn't want another lecture on right and wrong, the do's and the don'ts and last but not least, why are you doing this? That shit would kill my buzz.

I stood up straight and tall with my hands in midair while the band played on without a care in the world. I ignored Moe and continued to do me.

MEANWHILE...

A brown, four-door sedan was creeping up on the side of the apartment building. As it crept up, it came to a complete stop in front of my spot. Moe's mouth became dry instantly as the car came to a complete standstill. A rush of fear overwhelmed her as the rumors of someone hurting me flooded her memory bank. She didn't want to catch a bullet trying to save someone who really didn't want to be saved. She watched the car as two individuals carried on a conversation inside for a couple of minutes. A rapid heartbeat took a turn towards calm as Moe noticed it was two women. She scoped them out hard though, making sure neither one of them was that crazy bitch Lexus.

"Fuck that!" Moe mouthed, banging on the window again until the music cut off in the middle of the same song that had been playing since she had gotten there.

"Honey, everything is going to be okay, Porsha." Mrs. Bloom held onto Porsha's hand tightly, looking her dead in the eyes. You take this number and you call it as soon as you get into the house. She is waiting for you to call her. Ms. Joyce is a wonderful woman who will help you. I'm so glad you spoke up on the ride home and told me you were finally ready to move out of that bad relationship. It was only going to get worse because she is an addict wrapped up into her and is abusive in all ways. Ms. Joyce once stayed at the shelter she runs now as she fled the scene of her abusive lover, also a woman. She felt like you when I first met her. After she got on her feet, she wanted to give back to the place that helped her get a new life. I didn't want to tell you this, but I think I should. You know, Ms. Joyce tried to stay and help her girlfriend get off of drugs, but when enough became enough, she had to put herself first. When she finally got up the nerve to leave, she left on a gurney with broken ribs from being kicked in the back numerous times."

Porsha looked up and alert when she heard that. It scared the hell out of her. The thought of fighting me was going through her head. She wasn't going to let me go with my son without a fight.

"Porsha, look at me." Mrs. Bloom had to get Porsha to focus on her again as Porsha stared out the window at the apartment.

"I want you to do what's best for you and your son. You can't change someone that doesn't want to change. You can't save someone who doesn't want to be saved. So what I'm saying is, if you don't have the strength to save yourself, save your son." Porsha held on to Mrs. Bloom's tight grip and bent her head down, praying silently.

"Yes, ma'am," Porsha answered her, uncertain.

"Look at me, Porsha, pick your head up," Porsha looked at Mrs. Bloom, scared. But when she looked into her eyes, her soul felt at ease. "Now get in that back seat to get Shame Jr. Don't forget, honey, if you need me I'm just a phone call away. Let's pray before you get out."

"Egypt Winters, I know you can hear me, and I know you're in there! I can see you walking around in there, stupid! I'm not going anywhere until you let me in, dammit!" Moe stood with her hands on her hips, screaming. From the outside looking in, she posed as a love-crazed groupie as Porsha picked up on her radar. Moe had broken their prayer circle with her high- pitched voice.

"Please walk beside her Lord in her time of need. In Jesus' name we pray. Amen." Mrs.

Bloom raised her head to see Porsha ice grilling Moe. Do you know the young lady?"

"No, I don't!" Porsha spat with fear in her heart. Not the fear of fighting with Egypt to leave, but the fear of catching a case because she was ready to jump on the bitch, both the loud mouth and her baby mama. Then Porsha took a deep breath realizing this was happening way too often. There were so many different girls she couldn't name; the arguments over the phone were insane. And if she fought this bitch, there would be a lot more of them she would have to step to. It wasn't worth it. It was a fight worth walking away from.

"Go ahead and get Shame Jr. from the car seat and I'll walk you in."

"NO!!!" Porsha shouted out, startling Mrs. Bloom and herself. "I will handle this on my own, Mrs. Bloom, but thanks for trying to help." Porsha opened up the car door, removing herself nice and slow, locking eyes with Moe.

The energy between the two was generating fury. Even though Porsha knew the fight wouldn't be worth it, she was real tired of being disrespected. These bitches knew she was wifey. Porsha didn't let her guard down, though, not knowing the other female's motive. She picked Shame Jr. and the car seat up in one scoop ready for whatever.

Moe observed Porsha's every move, feeling the same way as Porsha, unknowingly. Carefully she watched, coming to a calm. The baby gave it away. it was Porsha and Shame Jr. exiting the car. Relaxing her attack mode, Moe smiled knowing she was getting ready to meet her godson for the first time.

"Here, let me help you," Moe shouted out, jogging over to where Porsha stood quietly.

"Who are you and why are you yelling for my woman?" Porsha didn't want to take no chances. She posed a threat first.

Moe looked Porsha dead in the eyes, and they were empty. She made sure to take the bass out of her voice before she answered Porsha. She didn't want no beef, and she could see the pain written all over her face. She felt bad for Porsha as she stood there face to face with the woman who loved Egypt the most and continuously got hurt for that.

"Please don't think I'm here to cause trouble, Porsha. My name is Moe. Me and Egypt been friends for quite some time now. You are Porsha, right?"

"Yeah, I'm Porsha, but how do you know my name, and how did you know that I was me?"

"Well…" Moe kinda rolled her eyes. She wasn't in the mood for a question-and-answer period. "Me and Egypt are friends, like I said before, and she told me a lot about you, and I knew it was you from the baby boy right here in your hands." Moe could see the uneasiness all in Porsha's body language. "Look, home girl, I'm not here to start any trouble, I'm just here to check up on my friend, your woman, Egypt."

Porsha heard Moe call Egypt by her name twice. She didn't talk about her in the alter ego stage, that damned Nikko. She then knew that Moe was an old friend and not a hood groupie. Mrs. Bloom's car was on stand point; she hadn't moved and Porsha felt good about that. For once since her brother died, someone had her back.

"Thanks, Mrs. Bloom, for such a nice day. I'm okay, and you can leave now. I promise if I need you, I'll call." That was Mrs. Bloom's cue to leave. She pulled off to the stop sign, made a left and went on home.

"I'm sorry, Moe, if I came off a little strong, but…"

"Stop it right there, home girl, I already know how the game goes down. I'm telling you woman to woman, there's nothing going on with me and Egypt. We are just friends. I'm really worried about her."

"Is she in there?" Porsha asked, dreading a yes answer.

"Yeah, her black ass is in there! She won't open the door!" Moe spat, placing her hands back on her hips with an attitude.

"Don't get mad at her. She's just stuck off the drugs. It makes her all paranoid and shit when she smokes too much." Porsha spoke to Moe while they were in movement towards the apartment building.

"So, I guess the rumors I was hearing are true. Damn, it's like I've been out here for a goddamned hour." Moe couldn't believe it at first and then reality set in. The life Egypt was living it was bound to happen.

I panicked as I peeked out the window, watching Porsha and Moe approach the building. Porsha was used to seeing the house trashy as hell, but Moe would pass judgment from the door. I was shaking in my boots as the confrontation was reaching its destination—her, me myself and I, up close and personal. Do you want an autograph?

Opening up the front door to the apartment, Porsha announced herself, not wanting to alarm me if I really didn't know if Moe was outside yelling for me. But for real, Porsha knew better; she knew I heard her and didn't want to face her. Porsha took Moe being there a sign from God. It was time to go, and Moe was going to pave the way for her to do so. As the door opened, I took off running out of the filthy living room into the bedroom, locking the door behind me. Anybody coming through that door could smell the toxic in the air. It was enough to get you high without putting anything to your lips. Moe walked in behind Porsha, jaw dropping to the floor. The stench made her flip her shirt up over her nose while she headed for the window she was banging on for over an hour. Moe opened the window, gasping for fresh air while Porsha broke for the bathroom with Shame Jr. It was the safest place in the tiny apartment. She didn't want him inhaling none of the toxic fumes.

The apartment itself was an embarrassment for the both of them, as Porsha and Moe stood in the middle of the floor surrounded by drug paraphernalia.

"Is it always like this, Porsha? This can't be good for the baby."

"Shit if it ain't. When she around, it's always a mess." Porsha knew that she was going to get that reaction. A friend or foe all, bitches are nosy as hell. She wanted to see me, and Porsha was going to put on a show. "You might as well leave Moe, Egypt isn't coming out of that room."

Porsha knew Moe would object to that fast. And she did.

Moe walked through the trash over to the bedroom door that held me hostage. She placed her ear against the door, knocking on it. When she didn't receive an answer, she knocked again.

"I wouldn't do that if I was you. She crazy when she high, for real."

The look on Moe's face when Porsha said let her know Moe had fell for my shit hook, line and sinker. She was about to see her friend in rare form. In the next minute, I started throwing things in the room.

"Whatever, bitches!! I'll punch you in the face! I'll hit you in your V.I.P..."

"What is she talking about... V.I.P.?" Moe asked, standing away from the door, dumbfounded.

"The question is, who in the hell is she talking to? But V.I.P. stands for very important part, which is your pussy."

"Ain't no balls there, bitch!" Moe mouthed just enough for Porsha to hear her. They both took on laughter until a loud crashing sound came from behind the bedroom door.

"Porsha you don't want to see me, for real. Put Moe's ass the fuck out of the crib right now!" While I screamed from behind the door, I threw a temper tantrum, throwing things against the walls and the bedroom door to get my point across. I wanted Moe up and out.

"Can I talk to you for a minute E? I'm ya bitch, your ace in the hole." Moe pleaded with met in her most calming tone. On the real, she wanted to kick the door down and slap the hell out of me.

"You ain't got shit to say to me right now. You just here to be the fuck nosy. I swear, bitch, get up out of my crib!" This time I put my foot through the door, kicking it hard as hell with a boot on to get my point across. Moe turned red in the face. She was ready to snap the hell out on me. I knew she didn't get down with people disrespecting her like I was, and she didn't care if I had transformed myself into a he-she or not, she would still smack the fuck out of me.

"Yo!! I swear you ain't shit to me, Moe! Get the fuck out NOW!" I put some bass in my voice, but neither girl cared.

Porsha looked at Moe as she slid down the wall and sat on the floor. Moe followed Porsha's eyes as she began to look around the apartment finding her bible in ruins. Page after page was missing from her book as she picked it up from the floor. She looked around again, looking for the pages on the floor, but there wasn't any, nor in the garbage can that she checked afterwards.

"Why did you do this to my bible? What did you do with the pages, you nut?" The apartment became quiet for a brief second. Porsha was in tears and her mind was made up. It was time to go!

Another crash came from behind the door, focusing the attention back on me. "You want to know what happened to your precious book?" I asked calmed and cool. "I tore out the pages and I smoked them to make a point to you and Raw. And while I smoked on one page, I munched on the others because I was hungry." Still calm, I spoke from behind the door until I screamed at the top of her lungs…

"!!THERE IS NO GOD!!"

Moe couldn't believe it, and she couldn't believe that Porsha had put up with Egypt for so long. She also couldn't stomach the fact that her friend was so gone.

"Fuck you and your God!" I continued to yell as I threw another temper tantrum.

"Have you ever tried to get her some help?" Moe asked in shock. She knew this wasn't the first time I had done this shit.

"Yeah, I love her and I blame myself. I've tried so many times, and you know how the saying goes—you can't save someone if they don't want to be saved."

Moe was still stuck on the "I blame myself," but nodded in agreement with Porsha about her last comment. "I know one thing, Porsha. We need to keep her locked up in there until she sobers up a lot." Moe was looking out the window as she spoke, trying to come up with a plan to get me to a rehab. She thought it could be done if she and Porsha stuck together.

When Moe turned around to tell Porsha what she was thinking, Moe couldn't understand why Porsha had a condescending look on her face, but became angry putting two and two together. Porsha was packing up her things and the baby's'.

"Where do you think you're going girl, with Egypt's son?" Moe now sported a scowl and her blood pressure was rising. She put her hands on her hips and that meant business.

"Moe," Porsha smirked while shaking her head. She was ready to go toe to toe with her. "You cool and all, and I respect you for only one reason—Egypt—but right now you out of line. I don't have no more fight in me left. I can't wait for her crazy ass to wake the fuck up anymore. I've been waiting too long already. She don't want me or my baby, and I'm the fuck out!" Putting emphasis on MY BABY, Moe knew that was a fight she couldn't win. There was no way she was getting her godson.

"Shit, Shame is my son... that's the best thing I ever did. It's because of me he was born, and if you must know, he's my nephew, now that's a fact. Another fact, my name is on the birth certificate and it resides right under the title Mother's Maiden Name, and my brother's name resides there as the father. Shame Jr. belongs to me. My brother's blood flows through his veins." Porsha made sure Moe caught on to her drift. She didn't have a problem with fighting about her son. She wasn't leaving him nowhere near me until I got my act together. "Shame Jr. is my son, and don't you ever forget that!" The sass in Porsha's voice was disrespectful as she walked away from Moe head up and ass tight. She walked into the bathroom to check on Shame Jr. He sat there in his car seat as comfortable as he wanted to be, sleeping through the noisy disturbance.

Moe went back to the door that I hid behind and sat next to it on the floor. "Is this what you want, Egypt? This small apartment can't hold any secrets. I know you heard every word Porsha just said to me."

I sat on the floor with my back against the same wall as Moe, with my face in my knees, thinking of the right words to say. I couldn't think of one....

"You don't have to explain nothing to me, but one day you'll have to answer to the little boy you gave birth to. Is this shit worth your family and friends?" Moe made one last attempt to talk some sense into me. She sat there waiting for me to answer her back while Porsha continued to go through the house packing up her and Shame Jr.'s things. Moe watched Porsha from out the corner of her eye, heated as hell. She couldn't believe the person Porsha was. You always supposed to be a ride-or-die bitch for you and yours. A sucka bitch leaves her man when the limelight turns dim.

"You's a stupid bitch! Damn, Egypt, you just going to let this chick up and leave you and take your seed? I thought you was 'bout it, but you ain't shit!" Moe tried to use reverse psychology on me. She wanted any type of reaction, good or bad, as she yelled at the closed door.

Porsha heard the word bitch and that made her place her eyes back on Moe, raising her brow. She felt the bad energy circulating between the two as Moe was passing judgment on her silently. She knew Moe was talking shit on her in her mind.

Moe seen Porsha's eyes staring and shrugged her shoulders, staring Porsha up and down. They sent unspoken warnings as their eyes okayed the beef if it was going there and down. Moe was with whatever about her friend. She wanted to help me, and she wanted my woman to help me, but my woman had her bags packed and one foot out the door. She felt Porsha was taking the easy way out.

"You know what, Moe?" Porsha broke the ominous silence. She put her hands on her hip and Moe followed suit. There wasn't anything between them but space and opportunity as they both continued to ice grill each other. "You can judge me for whatever reason you got, I don't care. Me and Egypt both done did wrong in this relationship. She don't want to stop getting high, MOE, but I the fuck do! This here woman ain't for me no more. Do you see this apartment, girl? As a matter of fact, would you want to live like this? I'm tired of this everyday shit you see here! I thought it was going to be hard for me to leave, but thanks to Egypt, it's not that hard at all. I see you standing there like you know me. You over there thinking about me leaving Egypt for the next free-meal ticket, but homegirl, like I said, it's not like that. I'm not moving in with nobody else. I'm not going to a relative because I don't have one to run to. I'm going to a god-damned shelter to save myself and yes, Egypt's son, too. Either I'm going to kill her or she's going to kill me in here messing around with these drugs. I WANT OUT!!" Porsha placed her hands in prayer position as her spirit crumbled and the tears fell.

"Do you know what it's like to watch a person destroy themselves and you can't do nothing about it, to be in the house with the person that you love and they don't see you, hear you, speak to you or touch you when you need a hug, because when they hug you it hurts them?" A long, uncomfortable silence took place as Porsha waited for an answer she knew she wasn't going to get.

"You all looking around stupid and shit without a damned thing to say. You don't know what goes on in Egypt's life, for real. You a side-step. You ain't nobody's friend until it's convenient for your ass. Let me tell you something, Moe!" Moe became nervous quickly as Porsha moved in on her. She balled up her fist, ready to do whatever.

"You can stay here with your friend, because a bitch like me is out of here! You can stay here if you want and wait for her to sober up, but you are going to be here for the long haul waiting for that. I bet you she got enough coke in there to last her about two days. PEACE OUT, EGYPT!!" Porsha screamed, carrying her voice toward the door. She looked Moe up and down once again, waiting for a response from me. In a way, she at least wanted me to say don't go, bye-bye or something. But when I spoke, I told the truth.

"It's cool, Porsha… do what it is you got to do. And Moe, she right, babygirl, you might as well follow behind Porsha because I have enough get high for about two days. And that's what the fuck I'm going to do—stay high. I'M NOT COMING OUT!!" My voice stared off faint, but by the end of my mission statement, I was screaming like a raging lunatic once again.

"HAHAHAHAHAHA…" Porsha was laughing so hard she had tears in her eyes. It was either one or the other, cry or laugh, because she was hurting with every tear she held back. Her laughter and cries held the tears of joy and pain.

"I told you, homegirl!" Porsha said sarcastically. "I'll see you around." Porsha grabbed up the rest of the bags she packed and headed toward the front door. Turning the doorknob, memories came back, flooding front and center. They were so bold and beautiful, it took her breath away. Her throat got dry and itchy and her feet couldn't move another step. Porsha gasped for air. "Am I getting cold feet?" she said discreetly. Scared of being alone for the very first time in her life, Porsha thought she should stay. Turning around, looking over the apartment, she came to grips with reality. Leaving was something she had to do. Opening up the door, the tears fell hard and fast, but Porsha continued to the car. She packed it extra slow, kinda wanting me to just say something. A please don't go, this is for the best, here's some cash to help you get settled, call me when you get there, a hug and a kiss to her or her son… but nothing. I stayed behind that closed door and didn't say a word. Since I wouldn't say anything, Porsha made one last attempt to see the woman she loved.

"Do you at least want to kiss the baby good-bye before I go? I'll take Moe outside so you can have some alone time with him?" Porsha stood there awaiting an answer as the silence grew long. Porsha then shrugged her shoulders, brushing them off. She went to Shame Jr. and looked at his beautiful face, making him the promise that she wouldn't leave him, kissing his forehead lightly.

Moe looked on, disgraced by what she had just saw from both me and Porsha. This was something she would have never believed if she hadn't seen it with her own two eyes. What more can you say? The fight was over and nobody was left standing but God. Who shall rise and who shall fall under, united we stand and divided we fall. But sometimes you must divide yourself if you don't want to fall.

Turning the lights off in the apartment, Porsha closed the door on that chapter of her life. She had done it. She finally moved the mountain as she climbed into the front seat of her car. Moe stood at the entrance of the building, looking lost for her friend. *Maybe Porsha's right*, she thought to herself. Maybe she was just a friend when it was convenient. She did fall off because of how her man felt about her friend that she knew before he came along.

Porsha seen the bruised look of confusion on Moe's face. She knew the look all too well from wearing the expression for so long on her face. NOW WHAT DO I DO? was plastered all over her face since she didn't become the super saver hoe she set out to be.

"Hey, Moe," Porsha said, hanging out the driver side window.

"What's up?" she replied, breaking out of her trance.

"I hope we can truly be friends one day, and if you want to see the baby, you're more than welcome to call me." Porsha put her hand out of the window, holding a small piece of paper folded.

"I'll keep you posted on Egypt and how she's doing, too. I'll keep you posted because I'm not going nowhere. I guess I'm on a stakeout until I see the bitch come up for air. She got to come out of the crib sooner or later and when she do, I'll be here waiting." Moe took the piece of paper. She knew the real reason why she wanted the number to be passed on, and she smiled taking it from her hand. She really wanted an update on me and knew maybe she had a chance to find out what was up through Moe. "I'm going to try and get her some help, Porsha, I promise you and Shame Jr. I'm going to get her in a rehab if I got to beat her ass all the way there."

Porsha knew it wasn't going down like that. But she said a quick prayer to give Moe the strength to pull it off.

"Good luck with that and… tell her I do love her…"

CHAPTER THIRTY-ONE

G oing to a nearby phone booth, Porsha prepared herself to make the phone call to the hotline. The day was growing long and weary and a headache was developing over her right eye. The temperature had fallen with the dark sky taking over, claiming the night. The streetwalkers came from out of hiding, placing dibs on their regular tricks. The early bird winos rested on the bus-stop benches in dire need to catch their next fix, and the dope fiends carried rank smells of trash and piss with a high stench of alcohol following behind them.

The chill in the air sent goose bumps running up and down Porsha's uncovered arms as she shut the phone booth door for privacy. She fumbled around in her purse, looking for the number Mrs. Bloom had given her, coming up with the piece of paper and a couple of quarters. She took a deep breath and put the change into the phone to place the call. Her fingers felt heavy as she hit the numbers on the phone and watched deals being made by the dealers flocking the avenue. She thought about just one more line of coke and a shot of rum to go with it before making a huge transition with her life. Shaking her head almost immediately to rid herself of the demons trying to take over, she dialed the number faster. She repeated the saying over and over again, "I'm a sober addict, but not a righteous one. I'll never know if I can do it if I'm scared of change."

"Domestic Violence Hotline for Women, can I help you?" The voice on the other end of the phone didn't sound any older than twenty-one.

"Can I speak to a woman named Ms. Joyce please?" Porsha's voice was shaky as the nervousness set in.

"This is she, can I help you, honey? Are you in trouble right now?" A lot of women call the hotline looking for Ms. Joyce. She had heard all the stories, and she kept an open call line just in case she needed to call the police while staying on the line with the victim. She had one finger on speed dial.

"My name is Porsha." Her voice was trembling, confused by the youthful voice talking back to her. "We have a mutual friend in common. Her name is Mrs. Bloom."

Instantaneously Ms. Joyce knew exactly who she was talking to. Mrs. Bloom had already put her up to speed on the young troubled lady trying to change her life.

"I'm so happy you decided to call, Porsha. I was waiting for your call. Do you need any assistance from the police?" Ms. Joyce wanted to make sure Porsha wasn't in any immediate danger.

"No, I'm okay for right now."

"I'm here to help you then. I already have a room for you and your son at one of the best domestic violence shelters set up."

Porsha then dropped the phone in a panic. She couldn't breathe as an anxiety attack hit her hard. She sobbed loud and uncontrollably in the booth as the receiver hung from the cord swinging in the air.

"Are you there, Porsha?!... Are you OKAY?!" Ms. Joyce herself began to panic over the phone as she screamed for dear life, needing Porsha to answer her.

Porsha heard the urgency in her voice and knew she had scared the poor lady. She picked the receiver of the phone back up, trying to pull herself together.

"I'm here, Ms. Joyce." Porsha finally answered after a terrified minute had passed.

"Are you okay, girl? Do you need a cab? I can see you're on a pay phone from the caller I.D."

"No, I don't need a cab. I have my own car... I just don't know if I'm making the right choice." Porsha began to sob again. She couldn't stop crying as good and bad memories came back to haunt her with ghostly chains.

"Now you listen to me Porsha!" The youthful voice became stern. "I want you to write down these directions and come to see me as soon as possible. RIGHT NOW! We will figure it out if you made the right choice when you get here." Porsha agreed, taking mental notes of the directions Ms. Joyce read off. Porsha hung up the phone, still crying and confused as hell. Her mind was made up, though—there was no turning back.

Before she started her new journey, she just had to do one last thing. Porsha was only on the Ave. she rode back up the hill and passed the apartment to see her old life once more and be nosy. Turning the headlights off, she crept by the building, sitting low in the seat. Moe's car was still there, but there was no Moe and the apartment was dark from the outside looking in.

"That bitch played me!!" Porsha thought the worst when she seen Moe was M.I.A. Moe was just another bitch Egypt had under her belt. Porsha didn't cry this time, though. She couldn't muster up one tear. She came to the conclusion that she had shed the last one. Porsha floored the gas pedal, pushing it down to the metal. She put the headlights back on and then honked the horn, putting her past in the rearview mirror and her future in the palm of her hands.

CHAPTER THIRTY-TWO

Raw was stroking the walk, looking and smelling like new money as he stepped foot into the hood bar. His name was becoming famous because of me, his boss. If the product you're selling is that flame, it sells itself and the name that stands behind it will be glorified.

The women in the bar cut their eyes at his slender physique standing six feet tall because they all knew he wasn't shit, the dressed-to-impress move didn't go over well with others. The hood politicians and the hoodrats looked beyond the spectacle, not aroused. John B and 2Pac played from the jukebox in the midst of the crowd of people who downplayed Raw's entrance. Eyes looked beyond to try and catch a glimpse of his rebel boss, who would've picked up his slack.

"Can I get a shot of V.S.O.P., Ray-Ray?" Raw asked with a toothpick hanging on the right side of his lip. He flipped it to the left showing off his tongue action for a groupie he thought might have been checking him out. Too cool.

"Sure can, Raw. Can I keep the change? I know for a fact you've had a good day." Ray-Ray the bartender had put over eight hundred big ones in his pocket alone as he was in charge of supplying the get-high and he picked him. He really didn't have a choice. I forced his hand, and Ray Ray had to deal with the prick. It was the only way he could get credit in the middle of the month when things were tight.

Many people worked with Raw, but only on the strength of me. Before I came into the picture, Raw was a two-bit hustler who sold burners to get by and stayed in and out of jail for robbing the elderly. His product was garbage and he was no good to the corners until I made him famous. He was my diamond in the rough.

"No, you can't keep my change! What!? Do I look like Nikko?"

Raw sucked his teeth with an attitude. "I don't give out handouts no matter how much you spend with the kid. Just get my damned drink!"

"I know your ass isn't Nikko, nigga. If you was, I wouldn't have to ask for a tip, I would just get one. Boney motherfucker!" Ray-Ray talked shit discreetly, but the customers close by heard him and nodded their heads in agreement.

"We all know you ain't Nikko. That's why he asked, you cheap-ass wannabe!" Somebody spoke up for Ray-Ray, but the voice was in disguise in the crowded bar. "You could never be the boss bitch!"

"Whatever. Can I get my drink please?" Raw asked, pulling down his volume because he didn't want no drama. He gave the peoples hanging around the bar a vicious look, grabbing his drink off the counter and took that change too. His facial expression did all the talking—fuck you!!!

Walking to the back of the bar, he could hear the whispers of criticism coming off the tongues of many. It really didn't bother him; he knew he would earn the respect of his peers one way or the other.

The hood politicians took up most of the space in the back of the bar as all twenty of them were in attendance and their seating arrangements were by rank. As Raw approached, they all ridiculed him to his face, showing no remorse. Raw had a few tricks up his sleeve, but he wasn't crazy. He knew when to play it cool, and this was one of those times. On the wall Raw held up, his face didn't carry an expression, but on the inside, he was grieving with envy, wanting the same love I was greeted with when I walked into a room. No matter what I did in my spare time, I still was the shit and you couldn't speak a bad word about me. I was the Robin Hood of the ghetto. Feeding the hungry, pouring out liquor for the winos, giving out Christmas cards with crack in them and sometimes giving out a whole 8-ball to a fiend who didn't have any money, just 'cause. I always had the fly chicks and the random whips to supply them with. Raw tried to do the same, but it wasn't popping off like that.

But what he didn't know was that's what I did. I didn't do it for the fame—I did it for the love. I didn't care about the saying "be feared rather than loved" because love runs out. I played the phrase backwards: fear will get you a bullet in the head when you're coming out the hood bar, but love will always send you a warning. I loved the streets because I wanted them to love me back, to fill the empty void of loneliness; to take care of the wounds others bestowed upon me. I needed the streets to be my motherly hug so I gave forth the upbringing the streets needed to get what I needed—a family. My true chase was love.

"Why you standing over here all by yourself?" Lexus ran her fingertips alongside Raw's chest. She posted up next to him, putting fire to a blunt to spark a conversation.

"What do you want, girl? I ain't got time for your shit. It's extra."

"Don't you want to hear what I got to say first before you dismiss me?" She was seductive as she licked her lips with the tip of her tongue massaging them slow. Lexus put the blunt to her mouth and puffed lightly, running the smoke up her nose. The chaser always got the fellas going. She passed off the blunt. "I want you to fuck me, flat out, but hit this weed first to relax a little."

Raw was already aroused by her touch. He spent so much time on the block, he couldn't remember the last time he parlayed up in the cock. A sly smirk danced across his lips while he took a puff of the blunt. Lexus didn't stop there neither, the fingertips just the beginning. As Raw hit the weed, Lexus' favorite song came on as planned, just in time. She swooped her hips from side to side, putting her ass all up on Raw. She teased his muscle nice and slow like Usher told her to. All eyes on her, she performed for the bar and her victim. Turning around, she replaced her ass with her hands fondling the throbbing muscle while caressing his neck with her warm tongue. The niggas paid close attention to the deep throat kiss Lexus put on Raw, grabbing their genitals, becoming sexually aroused themselves. Niggas had been trying to tap her sweet spot for a minute, but the girl wasn't having it. Lexus was grimy, but she wasn't no hoe. You had to be real special to tap that ass. Or real-ass crazy because the bitch was a stalker, a *Fatal Attraction* type—she'll boil your rabbit if you got one. And your pitbull. She'll hang his ass. Always carrying herself ladylike in the street, her looks could be deceiving. Her face held minor scars in a few places the blade cut majorly deep, but they didn't undercut her beauty. But everything that looks good ain't good, and Raw knew that going into this situation. Lexus had him by the balls, literally, and he just couldn't walk away. Showing no loyalty to his boss, Raw caressed her soft backside, pushing smoke from his mouth into hers, blowing a shotgun. One thing all niggas agree upon—if the ass comes to you, smack it, flip it and rub it down. Take it to the nearest rest spot and fuck.

Lexus knew exactly what she was doing when she approached Raw in the bar. This time she would stick it to me where it hurt the most, my pride and my pockets. Revenge is best served up with pussy in the play—it gets the prey every time. It's so cold when it goes down, and the blistering storm was coming in from the east, fast as the weather forecast successfully gave the order.

"Come on, let's get up out of here. We put on a show long enough for these clowns in the bar," Raw said, putting his arm around Lexus. He lifted his head up with the I'm-the-man attitude and put his swag into effect as Lexus worked the room going back towards the bar. Raw followed behind, picking up a six pack from the cooler. He put a ten dollar bill down on the counter, this time leaving Ray-Ray a four-dollar tip. The night was young and so was the pussy. Raw couldn't wait to get his face wet in between her second pair of lips.

Flashing lights were everywhere on the street outside the bar. It was total chaos from one corner to the next and the bodies lying on the ground in handcuffs proved it was going to be a long night for a lot of people.

"Where your car at, Raw? I'm not trying to get caught up in this sweep. I got a gun on me." Lexus pulled on Raw's arm as if they were on a date, trying to be low key. His eyes traced over her body after he heard what she said. He pondered on the thought of a sexy-ass young buck carrying a gun. He, himself, didn't have a gun.

"Come on, sexy. My ride is parked around the corner at the 24-hour store parking lot." Letting Lexus lead the way, he liked how she took control of the situation, draping his arm like a fine piece of jewelry.

"Why you carrying a gun, young buck? You planning on robbing me or something?"

"Don't talk to me like that, nigga! I don't have to rob you. The pussy itself will make you give it up willingly."

Laughing out loud, Raw shook his head, impressed by her answer. But he couldn't imagine himself tricking his dough away on a hood chick. "Whatever you say, young buck, that was a good answer. Come on and get in," Raw said, holding the passenger door open for Lexus. After he got her in the car, he put the seat belt on her, making sure she was nice and snug. For real, he didn't want any reason for the police to pull him over, while it was on the brain he did it, not wanting to forget and regret it later. He ran into the 24-hour store and copped a box of blunts and a pack of condoms for his best friend Woody. He was ready to complete his magnificent day with a glorious night. Raw got into the front seat of his ride and looked at Lexus skeptically.

"Out of all the niggas in the bar, why did you rub your ass up on me, knowing I'm cool with your chick, Nikko? You know that's my nigga, right?"

"Don't get in the car asking questions you really don't want to know the answers to. You know what?" Lexus spat, "I want to fuck with her head like she fucked with mine. I want revenge on that bitch because she played me. You wanted to hear me say it, now it's said. Can we fuck and get it over with?"

Raw was digging a grave on Lexus. She told the truth and it turned him on even more. Every time she opened her mouth, he was impressed with her sassiness. Even though she was young, she had a grown and sexy thing going on that would catch a grown mans' attention.

"Fo' sure baby, we can do whatever you like. Give me the address so we can roll out."

"613 16th Street and don't park right in front of my house. Park on the other side of the street."

"Why? Everybody in the bar seen you leave with me!"

"That's all they seen, stupid. They don't know what's up for sure; you got to leave something up to speculation. You should know to keep the peoples guessing at all times, being a top dog and all."

Once again, Lexus had impressed Raw with her antics. He was open. He was wide open, giving curbside service to Lexus. He dropped her off in front of her house. He sped around the corner to 15th and Hays, parking the rented car in front of a snaps' crib. The car was close but not in sight. He took all his money out of his pockets, placing it inside of the glove box with the rest of the p.k. that was left. A couple of early-bird pages on the hitter would kill the package so there was no need to crawl out the pussy anytime soon.

Walking up the steps to Lexus' front door, he had seen that it was open. You could hear the sweet tones of Changing Faces playing beyond the threshold. When he entered, the room was dim lit and the song playing led him upstairs to the second floor. The small candles on the side of the steps was the invitation to enjoy the moment and he did, walking into Lexus' bedroom. The scented candles gave off a baby-powder aroma, making her spot feel real comfortable. But before he got too comfy-cozy, he went back downstairs to double check the front door to make sure it was locked and checked for a back door. When he saw there wasn't a back door and the door was locked, he was ready to get down to business. Raw had heard so many stories about how females be setting up dumbass niggas that hustle so their boyfriends could rob them, and he refused to be a victim. Then he realized Lexus didn't have a boyfriend. She had a girlfriend so she had thought, and that is why he was there. He wasn't getting plotted on—he was the get back, he was creating the plot.

"They so quick to get some pussy, they never check the door twice. I will each and every time, baby." Raw talked to himself, going back upstairs, relaxed. "I'm on it like stink on doo-doo..."

Checking out the rest of the house before going back to Lexus' bedroom, he had to admit the young buck had a laid-out crib and her style was crazy-cool but tasteful, making any man real comfortable like.

"What took you so long to come to me baby? I was almost scared that you wasn't going to show up to join me." Lexus' body stretched across the neatly made sheets. Naked, she laid relaxed, smoking a blunt with her head resting on her arm.

"You wasn't worried about me. How you going to spark the blunt then without me? You could have come to see if a nigga was okay."

"Well, you look like you're okay. The only thing is, you are standing at the foot of my bed fully dressed. How are you going to make me cum like that, daddy?" Lexus posed on the bed with her back arched and her legs wide open like the 24-hour store down the hill. The smoke she inhaled on the rise up, she blew out on the down motion, touching herself very, very, very inappropriately.

"You always got something slick to say out of your mouth, and I like it, but I'm going to need you to pass that blunt and do that arch trick again... oh, yeah, I liked that shit." Climbing on top of the bed, Raw stripped down to nothing in the blink of an eye.

Raw made himself comfortable in between Lexus' legs. He took the blunt from out of her hand and headed straight downtown to investigate the pussy. He puffed the blunt, laying his head on her inner thigh. He wanted to get close enough without being obvious to give it "the smell and stick to taste test." Raw threw the statement at her knowing that Lexus couldn't resist saying something, but before she had the chance, she was surprised by a finger sliding into her hot spot, swiftly taking her breath away. His manhood rose to the occasion, feeling the heat of her warmth all over his index finger. Pulling it out slow, he hit the blunt and sniffed his finger. Satisfied by the scent , he ran his finger up and down his tongue, exhaling the smoke. Moans of pleasure overwhelmed the room as Lexus let out deep sighs of passion and Raw buried his face into a caramel spot so sweet he couldn't come up for air. Raw didn't even like going down on females, but the taste he had gotten off his finger gave him no choice. Deep-sea diving was going down.

Lexus could've won a Golden Globe Award for the stunning per-formance she put on in the bedroom with Raw. She felt she should downright have gotten paid for her acting skills. The intense moaning mixed in with the heavy breathing creating wet spots on the sheets the size of rain puddles making the orgasmic sensation the best Raw ever had. She wouldn't stop pleasing him until he begged for mercy. Every time he became soft, Lexus made sure she got it rock hard again by her possessed tongue. It was driven by a supernatural force. Raw and Lexus both had the thought one would give in first, but neither one was willing to be first to go down for the count.

Lexus used the powers she knew——the pussy always gets the job done. Breaking Raw down, he fell into a coma-like sleep a little after six in the a.m. She had succeeded with the succulent and powerful means of her pussy just like she had known she would do. *Phase One is complete*, Lexus thought to herself, running her fingertips over Raw's perfect inner belly button. He was fine as he laid there looking like a small child worn out on Christmas day.

Raw would soon succumb right into Phase Two. As he woke up to a beautiful woman standing over him completely naked besides a black silk robe hanging off her shoulders, his eyes widened. In her hand was a tray of food which consisted of steak, eggs, home fries and toast with jelly. It was topped off with a glass of orange juice, a cold beer and a rolled blunt. It was every man's fantasy to be fucked good and fed even better. CHA-CHING....

Along with breakfast in bed, he noticed his clothes washed and ironed, neatly folded on the edge of the bed by his left foot. Last but not least, the hot bubble bath drawn for her prey sent him over the edge. No woman had ever been so on point, not even his mother.

"Damn, Lex, I must have made one hell of a first impression on you last night to get the king treatment. Now who's putting on an act, woman?"

"This ain't no act, nigga. This is me all day, every day. Is the food good?"

"Yes."

"Are you full, daddy?" Lexus asked, this time with her hands between her legs.

"Yes, I'm satisfied. How 'bout you, young buck?" Raw peeped the crazed look in Lexus' eyes. She wanted him to eat her for a snack before he was out. He smiled at the lust written all over her face.

"I'm glad you asked because I am hungry for you to do that thing you did with your tongue last night." With no hesitation, Raw handled his business, giving Lexus that long tongue she desired. Twenty minutes later, he stood there holding his dick in his hands.

"Come on and bend over. Touch your toes and let me go deep!" Raw licked his lips as he watched Lexus rub herself in all the right places.

"Nope, I don't think I'm going to be able to do it." A sly smirk danced across her lips as she stopped her naughty fantasy routine. She bent over and showed him her ass before she went to her closet and grabbed up a pair of sweat pants. She wanted to hear him beg for the pussy. It still didn't matter if he did—he still wasn't getting another taste until he paid his dues.

We'll see if he doesn't trick no money away on me. Raw caught on quickly too...

"I knew it was too good to be true. Don't nobody put on a act like you just did without getting paid. I'll give it to you. You're worth a couple of dollars." Raw crossed his arms over his chest, dick still rock hard, he had to buckle to her terms and he knew it. He soooo wanted the pussy.

"I'm not a greedy bitch for right now. Just throw me two hundred for the moment, and we'll talk about negotiating another time. You know, you'll be looking for me to do that thing that you like. But I just want you to know I got my hooks in you and like a drug, you'll never want to cut me loose." Lexus spoke in a seductive tone in Raw's ear, licking his earlobe. She moved her body up against his to a random melody playing in her head. Raw couldn't do anything; she had his ass under her spell. The only thing he kept thinking about was the money. It was locked up a block away from the crib. In a blink of an eye, Lexus was in prayer position, staring at Raw's muscle. She would get what she wanted one way or another. Blowing on his muscle lightly, she watched it flex, and then she backed up.

"I got to go and get the money, Lexus, but I got you, boo, please hook a nigga up."

"Say it again." Lexus said to Raw in awe. It turned her on to hear him beg.

"I need it, girl! Damn!! What do you want a nigga to do?" Raw screamed, frustrated by the game Lexus kept playing.

"First off, I want you to go and get my money. Then we can pick up where we left off."

Raw pushed Lexus to the floor, anger stricken. As he got dressed fast, Lexus watched from the floor with a devilish grin.

This nigga trying to act like he don't want it, but you just watch and see. He ain't going nowhere with his no-pussy-getting ass but back to me. I got this weak-ass nigga by the balls. That cash flowing in his pockets will soon be flowing through mines without a doubt, she thought. Ten minutes passed and right before Lexus knew it, Raw stood in front of her. He dropped the money right next to her just like she knew he would. Just like me, she had the skills both ways.

After securing her money, Lexus made Raw beg for the pussy up until he threatened to kill her and take it. She thought, *Damn, the pussy must be real good if a nigga want to fuck it while I'm dead.* She gave him what he wanted, though, and he didn't kill her, but he did kill the pussy. As he broke her back, she couldn't help but to talk shit in her head. Changing her name from a money-getting bitch to the H.B.I.C., she smiled in between moans. Just as quick as it started, it was over. Raw was out of breath and winded for a couple of minutes, but had to pull himself together. I was blowing his pager up every five minutes.

Raw got ready to leave. "I'm coming through later on and that ass better be home since I'm paying for it. Here goes another buck on the bill to be at my beck and call. Go get some food and cook something to eat. I know a nigga going to be hungry when I get back."

"Don't you think you need to ask me if you can come back? You don't make demands around here, Raw. I run this shit. This here is my crib, and I do as I say and so will you."

Raw couldn't say a word. Lexus stood there naked and beautiful, mouthing off as usual. *She is breathtaking,* Raw thought, tuning out whatever the hell she was saying. But in all fun, he enjoyed her smart-ass mouth and played into her game.

"Damn, Lexus! Can a brother come back through when he get off of work?" Raw asked with sarcasm on the tip of his tongue.

"Yeah!" she replied, sassy as hell. "You can come back over, but don't park your car in front of my spot."

"And why in the hell not? Who you hiding from? What? You think Nikko is going to come up here and see my car at your crib?"

Lexus sighed irate by the comment. She shook her head annoyed. "This dude is stupid as hell. He can't be as stupid as he looks," she said under her breath.

"First and foremost, don't yell at me in my crib. And I don't hide out from anybody; bitches hide out from me, like your homie, Nikko. I don't give a fuck about what she thinks, but

I know you do. And about your car sitting in front of my house, that will never happen. I don't and you shouldn't neither, want anybody to know where you're resting your head at. The cops could be on your car. They could be watching your dumbass make moves, and I don't want my crib smacked because of you or anybody for that matter. You a dope boy; you supposed to know these things. You so worried niggas in the hood won't know you hitting me off. Soooo weak, nigga! Soooo weak! Bottom line—I don't want the cops to know nothing about me. Now you accept it or don't fuck with me. Walk a block or don't come through."

Raw rolled his eyes like a female tongue tied because he couldn't say anything. He didn't have a comeback line. Lexus was absolutely right about everything. Deep down he knew there was another reason and Lexus was up to no good, but she was innocent until proven guilty. On that note, he put her bullshit on the back burner. He would just keep his eyes open and his dick wet.

Picking up his car keys from the table, Raw planted a soft kiss on Lexus' lips. Smacking her on the ass before he walked out the door was just something to do to get under her skin. As he walked out the door, he knew nothing but trouble would come from their encounter. Lexus slammed the door shut behind Raw, locking both deadbolts. She laid down on her chaise picking up the remote to the television.

"Oh, yes... I will be the head bitch in charge, taking Nikko's right-hand man, making him my pawn. I'm going to make sure I get all the coke she got left, her corners, and all the clientele.

Shit, maybe even her baby momma, Porsha, fine as hell, too. Hell, yeah, I would do her anytime, anyplace, anywhere, just like Janet Jackson's song. She too fine for Nikko's dumb ass anyway. I hope she's prepared to look me in the face as I take her for everything she got. I will strip her from her worldly possessions, leaving her naked and embarrassed, just like she did me on more than one occasion. I'm coming for you, bitch. Oh, yeah, I'm coming for you."

Lexus flicked the channels back and forth under a spell of revenge, going over her plan once more. Checking Raw off the list in her mental Rolodex, she relaxed, thinking about Phase Two.

CHAPTER THIRTY-THREE

Raw sat in his rented car counting the money he made last night with a content smile on his face. He scrolled up his pager, noticing I had been blowing him up since this morning. It was time for Raw to pull his shit together and kill off the rest of the p.k.

A half hour later the p.k. was done and the money was made. He took a deep breath, knowing that he would have to hear my mouth for being three hundred dollars short. Lexus had him so gone he had forgot about what he had to do with the money, But I needed it all to flip, and if I wasn't right, he wasn't right, and that shit wasn't cool. Even though I had my shit with Lexus, I was good to him and he owed me his loyalty financially. I had put him on his feet when he had nothing and nowhere to go.

On the other hand, Raw was also tired of cleaning up the messy shit I left behind. He was so very tired of my malicious mouth making him feel less than a man when he was all the man I needed to run them corners.

He had to give respect where respect was due, though. I could make money when the corners were dried up and pagers wasn't pop, locking and dropping the cash. I always had the best product money could buy, even in a drought. Nobody in the hood knew how much coke I sat on neither because my connect was a mystery. Raw couldn't point him out if his life depended on it. Why go on his own to sell stepped-on product and be the last person you would call to get high? That's what your so-called homies did around PA. Like crabs in a barrel, the only person they want to see on top is themselves; that's why they always drag you back down. Ain't nobody have time for that. Raw had gotten him a taste of the best. Once you had a taste of the best, you can't go back to bullshit.

He had his own plan, though. He was just waiting to get his hands on the number of my connect. Then he could think about making some big moves with the hood politicians, becoming a boss of his own. Them niggas hated for real to see me do the things I did, but they gave respect because they respected the rules of the game and because I was a female with a baby. People paid close attention to me and the way I moved. I could do everything a man could do and better, even with a habit. Geared up from head to toe riding around in a Range Rover, a hundred thousand dollar truck, oh yes... niggas was envious.

When niggas was only selling twenties, I would sell dimes, and when niggas wouldn't give out deals, I gave out two for fifteen and three dimes for twenty. I gave out credit to big spenders, bought drinks for the thirsty, took rolled-up change and gave respect to the fiends for spending their hard-working money with me. I didn't talk down to them, but treated them the way I wanted to be treated. I took all the rules of the game and broke them up to work for me. I created my own flow, and niggas had to change up their stello if they wanted any of that corner money. I had shit on lock from sunset to sunrise.

You had two options for real when it came to the girl. Roll with the flow or kill a woman because of jealously. Every nigga took option A because they would never admit out loud that they were getting out hustled by a woman. I was greater competition alive than dead.

Pulling up to the stop sign, Raw noticed a lot of activity going on outside my apartment building. The curb was crowded with cars, making it hard to find a parking space up close to the building. But Raw made it happen, parking a block away from the spot. He had took little Lexus' advice about a couple of things. He smiled while he parallel parked his car. The clouds in the sky were thick, bringing in a storm from the east. They shadowed any sunshine trying to get through the skyline. Windows rolled up tight, Raw stepped out onto the street. The air held humidity, causing a light fog to take over the street. Walking up the block slowly, Raw tried to make out the strangers' faces wandering around the building. Raw thought from the door what a mess would he have to get me out of today. *Was this why she was hitting him up like a madman?* he thought, biting the corner of his lip.

Moe hadn't left from last night. She was keeping her word to Porsha. She wasn't leaving until she got to see me. Her boyfriend Tre came to join her to support his woman. He really wanted to keep an eye on his woman, though; he didn't care too much for me. Tre wished he had never intervened in the first place and wouldn't be spending his Sunday morning staking out a drunken-ass bitch's crib. All he wanted to do was watch a game, hold his woman and drink a beer. Something to eat would go great with that beer, too, he fantasized hard, hoping I would put an end to the stakeout. Tre continued to sit and daydream, checking the rearview mirror every couple of minutes. There was a man parked directly behind them a couple of cars down. He arrived shortly after Tre did, around nine o'clock. It was now eleven as Tre checked his watch and seen the man step out of his vehicle. The older man carried a funky expression on his face as he stretched long and hard on the curb. Moe watched just like Tre as the old man popped the hood of his car. He circled his vehicle, checking all four tires.

When Tre realized maybe the man needed some help with his car, he stepped out of his to see if he could help. I watched from a tiny crack in my window, still paging the hell out of Raw. I needed him to call me back or show up pronto because I had to pay my connect. I thought the man would have left by now, but it wasn't working out like that. I had missed too many appointments playing around with the work, and now the man wasn't leaving until he got what he came for. It was a family affair on the sidewalk of 12th Ave. and more and more people was joining the stakeout, waiting to catch a glimpse of me. Meanwhile, I page Raw again, putting 911 as my code. *Hurry the hell up and call back!* I think, watching the old man and Tre strike up a conversation up under the hood of the car. The police rode by making their routine rounds, paying no attention to the stakeout in progress. Moe was now joining everyone else up under the hood of the car when Raw came into bird's eye view. He stopped in front of the car, looking at all three people, puzzled.

I can just imagine what in the hell my partner has gotten herself into, Raw thought to himself, putting his hands in his pockets and poking out his chest.

"What up, ya'll? Did ya'll lose something? What ya'll doing around here?" Raw chucked his chin up, demanding an answer.

"I'm waiting for my sister round here, if you don't mind! So what? It's none of your business." Moe looked Raw up and down right before she broke out on his ass like a weave in a windstorm. Her neck rolled maliciously as she stood her ground. Tre and the old man wiped their smiles off their faces immediately.

"Look, man, don't mind her or her mouth. We just waiting for somebody in the building over there. We don't want no trouble."

"No trouble at all, young man." The old man chimed in after Tre was finished talking.

Raw stood there silent, looking at the three suspects. He knew I was an only child and didn't have no sisters. A sly smirk slid across his face as he checked his chin up once again.

"She ain't in there, homeboy, so check your girl and tell her don't talk to strangers like that. Anything is liable to happen when you let your woman shoot off her mouth like that." Raw eyeballed Tre long and hard as he spoke antagonistically.

The old man seen the jump off ready to go down as he stepped in between the two men. The old man asked Raw, "Could I talk to you in private?"

"Why? I don't know you! Fuck all ya'll, and you too old man." Raw waved his fist in the air like he was tough, ranting and raving.

The old man had had enough, taking the arm Raw was pumping, putting him in an old police choke hold he had learned when he was on the force. He bent him over and tangled Raw's body up like a pretzel. The old man whispered in his ear, "Do you know where Nikko is? My gut is telling me you do." Raw caught a queasy feeling in his stomach, embarrassed by how the old man hemmed him up without breaking a sweat. "It's very important that I see her, so tell me where she's at. I know you know where she is, too. Is she in the apartment building looking at us right now?" the old man said in a whisper with a slight chortle. Raw's pager went off and went off again as his face answered the old man's question.

I looked beyond the curtain in a distance, shaking in my boots. I didn't know what to do, but I knew I was going to have to pay the repercussions for having the man in charge outside of my apartment caught up.

"Who are you and what do you want with my partner?"

"How 'bout this? You tell me where she is, and I'll tell you who I am." The old man pushed Raw to the ground and didn't think anything of what just happened.

"Oh, my God, I'm not telling you shit, old man! You funny." Raw said, followed by laughter as he got up off the ground, dusting himself off.

"I'm more thought about than God, son. I'm the shining star in this surreal life show. I can make it rain, I can make the sun come out, and I can snatch the air from within a soul. You can say my name is Diablo." As the old man talked, he walked up on Raw. Raw was scared, but he didn't flinch when the old man placed his hand on his shoulder. In the next breath, an excruciating pain shot through Raw's body. The old man had pinched a nerve between his shoulder blade and neck. Raw screamed in pain as the shock wave lit up his upper body. Raw tried to break free, but the old man pinched his shoulder blade harder and harder until he spoke up.

"Yo, man... I think she's in the crib. She been blowing me up all morning. Now let me go!" The old man cramped Raw's style one more time, bringing him to his knees. "Are you telling me the truth, son?" His accent was demanding, running his tongue across his teeth.

"Yo, I swear to you on everything I love," Raw said in pain.

I glared back and forth at my connect, putting the finishing touches on the crib. I laughed aloud about how the old man was out there schooling my partner's young ass. I could tell right there when he had him on the ground that he snitched me out.

Tre had told Moe to go get in the car moments ago when he saw clearly the old man was here for me. After he watched the old man bring the six-footer to his knees, he was ready to go. He had told Moe they would come back later to check up on me. Tre had put Moe on to the window in the apartment that was cracked. He promised her he would climb in and pull me out himself if he had to. It was a lie, but she wasn't going to move without the promise being made and Tre knew it.

I watched Moe and Tre pull off. I wiped the sweat from my brow, sighing with relief. When they were out of sight, that was my cue to sneak out the back of the apartment building. Where Moe and Tre were parked, if I would have tried to do it earlier, they would've caught me red-handed. I had stumbled upon the trap door in the basement by accident getting high one night hiding from Porsha. And while I smoked my blunt that night, I planned an escape route just for a time like this. I hit the escape route just minutes before the old man's patience wore thin.

CHAPTER THIRTY-FOUR

Craze stands at the corner of Perrysville Avenue waiting for the pizza delivery guy to show up. His stomach is touching his back as he craves for a six-slice, white cheese pie. The Pasta Too Pizza Shop is tired of getting robbed by gun point when they send their drivers out to deliver on dead-end streets. After the fifth robbing by Craze and his crew, the owner decides to make their customers that live on the dead-end streets come to the main, lit-up avenue. There isn't light on the dead end streets because the drug dealers shoot out the street lights. Every time the city comes and fixes them, the D-Boys shoot them out again. Those boys in blue very rarely come down the one-way, dead-end streets just because of that. They are too dark and if they are ambushed going down there, they will be blinded and trapped. Nobody has respect for the police—the corner boys pop off at them every chance they get and there is no exception for the whack-ass pizza boy.

Ten minutes had passed since Craze got to the corner. He stands on the open street in broad daylight, hungry and nervous, flinching every time a car comes too close to the curb. He keeps his eye on his gun stashed between a curb and a parked car.

"General, where you at, fool? I could have been smoked this dude from right here. We got to get him before he goes back into that trap." Boo talks into his cell phone in a whisper. He ducks down low to avoid being seen by any witnesses with his eye on Craze.

"What I tell you about questioning my authority? You better not make one false move. I want that faggot to see my face when I light that ass up. I want to see the fear in his eyes when he hears the sound of the glock peel back."

"Whatever, man. If he gets back down that dead end street, he might never come back out. And I'm not going down there and neither are you. It's a whole set up if we even think about it. He got the street booby trapped from the only way in to the brick wall. Your ass isn't invincible, bro!" While Boo is ranting and raving on the phone, he never once saw General slither up behind Craze until the decisive moment takes place.

The cold hard steel cocks back, echoing throughout the phone, putting Boo on point. His eyes zero in right as Craze turns around to meet his maker. His eyes unrestricted, Craze tries to make a move for his gun. It's a bad choice for him to bend down like that towards the curb. The first shot dismembers his face and the second is a dome call to the back of the head. As General shoots Craze, the pizza boy pulls up to the corner. Hearing the gunshot, he floors the gas pedal with hysteria, not wanting to be a witness or a victim.

"Didn't I tell you you couldn't run from me, Craze?" General says, watching Craze's body shake from the aftermath of the bullet. General licks his lips, satisfied with his doings. He turns over the body with his foot, then bends down slowly and grabs Craze's dead weight body up by the collar of his coat. "Remember me, muthafucker!! I'm the one that did this to you!!" A sinister look rides General's face brazenly. He picks his pockets for a knife, never nervous, always anxious to carve, to disjoint, to slice, to kill at will and serve the dish cold. In the small of his back holstered up, the knife waits to be discovered. The light bulb appears over his head as he remembers where he put it at. Taking his good ol' time, General removes the knife from his back with one hand while holding Craze's body with the other.

"Fuck you, nigga!" General says to him and spits on the dead, half face, brains leaking out in the back grill piece. He opens up Craze's mouth, reaches in and pulls out his tongue, stretching it as far as it will go before cutting his tongue loose from his mouth. "You will roam the streets of hell deaf, dumb and blind." General laughs as he cuts off Craze's ears and then stabbed out both of his eyeballs. A satisfied demeanor takes over General's being as the savage beast comes alive right in the middle of the Avenue. Pleased with his demonic brutality, he walks back into the shadows from which he came.

Boo watches the monstrous act of ruthlessness still as a cockroach in the dark. He listened in on the phone as his brother took short, quick breaths, but couldn't utter a word, his mouth hung open in disbelief.

"I think you should pull off now, baby bro, before you become a number one suspect." Boo dropped the phone, hands shaking from the whispering voice that came through the phone from the other end.

"Am I my brother's keeper..." Boo said discreetly, trying to get his shaking hands to calm down so he can put the car in gear. Boo tries to pull off hitting the car in front of him. That wakes him from his trance, "WHAT THE FUCK ARE YOU DOING!! GET UP OUT OF HERE!!" Boo brushes off the dismay and pulls out into traffic.

General climbs into the front seat of the car he had stolen days ago to do the crime. He backed the car into a dark alley near the one-way, dead-end street. He knows wouldn't nobody grace the cut afraid of being robbed. General's crazy ass can't be more happier than a crackhead that hit the lotto. He never goes back on his word; he always gets his mark.

General pulls up to an abandoned warehouse, a factory of some sort, as the sun sets. He hits the lights off as he pulls around back, awaiting Boo's arrival. To his surprise, Boo is already there. This pleases General. He needs to be on point with every move he makes next. What he did and how he did it are considered capital punishment if he's ever caught, death by lethal injection.

In the dark, Boo sits waiting for the arrival of his brother. He has only been sitting there for about five minutes when he pulls up. Boo can't think straight, but knows he is in for a long night. They both exit their vehicles at the same time. Boo, not wanting to take another order from big brother almighty, hangs his head low. He doesn't want to be the man in charge that he so desperately wanted and needed to be at one point in time in his life. He just wants out; the bad dreams he runs from in his sleep have turned into a walking reality. Boo doesn't think he can stomach another killing, being in conspiracy with one or being the get-away driver. He just can't understand why General couldn't just kill a man. Just shoot the nigga and keep it moving. All the extra detailed shit reminds him of being a sick Jason Vorhees from the hood. What sequel was this he starred in? Boo shook his head. "Focus, dammit."

Setting up the gasoline cans, General hums the music of *A Night-mare on Elm Street*. Boo stands very still, wrapped in his thoughts. He doesn't want to disturb General's thoughts, not at all. All of a sudden the humming stops. An eerie feeling comes over General as he looks beyond the dark shadows of him and his brother. He starts taking off his clothes in a hurry and throws them in the back of the stolen car. Walking around to the back, he pops the trunk. Bare-ass naked, he stands on the gravel and rocks and broken glass without a blink of pain flashing across his face. He just smiles as he pulls the set of fresh clothes from the trunk.

He is totally prepared, with a wash tub and a gallon of water in the trunk, too. General thought of everything as he towel dries his balls. Without a care in the world, he goes over his to-do list, making sure everything is on point. Throwing all the evidence in the car, he soaks the entire car with gasoline without sparing a drop neither. Boo takes a Zippo lighter from his pocket, flips it open and ignites the flame. He throws the lighter in the car and the flames grow up full-grown instantaneously. He gets back in his car, and General follows right behind him fully dressed. Boo is ready to get back and put every detail that transpired on this night behind him. The burning car goes up in smoke and flames as they ride off looking through the rearview window, both were waiting for the boom like in the movies.

"What you think about that, Boo? I'ma pure genius! This shit right here has to make that show *Unsolved Mysteries* because a nigga like me you can't apprehend! I covered my steps too damned good. I'm too thorough for the weak-ass police to catch up with me. Them pigs don't know nothing but donuts and stale coffee!" General's adrenalin is pumping ferociously as he bangs on the dashboard, his voice loud and strong, in rare form.

Boo drives in silence, scared to blink his eyes for the sores that might appear when he closes them. His brother's twisted thoughts that come to life leave horrible images embedded in his eyelids.

"Take me to the crib, fuck boy. I got some business to attend to." General speaks to Boo while hitting him in the back of the head. He never misses an opportunity to shit on his little brother, another high he thrived on. The smack to the back of the head causes the car to sway to the left ,almost side swiping a parked car. The two of them never notice the cop car behind them until the flashing lights appear in the rearview window. "See nigga! You always on that hoe shit. You just couldn't take the smack like a man! I swear you better get us out of this. Man the fuck up!"

Boo pulls the car over, takes a deep breath and looks over at his agitated brother. Boo rolls the window down as the single cop approaches the car.

"Is there a reason why you're swerving on my road, young man? Have you been drinking at any time this evening?" The boy in blue plays his authoritative position very well. As he speaks, his hand doesn't leave his gun.

"No, sir, I haven't been drinking at all, and to answer your first question, it's my brother's fault, I swerved. We in here arguing about a female who chose me over him. When I told him he was being a punk about the situation, he hauled off and slapped me in the back of the head. He caught me off guard, and I swayed a little, but just a little officer." General's face is beyond angry as he was listens to Boo ramble on about nothing. He isn't handling the situation like General would do. He shakes his head in disgust.

"License and registration please." The boy in blue asks, never releasing his hand from his gun.

Boo looks over at General pulling the registration out of the glove box. He can feel the anger like a heat wave in the middle of summer as his animal instinct gets uglier and uglier.

"Here you go, officer" Boo says, handing the officer all the proper papers.

"Let me go and run this, and you over there," the officer points at General, "you keep your hands to yourself." The officer walks away. Boo doesn't notice the officer has a partner with him until he hands off the information he has given him to someone in the car.

"You is so stupid, Boo, why would you…" General speaks through clenched teeth, vexed.

"Shut up, nigga. The man is coming back, stupid." Boo cuts General off, getting a cheap shot off in the process. General can't do shit about it, and Boo enjoys his little moment, but he knows he will pay for it later.

"Can you step out of the car, please?" the officer says, opening up Boo's door.

"For what, officer? I ain't did nothing wrong." Boo's voice is shaky, and that's what the officer wants—to smell fear.

"I know you didn't do anything wrong and everything came back clean. I just need you to do a sobriety test before I can let you leave. I have to make sure I didn't send a drunk driver back on my streets. You kill someone, and I'll never be able to live with myself."

Boo gets out of the car and does what he is told. General calms his trigger finger down, watching them both do their thing. He was sweating bullets, thinking he was going to have to shoot his way out of Boo's bullshit, but surprisingly it worked. A few minutes later, Boo is back inside the car without a problem.

"Ya'll are good to go. I won't write you a ticket for putting another person's life in danger. I'm going to let you off with a warning this time, and next time solve your brotherly problems over a beer or two. That's what me and my brother do."

"Will do, officer," Boo says with a smug look on his face. He had pulled it off. He sat back in the front seat, awaiting sarcasm, but to his surprise, there wasn't a sly remark. A new Jay-Z song just played on the radio. And then General spoke.

"Now, that's how you man up. You took matters into your own hands and kept your cool. I can't believe it; I damned sure got to give you your props." General held out his fist and he dapped up his brother. "Now get us to the spot so I can handle my B.I."

CHAPTER THIRTY-FIVE

Boo left the door open on purpose. He wants me to escape, hoping I make it out while he and General take care of business. My days are numbered, and so it is written—even if I'm freed, I will forever be marked by death as long as General lives. It doesn't really matter to Boo; he just needs my blood off his hands. My escape might bring him some needed tranquility since he is the reason why I am in this bad situation.

Driving the speed limit back to the spot, Boo thinks about how bad he wants to be in control of the sick empire General has created. What kind of man has he become? A murderer, a rapist, a drug addict and a punk-ass follower who lives in his brother's shadow? Boo has just seen he isn't a man; he is a nobody trying to prove he's a man by kidnapping a female.

I had given Boo my word that I would stay sober and move as fast as I could to get out of the house once he got General out. The closer he got to the spot, the motion sickness kicked in stronger. His fate with death was knocking on its own door.

"Boo, why in the hell are you driving so slow? Dis ain't *Driving Miss Daisy*," General shouted, bringing Boo back to reality. "Come on, man, what's up? Grandma can drive faster than you, and she dead!"

"I got you, man. The police just got me a little shook. You know they be on our heels over here on the Hill. I'm trying to be careful with this heat in the car. I done already got us out of one bad situation." Boo and General nod in agreement, and General cools down.

"Yeah, I can see why you driving five miles per hour now," General says, smacking Boo in the back of the head. "Nigga, hurry up and get to the spot. I got to fucking pee!" General knows that something is up, but he can't put his finger on it. Boo is hesitating to get back to the spot for some reason.

The detective knows right off bat it is General at work. He looks at Craze's body laying at his feet, scared for his own life. *If the gutter rat ever comes after me, I hope my wife can have an open casket*, the detective thinks to himself right before he throws up for the second time. *General is becoming more dangerous and uncontrollable; shit, untouchable, like Elliot Ness.* He had told him to wait before doing the hit on Craze, but once again General took matters into his own hands on his own time. The mayor was on the police commissioner's back that was on his back, the lead detective, about all the bodies he was dropping, leaving no evidence.

General was emerging in his serial killer craft, and the lead detective knows he is getting worse as he allows him to get away with murder. But even if he wants to stop General, he can't; he has no evidence. General is the ill-famed, systematic psychopath. The fear causes a lump in his throat, looking down on Craze's brutalized body once again. "It's time to put an end to his reign of terror." There isn't no amount of money General can pay him to keep up these horrific murders in his streets. And the money isn't worth his soul burning in hell. First it was the woman the kids found in the woods that was gutted like a fish; now this young kid, no older than eighteen, laying here in the gutter, missing his tongue, ears and eyeballs. All this in less than a week.

News crews were starting to pop up, and the local paparazzi and crowds were forming to catch a glimpse of the young, deceased man. The detective hopes and wishes General leaves something behind so he can build a case. Combing the scene, he watches carefully as forensics picks up clues, bagging and tagging. And as he asks questions to the scarf-decked women and minors, just like every other murder that happens around here, nobody saw anything and nobody heard nothing.

"Did you hear that?" the detective asks as he walked back over to Craze's body that lays under a white, blood-stained sheet. He fumbles around in his pockets to retrieve his own, and when he does, it was calm. The similar sound continues to buzz in the detective's ear as he listens carefully.

It was like nobody else was paying attention to it; nobody else could hear it at all. He puts his ear to the ground.

"Is that you ringing, Craze boy?" The detective squats back down on his legs and uncovers Craze's body really slow. Pulling a pair of rubber gloves from the inseam pocket of his cheap suit jacket, he smiles. He checks Craze's pockets with caution. It is something he forgot to do. When he had seen Craze's body, it made his mind go blank. It is something he hasn't seen before up close and personal, and he has been a cop for a long time. The phone continues to ring. *Where is it coming from?* the detective thinks as he puts his ear to Craze's body. He travels from his chest down until he realizes the closer he gets to Craze's genitals, the louder the phone rings. A lump rises up in his throat. "Dammit!!" he says as he slides his hand down Craze's pants. The phone sits right before his penis, but something just made the detective pull down Craze's zipper. To no surprise, Craze didn't have underwear on, and his penis was missing action. The detective gags, places the evidence in a small plastic bag, tags it and places it in his pocket.

"Detective, we got a car on fire behind the old factory down on Sheffield Street in Manchester. I'm thinking it might be the get-away car that helped whoever did this get away without being seen. We also got a set of bloody footprints leaving the body from over here to back up around the corner to a dark alley. I believe he had the car parked around there. I feel since I'm putting the story of this plot together very well that maybe I can assist you if you're going to check out the car behind the factory."

The detective peered at the young officer in blue and vomit came up through his esophagus, landing on the officer's shoes. "A simple no would have been sufficient, sir" the young officer in blue says as he turns around and walk away. What he really wants to do is punch the old fart in the face, but as he goes to walk away, the detective grabs his arm.

"Hold up there, officer. Let me apologize for the unexpected shoe shine I gave you. Here," the detective roams his pockets until he finds some pocket change. "Take this and buy yourself some new ones." The detective is out of breath, trying to talk while dry heaving. Holding out his hand with the money, the officer glares at the fifty dollar bill only for a second before snatching it out of his hands.

"Come and take a look at this. Tell me what you think." The detective uncovers Craze's body. A light misty rain begins to fall and washes away the top layer of Craze's deep-rooted blood. Craze's mutilated body lays out in the open for the officer to see. The officer turns his head quickly, shocked by the dead body. He hasn't been so up close and personal with a dead body ever. He had only seen it on television, and this isn't a *Law & Order* episode.

"Look at him right now!! Boy, don't turn your head. This is your job," the detective yelled.

"Can you smell the feces undergoing his body? His tongue has been cut out, his ears cut off, eyes stabbed out, and the boy is even missing his dick. The stench of his blood provokes every weak nerve in your body, doesn't it, Mr. Boy in Blue?"

"Cover him back up, sir. Please, I've had enough" the officer says sympathetically.

"Do you think you're ready to smell burning flesh? It's grotesque to the senses of man. And knowing the sick bastard that done this, and if you're right about that car being a part of this murder, there might just be a burnt-up body in the back of the trunk."

"What the fuck is this? Are they at the spot, Boo?!" General gawks at the crowded sidewalk in front of his spot. The paramedics have someone stretched out on a gurney, which an EMS worker pushes into the ambulance. The townspeople stand their ground awaiting their fifteen minutes of fame. The news crews haven't showed up yet, but you can best believe they are nearby. Boo and General sit on the top of the hill looking down on the monstrosity. Boo's hands rest on the steering wheel as he shakes his head "NO" repeatedly.

RING! RING! RING! RING!

"Who dis?"

"You didn't look at your caller I.D., nigga. This here is ya number one."

"I cracked my screen saver and can't see shit on my phone. What's good with you?"

"YOOOO, the bitch you had in your crib got the hell out. She didn't get far, though, 'cause I just watched the paramedics put her in the back of an ambulance. She was laying in front of your spot naked, dude. And your door is wide open. The police is all up in your shit, dawg. I can hear them in there talking shit. What you better do is drop whatever it is you doing, grab up some loot and head straight for down south. You stay around here, your ass is going straight to jail, do not pass go, and do not collect two hundred dollars."

"Oh, yeah!! You think this shit is a joke; you think this shit is funny?! It was you that set me up, nigga, I bet. You always wanted to be me. What you doing over here anyway?"

"What, nigga?! I ain't no snitch, and if you thought I was, why in the hell did you make me your number one? Nigga, stop that shit, quit tripping and don't get paranoid schizophrenic on me. I came over to smoke like I always do. When I got here, I ran into the police. So go head wit that snitching, shit. Where you at anyway, playboy?"

While General is on the phone, Boo reaches under his seat to grab his heat. Feeling it with his fingertips, he can't quite grab onto it. He thinks quick on his feet, trying not to be conspicuous and drops his cigarettes on the floor of the car.

"Shit..." he whispers under his breath, but loud enough for General to hear that he did something wrong. Reaching down to pick up the cigarettes, he picks up the heat, also unseen. He places it in between the seat and the car door in hand's reach. His state of anxiety calms down, feeling the cold, hard steel up against his skin.

Don't worry about where I'm at, One, just know I can see everything. I won't be close for too long though. Thoughts of betrayal linger on and long..." General makes the comment with piercing eyes shooting daggers at Boo. Boo bobs his head to a mix tape, playing the part of not paying attention to General, but he is.

"General, you can't get in or out of the projects on the north side without showing some identification. They say they trying to keep tabs on the folks living up there, so stay clear. Oh, yeah, they got your boy Craze laying face up in the gutter missing some limbs over there on the Ave. Most definitely stay clear from that way, too. Well, you already knew that because you couldn't wait to run into him. Now that nigga? Straight snitch."

"I see you on your job One, but don't talk too much. You got any more info for me on that bitch's son?" General grits his teeth against each other.

"The only thing I came up with was her girlfriend took him and split because of her getting high. And she's in debt for about twelve five with some old-head dude she was running base for. But you need to let her and that shit go. You ain't got time to blow. You better get out of town before that hoe tell on your ass. And General..."

"What, nigga?"

"If you need some money or something, I got you, but after this shit, lose my fucking number. You hotta than a firecracker, dawg. You doing too much for me."

"What, dawg?! You can't quit me until I say it's over. I run this relationship, punk!! You disloyal motherfucker!! I'll slice your throat and piss down your neck!!" General screams like a madman into a phone that isn't connected to a line. One had hung up twenty-five seconds ago.

General is hot. If you threw cold water on him it would produce steam. He's ready to go up against any enemy he has in the state. It's all falling apart right before his eyes and he's in panic mode. It's no one's fault but his own for keeping my ass alive, but it wasn't his fault I escaped.

Boo puts the car in motion. He has his mind right for the last and final showdown between him and his brother. Making peace with God, Boo decides to do what his brother had been telling him to do his whole life—"MAN THE FUCK UP!" Boo says it aloud.

"What?" General said irate.

"Man the fuck up is what you always tell me to do all the time, right? You've been screaming it at me since I was about ten or something like that..."

"Yeah, and so the fuck what? You ready to man up, bitch? What, you ready to go against me? I'll cut you up so small the police will never find your ass." General spoke irate, but with a smile on his face.

"I left the door open so the bitch could get out. I didn't know she would pass out in front of the spot and make it hot. We agreed if I let her go, she would leave us out of it. I was going to tell you when we got back to the spot, so I thought."

General cuts Boo off. "See what happens when you think, motherfucker! Didn't I tell you to leave the thinking to me!! You made a pact with that bitch to rat me out, my own brother, you tried to set me up. Everything you said to that bitch I heard; I hear and see all things. I'm God!! She even knows our real names, don't she, Trace? You really think she ain't going to come after your bitch ass or me after what we did to her? You's a dumbass nigga!!!" General smacks Boo in the back of the head so hard he smacks it off the steering wheel.

"You's the one that started the whole fucking thing, and then it ends like this. It's over for your bitch ass right now!"

Boo pulls up to a red light, nodding his head yes to everything his brother says. But General didn't see a killer emerge right before his eyes. Boo picks up the gun he has stashed in the cut. He points it directly at General's head. The tip of the gun kisses General's temple. "Am I my brother's keeper?"

CHAPTER THIRTY-SIX

Shadyside Emergency Room is congested with the sick, the contagious, and the wounded. The EMS workers push the gurney with me on it fast, past everyone already sitting in the room. They both scream for the on-call nurse that is supposed to meet them at the door. My body begins to shake violently, drawing all the attention on me from all the different directions. Finally, the scene gets spotted by the on-call nurse who had forgotten about her trauma patient.

"Push her in here stat!" the nurse yells out, giving directions with her fingers. "Give me some room, boys," she says, busting through the crowd of cops following the gurney. "All these police, you would think she was the mayor's daughter or something. Why doesn't she have any clothes on?" The nurse checks my pupils, flashing a light into them. My eyes don't respond, but my body keeps shaking.

"We don't know what happened to her clothes, but we know she was in the freezing cold naked for about a half hour. She better be lucky a concerned neighbor placed the call after seeing her collapse on the sidewalk."

They push me into exam room number one. My body continues to have intense paroxysmal involuntary muscular contractions every two to three minutes. Pupils dilated, my small frame dehydrated, the convulsions worsen with every oncoming hit. Bruised from head to toe, patches of hair missing, the nurse finds track marks a mile long on both arms as she probes for an I.V. It takes an hour to get me stabilized. By the third sedative, the nurse is able to perform a rape kit on her suspected victim. The nurse looks into my vagina, oozing with a thick, yellowish pus to take a sample. Collecting three different hair samples and my ruptured walls forming genital herpes, the nurse hopes I have mothered at least one child because I won't be able to have a natural birth from here on out.

The machines start to beep uncontrollably, the flat line signal setting off a blue light as the nurse screams, "CODE BLUE...." My pulse is dead, my body still, my mouth frothy and then... everything stops. The crash cart gets pushed into the room just in time, my body only under for thirty seconds.

"The blaze melted the plastic of a fireman's hat to his face. The blazes temperature was in the inferno degrees as the man ran up on the blaze in search of a child he thought he saw. The fumes from the gallons of gasoline poured on and in the vehicle caused the poor man to see something that wasn't there. There wasn't any child in the vehicle." The fire chief spoke teary eyed for the man he had lost from the deliberately set blaze.

He continued, "We strongly encourage the people of the neighborhood to get involved with the crime that surrounds them, make a difference, stand up for something and don't fall for anything. If you've seen anything relating to this crime or any other crime, please call the number in the corner of your television screen. Any information leading to an arrest can possibly turn into a reward."

"There you have it, ladies and gentlemen, somber words from the Fire Chief. Stay tuned for more Channel 11 News.

The detective checks over the fire scene, finding nothing to link the car to Craze's death. The car is burnt down to the metal frame that held it together. Black soot clouds fill the night air, and you can smell gasoline a mile before approaching the scene.

"We aren't going to find anything here, sir, to link this car to the crime" the young officer in blue says.

"No shit, Sherlock Holmes, but I'm sure this was the getaway vehicle. It's the code he lives by. Fire and water destroys all evidence. I got to give it to him—the gutter rat is smart as hell." The detective talks to himself and the young officer at the same time. He walks back and forth, rubbing his five o'clock shadow in deep thought.

"What code are you referring to, sir?" the young officer asks, puzzled.

"Oh, nothing for you to worry about. I want you to stay here and knock on some doors. See if you can get any information about anything. Come and talk to me when you get back to the station. I got a lead I need to follow up on." The detective breaks out into a small jog back to his car. He thinks about his job and the sixteen years he has on the force. In all that time he hasn't killed anybody, but it was something he was going to have to do if he didn't want to go to jail himself for being a cop on the take.

"Sir... sir, wait a minute!" The young officer yells out behind the detective trying to get his attention.

"What is it?" he asks, being snatched back to reality. Running after the detective, the young officer trips and falls.

"What is it officer? I have to go!" The detective chuckles under his breath. He didn't feel so embarrassed anymore for throwing up on the young lad's shoe. Now they both had an awkward moment.

"The EMS workers just checked a young girl into the Shadyside Hospital. She was stark naked and passed out in front of your boy's, how do they speak?" The officer rolls his eyes to the left and points his finger at the detective. "Yeah, yeah, they found her in front of his crib, his door wide open. A blue uniform is requesting your presence in two places at one time. He said he has a neighbor who lives across the street willing to testify to what she has been seeing for the last year. She also saw the girl stumble from out of his building." The officer picks himself up off the ground and dusts himself off, ready to roll out with the detective. He didn't want to knock on doors; he wants to be in the mix of things. "I could do more good by your side, sir, than knocking on doors or sitting behind a desk. Let me roll with you on this one." The officer pleads his case, but didn't get anywhere.

"I agree, but this is a personal vendetta with a cop and a murderer. I don't want your blood on my hands. Next time." The detective unlocks his car door. He knows he has to crush the young officer's spirit.

"I will use my trigger finger for the first and last time to take out General's ass. But before I do, I'm going to kick him in the balls, hard." The detective shuts the door to his crappy Ford Taurus. He came to a conclusion—only Generals death would secure his freedom.

I laid in the hospital bed with no one to come to my aid. The police have yet to find out who I am. Brought back from flat line, I lay asleep as my eyelids move about rapidly, the constant nonstop dream of reality. *There must be a God,* I think, lying there unconscious, unable to move, I couldn't drink or do drugs to suppress the roaming conversations in my head. *Who else could have saved me?*

The man I cursed my whole life and blame for everything that went wrong, I call upon, praying for another chance to right a lot of wrongs I've made in my life. I don't want my life to end this way; I want to make peace with the person, the spirit that's giving me another chance. The Lord hears my cries, the cries I pray to spare my life, but the Lord will not allow me to awaken. I made my bed and now she have to lie in it. The Lord wants me to see every last mistake I've made in my life for that's what brought me to him. He wants me to appreciate life and know that he is real and always there for me.

Wanting to awaken, I lay there still as the angels slow down my life as a movie. It's chopped and screwed, but the story must be finished.

"The only man I need in my life is Jesus...."

"What did you say?" the nurse speaks to me as if I were awake. She had thought she heard me speak, but when she turned around, my body lay there still as calm waters. The nurse just shakes it off, damned near crazy from being up for eighteen hours straight.

"Only the Lord, God himself could have saved me from me. I should be on my way to being a spokesmodel for the Hell's Angels, but he saved me, he saved me..." My mind continues to talk, forced to watch the rest of my mistakes I made through my journey of not believing...

CHAPTER THIRTY-SEVEN

Raw stood across the room while the old man sat on the couch with his gun in his lap. Raw couldn't believe how clean my apartment was as he smelled the scented candles burning.

Where in the hell was all the drug paraphernalia at? The bitch never cleans up, Raw thought after using the spare key I had given him to let the two of them in. Checking out the small apartment, the old man made himself at home. He decided to relax a bit, He had a feeling his meeting with me was going to be very long. Raw knew I couldn't be far, but he wondered how long I would make the old man wait. He had already pieced together that the old man was the connect, and he felt bad for betraying his friend.

"So how long do you think you can keep me here? You might as well let me go! Egypt will show up sooner or later!" Raw spoke with bass in his voice, giving direct eye contact to the old man. His eyes demanded an answer.

Diablo crossed his legs, placing his trigger finger on the shooter. "Look over there in the ice box and fetch me something to drink. I prefer that it's cold, you fucking rat." As smooth as he wanted to be, he didn't raise his voice. His accented voice was so calm it was creepy. "There's nothing tough about you. Nikko got more heart than you, and he is really a she, a damned woman. I don't think she would've turned on you like you just turned on her, and so quickly, without a fight. She's a good girl," the old man said, taking a deep breath and sighing disappointed, "but she's not making wise decisions. She needs to pay me my money. But You... you don't ask me no questions, just do as you're told. And all that tough talk? Save it for someone who cares."

Raw ran his tongue across his two front teeth debating on saying something else or not. But when Diablo stood up from his seat to his feet, he thought to himself he'd rather not.

The old man shifted towards the window and took a couple of steps to take a gander. He dwelled on the thought that Raw would be more than enough if I didn't pull through with the money. Turning back around to put his eyes on Raw the Rat, he stood before him holding a long, tall glass of orange juice on ice.

"I knew you were good for something." The old man took his glass of juice and shook his head, repulsed by the sight of Raw. "Me, personally, I wouldn't let you be anything else but a bottom feeder." He sips from his glass, "I'm going to have a long talk with my girl when she gets here about you. You cannot be trusted. Under pressure you will fold every time. You're not built for this game here." He finishes the glass of juice.

"And you think she is? I think not!" Raw shot back angry. "She owe you money, not me. I'm not dying over nobody else's bullshit. You really think she would do it for me? I think not."

"I know she would. She's a lot of things, but loyalty to the game is her. It's the blood that flows through her veins. She doesn't have anything else. She has to love the streets because she needs them to love her back."

The door knob turned slowly until the door opened and there I stood. Nervous as hell, I stepped foot in the house, giving direct eye contact to Diablo.

"It's so nice for you to join us, Nikko. We were just talking about you." The old man took back on his sitting position. He motioned for Raw to remove his glass from his hand, and he placed his gun back on his lap, trigger finger on shooter. "Come on in, don't be a stranger. You do live here."

I shut the door behind me. I looked at Diablo's gun and instantaneously fear grew immensely inside of me. I only had half the money and no explanation why. "You right, D, I'm tripping." Playing it cool, I walked into Diablo's now open arms as he still sat. He put his arms around me and squeezed tightly as if he was my daddy. The hug was warm and comforting. It confused me, but that's what the devil does best—pulls the wool over your eyes.

"Now that we got the thoughts of bad feelings out the way, where in the hell is my money, Nikko?" His voice didn't rise, it didn't fall, it didn't carry any emotion. Neither did his eyes.

"I got you, D. Just let me holla at my man real quick." I looked at Raw and nudged my head to the right. "Let me talk to you for a minute."

Raw couldn't look me in the face. Head to the floor, he followed behind me. "Pick ya head up, nigga. You done did what you did and now it's done. Give me the money from the pack."

Raw reached down in his draws and pulled the money to the full front. "It's three hundred shy, but here goes the rest." Raw pulled out two knots of money, one containing a straight G.

"So this is twenty seven hundred? You sure all of it is there, nigga?" I asked, sickened by how her boy made the both of them look bad.

"Yeah, that's all the money."

"Aiight, aiight, let me get my shit together."

The old man sat very comfortable, very relaxed. "Are you going to keep making me wait on you after I've been waiting all morning? You know we did have an appointment. You must be real special to me, Nikko. I'm real surprised I've kept my cool."

"I know I'm special to you, D. I'm the one who keeps you connected with the hood politicians round here." Egypt counted out the money she had gotten from Raw, and it was twenty-seven hundred on the nose. All together, she had eleven thousand and no product left. She pocketed the seven hundred because the old man wouldn't take a knot of money unless it was a straight stack.

"I'm going to be straight with you, D, I only got half of your money." I sat next to the old man on the couch, my elbows resting on my knees.

"Before you give me a sob story, your man over there, as you say, has to leave my presence. He's a parasite. I can't have people around me that can't hold their ground."

"He cool, D," I tried to protest, "He helps me get that corner money, you know what I mean?" I continued, but the old man's facial expression spoke highly. It wasn't an open discussion. I was to do what I was told—get rid of him.

"Aiight... aiight, get in the bathroom, Raw!" I spat.

"What! I'm leaving up out of here! There ain't no other reason for me to be here. Shit, I was only supposed to be here until you showed up."

"See what I mean?" the old man interrupted. "Forget about him running any corners. If you keep him around, he'll betray you. He's weak, Nikko."

Egypt knew Diablo was right, but he was all she had left. She had to keep Raw around for as long as she could to get the product off.

"D, please, let me handle this! And you," I gripped Raw all up in his collar, "get in the fucking bathroom." I let him go and smoothed out Raw's shirt. Raw eyeballed the old man, and the old man turned away from the eye sore. Raw knew he shouldn't leave his homie, but he felt too embarrassed to stay. He fucked up and he knew it. "Just get in the bathroom nigga before we both get shot." This time my tone was calm. I meant business and he knew it. Raw walked a couple of steps to the bathroom with his chin in the air, a high-strung bitch, and then slammed the door.

By this time, Diablo stood by the entertainment center, admiring the expensive equipment inside. "This right here is high tech," he said, pointing at the system. He ran his fingers over the speakers that were as tall as him. "Look at all the CD's you've accumulated. What, is this a hobby of yours?"

"Yeah, it is," I smiled. I loved music more than life itself; it really spoke to me. "The last time I checked, I had about three hundred and counting. I even got some old-school in here that could remedy any fight you and your honeys get into. Let me put some emphasis on the word 'honeys.' You know just as well as I know that you are the man." The old man smiled, pushing the on button to the expensive stereo system.

"Earth, Wind and Fire is what I would like to hear. I'm old- school, baby girl. You got some of that?"

"Sure do. I got it right over here." I pointed to a CD tower to the left of him. "It's right on top of Marvin Gaye's *Greatest Hits* CD. My favorite song on that is *Sexual Healing*." I loaded up the fifty disc CD changer with some old-school funk and a little bit of new-school R & B, just showing off my taste in music, because it was most definitely well rounded. Programming some tracks in, I pushed play, turning up the volume to a reasonable level.

"I'm impressed that you have my favorite CD. Well, one of them." The old man eyeballed me and thought of a couple of ways she could make up for being late with his money, only half the money at that.

Reasons came on, blaring out of the speakers crystal clear in the surround sound. Diablo shut his eyes and pondered on a thought, a raw moment way back when. "You can never go wrong with the three elements: Earth, Wind and Fire."

I ruined his moment, "So what's up? Are you going to let me work off the money I owe you?" The old man took a seat back on the couch. He motioned for me to sit next to him. He ignored my question and touched my inner thigh with the barrel of his gun.

"The reasons... the reasons why we're here..." Diablo sang off-key with his eyes shut, putting the verse to bed. I never saw the back-hand smack land across my face until his hands crushed my throat cutting off her air supply. My eyes widened with fear as he pushed his weight down on top of me. He commands me to just listen, don't talk. His hot breath made her earlobe sweat as his tongue probed in and out of her canal.

"For making me wait so long, you have to do something for me. If you agree, shake your head yes." I shook my head yes, then pounded on the old man's chest in dire need of air. "Calm down and don't panic," he whispered, "it will only make things harder for you. It will also drain your energy, and you're going to need it." He loosened his grip, but doesn't remove his hand. The old man gave me a set of instructions to follow. When he finished, he removed his hand from my neck. I struggled for a breath deliriously.

By this time, Marvin Gaye's *Sexual Healing* came across the speakers. Diablo took his position back on the couch. I laid on the floor, scared as hell, ready to cry but unable to produce a tear. He pulled out his organ. It was thick and healthy, but his balls were small and withered up like old prunes. The old man motioned with his finger to come closer. I couldn't move, sitting there looking at the profile of the old man. My face frowned with disgust, knowing what was getting ready to happen next.

Down on all fours, I finally caught my breath. I made a purring sound as if I were a cat, a lioness. I moved in a sleek manner, shaking things I forgot I had. As I made my way to him, his muscle stiffened. It grew another inch right before her eyes, the excitement of his command turning him on profusely. "Fuck it," rolled through my head. It was the price I had to pay for breaking the number one rule—never get high on your own supply. I did as I was told, taking the old man's dick and swallowing it deep down my throat. I gagged from the tip touching my tonsils. It had been a long time since I swallowed, but not long enough. The old man stretched his arms out over the frame of the couch and tilted his head back in pleasure. I looked on, rolling my eyes at Diablo. I snickered on his muscle as my long lost skill came back to me, the skills I possessed in my dick-sucking era coming in handy as I felt his legs begin to shake. It was only three minutes in before it was over, the eruption like watching paint dry. I didn't know I had it in me, but the memories came back in full circle when he palmed my head up and down his shaft. This shit was easy, like taking candy from a baby. I could have fucked my way to the top a long time ago. But damn, is this what I've become?

As I wiped my mouth, I tried to look the old man in his face. I needed him to soften the blow. I didn't want Raw to see me on my knees bobbing and weaving, but I was too afraid to be in the apartment alone with Diablo. I just knew he wouldn't risk killing two people; the choice was made. He had to go in the bathroom——Raw risked my life, and now he had to save it by just being there.

The old man didn't soften the blow. He had no mercy, pushing my body down to the floor. "Turn over like a good little pussy cat..." The old man didn't waste no time; the motherfucker wasn't that old neither. He pushed his hard hat inside my untouched exit. I could feel the flesh rip around my anus. He pumped as vigorously as a dog in heat, erupting once again. Violently the deed was done as he collapsed on my back, sweating, out of breath. I gritted my teeth, sucked up the tears, grinned and bore the thought of stabbing the old man over and over again a thousand times for the willing rape that took place. Diablo regained his strength and stood to his feet, "I had to make you feel less than a woman; you made me feel less than a man. You don't cross me for nothing or nobody, you better recognize, this is really a man's world. You want to stomp with the big boys, you get dealt with like a big boy."

I cut him off. "So you're telling me that's what you do? You fuck people that owe you money?"

"Literally, bitch!" The old man showed his first sign of emotion. He kicked me in my mid-section, his forehead wrinkled with anger. "Better yet, little whore, I kill them. I just gave you life support, so thank me." Diablo's grip was tight on the tails of my braids as he snatched my neck back. He wanted my full attention. His eyes was piercing through my soul. He meant what he said.

"Thank you," I humbled myself and cried while doing so.

"Now, the next order of business is what to do about your debt. Your body only granted you time." Diablo mugged me in the face. I was in so much pain I doubled over on the floor. My asshole was ripped from the inside out.

"Give me the even amount of money you got. I only want stacks of a thousand. You're not getting any more of my product until you pay me the rest of my money. I will no longer support your habit. And by the way, you should eat more, m'love, you're looking kinda.... uh.... how do ya'll say it... crackish." A belligerent smile crossed my lips but it subsided very quickly after the old man smacked the grin right off my face.

"Don't look at me like that. It's a sign of disrespect. I want the truck you got sitting outside for collateral."

I rub my face with the palm of my hand, pushing the anger I have towards Diablo deep down below my soul. "Collateral, D, for real? Come on, please.... my baby daddy gave me that truck. That's all I got left from him."

"That's even more reason for me to take it. It holds sentimental value, and if a truck is all you have to remember your baby daddy by, I must say, that's a shame. Material things come and go, but memories last a lifetime."

"Yeah, I hear you, D." I fumbled around in my pockets, then walked through the apartment turning up pillows, but found no keys. The old man wasn't buying it. He had sympathy on me, but it was the last time. He pointed to my jacket. The side pocket held a bulge from the keys. I walked over to my jacket casually. It was no sweat off my back. I couldn't let the old man see he had gotten the best of me, but really he did. I knew it, and so did he. I wanted to break down, but chin checked my emotions, pulling myself up from the crying game.

The CD's I had programmed doubled up to play again. I retrieved the keys and threw them to the old man.

"Before I leave, I'll take that Earth Wind and Fire CD, too. And as for your homeboy you got stashed in the bathroom, get rid of him, Nikko!"

"Whatever, Diablo. Leave my corner boys to me. I can handle it, okay?"

"You mark my words, Nikko, he's a rat with a see-thru disguise. He sold you out three minutes into our conversation."

Just in the time it took you to bust that nut, old-ass man... "Don't worry about it, D. I said I had it. It's time for you to go." I pushed the CD he requested in his hand, took a couple of steps to the door and opened it.

"Okay," the old man said, patting the air with his hands, "I can see I've worn out my welcome. Maybe I extended my stay too long, like you're doing my money. I'm gone, but if I don't hear from you in a week, you're going to wish I killed you, bitch."

"You got my word, and my word is bond." I shut the door so fast I damned near hit Diablo with the doorknob in his back. I headed straight for the bathroom, knuckles blazing. I didn't use the doorknob this time. When my foot connected with the door, I kicked it right off the hinges. The door smacked Raw to the floor and almost knocked him out. He didn't hear me coming even though he was ear hustling. I jumped on top of the door with him under it. I could hear the heavy moans from up under there. The strength I possessed was Incredible, Hulk like. The pain ripped through my body as I continued to stomp out Raw. Raw couldn't escape the beat down of the boots—the door took everything out of him. The only thing he could do was try to protect his face, and that wasn't going too well, neither. I didn't begin to get tired until I saw I drew blood. "Be lucky I'm crashing your cranium with this beating of disloyalty, because the next time you're not going to see the spark of the flame, you're only going to feel the burn."

CHAPTER THIRTY-EIGHT

"**D**id you and your son sleep well last night?"

"Yeah, we did. I hope we didn't wake you. I tried to be as quiet as I could be when I came in."

"Naw, you was cool. What's your name?"

"My name is Porsha, and this little guy here" she patted the baby on the butt, "is Shame Jr."

"My name is Roxxie, and it's nice to meet the both of you." She smiled at the baby laying on the bed asleep and extended her hand for a formal introduction. Porsha obliged and shook her hand.

Roxxie continued, "This place got some shit with it, but don't we all, so don't judge. That's the only tic in this operation. We women tend to be messy, but this place will help you get out of a bad situation if you want to get out."

It was a bit much for Porsha to handle. She had just checked into a women's domestic violence shelter. Roxxie didn't look like she was abused, but then, neither did she. Porsha just stood there in the middle of the floor not knowing what to say, and she wasn't about to tell her story with a complete and total stranger. Roxxie was most definitely waiting for Porsha to chime in with some sort of detail of her life. An answer everybody wants to know in a place like this—what was the straw that broke the camel's back?

"Alright, then, I'll show you around later, and if you need me for anything, just give me a holler, okay?" Roxxie ended the conversation with a smile. She had seen Porsha was going to have to warm up to her before she started telling her her business. Roxxie liked a challenge—it gave her a chance to play I spy. Most of the females that came through the door couldn't wait to tell their story in dire need of a pity party.

Porsha checked out the room in the morning light as Roxxie walked out and shut the door behind her. To her right was a gigantic window that overlooked the Oakland area in peace. The streets were busy with traffic, and the people had smiles on their faces as they walked to and from their destinations. As Porsha watched out the window of opportunity, she took a moment out to do a small prayer for strength. She so desperately needed to be a part of the moving people on the sidewalk with her own destinations. "Where will this whole experience lead us, little man?"

"It will lead you to wherever it is you want to go. This place is a stepping stone, girl, all you have to do is take the first step." Roxxie reached out to touch Porsha on the shoulder, but as she tried, Porsha flinched, turning around to face the familiar voice talking behind her.

"I was just talking to myself, but thanks for the advice." Porsha went back to the bed to check on Shame Jr. when a door flew open and a teenager appeared.

"Roxxie, can I borrow your orange sweatshirt to go to the mall?" A very thin sixteen-year-old girl stood before Roxxie and Porsha with her hands on her hips. Her weaved in, glued up tracks looked horrible and she wore too much make-up. She must've been going for the cheap whore look. In shock, Roxxie and Porsha stared at the blur. She had caught the girls off guard.

"What?" She looked at the two staring at her like she was crazy. "Do I have egg on my face?" the young girl asked, scarred by their scrutiny.

"Where the hell do you think you're going looking like that, Chrissy?" Roxxie asked the too- thin teenager, giving her a name. She pulled the orange sweatshirt from a duffle bag under the bed.

"I told you I wanted to go to the mall."

"And where is your mother at?"

"Somewhere doing what trailer trash mothers do—prepare for *The Jerry Springer Show*." Chrissy jumped up into a cheerleader pose with her hands pounding the air as if she had a set of pom-poms.

Porsha's mouth hung to the floor right after she laughed at the girl's remark. She wondered if Chrissy would have said that to her own mother's face. Roxxie just shook her head and shot Chrissy a distasteful look.

"And who's going to look after your little sister until your mother comes back? I know you're hot ass will not be back no time soon." Roxxie scanned Chrissy up and down, her lip snarled up.

"I was hoping you would do me a big favor and watch the twins for me. I have two sisters remember."

"Yeah, that is right... I can only remember the one because she is Satan for real, and no, I'm not watching the bad seed today."

"Pleeeeeeaase, Roxxie...."

"I most certainly will not. Don't ask me again. You won't have me caught up in one of your hair-brained schemes, young buck. The last time I done that shit, me and your mother got into a fist fight!"

"But..." Chrissy tried to cut in.

"But nothing. I told you no, you're not going anywhere with a boy. If your mom won't put her foot down, I damned sure will." Roxxie ended the conversation by turning her back towards her. She dismissed Chrissy, who stomped back through the door she came from.

"What are you around here, Roxxie?" Porsha asked, observing the bathroom that had two doors.

"I'm a friend to some, a counselor to others and for you as of right now, a tour guide of our spacious domicile."

Porsha shook her head; she liked her answer. So, both rooms have access to the bathroom?"

"Yeah, so hide your shit. As you can see, every two rooms share a bathroom, and each room has a door to access the facility. I should add I'm a mentor, and a mother to most crossing my path in here."

Shame Jr. began to squirm on the bed. He was waking up from his nap. A small whimper escaped his mouth as Porsha went to his aid.

"Now, now, now, come on, girl, you're going to spoil him. Give me that baby and let me spoil him while I give you this tour." Roxxie picked Shame Jr. right out of Porsha's hands. "Did you do your paperwork last night?" she asked, giving the baby a smile.

"No, the woman last night told me I'll do it today once I'm settled in."

"Alright then, let's roll." Roxxie walked out the door and Porsha followed behind her closely. Walking out the room, she stepped into a long corridor. Kids ran up and down it, sliding on the freshly waxed floors. You could smell green peppers and onions being cooked throughout the spacious living arrangement. Fifteen rooms were held up in the corridor with three to four beds in most of them. The smaller rooms had only two beds in them, and they were real homey looking. The women residing in the shelter were being well taken care of. And domestic violence wasn't about color neither. Porsha was being introduced to the different ethnic groups of women. She learned very quickly the help was offered to the women to get their lives back on track, but what Porsha didn't like was that there were many addicts there. Benefitting in a program for domestic violence, their appearance spoke loud and clear. Then she stood down, "I turned to drugs, too. I'm no better than the next woman."

Black, white, young and old, they all were running from something to end up in a place like this. Dinner time came about in a matter of a couple of hours; it was around five o'clock. Porsha stood by in the colossal kitchen watching Roxxie with others prepare a meal for close to forty people. It was amazing to see women together helping each other out instead of stabbing each other in the back. She felt proud, and she wanted to be a part of something positive.

There was a lot of opportunity knocking on the door in the shelter, and whatever they had to offer, Porsha was willing to try with all strings attached. From helping women change their way of thinking about themselves, to pushing through section eight vouchers for emergency housing, if you were sick, the women's shelter had the cure. That was only if you wanted to be a better person, live better, and make a safe emotional balance for yourself and children. They had mandatory classes on abuse, self-esteem, family values, addiction and money management. If you didn't have a high-school diploma, they would pay for you to obtain one, and help with furthering education if you wanted to better yourself for a career. Who knew the city had a place like this, a safe haven?

Everyone had chores they had to do within the shelter, and by doing so, you earned currency, a shelter dollar. In the lower level of the shelter was a storage room filled with donations from people and churches within the city. Everything from soap to video games was stored down there. Most of the women saved their dollars up until it was time to move on, to start all over again. Preparing for a new apartment, they would go to this big storage room and buy dishes, pots and pans, glasses and silverware to get off to a good start.

It was certainly a different way of living for Porsha and Shame Jr. Jumping in feet first, Porsha knew she was ready to take the first step.

"Are you okay? You sound so sad."

"Well, I just left the woman I love. I miss her, and I'm worried about her Mrs. Bloom. I don't know why I miss her, but I do."

"Because once upon a time the two of you loved each other very much. It will get easier, baby, do you hear me?"

"Yeah, I hear you."

"Do you like the people here? Are you settling in well, honey?"

"It's different here, and it will take some getting used to. The people... in a way we are all the same. We're all in a struggle with something. They're okay with me."

"That's good to hear. Now all you have to do is relax. Ms. Joyce will be around to talk to you very soon. Porsha, you never know what you could learn from another person's struggle. You can find out things about yourself you've never known until someone sheds a light on it. This will be a challenge, but I know you'll pull through just fine."

The line was growing to use the pay phone in the lounge area. The limited fifteen-minute call went by quickly. Porsha held her hands over her face finishing her conversation with Mrs. Bloom. Roxxie stood by closely, trying to listen. She couldn't wait until Porsha hung up; she wanted to gossip about everybody else's business. She didn't mind putting her own out there neither, leaving nothing to the imagination. After Porsha finished her phone call, she took on Roxxie and her stories. It was like the woman wouldn't shut up.

The day was growing long and Porsha's body was calling for a bath. She went back to her room and, of course, Roxxie followed behind, toe to heel. Porsha laid Shame Jr. down on the bed. Her next step was to the bathroom. She locked the door that lead to the other room. She could hear the kids screaming on the other end, but it didn't bother her that much. She knew they crave their mother's attention. And for Roxxie, Porsha was getting ready to hide out from her. She turned the hot water on full pressure so the tub could fill up.

"Can you look after little man while I soak my body in this tub of water? I haven't had a chance to freshen up," Porsha spoke, pulling off her shirt. She had a tight t-shirt on under it that hugged her waistline. "I'm going to go crazy if I can't get at least thirty minutes of alone time."

"That's what I do, girl. I'll keep an eye on him for you. You go and get right. I'll keep everything under control. But make sure you lock the other bathroom door."

Porsha gave Roxxie a sly smirk. "It's already done."

The hot water steamed the mirrors. Porsha needed not to look at the reflection that would stare back; she was too afraid of what she might see. The scented oil she dropped in her bath took all the anxiety away when her body went under the influence of the water. Her weary bones gave in to the hot water as she relaxed in the tub. Replacing the calmness with worry, Porsha cried out for me and my touch, the thought of getting high she couldn't escape.

"Where's a good Mary J. Blige song when you need one?" Porsha said aloud, taking a long sigh afterwards. The body wash and the oil comforted her skin as she washed slowly in peace until the bathroom lock was popped. A woman in her mid-thirties came rushing through the spot, pushing the door back shut and placing the lock on it. She didn't pay any attention to Porsha in the tub as she rambled through her purse.

"Excuse me, miss! I'm, like, sitting in a tub of water, naked. Can't you see the door was locked for a reason?" Porsha grabbed a nearby towel to cover up her body as she stood to draw the shower curtain.

"Mom!! Open up the fucking door now!! I can pop the lock too!!" Porsha remembered the teenager's voice. It was Chrissy outside of the door, banging on it viciously. The lady didn't pay attention to Porsha or her daughter. She only could focus on her purse and what she was looking for. Porsha knew the dope fiend look a little too well; she was jonesing herself.

"No, you will not pop the lock, young buck. Just cool down. And don't bang on the door again!" Porsha wanted to scream and curse, but she didn't. The teenager was not hers to be screaming at. And to her surprise, Chrissy had stopped. Porsha peeked her head around the shower curtain to see the woman sitting on the toilet seat rummaging through her purse.

"Do you not care, miss, that I'm in here trying to wash my ass?" Porsha remained calm, but underneath she was hot, ten seconds from snapping the hell out. She watched the woman awaiting eye contact, but instead the woman kept right on looking through that damned purse.

"Chill out, Roxxie, you don't have nothing I haven't seen before, but I do got a bag of that shit to push if you want some."

"What?" Now Porsha was upset. This bitch was fucking with her sobriety. "You need to make sure who you're talking to before you start running off at the mouth."

Finally, the woman looked up foolishly, face flushed with humiliation. She didn't have nothing to say as her heartbeat was chaotic and a rising knot sat in the middle of her throat. Breaking the awkward silence, Porsha decided to introduce herself. She saw the lady had something serious really going on with her. She could tell from her tear-stained face. The lady was a white woman, so she was doing some serious crying.

"My name is Porsha." She introduced herself, opening up the floor to find out who this lady was hiding out in the bathroom from her kids and cutting in on her quiet time.

"Okay, Porsha." The lady gave a shy smirk. "It's nice to meet you, but I really thought you were Roxxie. Just let me push this in my nose, and I'll be on my way."

The desperation in her eyes was heartbreaking as the constant crying for mommy and the incessant knocking faded to mute. Porsha didn't have an answer; her mouth watered, but she didn't say a word. The lady that busted in on her quiet time was now sitting on the toilet snorting coke in front of a stranger. As she watched the white powder being sucked up the right nostril, her body tingled with heat. It was damned sure enticing and Porsha wanted a taste. The allure had set in and temptation was taking over strong.

"Here, you look like you want a taste bad." The bag dangled from the woman's hand in mid-air, then Roxxie came in the door and saved the day. She popped the bathroom lock from her side and busted up the little party.

"Yo, give me that shit!" Roxxie snatched the temptation right from up under her nose.

"What in Sam Hell do you think you're doing?" Roxxie came in and slammed the door shut.

"Have you lost your mind, Kay? You better pull yourself together now. I done told you don't bring this shit up in here no more. You fucking with my addiction." Roxxie's eyebrows were arched with anger, beads of sweat spotted the tip of her nose, and a light sweat broke out on her forehead.

Porsha had given up on her bath and her thirty minutes of alone time. There was a silent moment between the three. Porsha knew Roxxie's speech was just an act. Her fluster gave away her secret— she had never stopped getting high. But at that moment, Porsha knew she was finished for good.

"Thank you, God. Everything happens for a reason." Porsha hugged Roxxie and gave a wide smile to the lady as she drained the water out of the tub. She left the bathroom with a burden lifted up off her shoulders. Blunted on reality, Porsha spoke softly, "I'm an addict. I'm a sober one, not a righteous one." She felt free and walked out of the constraint placing judgment on no one but herself. This was real life, and real life doesn't stop because someone wants to change. The seduction of wrong is always around the corner, always two steps in front of you and in the back of you. Every time you think you're safe and you let your guard down, the devil comes a knocking in a head-to-toe disguise.

Porsha checked on Shame Jr. Just like a good little baby, he laid there in the middle of the bed asleep as Porsha kissed his cheek. Roxxie had slammed the door behind Porsha as she walked out. Her and the lady had it out, with the kids back to yelling and banging on the door. Porsha returned to the big window overlooking Oakland. "Before you start pointing fingers at others, look at yourself. You gotta start looking atcha self, Porsha. Porsha must die, the old me has to go... I have to start peeling off this flesh so God can work with me. YES, ME!! I have to fight for my life. The battlefield awaits me, and I have to be ready. I got to have a sword. The enemy is me, Lord, but no more.

SENSIBLE INSTRUCTION IS A LIFE-GIVING FOUNTAIN THAT HELPS YOU ESCAPE ALL DEADLY TRAPS

Proverbs 13:14

CHAPTER THIRTY-NINE

"**W**hy in the hell did you just run in the bathroom without checking to see if it was me in there? Kay, that wasn't really smart. You can't let that shit cloud your brain—you gotta think, mami."

"I don't know why I did it, Roxxie. Shit, yes I do. I'm lying."

"Why?" Roxxie asked in a quizzical manner.

"I wanted to get away from my damned kids." Kay put her head down. "And I wanted to get high. I had a rough day, honey."

"Do tell." Roxxie said, copping a squat.

Kay shook her head in disbelief as she opened her mouth to speak. "My husband told me today he was in love with his stepdaughter from his previous marriage, and he is now going to divorce me and marry her."

"Stop playing, Kay. You're kidding me, right." Roxxie couldn't believe what she had just heard. It brought her back to what Chrissy had said earlier. Her mother was somewhere doing what trailer trash do—prepare for *The Jerry Springer Show*, and that was some Jerry Springer shit. "What did you say to him?"

"I couldn't do anything but laugh. I was in so much pain from the jerk, and I did the first thing that came to mind."

"And what was that?"

"I snapped clean off my rocker. I tried to burn down that dirty-ass trailer home to the ground, but before I could, Jack put my ass out and sat me by the trash. 'Pick up is tomorrow,' was the last thing he said to me before he shut the door and locked me out. I could hear him laughing at me in the house, loud as hell. "You won't get a dime of my money neither, bitch," he yelled at me through a window.

"How much money could he have living in a trailer park, Kay? Come on, let's be for real!" "It's not funny, Roxxie." Kay's feelings were hurt, Roxxie made matters worse, laughing in her face.

"That bastard put me and my kids out, I don't have nowhere else to go, and you think that's funny?" Kay was growing angry. "I don't have any family to help me. I told you once before I burnt all my bridges with my family when I married him. He was my cousin for Christ sakes. I should have listened to my momma; I shouldn't have married that fool."

Roxxie continued to laugh at her absentminded friend. Kay began to cry and her high was gone. She slapped herself in the head and with light punches.

"Don't cry, Kay, you deserve that shit for marrying him anyway. I don't feel bad for your white ass." Roxxie got up and smacked Kay right across the face. "That's for not being aware of your surroundings. I don't want to have to explain shit to nobody about you, and I don't need anybody asking any questions neither. That girl you just sniffed coke in front of is cool, but we don't know her from anywhere. You got to be more careful, or you and your family won't have a place to stay for real." Kay shook her head, comprehending every word Roxxie said. Roxxie hugged her, trying to nurture her bruised ego. "Don't cry," she said. "Everything will work itself out."

Immediately Roxxie remembered she had left Porsha alone. "Go and check on the girls, Kay, while I go and check up on the new chick on the block." Their moment only lasted a hot second, but it was needed—Jack weighed heavy on her heart.

Roxxie only found Shame Jr. sleeping on the bed when she walked into the room. The worst entered her head from the door. "Where the hell is she at?? Could she be telling on me and Kay right now?" Roxxie was in a panic as she walked around in a circle.

Kay walked into her room, hanging her head low. She didn't know how to tell the twins that they weren't going to see their low-down, dirty daddy no more. She really didn't want to be bothered. Once again, she didn't pay attention to her children. Kay's body just went splat onto her bed.

"Mom, Mom, look! This is Porsha, and she's cool. Can you believe she got the twins to stop fighting?" Chrissy had a glow about her for the moment, until the scowl raised up from Kay.

"Who?" she asked coarsely.

"It's just me," Porsha answered, making herself seen. "I wasn't trying to pry when I came over. I just thought you needed a minute to yourself to get right. I thought I would help out by coming over here and calming the kids down."

Kay was thankful, her face relaxed as she properly introduced herself to Porsha. Before Kay could utter another word, Porsha assured her there wasn't any need for an explanation. What she did with her life was just that—her life and her business. Porsha had her own set of problems and refused to be the next Roxxie. Cutting all conversation short, Porsha returned from where she came from, the bathroom, to try again for a little R & R.

The lukewarm water soothes the rupture on my backside as the sweet sounds of Sade whisper in the background. I have lost all control of my life. I bet against myself by letting a narcotic think for me. A sober mind in wonderland tracking its next fix isn't a good look. Paying back the devil was the furthest thing from my mind, but I had to handle business.

No product, no money and no fuck boy to make things happen produces nothing. I crave for the craving as a wino cringes, lusting for the next drip of that sensation, alcohol. I have no way out. The rent's due, the trash needs taken out and there's no money to put food on the table. The woman I once knew and loved has walked out on me, and I sit here in a tub of water, asshole bleeding.

I throw myself a pity party. I'm no stranger to pain—I'm the blame, nothing will change, but the days into months, into each individual dying season. I sing a bittersweet symphony as I run from the present to no future. What lies ahead is what lies beneath; nothing but the inevitable, trouble I seek... I can't even understand myself. Who can I run to? How can I stay down? I got to get back on track before my time runs out...How could I have someone so close to me so incompetent? Can I not see with my own two eyes that this nigga is weak? There has to be some reason why I keep him close, but what? His weakness is my vulnerability and having him on my squad is a straight wrong move. I got to make my move, though, and make it fast while I'm invited to the occasion. It's time for me to get back on point around here. My ass should have paid attention to the gangster flicks. Never get high on your own supply.

"What you doing up there, girl? You paying attention, Lexus? You almost put that shit in my eye," Raw says brazenly.

"My fault, nigga, but don't get mad at me because you got lumped up by a female," Lexus chuckles. "She lumped dat ass up pretty good, too."

"It ain't as bad as her using your face for a knife sharpener," Raw shoots back with a snicker.

"That was some real fucked up shit to say, Raw, but I'm going to let it slide since we both got a mutual vendetta against the bitch."

Lexus continues to put hydrogen peroxide on Raw's bumps and bruises, disgusted by him. He is weak, a two-bit hustler with no backbone, and for the life of me, I can't see how he stands on his own two feet. He ain't shit but a cripple. Lexus shakes her head trying to overlook Raw as he flinches every time she tries to clean his wounds.

"Are you going to tell me what happened with Nikko?" There isn't any tactful way to ask, so Lexus gets to the point.

"Did you go get that food like I told you to?" he says vexed.

Lexus spots the hurt ego and eases up. "Yes, I got what you wanted. I did what I was told. Now, what's up? You can talk to me." She
massages his shoulders while droning in his ear sensuously.

He relaxes, trying to find the right words to say out his mouth.
"All I know is I could have stolen her connect today, but I done something stupid and fucked it up. She owe him money, and she ain't got it
neither. I know that, too."

"What else?"

"Nothing! Damn you nosy."

"Who you think you talking to, nigga? This here is my crib.
Check your tone in my house Raw. You need to be on America's Most
Wounded." Lexus laughs in a frazzle, and Raw can't help it—he has
to laugh at her smart remark likewise.

"For real, she caught me off guard. My face is the end result of
that. I won't let it happen again, though. The little bitch is strong as
hell, too. She kicked her bathroom door off the hinges. When the
door hit me in the head, it was a wrap for my high yellow ass."

"You let a bitch beat you up. You do know that, I hope."

"She ain't beat me up, girl! You better stop cursing at me! And
that bitch is half dude anyway. She can pump just as much weight as
me, and I was in prison before."

Lexus rolls her eyes in the back of her head with a scurrilous speculation, *Now who's the bitch?* "It's okay, baby, just be cool and tell me
what you plan to do next."

"It's cool and I know it's okay. Nikko needs me. She'll be back,
you just watch and see." Raw ends the conversation by placing Lexus'
hand on the bulge in his pants. He sits back with a beer and a smile.

CHAPTER FORTY

S weat pours off the detective's face and neck as he sits behind a desk off in a secluded area in the police station. The confinement of the small room puts more pressure on the man while he smokes cigarette after cigarette. The once fresh coat of paint is discolored and withered from dry heat, and the white walls have turned smoker's yellow from the constant smoking of the innocent until proven guilty and the hard-working detectives. Blood stains the floor beneath his feet in distinction to the beaten-out confessions the interrogation room holds. Forensics file case #L08770 is scattered about the desk with more than enough DNA on it to put whoever the person was away with a sentence that has letters behind it.

Diane James had died a brutal death by the hands of General, a.k.a. Trap Burrow. The detective has General right where he wants him—by the balls.

"I got you now and my fifty thousand dollars you sick, crazy son of a bitch," the detective speaks aloud, scratching his scrotum sac.

The phone he pulled out of Craze's pocket was close by in the evidence. He sends out mental telepathy in dire need for it to ring. The detective begins to tread the floor when a knock startles him. He tries to cover up what he can as the young officer enters the room, but he is caught red-handed trying to cover up the phone he pocketed without processing it through the proper channels.

"What is it, Officer Blue?" the detective asks, irritated.

"Well, sir," the officer moves about the room, giving off a peculiar vibe. "You forgot to pick up the rape-kit report on our female victim found in front of your suspect's apartment building.

I went to pick it up for you." The officer's chin is tucked into his neck, his eyes leery as he gives the detective the stare down.

"How did you know I was here?"

"This is the only light on over here in this corner, sir. I didn't know you were here; it just worked out in my favor since I was on the prowl for you." He placed the paperwork onto the desk with the others. The officer lightens up his strenuous expression while looking over the shabby room in the dim light. His eyes wander around the desk until he seen something colorful lighting up. "Sir, this phone is ringing. It must be on silent ring, that's why we can't hear it."

"Well, thank you, Sherlock Holmes, and if I need you, I'll make sure to yell, okay? Is there anything else that I can do for you, or maybe that you can do for me?"

"No, sir, I guess my work here is done."

"That's great!" the detective chimes in maliciously. "Like I said officer, if I need you, YOU OFFICER, I'll come and find you!"

As soon as Officer Blue leaves the room, the detective takes a dive towards the desk to obtain the phone. The screen saver, reads MISSED CALL, pissing him off. Fighting the air with frustration, he thinks he won't get another opportunity to answer the phone, but to his surprise, the phone lights up again.

"Hello..." The detective says into the phone in an undertone. The phone goes dead, there's no line, and no charger. In the heat of the moment, the detective didn't think; he just reacted. He throws the phone up against the wall, overwhelmed by derangement. It shatters on impact off the wall.

"SHIT!! WHAT HAVE I DONE!!" the detective cries out, looking at the pieces of the phone on the floor. He feels defeated, hanging his head low. He has let his anger for the nosy officer get in the way of his thinking. Now he can't get to General before General gets to him. He has to await his call.

The detective sits back down behind the desk. Time is on crack, and is running down to the last minute. Officer Blue was really beginning to get up under his skin as the continuing coincidences of him popping up at the wrong time turned suspicious. "Where did the over- anxious rookie come from?" he thinks, rubbing the stubble on his overdue shave. His head shakes in awe as he pushes his feelings to the side and picks up the report on the rape kit. Investigating the report, the detective's heart begins to weigh heavy for the victim. It could have been his daughter, and if it was, what would he do? He read over the part twice where it said she wouldn't be able to have any more children and he pondered, *How will she come to grips with being foully raped and contracting several sexually transmitted diseases?*

"The diseases!" The light bulb went on over top of the detective's head. His victim struck a nerve in his brain as he reads up on the sexually transmitted diseases she contracted. It's staring him right in the face.

"Son of a bitch! DNA don't lie! Hot dammit, baby!" The detective drops the report on the desk, clapping his hands together like he discovered a new titty bar. The wheels in his head go round and round, turning about the new information he has in his mastery.

Cracking the door to the small room, the detective pokes his head out to take a glimpse as far as his eyes will take him to the left of the hallway and to the right. He is trying to avoid running into the Robocop, convinced that he is being followed by the man who just suddenly appears from out of thin air. It is late, the police station is empty and from the looks of things, the coast is clear. He evades him out the back door, the brisk air giving him a wake-up call. The detective begins to relax as he opens up his car door, then, from out of nowhere...

"Sir, you don't need any help with anything, do you?"

The detective damn near jumps out of his skin. He turns around indignant. "Where in the hell did you come from, Officer Blue!?" The detective completely flies off the handle, banging his fist on top of his vehicle. "Are you following me?"

"No sir. I was just calling it a night when I seen you rushing out of the back door of the station. Did you find something new with the case?"

"No, I didn't find out nothing new! Just like you, I'm calling it a night!" The detective responds, unsettled and sarcastic.

"There's no need to catch an attitude, sir. I'm just trying to do my job, okay?" The frivolous officer sees that he's getting up under the detective's skin, and that's right where he wants to be—a Band-Aid laying in the cut."

"You're not just trying to do your job; you're trying to do everybody else's, you little punk! You stick to traffic violations and domestic relations and let the detective handle the murder cases!" Under pressure, the detective climbs into his front seat and slams the door behind him. He can't stand to hear another word fall from his mouth. The detective waves his hand in front of his face, giving the assumption to piss off. He didn't think giving Blue the finger was enough. His engine roars in the still of the night as he pulls off into the dark, kicking up dust in the young lad's face.

****

General sits in the front seat of the car, bleeding from the ass-whipping he never saw coming. Unconscious, he sleeps while his head rests on the window in peace. Boo is cruising the naked streets smoking a spliff. He rides two miles an hour, keeping his eye on the rearview mirror, in search of a place to collect his thoughts. Nothing is really popping with the late-night life, besides the knockoff boys rolling hard throughout the hoods, chasing the corner boys off the block and back behind closed doors. Boo cuts his eyes over to a sleeping General with apathy. He takes a drag from the spliff and inhales the smoke deeply, causing himself to choke.

"It was all good just a week ago when you caught me off guard smacking me in the face wit your piece. Yeah, muthafucka, you going to feel my pain when you wake up." Boo peeps at General, his eyes slightly open as he talks shit. Man up, bitch…. you ain't nothing but a homo, bitch…. you can't stand your ground, bitch. Well, it looks like I'm coming up in the world. AM I MY BROTHER'S KEEPER?" Boo pauses and takes another glance at his brother, then continues, "YOU DAMNED STRAIGHT I AM! THAT'S WHY I'M ENDING THIS SHIT WITH A BANG!!"

You can smell the flesh of the dead opening up the double doors to the autopsy lab. The slab tables are covered with crisp, all-white sheets; underneath lie the decomposed cadaver ready to undergo an autopsy. The lab stands at a standstill at two o'clock in the morning. Anita Baker nibbles at the ear to take the edge off the cold slabs of human flesh just laying around.

The detective waits in the distance, watching Ms. Yorkshire from afar do what she do— crack cases. She is the best in her field and the best lay he's had in a long time. The wife was on strike, as usual.

"I see you standing over there, detective. Can I help you with something?" Even though the space is fairly large, he can still hear her soft voice in the deadly calm. "Come closer detective, I swear she won't bite." She stands over a body, steady at work. Her eyes never leaves the cadaver. She is the person to call when you can't find anything to crack a case. No husband, no children, she is married to her work, the love of her life.

"I see you still listen to old Anita Baker while a genius at work." The detective stays behind Ms. Yorkshire, caressing the small of her back through her white lab coat. Overlooking her shoulder, he studies her technique very careful, as if he is trying to learn something. Her slender body feels so good in his hands and the sweet smell of her hair follicles sends all the blood from his brain and feet directly to the muscle in between his legs.

"What is it that I can do for you detective? I'm very busy at the moment." She feels the rise from behind and in an instant is turned on, but she really isn't in the mood for another night of meaningless sex with a married man. Still, she must admit she misses his passionate touch. "The investigation report on your victim, Ms. James, came back inconclusive in my book, so I have to start from scratch. I should have done it myself, but I let one of your good friends do the job after he persuaded me he could handle it. I thank you, Reggie, for having me stay here all night."

"Good ol' Reggie, I can always count on him to mess something up. But listen, I need a big favor from you, and I'll do whatever it is you want me to do."

"Even leave your wife you claim to hate so much?" Amusingly clever, the medical examiner forces the corners of her mouth up to form a smile she didn't want to wear.

"Come on, York Peppermint Patty, that's kinda to the extreme, don't you think? You really don't want to be in a relationship with the living when you're married to the dead. You love your work more than anything. Anybody can see that, even Ray Charles, and he's blind."

She can't help but to smile and appreciate the way he approaches the situation to let her down easy. For the past year, the late nights turned into mornings, the mornings she often slept recovering from the undeserving touch of the detective. His smooth jive talk and pecan- buttercup skin made him solely irresistible; it shut all doors that compromised his infidelity. The truth is, it isn't problematic for her to be seeing a married man when he is comforting the essence of her naked body, but she knows it is wrong fornicating with a married man when he is in God's eyes. The temptation—so sweet, so alluring, like a moth to a flame, his tantalizing touch tainting her apprehension. Nose wide open, she makes her body reject the finesse of his stroke. She doesn't want to fall victim to his pastime influences.

"Are you going to play hard to get tonight? You know what I want, and you know what I can do. You do me a favor and I'll do you one even better." The detective pulls at her lab coat playfully. He wants to taste her sweetness between her legs; yes, indeed, it was soooo sweet.

"I'm having a bad day, detective, and having sex with you will complicate things. , Look, I'll do whatever it is you need me to do as long as this is the last time."

The detective is stunned! He can't believe he just got shot down; the joke was on him. He wants to have sex with the woman he had grown to love despite his hand in marriage. He has no choice but to stand down, though the facial expression of "it's over" are written all over the front page of her demeanor. She and he have ran their crash course, and it was back to business as usual.

"I got a report here on a young lady, and I need to find out who she is. When you find out who she is, I want you to run her DNA up against Ms. Diane James, the lady you're cutting on now. I need to know what you come up with ASAP."

"That's funny how fate works. It was meant for Reggie to forget to upload the conclusions he found from the fibers and nail scrapings onto the computer. She would be gone if he hadn't done that."

"Good ol' Reggie. Like I said earlier..." the detective says, following up with a slight chuckle. Then a moment of silence takes place.

"I've heard your name coming up in some internal affairs stuff," Ms. Yorkshire says, trying to break the awkward mood, but she only made things worse. "What are you getting yourself into?"

The detective plays it cool. "I'm clean as a whistle, I swear it on the Lord above. Don't worry about it; it's just a rumor I'm betting. Don't you worry your pretty little head about it. I'm fine."

"Then why are you talking repetitively? Don't worry about it, huh?"

Brushing his shoulders off, he ignores her last comment and hands over the rape-kit report with worrisome eyes.

"I've been doing small favors for you for a long time. I better not get mixed up in any illegal activity surrounding you or any of the past cases I've so called "done favors for you on." Ms. Yorkshire seizes the report from his hands, taking a glance over it while giving him guilty eye daggers in the process. "Why do you need this?" It is another question she has to ask, but she doesn't really care for an answer. She just wants to bust his balls for making her fall in love with him.

"It's just a hunch I'm working on." The anger rises in his tone of voice. "Are you going to help me or not? I don't have time for this." The detective's eyes hit the floor. His emotion give him away. The guilt just seems to pour out of him as he stands as still as an untouched pond. "Don't be pissed off now because I won't leave my wife."

"Don't get beside yourself. You're cute, but not special." Fist clenched, she smashes it down into the palm of her hand as she speaks, her voice calm. "Let me quote you—'I love my work more than anything,' right? 'I'm married to the dead.' Remember? I don't want your wife's sloppy seconds, you selfish asshole."

The detective pulls Ms. Yorkshire close to his waist, forcefully. "That woman laying on that table could be this girl's mother!" He points his index finger to the file she holds in her hand. "I'm right about this one." The detective opens up the report still in her hand and points to a fact, "but the proof is in the pudding." He takes both of her hands and pushes the report closed. "I need you." His demeanor humane, his attitude prudent, his eyes staring into the depth of her soul.

"When do you need this?" Ms. Yorkshire has given in.

"I needed it an hour ago."

"It's done. Come back and pick it up at 3 a.m."

"I'll be here at 2:59." The detective turns around with swag. Arrogance fills the pep in his step walking out the double doors.

The hospital room has a chill in it. It took hours of nursing before I had finally calmed down. Moving me from the emergency room wasn't easy with the constant trembling that kept occurring. From the physical weakness, emotional stress, the drug withdrawal, the dehydration… my body is reacting harshly from the trauma.

Heavily sedated, my body lays at peace for the moment. The morphine drip plays a part in the mean cravings my body subdues as I desire the taste in my sleep. Asleep, beads of sweat form on my forehead, my closed eyelids moving rapidly.

Officer Blue stands over me, suffused with anguish. He can't go home and face his wife and kid without coming to see if I'm okay. He feels obligated to do so since he let dirty cops run the streets. It has taken months for the IA officer to get close enough to catch the cat putting his paw in the fishbowl. But the moment has arrived. The officer doesn't know who, what, or why he feels a strong connection with me; however, he feels I am the breakthrough for him to catch his fat cat with dirty hands.

He keeps imagining me as being his own daughter, laying all alone in a hospital bed recovering from God knows what. To protect and serve is the oath he took coming into this profession, a public declaration. *But what have I done to honor that?* he thinks to himself, looking down on a little girl lost.

Interrupted by the buzz of his pager, he focuses his attention on the number in his beeper. He reads back his home phone number and the time storing it in his mental notes. There won't be no sleeping in a bed next to his wife tonight. It is already three in the morning and he hasn't been home in two days, chasing a case which could sit him at the governor's table.

The Conclusion….

CHAPTER FORTY-ONE

Searching for the right words to say, I stood before Joe Crack. He sat there and listened to each and every lie I told. The only thing I could remember him telling me the last time I was in his office was I would need him for a favor. The streets were talking and the corners were watching. Hear no evil, speak no evil, see no evil, but behind every corner evil lurks. Be careful and take heed when you start to tell lies.

Through the wires on the street and the hidden cameras Joe Crack had posted up within the block radius of the store, he didn't miss a beat. I knew he knew I was lying, but shit, I had to try and get work from somebody.

"I told you one day you would return to my office. However, I thought it would be to seek knowledge of some sort to get up out of this game. Just like my daughter, you don't listen to nobody." Joe Crack turned about in his swivel chair, checking out his surveillance cameras. He strong-armed the quote, "The streets are talking. You standing here before me rambling on and on about nothing girl. Just get to the point, Nikko—you want product from me." Joe turned back to face me. He leaned back in his chair and locked his fingers together. "I have to say, Nikko, you've gotten yourself in a nasty situation. I say you're stuck between a rock and a hard place. Nonetheless, I'm not in the distribution game anymore. I evolved from all that nonsense a long time ago. I had to get up out of all of that feeding myself knowledge. Not no text book shit neither!" Joe Crack disputed, banging his fist against the office desk. He had to snatch me back to the moment, to focus my attention back on him. My eyes had fallen to the left when he said he had no product to sell. My head began to throb as

I thought of another way to make a come up. I damn sure didn't want to hear another drawn-out speech. Restrained to his office, I had no choice but to lend an ear since I had the audacity to ask the man for a favor in the first place.

"I taught myself about the different definitions that the word hustle carried in the streets, and all the differences in its nature. My brain and my soul was starving. All three of us needed a way out of the drug game. It was sucking the life out of me and cost my daughter her very own. Stubbornness must run in my gene pool, or it just might be that young mechanism that we're all wired up with. I wouldn't listen to nobody.... and when they killed my daughter to send me a message... I didn't think I would ever find the light at the end of my dark tunnel. I was drunk with revenge." A single tear fell from both eyes for his loss and to whatever his cause he had found.

What Joe Crack didn't realize, though, was I didn't give a damn about his lo- end theory or the story of his long-lost daughter. I prayed the story would end with a happy ending, my hands being blessed with a big chunk of work. I did feel fiendish for not having a sympathetic bone in my body, but I didn't care about myself let alone somebody else.

Joe picked up the picture of his daughter off his desk. "She never seen the muthafuckas coming when they pushed my Cherish down thirteen floors. It was an old elevator shaft. It goes the same for you, Nikko—you will never see them coming."

"What, Joe?"

"When they come for you, you'll never see it coming!" Joe cuts me off, irate. "You can't hear anything I got to say. You can't focus because you're plotting on ya next move. I bet you wish I would shut the fuck up so you can bounce."

The room fell ominously quiet.

"Here's the deal because I'm tired of wasting my breath. You're not one of the smart ones, I see. I'm going to let you keep going down this path of destruction until you're done. I can't stop you if I wanted to. I got peoples who know some peoples who know the people. I can vouch for you and get you about two ounces of blow, but you will be taxed. I want a thousand dollars per ounce and two hundred for me for the hook up. You can say it's a finder's fee."

"Are you crazy, Joe Crack? You want twenty four hundred off of two ounces? I can't make no money on those terms."

"Yes you can if you keep your hands out the cookie jar. Don't get high off your own supply, and DON'T get high off of somebody else shit. You can get killed out there doing that shit. I don't want to see you dead in one of my trash cans out back."

"You're right, Joe. I'm done with all that, and I promise to get the money back to you in two days. Make sure your man got more. I'm about to make him a lot of money. I'm on the grind for this paper, J. Crack."

"You better be, Nikko, because this boy you dealing with ain't no old man. He won't settle for no pussy if you don't have his money. You better take heed to the words I said to you before and now, if you fuck up, you'll never see it coming."

I threw up my hand and Joe Crack extended his. We shook on it, and I agreed to move the product on his terms. I had confidence in myself, and told myself I could do it. It wouldn't be no problem with having the coke in hand without getting high.

"Give me a number where I can reach you at." Joe Crack pushed a piece of paper with a pen to the edge of the desk. I scribbled down my seven digits with the quickness and pushed the paper back to him.

"Aiight then, Nikko, I'll call you with a time and place to pick up the work. Don't make me wait too long for a call back. I see this is a pager number. Time is money, you heard me?"

Shaking my head yes, I threw up a deuce sign and walked out the office door.

"I want everybody to stand to their feet and recite the twelve steps."

Porsha stood up proudly with a newcomer by her side. Kay stood to the left and Chrissy to the right of her. They both held Porsha by the hand, watching her lips recite the twelve steps with a breeze. It was a graduation ceremony for those that were clean for three months from drugs and other addictive behaviors. Kay's youngest daughters resided in a daycare center with Shame Jr. close by. The center that Mrs. Bloom had put into the Hill House was flourishing with all different ages of children. The daycare center was called the Rainbow of Life. The center gave some of the women and young girls without a record of child endangerment a chance to get job experience. For some of the recovering addicts, it was their first place of employment. It was a starting point for some who hadn't worked a day in their lives. Boosting self-esteem and job resumés all in one was the goal Mrs. Bloom was striving for——and she succeeded.

Porsha and Shame Jr. inspired the whole production of the daycare center Mrs. Bloom told the press on opening day.

"I was an admirer of how much devotion Porsha put into her recovery. She was always on time for a meeting, most of the time the first one to take a seat in the first row for NA meetings, prayer meeting and church worship, and she did all of it with her son, Shame Jr., on her hip. When I told her we would work things out here at the Hill House to get her as much help as she needed, I never thought it would end up like this. Through the blood, sweat and tears of testimony, I watched this young lady become a woman. Her strength, might, and backbone was brought to us and today to open the doors to the children who go through addiction also. The Hill House is here to help the community and the people in it. We aim to help anyone who has the courage to live beyond the pain of addiction. I had told Porsha when she first came here that we didn't have a daycare center for her when she called us for help, but it didn't stop her from getting what she wanted. That's another reason why we're here today. Your determination is what got us here. Give a round of applause for Porsha, the inspiration behind this project." The crowd was live with clapping and whistling. The press took their snapshots as Porsha stood to her feet, and as she rose, the crowd began to bring their volume down to a minimum whisper. Porsha looked out at the guests attending the event. A lot of people she had grew to love had fallen to the wayside back into the arms of the street. Taking a bow, she walked up to the spotlight where she and Mrs. Bloom embraced in a hug.

"I'm so proud of you," Mrs. Bloom said in a whisper, squeezing her tight.

The speech Porsha gave put God first. The crowd gave a standing ovation. Mrs. Bloom watched her face glow as the press ate her up with lights, camera, and action. It was a beautiful thing to see Porsha complete the twelve-step program. The day was wonderful and a success. Afterwards there was a dinner for those who completed the program and for family members who came to support the graduation and grand opening of the daycare center. Every seat was taken, and every being was filled with a sense of purpose. And everybody enjoyed themselves while dining.

"Are you two enjoying yourselves?"

"Yes, we are," Kay and Chrissy answered in unison. They both hugged Porsha, happy to be a part of her accomplishment and honored that they were invited.

"Look!" Chrissy said, pointing her finger.

In the center of the dining hall sat a spacious table with a black tablecloth trimmed in pink. There were name cards placed on the table, and Porsha's sat amongst them along with Mrs. Bloom the program director, Ms. Shields the director and Sister Smith, the head honcho in charge of the big picture.

"Where is your family at Porsha?" Chrissy asked, warmhearted.

Porsha looked around the room, stagnated from the question. For a brief second, she allowed herself to feel alienated by not having any family support. Then she looked over the room again and realized how much family she had supporting her. Mrs. Bloom, the mother she missed, smiled gleeful. God was all the family she needed.

"Right here standing next to me and Mrs. Bloom." Porsha put her arms around Kay's and Chrissy's shoulders, at peace with the family she had. And she smiled big for Shame Jr. She had changed her life to save her son.

"I'm so glad you consider us as your family. You know the deal with me just as well as I know the deal with you. You're better than the sister I never had. I'm proud of you and everything you've done, and what you're about to do. I'm always going to be here for you because you were there when I had nobody. You told me the truth, and you led by example, Porsha. Everything you said to me and everything you did for me was positive. You showed me what a real friend is. Thank you." Kay embraced Porsha, overjoyed. "Everything happens for a reason, and I was meant to meet you. You saved my life," Kay continued to say discreetly while she and Porsha embraced. They had a moment, and it was beautiful for both, food for the soul and strength beneath the wings.

Joe Crack let a couple of hours go past before he served up the coke on a silver platter. A cousin of his was a hood politician and he knew he wouldn't turn down any opportunity to make some money. Joe paid six-fifty a piece for the two ounces he grabbed up for me. He had confidence in me the first go round because he knew I needed the money to get out of the hole, and I needed a connect to the work. He thought I would never know the huge favor he was really doing for me. He wanted to save my life, even if I didn't. Joe Crack knew the old man she I dealing with and was surprised I wasn't already dead. He knew the only reason why my life was spared was because I was a woman and a mother. He reached out knowing that I didn't need another target on my back. The money he had put up wasn't nothing compared to saving someone's life, and he had to make an attempt to try and do something.

The spirit of his daughter wouldn't let him rest, and if I wouldn't have showed up at the store, he would've combed the streets until he found me. He had to give me the drugs to keep me from owing on more killer money.

"Money is the root to all evil. Look what has become of your life chasing this American dream as they say out here on the streets. This game and that dream will make the next man kill his brother, sell drugs to his mother, set up your best friend to go to jail or death, all in the namesake of the almighty dollar. It's the same for legal money, too, don't get it twisted. A spouse will kill its other half for the insurance money, the children of rich folk kill their parents for the family fortune, so on and so on. I hope you can read between these lines, but if you can't, I'll say this—don't let your greed for money ruin your life anymore. This American dream you're chasing is going to kill you. Do what you got to do and get out." Those were the last words Joe Crack said to me, knowing there was only a fifty-fifty chance he would ever see me again. As I walked out of his office, he picked up his daughter's picture.

"My good deed is done, baby. There is nothing else that I can do, so you go with her and watch out for her. Make sure she doesn't suffer when she dies." Joe Crack hung his head and cried for his daughter and me.

Sweat poured off of my body as I sat on the floor in manufacturing mode. Nose runny from standing over the stove, whipping the work into fast money, the sweet aroma of the product melting down triggered a soon-to-be relapse. Struggling to put the coke in the corners of the baggies, Diablo came back into play.

"Twelve thousand is not hard to make if I just stay focused. Get money first, Nikko, and get high later. You got a lot of people depending on you to come up with their money. If you don't do this right, you will be running for your life."

KNOCK! KNOCK! KNOCK!

"Damn! Who is it?"

"Open the door, Egypt!!"

"I said who is it?!" I had just put the flame to the spiff. Temptation won the battle as I took a nice pull on the smoke.

"Don't piss me off, Egypt! Open up the door now!"

I dropped my head when I caught on to the voice. I crushed the cherry on the blunt and blew out the scented candle that sat on the back of the toilet. I knew I had to open up the door for Moe; she wasn't leaving until she got whatever it was she wanted to say off her chest. I was happy, though—Moe's timing was perfect. I had only hit the spiff once and wasn't high. The hit calmed the craving, and I would be able to withstand her for at least ten minutes.

Who is it?!" It asked once again, this time pissing Moe off. That's what I wanted to do because I had to get up under her skin.

"It's Monica, and if you don't want the neighbors to call the police for disturbing the peace, you better open up the damned door." Behind her loud talk, she kicked the door so hard the pictures on the wall shook.

"Stop kicking my door, girl!" I yelled, opening up the door. Moe didn't waste no time pushing past Egypt into the apartment as Tre followed right behind her.

"Well, come on in, why don't cha!!" Egypt added brazenly.

"I don't mind if we do!!" Moe spat back.

"What do you want, Moe?"

"I want my friend back."

I shut the door and took a deep breath, sighing out loud and slow.

"Didn't you hear what I said? I want my friend back." This time

Moe said it with irritated eyes, pushing me back up against the wall. It took everything in me to hold the tears back.

"What do you want me to say, Moe?" I asked genuinely. I seen how much I was hurting my friend. "Seasons change, just like people do. I'm still your friend, but our lives are on different paths right now. I don't have time to hear shit about nothing, not unless you got twelve g's to get me out the hole."

Moe fell onto the couch like somebody punched her in the stomach after hearing how much money Egypt had owed out. "Twelve thousand dollars? Are you for real, E?"

"Yeah, I'm for real. So you can stop all this intervention shit because you ain't getting your friend back today. I gotta get this money before I get a bullet in my ass."

Moe looked at Egypt sideways. "I don't believe you, Egypt. I think you don't want to grow up. You just want to be a hood rat for the rest of your life. This ain't nothing but an excuse to keep getting high."

"Yo!! I'm not trying to hear your theories about my life or my decisions! I'm glad you stopped by, but you and your man gotta get up outta here." I was starting to tweak. I needed to get it in as my body began to sweat, knowing the spliff was nearby, ready to be smoked. I spoke as calmly as I could, but callous.

"You know what, E, you're right." Moe stood in front of me and broke down in tears. "I can't help you until you want to help yourself. I love you, and whenever you need me, I'll be just one phone call away. I don't have no money, but I'll pray for you to stay safe out here in these streets."

I didn't really pay attention to the tears. I couldn't because if I did, I would have to care about someone else besides myself. Instead, I walked Moe and her man to the door. "I need money, I don't need no prayer. You can keep that shit. Don't waste your breath…" I opened up the front door to let the two out, and to my surprise, more unwanted company stood toe to toe with me.

"Move your bitch ass out the way and let her bitching ass pass so she can roll up outta here."

"Our conversation done, E?"

"Hell, yeah Moe, it's done for now."

Moe turned her back on me and walked away, hand in hand with Tre. I sucked my teeth as I watched her exit the building. I then looked Raw up and down and tried to slam the door in his face. He knew that I would try to do it and got his foot caught in the door just in time. It slammed on his foot hard as hell and it hurt, but he didn't let up.

"Get away from my crib, nigga. This time I'm going to shoot your bitch ass. You better move that foot before you lose it."

"Come on, Nikko, you know you need me to help you get that money, and I got a way for us to get it."

"What do you mean by 'us'?"

"I got a plan on how we can get paid, but I need you. I owe you that, Nikko. Plus, I got some info you need to know a.s.a.p."

I moved away from the door. I wanted to hear what Raw the rat had to say about everything. And if his plan was good enough about the come up on the money, I would cut him out and do it myself. Why not be entertained while I smoked?

"Don't get no flashbacks coming up in my bathroom. I got to smoke, and I got too much traffic coming through my crib to be out and about flossing..."

"It's cool. I deserved that shit anyway for ratting you out to that old man. I was wrong, Nikko—I should have had your back."

"Aiight, aiight, you can stop kissing my ass. Tell me what's up with seizing the loot. Lawd knows I need it."

"Hell, naw, I don't know. I ain't never seen no spot in there, and I been hustling in there forever."

"I just found out about it myself. That's why all the H.P. niggas be holding up the wall back there. They be watching out for their invest-ment, you know..."

"Oh, yeah, I don't believe you. I think you trying to set me up to get in bad with the hood politicians. You know, they never did like you."

"Look, I got somebody to put me on who knows what goes down behind that wall the H.P.'s be holding up. You gotta believe me, and NO, I'm not trying to create no bad blood. The young boy that's on the inside is going to be in there gambling, pulling the strings so we can get in and out."

"And after it goes down, how are we supposed to get back past the H.P.'s without being seen? As soon as they find out they been hit, they coming straight for us. I'm guessing we going in there bare-faced because if we don't, we will never make it past the bar." I shook my head. "This shit don't sound right at all." I put the spliff out and began to wash my hands.

"It's a good plan, Nikko, but you ain't trying to hear me out. Just…"

"Just nothing. I'm cool Raw, and I don't want to hear nothing else about it. You trying to die quick, fucking around with them H.P.'s. I already got one death wish, I don't need another."

"Whatever, Nikko, you sound scared to me." Raw stood to his feet, eyeballing me.

"Don't try and bait me, nigga. I'm not falling for that reverse bullshit. I'm way smarter than that." I lifted up the toilet seat and flushed the roach I put out down the bowl. "There goes your plan with me in it, right down the crapper." I looked Raw right in the eyes and didn't blink. "I don't have nothing for you. You might as well get up on out of here, I got work to do."

Raw didn't argue with me. He opened up his arms and tried to go in for a hug. "Aiight then, I'm out…"

"Don't try and touch me, Raw! We ain't brown like that no more. You gets no love!"

"You right, you right." Raw backed away and put his arms down.

"Just to let you know, though, your girl Lexus is out to get you. I advise you to watch your back."

"Tell me something I don't know! I better not do shit but stay black and die! Fuck her and fuck you, too. You know your way out, and don't let the door hit you on the way out." Hitting the block hard was the next move. I didn't entertain anything Raw had to say. Him showing up was a sign of bad luck; he was up to something, but she didn't know what and didn't have time to investigate. I had to get at a dollar and do it quickly.

The Ave. was popping, and the money was there to be made. The street was paved with clients ready to get high. It was about two in the morning and the bars were getting ready to close, and that would let out more money to walk the streets. I took her spot on the bench to wait for the money to roll in.

"What's up? You working with something?" a white man asked, taking a seat next to me on the bench.

"You waiting on the bus, sir?" I asked, playing it up.

"No, I need a couple of twenties," the man, said looking around.

Right then and there I knew I should have let that man keep on going, but did I? Hell, no, I needed money.

"How much money you got on you?"

"I got a hundred dollars, and if the shit is good, I got a lot more where that came from."

"It sounds like a plan. I'll give you thirteen dimes for a buck twenty. Something tells me you got another twenty spot, and I need that, too. Plus, if you spend the extra twenty, I'll throw one in for free."

"Now that sounds like a plan," the white man said with a smile. He pulled his money out to make the exchange.

As soon as the deal was made, I was surrounded by the police. There was no way I was escaping jail. They slapped the cuffs on me so fast my head spun. It was the beginning of the end of my world as I knew it. When the police door shut and the flashing lights turned off, Officer D. Ho-Mo was satisfied.

Already out on bond, the judge hiked up my bail to twenty thousand straight. A half ounce of crack was gone and two hundred dollars just occupied a dirty cop's pocket. There was no one to call, no back-up plan and most of all, no money.

"What if I just did right by my woman and my child? What, am I being punished for sleeping with women, shit, let alone my baby-daddy sister? What am I gonna do?" I talked to myself, rubbing my head in a circular motion. The holding cell was dirty and cold with graffiti all over the four walls. It was also filled with the ho's from down on Fifth Ave. About four of them conversated amongst themselves until they heard me say that she slept with her baby-daddy sister.

All attention on me, she gave the judgmental eyes and her middle finger. Then I thought of one person I could call to come and get me out of jail. I stood up from the cold bench and walked to the pay phone without a quarter in my pocket. I took a chance, calling collect. It wasn't a good idea to have collect calling nowadays because sisters knew if they had it somebody would run it up until the phone got cut off. I sighed, pressing zero to get an operator. I sounded off the number once, twice, three times and then again, but couldn't get it right.

"Dammit, Moe! What's the phone number?" I cried out hammering the phone receiver into the phone box until a guard yelled for me to stop. Out of breath, I held back the tears, taking my place as a prisoner. I knew I wasn't leaving.

"When this car goes past, I'm gonna push you through the window." Raw instructed Lexus with his hands underneath her butt.

"You better not push me hard, neither. You better be sure she ain't coming back no time soon, too."

"I told you she got booked a half hour ago! There's no way she's making it back here until tomorrow evening, if she makes bond!"

The car slowed up and went through the stop sign. Lexus opened the window and Raw pushed her through in a matter of seconds.

"You cool in there?" Raw asked when he heard a thud hit the floor.

"Yeah, I'm fine. Go around to the front door so I can let you in." In the next breath, she stood in front of the apartment building door with her hands on her hips like she lived there.

"It's like taking candy from a baby, stink butt. Let's rock and roll" Lexus said, inviting Raw into the apartment.

"I want every CD that bitch own, and everything else… trash it," Lexus said, demanding authority. She was running the show and wanted Raw to know that. "Find the coke while I pack up this stuff, and I bet you any money it's up under the couch."

Raw was a good little flunky. He finally had did something right. The old man and I were right about one thing—Raw was foul and couldn't be trusted. The whole thing was just a plot to get back in her crib. In the grand scheme of things, the set up to rob the H.P.'s was a diversion. He just had to find out if she had work and unlock a window to get into later on. The only person who was getting robbed was me. And Lexus was one step closer to getting what she wanted, revenge on a bitch that broke her heart. Raw obeyed her commands and just like she said, the coke was underneath the couch. Lexus pressed play on the CD player and Mary J. Blige poured out the surround-sound, crystal clear.

"We should steal this big-ass system, too. It would sound so good in your room while I'm hitting it from the back." Raw smiled, humping on Lexus from behind.

"Nope, it would kill her to have to pick up the broken pieces of her other woman. I'm smashing everything."

Lexus started dismembering the stereo while Raw collected all of Egypt's clothes and shoes, placing them in the bathtub. Raw loaded up the car with the CD's and some other things he pocketed for himself, bringing back in two gallons of bleach. He ran the water in the tub and poured on the bleach with a smile. In the other room, Lexus took a gold necklace that was on my dresser which I wore on the regular and put it around her neck.

"I got you, bitch," they both said in unison.

Standing in the middle of the mayhem, Raw and Lexus were ecstatic by their petty tactics. Turning on all the running water in the apartment, they got what they came for——revenge.

Locking the door behind them, they walked out like they owned the joint. The night air never felt so good...

The cold shower was a wake-up call. After being stripped buck naked, having to spread my butt cheeks wide open for the female officer to peek at, I didn't want to do nothing else but go to sleep. The reality set in when I reached cell 224 and was told breakfast would be served at six a.m. The cell door closed behind me, cutting off the fresh air. It made the cell smaller than it was. Just looking at the thin mat that was supposed to be a bed made my body hurt. The walls were similar to the holding cell down in the tank. They were sprayed with numerous names of the prisoners before me. I took a deep breath and sat on the floor, Indian style. The path I was following only left me two choices: death and incarceration, and the angel of death followed behind me close. The grim reaper painted the path of the American dream of selling drugs with golden streets and lots of respect, but what honor do you get for becoming an undercover smoker playing drug dealer?

CHAPTER FORTY-TWO

It was Saturday morning. Porsha was relieved the end of the week finally came. Her week had been filled with demand after demand. Shame Jr. having a cold, didn't make things any easier as he kept her up for three nights in a row. But today was the day of rest, and God proclaimed it that way.

Kay was already up with the kids ready to go, while Porsha moved slowly to get dressed for church. The breeze was delightful as the sun shined down on her face and she cracked her window open for some fresh air. Sadness overwhelmed her this morning and she felt the need to cry, but the tears wouldn't fall. I was on her mind, weighing heavy on the heart, and Porsha couldn't shake it. But she refused to shed another tear on a love she once knew.

"What are you doing up there, Porsha? You gonna make us miss the choir singing, if you don't hurry up." Warmhearted Kay shouted up the steps. She and the kids were ready to go.

Porsha stood in front of her bedroom mirror. She forced herself to smile, then her smile became majestic. Putting on her top, she giggled from the thought of being rushed to get to church. Never in a million years would she have guessed her life would have turned around like this. In a rush to get to the club, yes, nut a church? No.

"Give me ten more minutes, and I'll be ready, okay?" Porsha knew it was going to take a little longer than that, but it sounded good. Nevertheless, she put some pep in her step to get ready faster. Fifteen minutes later, Porsha descended the steps, dressed in an all cream Donna Karan pantsuit. Kissing the gold cross that hung around her neck, she was ready to go like everyone else.

"I'm ready to go."

"Well, it's about time. You look good as always," Kay said to Porsha, truthful. "Come on kids, let's go, and Chrissy, don't forget to pick up Shame Jr.'s diaper bag on the way out the door."

Porsha started up the car as the bodies filled the seats. The radio was playing a classic Mary J. Blige song that drifted back a memory of bliss her and I shared. *Not Gonna Cry* played for a millisecond until Kay changed the station.

"Why did you do that?" Porsha asked on edge.

"You couldn't see the expression on your face, but I did, and I didn't like what I saw. Come on, Porsha, I know Mary is your ex's favorite, and when you hear her, it makes you think of her. The thought of her becomes written all over your face. She makes you wear your heart on your sleeve. Bottom line—you hearing that song is no good for you right now."

Porsha knew everything said out of Kay's mouth was the truth. Vulnerable, she wished the memories of her and me singing over the tracks drunk away and away and gone. Kay pushed Porsha's hair behind her ear, caressing her cheekbone lightly with the tip of her fingers.

"Let's go. You're right. I don't need to hear no old Mary J. Blige songs to make me ponder on something that's gone. What I really need is to not miss out on that choir singing this morning." Porsha put the car in drive, finding peace within herself.

The organ played heavenly loud music. Porsha could hear it pulling up in the church parking lot. It was a relief to see the house of the Lord. Hillcrest Seventh Day Advent Church had become a second home for Porsha and Kay leading a new life. They came to the conclusion only God could judge them and shine light in their dark tunnel.

As soon as Porsha and the family reached the double doors to enter the church, Porsha felt uneasy but didn't pay it any attention. You could feel the presence of the Lord stepping into the temple, and Porsha embraced it like the sick needing medicine. Just as they waited for an usher to be seated in the sanctuary, Mrs. Bloom came rushing through another set of double doors that led to that very place with tears in her eyes.

"What's wrong with Mrs. Bloom?" Porsha asked a deacon following behind her toe to heel. She had never seen Mrs. Bloom without a smile on her face.

"That's something you would have to ask her. But this is the side she never lets anybody see. You two have become close over the months. I'm glad you're here, and you came when you did."

Mrs. Bloom was held up in the pastor's study. "Do you think I should go and check up on her? I know she would do the same for me."

"I know she would do the same for both of us," Kay interrupted.

"You're right, Kay." The deacon and Mrs. Bloom's husband's answer didn't count anymore. "Take the kids and sit down. I'll be out in a minute."

She could hear Mrs. Bloom crying, approaching the door to the pastor's study. She didn't know whether to knock or just go into the room. She decided to go in because if she knocked, Mrs. Bloom could turn her away and she didn't want that. Finally gaining enough courage to open the door, Porsha sighed, seeing Mrs. Bloom on her knees, crying uncontrollably. She didn't bother her. She just stood in the shadows while shedding a tear. Porsha wasn't ready for what would come next.

Mrs. Bloom knew she stood near. She could feel Porsha's eyes piercing her back. She needed an explanation for why a woman so happy all the time sits here on the floor knee bound, in tears. Mrs. Bloom motioned for Porsha to come near with her hand. Porsha, now in tears herself, came closer. Mrs. Bloom placed Porsha's face in the palm of her hands and brought her down to her knees until they were eye level.

"I walked out of my daughter's life twenty-four years ago on June the second in Magee Women's Hospital. Not looking back, I turned to a life of prostitution, drugs and alcohol to heal the pain of leaving my baby. Porsha, I really never thought I would change my life. I never thought I wanted to see her again because of the hurt her father put on me, and when my mother died, I thought there would be no hope to seeing her ever again. And when I heard about my sister's violent death, I prayed that my daughter was dead so I wouldn't have to answer to her. But you brought her back to me, Porsha." Mrs. Bloom stumbled over her next words. "Porsha, my daughter is your girlfriend. My Egypt is your lover. Egypt Winters is my child!" The tears came crashing down like a ton of bricks as Mrs. Bloom held onto Porsha's face for dear life.

Awestruck, Porsha sat in silence as her tears tumbled down her face for me and the mother I never had. Immediately she pulled her hand away when the words sunk in further. She was in disbelief from the words that fell from Mrs. Bloom's lips. She stood to her feet without saying a word. What more could she say? Face to face, Porsha and Mrs. Bloom stood at attention with blank stares.

"Please repeat for me one last time what you just said to me," Porsha muttered.

Mrs. Bloom put her head down. "She's my daughter, Porsha."

"I can't believe you." Porsha backed away from her reach, rejecting Mrs. Bloom's invitation to embrace. Shaking her head, Porsha became faint. The news was creating a dizzy spell. Trying to grab the chair behind the pastor's desk, she settled for the desktop to lean against.

"Please, say something, chile" Mrs. Bloom said distraught.

"How long have you known about her, Ms. Lola James?" Hatred roamed Porsha's eyes. "How could you do something like that? How could you leave your own daughter?" she mouthed, but the words didn't quite come out.

"I've known ever since the night you moved to the shelter. I heard the young lady that was in front of the apartment building you two lived in scream her name out when I dropped you off from church that evening. When she said it, something in my soul shook and anchored. I knew in the next breath it was her. After I made sure you were at the shelter, I went back to your apartment. I fished through some mail in the box and seen her birth name staring me right back in my face. I always thought about her, but I never..."

"You never what? You never did nothing, Mrs. Bloom, or should I say Lola?" Her eyes pierced through the lady that stood before her. "Who are you, for real? You can't be the person that would do something like that. You're supposed to be a drunk, a crack head or something. She'll never accept you being this perfect." Porsha spoke with the venom of Egypt's hurt.

"Please, can you make this a little easier for me? I know..."

"You don't know nothing! You're the reason why she doesn't know how to love me, or to love her son for that matter. You might as well killed her, because the drugs she does is to subdue the pain of being a motherless child. Why should I help you? You tell me why!!" Porsha raised her voice, enraged but remembering she was in the house of the Lord. Mrs. Bloom was lucky, too, that the two were not brawling right now. "Ain't nothing for Egypt been easy."

Mrs. Bloom didn't know how to answer Porsha. Every time she tried to open her mouth, nothing came out. She turned and faced the wall to avoid Porsha's malignant eyes.

"You're going to turn your back on me, really? Please tell me this, Lola—how can you be a person of God and do something like leave your child... your own child?"

"I wasn't always this person, Porsha," Mrs. Bloom said, trying to come to her own defense. She turned back around to face her. "Don't judge me on this, leave it to God. Don't question him or your faith by my wrongdoing. You'll never understand how it feels to be me. I'm the one that has to live with the awful decision I made twenty-four years ago. But I left her because I couldn't see past the hate for her father. I didn't know how to love her without being constantly reminded of the dogmatic man he was. She looked just like him, for Christ's sake. Her father was horrible after he lost his parents. He became a drunk and so did——I because I thought that would keep us together. I thought Egypt would keep us together, but when he left, what did I need her for? I know I was wrong ,and it took me years to forgive myself for what I did wrong. I tried to find her once or twice, then I thought she would be better off without me. I don't know if it was fate, however, I know the Lord sent you to me so we can save her. I can't do it without you, Porsha. You are the rock…"

"Do you really think you can come back into her life and make things right?" Porsha's voice went from calm to antagonistic, her fists pounding on the desk as she spoke. Porsha stood tall while Mrs. Bloom fell back on her knees.

"Please forgive me," she said in prayer to the man upstairs and Porsha. "Help me, Porsha. Please bring us all together. God crossed our paths for a reason, and I'm ready to fix things now that I know she's my daughter. Doesn't that count for something, Porsha? I was sent to you for a reason, and you the same. Just look how far you've come. Look what you've done for me. You brought my daughter back to me. I didn't turn my back on you; please don't turn your back on me."

Quietly, Porsha investigated Mrs. Bloom down on her knees. She was livid, feeling inconsiderate for the lack of emotion she felt for her cry for help and confused by a woman she thought could do no wrong. Porsha walked away from Mrs. Bloom and right out the door of the pastor's study. She took three steps outside the threshold, and Mrs. Bloom groveled at her feet, ankle biting. All her pride was aside.

"Please, Porsha, I beg you, don't walk out on me."

"You walked out on Egypt, your only daughter." Porsha made a mad dash past the deacon, disregarding the fact it was the morning prayer in progress. The congregation was down on their knees, giving thanks. Kay did the same as Porsha approached her from the back.

Placing her hand on Kay's shoulder, she raised her head annoyed. Nonetheless, the swollen eyes, face stained with tears and the imperfect make-up gave away that there was something wrong...

"What's wrong with you?" Kay asked discreetly.

"I don't have time to explain. I have to go, and I gotta go now. Make sure you find a way home. As a matter of fact, ask Mr. Bloom to do so as a favor to me, and he'll do it. I don't know where I'm going or when I'm coming back." Porsha placed her hand over her chest, trying to catch her breath. Kay took in the directions, giving an okay nod. She didn't ask any questions; she just did as she was told.

Porsha escaped the four walls of the church that was closing in on her. Almost falling out the exit, she breathed in the fresh air profoundly, standing in the middle of the parking lot. *What am I to do?* she thought with her head held up to the sky. *What are the odds of something like this happening? Fate rode in on a huge horse, making a star debut in my life, Egypt's and Mrs. Bloom's.*

CHAPTER FORTY-THREE

M y name is Brook. Now, is she dead or alive?" Porsha asked again, imperiously.

What am I going to say? How is she going to react? More than likely, she's going to snap out.

This will either make her or break her. The bombshell Mrs. Bloom dropped was propped in Porsha's viewpoint. Speeding down I-79 doing twenty-five mph over the speed limit, she weaved in and out of traffic, sweating bullets. Was this something good, a sweet dream? Was this something that would blow up in everybody's face, a beautiful nightmare? Who was to say? Porsha rambled on in, pulling up in front of the apartment building her and I lived in once upon a time. Police cars surround the premises. Panic took over instantaneously. She couldn't get the front door of the car open fast enough.

"Is she dead?" was all Porsha asked as she fell out of the car, making herself a spectacle. "Please, God, let her be okay." There she stood staring at a cop, who didn't even try to help her up. He didn't answer her question either. In that case, she decided to speed walk right past him.

She approached the front door, which was kicked in off the hinges. Three more police officers were walking about the trashed apartment. A water-soaked rug sank Porsha's heels into the carpet as she stepped in.

"Somebody please tell me my girlfriend is alive!" Porsha pushed out, terror-stricken. She wasn't noticed amongst the cops until they heard her shriek. In a whiplash turn, one of the cops put eyes on the voice that startled him. "And who are you, ma'am?" he asked, writing down something in a small notepad.

"Did you say she was your sister?" the cop asked, flipping his small notepad closed. He snickered at the next cop that held his full attention on Porsha.

"I said she was my girlfriend, Mr. Officer."

The cop snickered again. "This fine piece of ass is a dike," he tried to whisper to the cop, but it didn't work out that way. A sly smirk danced on his lips while he stared at her crotch. "Your girlfriend is in jail. So what? Did you find out she was cheating on you with the female up the street and you came here and trashed the crib?" The other two cops just stopped and stared at him with an idiotic expression.

"Are you really serious?" she asked, belittling them. She was relieved to hear Egypt was in jail and not dead in a ditch somewhere. She didn't know what in the hell happened to the apartment, but thought it had something to do with money. On that note, Porsha knew to keep quiet.

"Do you know anybody who would want to do this to her apartment?" another officer chimed in. "By the way, my name is Officer D-HoMo. I'm the one who locked up your girlfriend who was banging the broad up the street." Officer D-HoMo was trying desperately to get up under Porsha's skin. He wanted any information on me and maybe my connection to the drugs I sold. He knew if he asked straight out he wouldn't get a word. He had a better chance playing the jealousy card.

Porsha turned red in the face, blushing with anger. "I don't know nothing about nothing. I don't even live here anymore. How did you get in here anyway? And since we're asking questions, what's up with all the water on the floor?"

"Funny thing about that is, you don't ask the questions, ma'am, I do," Officer D-HoMo said, placing his undivided attention back on himself and the other two officers. They whispered amongst themselves for a brief second.

Porsha was annoyed. There wasn't nothing else at the apartment she cared about. It was time to go and she turned to walk out the door. She figured she didn't have to put up with the pig's bullshit. All she wanted was me, and now she knew my whereabouts.

D-HoMo watched her as she turned around to head for the door. His facial expression turned from cop instinct to a horny man with power. The flesh between his legs stood erect, overseeing the sashay in her step and her slender body filling out her suit.

"You know you can cut a deal to get your girl out of jail and all the drug charges and the assault charge will be dropped. You know, she really needs someone like you to look after her because right now she's not being smart. She's facing a lot of time if convicted on the drug charges. And oh, yeah, that assault charge is going to get her sent straight upstate, where the real dikes are at."

Porsha stopped dead in her tracks. She turned around slowly. "Hell no, I don't have nothing to say to you!" Porsha stood directly in front of the apartment door. As soon as the words fell off her lips, two more police officers appeared in the threshold. Jittery, she stood back.

"You need to watch your mouth before we take you downtown, too. We make things appear when in need to get the job done." The stubby officer flexed his muscles but didn't scare nobody.

"Leave her alone, guys. She's been through enough," unknown cop number two said. But everybody know how the police get down— good cop, bad cop. He wasn't like the other cops on the scene; he was clean cut and shaved down to his fingernails. His suitable attire almost made him look like he pushed some cocaine on the side as a night job. Another thing everybody knows—a cop don't make no money.

"The neighbor upstairs said she heard a noise come from down here around twelve-thirty a.m. and nothing since," Officer D-HoMo said, walking back up on Porsha. "You know the old lady seen you breaking in here. She saw everything. She's too damned scared to talk."

"Go ahead with that. You didn't see me do anything. I was at home with my son."

"A dike with a kid. That's gonna be one messed-up little dude." A horrific laugh erupted from D-HoMo. It must have been a cop joke because they were the only ones laughing. "You can tell your dike, carpet muncher whenever you see her, the landlord is taking her to court for water damage on his apartment." After talking shit, the man took his hand out of his pocket to shake Porsha's. She stood there, flushed with fever, wanting to smack the disrespectful pig right in the mouth and stomp on his nuts. She looked at his hand and rolled her eyes in disgust.

"I'll make sure she gets the message." Porsha sucked up the intolerable officers and put a smile on her face. "I hope you officers have a nice day; I know I'll do the same." Kill them with kindness is what the Good Book always says, Porsha chuckles as she swayed them hips against the wind on purpose on the way to her car.

In her car, she let the anxiety fall from her shoulders and tears came after. She only wondered how much money I owed and to whom. She also thought about the possibility of another woman doing it. "I will not cry no more!" The thought of me being with another woman cut the waterfall off. Her mind switched gears as she started up her car. Uplifting her head, she peered out the windshield laying eyes on Lexus, squinting to see what it is around her neck. "It can't be." It was my gold chain. The sun hit the encrusted diamonds, lighting up Porsha's eyes.

She put the car back in park and exited the vehicle. Lexus knew from the door who Porsha was, but Porsha only had a highly educated guess on who she stood before. The thick redbone female was only the latest edition of my toy collection. It didn't bother her, but the necklace around Lexus' neck did. Porsha had bought the chain for me on her twenty-first birthday.

Lexus stood at ease with her arms folded across her chest. Walking to the middle of the street, she flung her eighteen-inch weave from one shoulder to the next. Suggestively, she took the tip of her tongue and wet her lips. Porsha thought she was at a hoedown.

"We finally meet after all the phone conversations, WIFEY." Lexus didn't waste any time letting it be known who she was.

When Lexus opened up her mouth, it sent chills down Porsha's spine. She caught on quick and her guess was confirmed—it was Lexus. Porsha kept God in her presence with every little step she took closer towards her. In reality, she wanted to act like the devil bitch she once was and choke her out.

"Don't let the dress fool you; I will get hood on your young ass. And yes, I'll always be wifey, and you, you'll always be that bottom bitch." As soon as Porsha opened up her mouth, she forgot about the Lord. Palms sweaty, jaw clenched tight with rage, it took all her might not to snatch the chain Lexus possessed around her neck. Porsha could smell the cherry-flavored bubble gum Lexus was chewing from being so close to her face as they stood toe to toe.

"What's up, Porsha?" Lexus took three footsteps back from her. "You sure about that because you don't look too sure to me 'bout who's holding the wifey title." Confidence wrapped Lexus' demeanor as she slid the encrusted diamond charm back and forth across the chain, popping her bubble gum.

Once again, Porsha caught herself. She was about to go there with Lexus just because of the disrespect she displayed, but a higher power wouldn't allow it. *Kill them with kindness...*

"That is absolutely true. You've won. I don't want the title of being somebody's wife that I have to fight about every day. That's your job now. I refuse to fight with you any longer. Look at you standing there like you're untouchable, but for real, you don't want to see me or you wouldn't have backed up. In your heart, you know that Egypt don't want you, and if you don't, that's sad on your part."

Lexus didn't respond with a comment. She rolled her eyes and popped her gum. She sucked her teeth as if nothing even mattered. The words Porsha spoke was the truth, and she knew it, but couldn't show it. The only thing she could do was brush her shoulders off and wait for Porsha to return to her car. And as Porsha turned around to do just that, Lexus exhaled the deep breath she was holding. She felt she got her point across and killed any chance of her and me getting back together. Then Porsha stopped dead in her tracks.

She turned back around for one last word. "I need you to get a message to Egypt if you see her. Tell her her mother wants to see her. She can find her at a church called Hillcrest Seventh Day Advent Church. It's on the Hill, right in the middle of Wiley Avenue."

"Her mother..." Lexus replied, confused. "She doesn't have a mother."

"She does now, so make sure she gets the message." Porsha continued to walk back to her car. She knew the young girl didn't have a clue about who I really was. And if they were in love as she claimed, why wasn't bailing me out of jail.

"That's it..." Porsha said, starting up the car again. "I can bail her out of jail before someone else does." Talking aloud, she put the car in drive and the pedal to the metal.

This can bring us back together once again. I can have another mother, a mother-in-law sounds good. And after I help Egypt get past the pain of her mother leaving and then coming back, we can truly be happy. We can all be a happy family. Finally my baby is going to be okay, Porsha thought as she pulled up to the Allegheny County Jail. The sun was shining down on the revolving doors of the criminal mischief that entered all hours of the day and night.

"I would like to make bond for a Egypt Winters please." Porsha stood at the window, legs shaking. The overweight black woman sitting behind the Plexiglas didn't give eye contact. She nodded her head to Porsha's question, confirming she heard the request. Her perfect manicured fingernails stroked the computer keys slow and unwanting.

Looking over her reading glasses, she asks, "Are you the last to find out?"

"Find out what, ma'am?"

"The person you're inquiring about got released over an hour ago, so the computer says."

"Who made the bond?" Porsha quizzed.

"A Larry Cash from Liberty Bails Bond. If you want to know anything else, you'll have to talk to him. The number is over there on the board hanging up if you need it." The woman pointed her sausage finger over to an information board by another booth. She pushed her glasses back up on her nose, put out her smoke and picked up the telephone, finalizing the end of their conversation.

That was it. Egypt was gone. Porsha figured she wouldn't go back to the apartment if somebody was trying to hurt her, and if she went back to Homestead it would be to Lexus.

"Should I cry?" she asked herself, walking back to her car. Taking it home, she cruised the back streets of Downtown, hoping to see the familiarity of her lost love.

I watched every step I took creeping off the 53F Homestead bus across the street from my apartment. The only thing I could think about was a hot bath and a spliff to ease the pain. Fuck everybody money, I'm going on the run. CATCH ME IF YOU CAN...

There wasn't a doubt in my mind I was smoking whatever product I had left that Joe Crack had assigned. From the shadows, unknown voices caused ,y blood pressure to rise, my feet to move faster and my mind to jog. Putting the key into the apartment building door, I began to relax. My feet sank into the wet carpet as I stood in front of my door to open it.

"What in Sam Hill? Why is the carpet wet?" Egypt spat as the door swung open to the apartment. Her eyes ran over the ruin in the apartment. "What the fuck?" My mouth hung open and my brain draws a blank. "Hell, naw..." I yell, running over top of the rebel on the floor to the couch, using all my might to flip it over. "It's gone!! It's fucking gone!!"

A noise causes my head to turn towards the door. I feasted my eyes on Lexus. Bold and beautiful, feet planted firmly in the wet carpet, she pops her bubble gum. The chain hanging around her neck was flawless as she rubbed the charm up and down the gold.

"What did you do with my shit, bitch?" I yelled, running straight towards Lexus. She didn't waste any time jumping on the young girl. The eighteen inch ponytail got wrapped around my fist. I threw her to the ground and put my knee in Lexus' back. "Bitch, if you don't tell me where my shit is at, I'ma kill you!!"

Lexus tried to answer, but the smelly wet carpet was making her gag. "I got something even better," she managed to utter in excruciating pain. My fury couldn't help but to strike Lexus in the back of her head with a closed fist. "I don't want to hear nothing from you besides where my shit is." I pulled on her ponytail, stretching her neck out.

"Please listen to me, baby. I know where your mother is, Nikko. I know where you can find her right now," Lexus blurted out, her words rambunctiously trying to escape the next head blow.

"What did you say?" I asked awestruck. Lexus had all of her attention.

"Your girl came past here looking for you earlier today. I was stalking your apartment to show you what Raw made me do. He put a gun to my head and made me break in here with him when he peeped me hiding out in your bushes. He trashed the crib, took all your music and the blow you had stashed under the couch."

I punched Lexus in the face and spit on her. "You think I'm dumb, bitch? You was fucking the nigga!" One hand around Lexus' throat, the other wrapped up in her ponytail, I squeezed on her neck while pulling her hair so hard her scalp began to bleed.

"I swear to you, baby, I didn't have nothing to do with it. I love you, please… please stop…" Lexus cried out in pain. "Your mom is at a church called Hillcrest on Wiley Avenue on the hill. You got to believe me. Just call Porsha. I swear I'm telling you the truth."

I dropped Lexus' face back down in the moldy rug, rubbing it into the car[et. cutting off her oxygen. Lexus panicked, kicking and screaming for dear life until I let her up. I untangled my hand from her head and got up off her back. Kicking her in the gut, I asked, "What is the name of that church again?"

"Hillcrest," she answered, doubled over in pain. "Porsha told me to make sure you got the message."

I stood in the midst of her foul apartment staring at Lexus. "I got it! That's the church I walk past every Friday to get to the gay club down in the next block. I hustle over there sometimes when the money is low. Is this some type of a joke?" I kept a close eye on Lexus for any little sign of a lie. She held eye contact with me, shaking her head no.

"It's not a joke, baby. I'm telling you the truth," Lexus said, reaching in for a hug. Stunned, I allowed her to do so.

Speechless, the two held each other for a moment. The urge to get high was subdued, and the thought of finding Raw wasn't a given, it was nonexistent. I pushed off Lexus and ran to the bathroom. You could hear me throwing up and crying at the same time. I believed Lexus, every word. I had to.…

A supernatural force came over me while I stared at myself in the bathroom mirror. I stood face to face with the devil, me. The devil was me. I walked like him, talked like him and I thought like him. I broke the mirror with my bare hand with so much hatred for the reflection that stared back at me. Faced with the moment I've been waiting for my whole life, I turned away and ran.

I went back to the living room where Lexus was at and smacked her once, twice and again. I went in her pockets, taking a nice knot of bills and snatched my chain off her neck. I didn't even notice it was her own chain. The craving to get high called as an almighty necessity as I fled the apartment, leaving Lexus behind.

Lexus opened up the door to her house tired but satisfied with her meet and greet with me. Flicking on the light in the room, shock overwhelmed her. Raw sat on the loveseat, arms stretched across the back while three more men made their way to the living room from the kitchen. Her black track suit was soaked, her ponytail hung from the side of her head by a thread, face bruised with a pounding headache, Lexus played the victim right into the arms of Raw. Crocodile tears rolled down her stone-cold face as she buried her face into his chest. Raw consoled her while pulling a gun from up under a pillow on the loveseat he'd stashed before she got there.

"There, there baby, everything is going to be alright," Raw said, putting the gun up under her eye to wipe away the tears.

"What the hell are you doing with that?" Lexus spat.

"What does it look like?"

"I don't know, you tell me!" Lexus rubbed the fake tears from her eyes to make things clearer. Anxiety set in as she awaited an answer.

"It's a stick up, bitch. Now what?" Raw pushed Lexus to the couch, knocking what was left of her ponytail on the floor. He motioned to his homeboys with the gun to proceed with the plan they talked about a day ago. "You a smart, bitch, I think you know what that means— I'm taking everything in your crib you own. You should remain seated on the couch and just count this one as a loss."

Lexus didn't say a word. She had underestimated Raw. She didn't have a plan and was too nervous to think of one. So she sat there watching the three men take her belongings. She eyeballed Raw with disgust; however he enjoyed it, as it turned him on.

"Awe, you mad at me, Lexus?" Raw smiled a devilish grin.

"You crazy as hell if you think you're going to get away with this."

SMACK!! "You do what I say and I'll let you live. Plus, look around you. I'm already getting away with it, young buck."

Blood dripped from the corner of Lexus' mouth while Raw's homies watched and laughed at him playing Big Willie style pimping. He was getting off being the boss, the rush going to his head.

"As a matter of fact, I got something to keep your mouth shut." Raw massaged the bulge in his pants as the thought of Lexus sucking him off in front of his homies made him harder.

Lexus knew the look oh too well. She seen his vein swelling, and even though she wasn't keen on sucking dick, she knew she had no choice. She kept a mental note tucked in the corner of her brain— never underestimate anybody and always have a plan B. He removed the flesh from his pants without saying a word. He motioned with his gun for Lexus to come closer to him. She did what she was told, moving up on him until she was eye level with his penis. She looked up at him, and he was staring down on her with no mercy. She opened her mouth and he eased on in as she deep throats.

Yes, yes, yes, do that, boo, like you know how. You thought you had me pegged from the start. I was just another dumb corner boy you was going to fuck, suck and use. Caught you by surprise, didn't I Lexus? I'm smarter than the average bear, Boo-Boo the bitch." Raw gloated as he put on his show for his homies. He ran his hand through Lexus' hair, gripping up the nappy roots in the back, forcing his muscle deeper down her throat as he controlled her head movement. She clutched his waist trying to find his rhythm, sickened by the whole ordeal and wanting it to stop. Stupidity is what she felt down on her knees with a dick in her mouth, her house invaded, her egoism brought down a notch by a man she thought she controlled. Karma is a bitch... what goes around comes around... the trap you set for someone else is the same one that catches you...

CHAPTER FORTY-FOUR

"**M**s. Lola James… Yeah, that's her… My mother. As I sat there in the back row of a church listening to my mother preach the word of God to us devils that just stepped in off the street to get warm, I cried. She was so beautiful to me; she hasn't aged a bit from her picture.

Her full-length hair was wrapped and pulled around her high cheekbones, causing a glow to come about her face as if she has found her calling. The night air was chilling to the boneyard as I wait on the Candyman to come through the streets. The cold was what drove me here to this pew. Could it be that thing, drugs that drove us away that will bring us back together today? The words spilling from her mouth gave me butterflies in my stomach. Was she talking directly to me? Even though the church was packed and you could hear the "amens" bouncing off the walls, I couldn't see or hear anybody else but her. Did she notice me sitting way in the back?

The manifestation of a man was how I'd carried myself for the last couple of years of my life, shedding very few tears, all alone taking life as it was dealt—FUCKED UP!! Her daughter, her little girl… that's what I was the last time she saw me, the last time she held me in her arms, and the last time she saw my face. Only by blood was this woman standing up there on that pulpit anything to me. I stood before her a grown-ass dike with issues as she stared past me. Only if my grandmother could see how my mother, her daughter, had overcome so many demons she had controlling her emotions. To see her first born she cursed until the day she died make something of herself. As she stood there, preaching, I couldn't believe it. My stomach muscles went from calm to reflex, ready to throw up the 40 ounce of beer I drank a half hour ago. I needed a hit of crack.

"The only man you need in your life is Jesus. I know that's the only man I need in mine. He is my rock, my faith and my friend when I have no other. He is my wing when I don't have the strength to go on any further. I know some of you way in the back just came in here this evening to get warm, and you are welcomed in the Lord's house. God loves you, too. He made it cold to bring you to me so you will know the Lord loves sinners, too."

The preacher woman came down from the pulpit. She spoke, but I can't hear a word coming from her mouth. Our eyes are focused on each other, my heart pounding tremendously.

"Come to me my love.... come to me, my only daughter...." The preaching lady came close... closer... closer...

"I..." I try to talk. My eyes open up, my vision blurs, my mouth grows pasty, my throat is itchy and dry as I try to speak a syllable. I blink repeatedly to try and focus, moving my hands to my face to rub my eyes. Finally I begin to see clearer.

A young white male sits in a room that I figure is in a hospital from the tubes hanging from my body and the beeping machines. Right off the bat, I know he is trouble. Cop is written all over the young man's posture. His dusty blond hair covers his right eye. He sits in the chair asleep on the back of his hand, which rests on the arm of a recliner.

"Hello..." I said under a raspy voice. My throat is extra dry and it hurts to speak.

"What did you say?" he asks to my surprise. I didn't think he heard me. In a blink of an eye, he is on his feet, standing next to my hospital bed. He asks again, "What did you say?" as he wipes the corners of his mouth.

"Water, please" I ask. He is on it, quickly pouring me a cup that sits next to my bedside.

The water I drink gives me strength as I look at the white man. I know it is time for me to go before the police show up. Another glass of water and I'm sitting up. I swing my feet around to hang off the side of the bed. The white man runs towards the door, demanding more water from a nurse walking by. Next thing he is right back in my face.

"My name is Officer Blue."

"I knew you were a cop." My voice doesn't crack.

"I'm here to find out what happened to you the night you were found naked on the sidewalk." The officer runs his fingers through his hair; I run my fingers across my trachea as if my throat begins to hurt again. The officer makes an attempt to get more water when a nurse appears right on time with a fresh container and cups.

"Can you find me some clothes from somewhere nurse?" I ask respectfully.

The officer holds out both of his arms between the nurse and me. "You can't go anywhere until you answer my questions." The officer puts his hands down and nods to the nurse to get lost. Standing firm, he pours water into the three-stacked cup while I jockey the cop out the corner of my eye.

"What's your name?" Officer Blue asks.

"My name is Egypt, and if I'm not under arrest I would like to leave. I got more important things to do than talk to the police."

A flashback of that ugly fucker flashes before my eyes; seeing Boo's face turns my lip up, however, his brother, my long-lost first love sends a quiver through my soul.

"Are you cold?" Officer Blue asks, seeing the chill run across my body.

"No, I just had a bad feeling about something. I need to find my mother and make things right."

"So, that's the more important thing you have to do rather than talking to me?"

"Anything is more important than talking to you." As I sit on the edge of the hospital bed, my heartbeat is fierce. All I can think about is General coming to find me and kill me if I ever utter a word. "Even if I did open up my mouth to tell you something, it wouldn't be nothing but a lie because I know no truth."

"Why wouldn't you want to tell me what happened to you? What kind of person would protect the monster who done this to them?" Officer Blue looks at the cup he still has in his hand, dumbfounded as if searching for an answer to his own question. He hands me the cup of water like the contents have the answer.

"You can't protect me from the streets, from this man who done this to me. He's been a part of my life always, watching me, watching my family for many years, and I didn't know it. I live in the streets, and I'll handle my beef in the streets. I'm no snitch, raped or not." Disgusted by my own answer, I can't do anything but hang my head low. "I just really need to get out of here so I can get with my mother..."

"Well, Ms. Winters, your mother is dead." A domineering voice cuts the moment with a knife, creating a brazenly introduction. Me and Officer Blue turn around to put a face to the voice.

"Another fucking cop!" I spit under my breath. "You don't know nothing about my mother! How do you know she's dead?"

"Yeah, detective, I want to know how you came up with that information, also," Officer Blue adds.

"Good ol' fashioned police work, Mr. Rookie of the Year." The detective makes one hell of an entrance. Suave, he walks into the room, removing his stale suit jacket. He moves about the room like he cracked the Cold Case File. "Your mother is Ms. Diane James, right?" the detective speaks shrewdly; he just knows he has all the answers. Opening up a folder he has in his hands, he licks his index finger before he starts looking through the papers.

I can't believe how humorous the funny-looking cop is. I want to see the rest of his performance of super detective, but I don't have that much time left, so I decide to crush his dreams.

"See what I mean?" I speak directly at officer Blue. "The punk-ass police don't know shit. Diane James ain't my mother, she's my aunt, silly Mr. Detective. How dare you come in here, smug as hell, trying to show your partner up," I crack a smile at Officer Blue, "with the wrong damned info? You supposed to have your shit straight." Now I'm angry. "I'm really not telling you shit now! You can't protect me or my family! I'm the fuck up and out. I don't care if I'm naked or not."

"What in the hell is wrong with you?!" Officer Blue shouts, pushing the detective in the far-end corner of the hospital room. "Where did you get that fallacious information? She didn't trust us before, but with that stunt you just pulled, she won't trust us ever" Officer Blue whispers, but nonetheless, I can hear him as I find some clothes to put on in a large double-door cabinet.

"Fallacious," the detective sneers. "Such big words for a little sneaky son of a bitch like you." The detective removes himself from the small corner Officer Blue tried to hold him in.

"Look here, Egypt! I don't care about little black girl lost and you having to find your mother, whoever the hell that could be. The only thing I care about is the monster, and General is his name that done this to you!"

"Well, if you know his name, why you in here fucking with me? Go and get him!"

"You admit that General is the one that held you hostage in that apartment?"

Shit!! He had me. Even though I didn't want to tell, it still got out. I stand there, my mind a blank. I don't know what to say.

"If you don't tell me what happened in there, Egypt, he could hurt another girl and that would be your fault." The detective speaks, walking directly towards me. Our eyes are locked on each other as his words sink in. I try my best to get the clothes on I found in the cabinet, but the shirt or pants don't seem to fit. Frustration begins to set in, and I can hear the calm in my fault. I have made up my mind.

"I'll talk if you buy me something that fits."

The detective smiles. I can see all thirty-two of his teeth. "You got it, little lady. I can get the rookie to get whatever it is you want." Pen and pad in hand, his smile resembles the Cheshire Cat.

"Hold up here, I'm not your errand boy!" Officer Blue disputes.

The detective gives off a look that says you're going to do what I tell you to do.

"I need a medium-sized sports bra and a pair of boxers." For some reason, when I speak, I look directly at Officer Blue. He makes it a little bit easier to do what I have to do. "And I'll take a large white tee and a pair of large sweat pants. Please have me matching."

The detective nods to the rookie to fulfill the task so he can be alone in the room with me.

"I'm not going to play with you any longer!" The detective starts in as soon as the rookie leaves the room. He throws the malicious pictures of my dead aunt onto the bed.

"I want you to look at them, Egypt! The same man that did that to you has killed your aunt and is most likely onto his next victim. Do you really want him to get away? Go ahead and look at what he did."

I am sick to my stomach. I can't move a muscle, my mind racing with the thoughts of me having sex with him when we were kids. Once upon a time he was my baby, and now he's this monster.

"You know, Egypt, I'm sorry for confusing her, your aunt with your mother. It was a simple mistake. I just assumed she was your mother because the DNA ran together perfect, and that's because she was your mother's sister. This could be your mother next if we don't find him." The detective picks up one of the photos off the bed and places it on my lap. "If he found your aunt, and did this to you, your mother is bound to be next."

I look down at the photo of my aunt. Her body lays on the dirty ground mutilated. I can't stand her ass, but didn't nobody deserve to die like that. I can't believe it. I haven't seen my aunt in years and now this.

"It's really her...." I mumble underneath my breath, tears welling up in my eyes as I look at all the puddles of blood on her body. It sends chills up my spine when I look in her open, dead eyes. I drop the photo to the floor, stumbling to get to my feet.

"I don't know where he is now, but you have to help me and my family, the little bit of family I got left. He's my ex-boyfriend from when I was a teenager. His brother is the one who raped me first. I thought I knew him, but I knew nothing about him. From beginning to end, I was at the wrong place at the wrong time, getting high. Me and Boo started off getting high together, and then he drugged me with heroin, and that was all she wrote." I continued to tell the detective everything I knew—all the gory little details. I even tell him about the hit he put on my baby daddy. The misguided detective stands before me awestruck. He is hanging on my every word, intrigued more and more by the end of each sentence.

My body became marked for death as the cop became an eyesore, asking question after question. I have gone out of the way to break the street code I lived by. I am now a snitch as I sit here and tell it all like I'm a guest on Oprah. I ask myself—am I justified to go this route? Vividly my memory bank overruns the mental blocks; the harshness of many situations I choose to do wrong ring loudly. My short life becomes an illusion, a mistaken perception of reality, a false belief, and a misconception of my entity. Revealing the truth about what happened behind those closed doors makes me realize I would have nightmares for the rest of my life. Not just about being raped, but about the way I lived and cheated death so many times.

"Maybe you would like to take a break and try these clothes on I got you." Officer Blue stands at the door holding a bag of clothes. He is only gone for forty-five minutes, but it seems like a lifetime.

I never thought I would be happy to see a cop. The rookie slides past the detective and hands me my bag with the clothes in it.

"Is he treating you okay?" he asks with a small grin. I nod my head yes and return the same small smile.

"Go ahead in the bathroom and get dressed. I hope the clothes fit you well."

"Who are you to come up in here giving orders, rookie? I would have told her when I was ready when she could have gotten dressed."

Officer Blue held his tongue. Nonetheless, if looks could kill, the detective would be one dead son of a bitch. For real, the rookie really wants to beat shit down his leg, but has to take a different route.

"Come on, old man, you don't have to keep disrespecting me like that. I'm not giving orders, sir, I'm just trying to help you out." Officer Blue puts on a smile. He wants to bust the detective right there on the spot to check his pride; however, he has a job to do and he is going to do it.

"I don't trust you, rookie!" the detective says, irate. He moves in very close to the rookie and smells the crook of his neck,."You smell kinda funky to me." The detective runs his tongue over his teeth and backs up slowly. They eye each other viciously.

"The clothes fit just right," I say, opening up the bathroom door, stepping into a duel.

"I think I'm going to go get me a cup of coffee" the detective says, and with that, he was gone.

"He's an asshole," me and Officer Blue say at the same time. We can't help but to laugh at his dumb ass.

"You've been a great help to the detective, and I know this because he left. And I'm not going to sit here and take you down a long line of questions neither."

I can't help but to sit back down on the bed. I am lightheaded and need something to drink. I hang my head.

"Pick your head up, honey. You don't have to be ashamed of. I think you're damned brave for making it out of that apartment alive. I believe you got a second chance at life—you better take it and run, honey."

I can't help it. The tears are running down my face nonstop. I look the cop in the eyes. They are warm and soothing.

"His brother helped me escape in the end, you know. And he doesn't like his older brother General that much. Boo left the door open for me when he left to carry out a hit on some boy named Craze. He felt bad because all he wanted to do was shit on me to feed his ego; he never thought I would die because of it. If you can get to his brother, Boo, I know for a fact he'll help you set General up for his downfall."

The rookie cop soaks up all the information. I tell him what I didn't tell the detective. For some reason, he is the one I trust; the rookie seems aiight. I want him to win the case.

"Thank you, Egypt," he says gratefully.

"You're welcome."

A nurse enters the room with a tray of meds and more water. I ask questions about every different pill on the tray and what it was going to do to my body. The nurse smiles and answers all of my questions. I learn I will never harvest another child in my womb, and I am a carrier of the hepatitis C virus that could take my life quicker than AIDS if I don't take care of myself.

Even though I caught a nasty backlash from the choices I made throughout this whole ordeal. I can no longer blame my mother or curse God—I can only put the blame on me, myself and I...

As I discuss my medical condition, Officer Blue has a heads up on the detective and his next move. All he has to do is make one phone call and everything will be set into place. As he steps outside of the hospital room, he walks right up behind the detective holding a phone conversation.

"Hot dammit!! You are the man, Henry!! I got to buy you a drink as soon as I close this case. I can't thank you enough for finding the plate number for me. When I catch up with him this time, I'm going to put him to sleep for good. Believe me when I say we're home free, buddy." The detective hangs up the phone with all his teeth showing, standing a few paces from in front of Egypt's door. Turning around, he's face to face with Officer Blue, who was riding his back. Catching him off guard, the detective stumbles back, almost losing his balance, using the wall that's close to him to break his fall.

"See what I mean, Rookie of the Year? You're always creeping around."

Officer Blue shakes his head, piqued. "I smell a rat detective, and it's you. You're always up to no good. But you're right, I am always creeping up on you, and it's not hard because you don't pay attention. You're a bad, crooked cop, and you should work on your creeping skills."

The detective waves him off. "Whatever you say, young blood."

"You know that I'm right, old head!!" Officer Blue speaks in a whisper, barely parting his lips. The scowl on his face lets the detective know how he feels deep down inside about him.

"This conversation is through," the detective says, turning around and walking away. Using the same telephone, Officer Blue dials zero to get an outside line.

"He's on the move right now. Make sure you put a man on him, and you tell him if he loses the detective, he'll be frying fish tomorrow. This is it. He's about to take himself down; I can feel it. He's going to lead us right to the General."

When the rookie returns to the room, he finds I escaped room without him seeing. He calls my name out...

"Egypt!!" In the room and then next in the hallway, doctors, nurses and patients look at the officer with confusing stares.

"She's gone..." he mumbles under his breath. His feet moved quickly to the elevator to see if he can catch her at the opposing side of the hallway, but there is nothing. "I hope she finds what she's looking for," Officer Blue says aloud, pressing the elevator button.

I walk out the double doors of the hospital, seeing the world in a whole new light. The breeze is cool, but the sun is shining down on me. I glance over the cheap sweatclothes I have on. It doesn't bother me. For the first time in my life, I don't care about what someone else is thinking about my outline; I am perfectly fine with the reality of breathing. Today, and from this day forth, I'm going to live my life to the fullest and happiest through prayer. I will be a living testimony for the next lost soul.

CHAPTER FORTY-FIVE

The naked room was quiet. The beam of sunlight crept through the window, warming Lexus' naked body. Raw and his crew have their way with Lexus and make a perfect getaway with all of her belongings in her household. Every time she shut her eyes, she would relive a different part of the pain. Because of this, she has been laying awake for the last twenty-three hours paralyzed with agony.

"Do you see me in this pussy, homeboy?" Raw shouted at his team as they walked around him having sex with Lexus. "I should be in a porno movie!! Where the camera at in this motherfucker?!!" He pumped harder and harder, tearing up her insides. "Say my name, bitch, say my motherfucking name!!" He continued to pump as his homies cheered him on, waiting for their turn. Raw stuck his dirty fingernails in the skin of Lexus' ass and clawed it until he drew blood, pumping in and out faster and faster as she pleaded with him to stop. The more she said his name, the rougher he became. The more she begged him to stop, the harder he dug his fingernails into her skin until three of them broke off.

"You thought I was stupid, didn't you, bitch!! You thought I wasn't capable of being a man. You tried to use me; you tried to settle your beef with Nikko by fucking me, but now I'm fucking you! Raw was still beating it up from the back. But now a horny spectator had forced his vein down her throat. She gagged, unable to breathe from her nose being stuffed up from crying so much.

"Your little plan didn't work out, now did it!!?" Raw laughed and his team followed right behind him, laughing even louder. Raw's legs began to buckle; he couldn't calm the tingling sensation his balls were having any further—he was going to blow.

"AWEEE," Raw screeched, and his voice bounced off the empty room. Raw walked around to Lexus' face and made his boy pull out of her mouth.

"Clean off the tip, bitch!!" Raw ordered her. She didn't have a choice as he forced his semi-erection in her mouth.

"Everybody gets got playing around in this game. The twist of fate won't have it no other way, baby." Raw patted Lexus on top of the head like she was his pet, a good little puppy. He placed his dick back into his pants, and it was a wrap.

He sat his ass down on the floor, sparking a blunt to watch the after show. His boys took turns raping Lexus over and over again. They showered her with piss and semen until she was too vile to fuck any longer. The only thing she could do was blame Nikko. *This is all her fault*, she said to herself over and over again. If only she wouldn't have hurt me, I wouldn't have gotten myself into this situation. Anger grew from deep down within.

"You'll never break me, Raw, you'll always be a weak-ass nigga to me that got beat up by a bitch!!" With the last breath, she took Lexus spoke her mind. Three seconds later she got kicked in the mouth.

Lexus moved her stiffened arms from around her legs and mustered up some strength, overthinking everything that went down twenty-three hours ago.

"Oh, yeah. I'm going to kill that bitch. If it's the last thing I do, I'm going to kill Nikko." Boo has found a back street from off of Route 279 leading straight to the projects to where it all started. The cops often forget about the long dirt road that reaches from the highway to the backwoods, so Boo felt safe. It is time to finish what started years ago down in the dark basements. Manhoods were taken, lives were brought to their end, soldiers were created and young boys lost their sensitivity for life itself, deep down, way in the back of those dark basements.

Monsters warp Boo's mind as he pulls up to the old rowhouse his grandmother lived in once upon a time. The middle house in a row of six sits boarded up just like all the others. The rain has gone away and the shining sun is taking over, but you can still smell the stench of death in the air. Little kids ride their bikes up and down the sidewalk of abandoned houses on a strip called Hope Street.

"Get the hell up, nigga!!" Boo whacks General in the face, causing his head to hit the passenger side window. "The devil must be down there beating the hell out of his wife!"

"What..." General asked, disoriented.

"Come on, you remember that old saying grandma always said before the sun shined bright after a hard thundering rain, don't you?"

General mumbles something of no understanding towards Boo feeling the lumps and the bruises all over his face and busted lip.

Boo smacks General again. "Come on, nigga, get the fuck up!!" He shakes his head, laughing. "Don't tell me you can't take a hit."

"What happened to my fucking lip?" General asks, patting his lip and then looking at his fingers for a spot of blood. General's vision is blurred from the thick cut resting over his left eyelid.

"I knocked your bitch ass out cold last night, and you was sleeping like a baby, that's what happened to you." Boo picks up a napkin from off the floor of the car and hands it to General to wipe the blood.

"I guess you finally grew some balls, lil' nigga." General isn't talking his words, he is growling them, his jaw clenched with anger.

"So," General pauses, "what the fuck are you going to do now?" He pulls down the flat sunshade attached to the top of the car. "You gonna kill me, nigga? Is that really what you're going to do?" General examines his eye in the mirror of the visor unamused, and Boo doesn't answer none of his questions.

"We home, General," is all Boo says, nodding to General to take a look out of the window.

RING! RING! RING!

A cell phone underneath the passenger seat of the care startles Boo and General. General looks at Boo and Boo looks at him, as if General is asking permission to answer it. Even though his dick is rock hard to kill his brother, for the first time in General's life he is scared to make a move. Boo is too relaxed, too confident, and today he doesn't hesitate to look him in the eye.

RING! RING! RING!

"Get the fucking phone, man!" Boo yells demandingly, letting General know he is running the show.

General glares at Boo with hesitation. "And if I don't, what you going to do wit ya bitch ass?"

Boo takes a deep breath, shaking his head for his poor brother. He realizes at that moment he didn't get the memo that little bro was running shit now. Everything General has ever done to him flashes before his eyes. As Boo blinks repeatedly, tears falls from his eyes. Not wasting another minute and without saying a word, he smacks General again in the face with the butt of his gun. Without aiming, he knocks out two of his teeth.

"Don't you understand, Trap!? It's over for you. Your time is done." Boo goes from dramatic to calm in thirty seconds. "Your time is up, man..." Boo whispers again. And General can't say a word. His mouth is busted wide open and he is spitting out bloody teeth.

RING! RING! RING!

The phone continues to ring and General continues to spit blood out of the window. He is in hella pain, but he won't let it on to Boo. He isn't thinking about pressing his buttons again neither.

"Clean yourself up, nigga, and get the phone."

General looks at Boo with disgust and spits another glob of blood out the window. He presses the reclining button on the side of the seat to push it back so he can get the phone.

"Don't make no plans," Boo says smirking. He is enjoying every bit of his freedom. He is no longer going to be up under another man's thumb.

"Holla." General barely got the word out his mouth. The open holes where the teeth once resided is on fire as his gums thump with throbbing sensations every time air hits them. He doesn't want to say a word, but he isn't going to bitch up in front of Boo. General knows at that moment Boo has him by the balls, but he won't let up to make Boo even think he has it like that. NEVER!!

"It's me," the voice says on the other end of the phone.

General takes the phone from his ear and looks at it strange. "What the fuck is this?" He can't believe whose voice he is hearing on the other end of the phone, a voice that is only supposed to be heard on his terms. "I need to know when I lost control of this situation. How in the fuck did this happen?" The detective is to never catch him by number.

"You lost control of the situation as soon as you let your little girl-friend get away," the voice continues. And the detective is taping the conversation, putting his own plan in motion.

General pushes the speaker button so Boo can hear. He looked at Boo ill-willed. "Repeat yourself, Mr. Detective, for my brother."

"You lost control of the situation as soon as you let your little girl-friend get away. Did you hear that, brother? I hope I got both ya'lls attention because what I'm about to say I will not repeat twice."

Boo's facial expression never changes. It remains cold and unfazed. General's heart is in his throat, and he can't believe that Boo isn't shook. General is beginning to get mad at himself for being afraid.

"I knew I should have killed that bitch myself," General says up under his breath.

"That's exactly what I expected you to say you, dumbfuck," the detective said nonchalantly. "You're going to make this so easy."

"I have your little girlfriend locked away in a hotel room ready to bring you down, Mr. General, and your whole out-of-control crew. She couldn't wait to spill her guts about how you and your brother raped her and pumped her full of dope continuously. The pictures we took of her at the hospital will get you 20 years, no doubt. But oh, there's more. I have you connected to the Diane James' victim, the aunt of your latest victim. Your DNA is all over her body, and the hairs found on your little girlfriend match Diane James'. Now, you're looking at life Mr. Trap Dixon. You're not going to have football numbers, you're going to have letters—big, bold and black letters. Are you getting all this homeboy?!" the detective finishes up abruptly.

General plays it cool, eyeballing his brother. "And so what, Mr. Detective, you work for me. Make it go away or I'll rat you the fuck out." General picks up a blunt from the ashtray and puts fire to it. He cracks a smile as if he has everything under control.

"You think you know everything, don't you?" the detective asks with laughter behind his voice. "They already know I was working for you as a dirty cop, General. That was the role I was supposed to play, being undercover. I truly have you by the balls, bitch! It's over for you, unless you can come up with one hundred thousand dollars. Checkmate!"

The detective lights his cigar and places his feet up on the dashboard of his car. He is holding all aces and he knows it. The phone line is still open, but it is as quiet as a church mouse.

General sits with a blank stare. He is as furious as a raging beast. He wants to kill Boo with his bare hands, but the gun on his brother's lap makes him think different.

"I told you to kill that bitch, Boo. Now look, she done came back to haunt us." General is irate, although he speaks calmly. "Since you're in charge now, how do you plan to handle this situation? You got this man's money? I ain't doing life behind your dumb-ass mistake. Fix it and fix it now."

Boo snatches the blunt out of General's hand and raises his fist at him. Caught by surprise, General flinches, and it was a wrap. Boo grows an ominous smile; he has the fear in his brother for the first time in his life. He hits the blunt and then snatches the phone out of

General's other hand. He takes off the speaker and places the phone to his ear.

"I got your money detective, but how do I know you'll hold up your end of the deal? After all, you can't be trusted; you're a fucking pig." Boo is gruesome and fearless. Posture erect, his eyes are on point. He nods his head listening to the detective's response, insinuating that he will follow his lead.

"Get the fuck out of the car," Boo says to General, pointing his gun at him. General does what he is told and opens the door. When he does, Boo whispers something to the detective and hangs up the cell phone. Just as General shuts the passenger side door, Boo comes up from the rear.

"What in the hell are we doing here, Boo?"

"I got a surprise for you, big bro. I'm sure you won't like it, but who gives a damn." Boo puts the gun into General's back. "Now move, bitch. We taking it back to the old days. Remember what we used to do down in Grandma's basement? It's gonna be just like old times." Boo pushes General down the back sidewalk leading to the rear door of their old dwelling place.

"I'm not going in there, nigga!!" General says pulling up to the door. He can feel it deep down that something isn't right. If he goes in that basement, he knows he won't see another day.

Boo doesn't respond with words, he responds with force. From the back, Boo smacks General again with his gun. This time, General turns about and tried to take a stand, but Boo wasn't having it. As soon as General spins around and swings, Boo ducks and comes up with a stiff uppercut, knocking General to the ground. The blow to the mouth is too intense, the punch hitting a nerve, numbing his whole mouth and ringing his brain with a constant thrash of agony.

"Man the fuck up, bitch!! Ain't that what you always said to me? Well, look at me now! Yes, I am my brother's keeper." Boo grabs General by the collar of his jacket and pulls him into the abandoned house they grew up in. General can't put up a fight. His mouth is in excruciating pain as the rest of his body falls victim to it. He fight off the new strains of infection residing in his brother.

"You going to kill me, ain't you, nigga? You let a strange bitch go and get us caught up, but you going to kill the only family you got left," General cries the words out of his mouth. Blood drips from the bottom of his swollen lip. It is a pitiful sight. Boo regrets lighting the candles to bring vision throughout the basement as soon as he seen his brother at his weakest moment. He thinks the ultimate high would be to fuck his brother slowly as he did him for years, to strip him of his manhood and make him beg for mercy, but as the light trembles upon his distorted face, Boo seen the lost soul of his brother. He knows at that moment what he has to do.

General lies on the floor, moaning in pain. Boo moves about the basement, lighting the remainder of the candles he set up on previous trips. His grandmother's basement became a permanent fixture in his life once he started pumping dope in his veins. The warmth of the drug would take effect and draw him to his pain, flashing back to his life before his parents and then after, before his brother raped him and took his manhood. The dope was a secret for many years as Boo started doing it at the tender age of thirteen. The basement kept his secret just as the many others, and it soothed the nightmares his tormented soul couldn't let go.

Boo is drawn to the darkness, letting demented memories tear through his conscience when he realizes he'll kill himself before he becomes the monster his brother is. Then he thinks about what he has done to subdue his own ego trying to be his brother, realizing this time he is already him, maybe worse than him because he is a follower, the filth of the beast.

"We got to get this crooked cop's money, Boo, or we both going down in a matter of hours," General moans in between his words as he whispers them slowly. Lying on his back, blood drips down the back of his throat, causing him to choke up phlegm.

Boo hears every word his brother says, but ignores him. He inhales the scent of stale urine, molded wood and mildewed walls, eyeing the old, rusted pipes that run along the ceiling.

"Don't you worry about getting that money, General. Neither one of us is going to do a day in jail, and that detective ain't getting one penny of anything with his crooked-cop ass. I'ma take care of you..." Boo says, walking towards General.

"What do you mean you're going to take care of me?"

"Don't ask me no questions, and I'll tell you no lies." Boo approaches General, standing over him. General can see his empty eyes. He is sure he is going to die at this moment. Instead, Boo bends down and begins to strip General of all of his clothing.

"Oh, I see!" General says irate. "I knew you was a fucking faggot, bitch!!" He laughs for all of about five seconds when Boo's foot rests on the crease of General's neck.

Very calmly he says, "I am you, Trap. You taught me to be this way, a faggot, a drug addict, a gangster..."

"We both know you ain't one of them, nigga!!"

"You know, you right, " Boo says, grinning "I'm not a gangster, but I am my brother's keeper." Boo pulls off General's pants and removes his Polo 45-inch-waist belt. "This should do the trick. . ." Boo says as he kicks General in the kidney.

The bad blood boils between the two as their eyes lock with deep indignation to punish each other.

"I was only. . . I was only eight years. . ." Boo tries to get the words out of his mouth, but General finishes his sentence for him.

"You was only eight years old when I made you my bitch, bitch!" His smile is obnoxious, his voice wrathful. General knows he is staring down the barrel of a gun and can't fuck around with fate any longer. He is ready to die. "Yeah, I remember that shit like it was yesterday. Yes you were eight, but the way you handled my dick I thought you was a lot older than that."

"I was your little brother, you sick motherfucker!!" Boo yells in a crying rage. I didn't ask for none of this..."

"Neither the fuck did I!! This is just the hand we were dealt.!" By this time, General has made it to his feet. He stands before Boo naked with his hands to the sides and his palms up. "I did to you what your father did to me. He stole my youth and killed our mother long before I set fire to the house. I only saved you Boo to kill you, to steal every innocent moment you could have possibly ever had in your life. And you see, I got what I wanted—I'm your nightmare just like your daddy was mine." General talks his way up to Boo and makes his move.

General swings wildly with the left hook, missing but coming back and punching Boo with the right in the stomach. Next, General tries to go for Boo's gun, but fails. Boo knows his tactics too well. That is one thing Boo did—paid attention to the detailed ass whippings he got on the regular awaiting the day to be a man and stand up on his own two feet. It is time.

As General reaches for the gun, Boo sweeps him off his feet, bringing him down on his back. He takes the gun and lets off two shots in both his brother's kneecaps. The sound of the gun echoes through the hollow basement as General's cries bounce off death's opened doors. Boo doesn't waste another minute. It is time to do what he has to do and show General why he was brought there. Boo comes from behind strapping up General's neck with the belt. Cutting off his air supply, he punches General repeatedly in both kneecaps to hear him scream. General can't scream, though, pulling at the belt with his bloody fingers, fighting for a breath until Boo loosens the reins. Boo looks above his head, laying eyes on the rusty pipe running across the ceiling. Boo choose one of two chairs sitting in the midst of the filthy basement and checks the weight of the pipe. He places his hands around the pipe and lets his body hang from it like dead weight. Doing two pull-ups, Boo is convinced the pipe can do the job.

Boo hops back down off the chair and pursues General once again, this time taking his shirt and tying his hands behind his back.

"Get up, motherfucker!!" Boo whispers, pulling General up by the arm. "I want your ass up there on that chair."

Knees shot out, all General wants is for it to be over. He wants Boo to kill him and put him out of his misery. He finds the strength not to fight but to do what he was told, sitting down on the chair.

"I didn't tell you to sit, nigga," Boo says, tightening the reins once again around General's neck. Boo stands on a chair behind him, pulling General up as he wraps the belt around the pipe. General has no choice but to stand to his feet if he wants to breathe. General looks like he is ready to commit suicide, standing on a chair asshole naked with his balls in his hands.

"You better kill me, nigga, 'cause if you don't, I swear I'm going to kill you." General's lip shakes with all honesty.

"Don't even worry about it, nigga." Boo pours liquor on General's feet and then takes a swig. He looks him in the eye, then seconds later a big smile dances on his lips. "I'ma set you on fire."

General spits at Boo. "Do whatever it is you need to do to make yourself feel better. I don't give a fuck if I live or die, you know why? Because if I'm alive men fear me, and when I'm dead, I'll always be in the back of nigga's heads. They will still shiver when they hear my name."

Boo nods his head. "You're so right." At that moment, he despises his brother, pouring the rest of the liquor all over his naked skin. He slowly walk toward one wall and then returns. He stares at General with fierce eyes, then throws a candle on his body.

General screams for help, trying to put the fire out with his bare hands. Boo kicks the chair from up under his feet and watches his brother hang and burn to his yelping, sounding like a wounded animal, the beast that he was, dying. Seconds later, Boo suffocates the flames. He shoots the belt, and General's burnt body falls to the floor.

"I don't have to worry about you trying to get bucked now. Your Freddy-looking ass ain't going nowhere. Ain't that who you wanted to be nigga? Freddy? Now you look just like him."

"Help me…" General utters in agony.

"FUCK YOU!!" Boo yells, spitting back on General. The burning flesh makes him throw up as he put the last flames out on his body. "You said you wanted to come back and haunt niggas in their sleep. You tortured me so long, all my life, I hope I can have peace in the afterlife." Boo takes a blunt from behind his ear and put fire to it. He has to do something to cover up the stench of burnt flesh. General lays on the floor smoking, barely moving as a murmur escapes his lips every couple of minutes. He is ready for his final execution.

Everything in place, Boo takes his position awaiting the cavalry to come. Soon, the detective will be coming through to collect on his ransom.

"What a rude awakening it's going to be when he feasts his optics on General and no money." Boo pulls his last package of dope from his back pocket. He has his kit set up ready to get high. He watches his uncut smack bubble up and turn brown, his veins screaming for intoxication. "Crooked-ass cop. He deserves a bullet for every move he made with General and got paid to keep his mouth shut. For once, I'm going to do something right.

The detective is close to the destination, calling the same number back time and time again for General, but no answer. Bobbing and weaving through traffic, his foot doesn't let up off the gas pedal. Tearing up the road leading to the projects, the detective takes the same route as Boo, taking the same precautions to avoid being seen. He wants that money so bad his muscle is standing at full attention.

"Hope Street, this is it," the detective says, pulling up behind Boo's parked vehicle. It is parked right outside of the address given by Boo. Before exiting the car, he makes a mental note of the plate number and unlocks his gun while loading his steel. Feeling down his left leg, he checks on his back-up plan to reassure himself he is ready.

Taking a deep breath, the detective psyches himself up and gets out of the car. It isn't a smart move doing business like this without a partner watching his back, but for the love of the money he isn't thinking straight. Greed makes the detective tough and the ransom money will only be shared with his family.

The street is quiet with limited activity, which wasn't unusual since the police was combing the streets hard looking for the same man the detective was getting ready to see. He chuckles at the marked cop car. *If only they knew their man is right under their nose*, he thinks to himself.

The detective follows the directions Boo gave him while he tried to call the cell phone number once again. He takes the same path until he comes face to face with the backdoor. Once again, the detective takes a deep breath and looks around to check his surroundings. He bangs three times on the boarded-up window as he was told.

A startled Boo caches himself in mid-nod hearing the third knock. In one hand, there is a needle piercing his vein and in the other, his gun. It is the end of the road for him and his brother. Boo knows the detective is going to come in if he answers him or not, so he pushes the hot dope into his arm. Disrespectful as hell, Boo doesn't remove the needle as he coasts on the ride of the get-high. The detective enters the basement just as Boo knew he would, gagging on the smell of burnt, dead flesh. His heartbeat fierce, it ricochets through his conscience. He pulls his shirt up over his nose, holding his breath from the foul stench setting his eyes on the cause of it.

General's body looks like something out of a horror flick as the detective glances around, taking in the sights. Boo watches from the shadows undetected with a smirk on his face.

"What the hell is this?" the detective says loud enough for somebody to give him an answer. "General, where are you?"

"That's him laying right there in front of you. You should help him like you've helped him so many times before. Work for your blood money, crooked officer."

"Who's there? Make yourself seen before I start shooting." The detective points his gun into the shadows, nervous as hell.

"You start shooting and you just might kill me. Then how will you get your money?" The monkey begins to ride Boo's back hard, the dope breaking down his body.

"I'm tired of playing with you cocksuckers, Last warning, give me the money and get the fuck outta town. I'll kill the witness, your little girlfriend as a perk, and in a couple of years, we can start doing business again."

"I got something even better for your crooked ass." Boo puts a flame to the wick of the candle he is holding to show the detective his whereabouts. "You can see me now as I can see you." Boo raises his head, even though it is heavy from the nod of the dope. He looks the detective in the eye as he pulls the trigger of his gun, shooting General in the top of his skull. You can hear him take his last breath over the ominous quiet.

"You gets no money, you gets no immunity and you're going to get what is coming to you for making a deal with the devil." Boo turns his gun on the detective. "I'll see you in hell with gasoline boxers on, motherfucker." Two more shots go off in the dark basement where Grandma once lived as Officer Blue and a team of ten come in from the east and the west, saving the day.

CHAPTER FORTY-SIX

I lay awake in the company of my woman, the person I love, and I'm ecstatic she has given me another chance to do right by her and our son. He is asleep across my chest as I gaze into his sleeping beauty holding his head in my hand. "Thank you, Jesus…"

It's been a long journey getting my life back on track and restoring my health. However, I've accepted the fact that I'll be an addict for the rest of my life. Porsha got me going to one meeting every day, and I must admit, it's working for me. I haven't been out of her eyesight since the day fate brought us back together. Who knew she would be riding down the same street I was wandering down trying to figure out where do I go from here as I left the hospital? Taking me as I was, broken down and beat up, she gave me the unconditional love I needed. She brought me back to life.

The nightmares of my bad choices, though, have taken their toll on the both of us as the constant night sweats get worse and the unexpected middle of the night screaming gets louder. I can't ever outrun General's voice. He haunts me in my dreams every night, burnt to a crisp. It causes a wedge between Porsha and I in our lovemaking rituals, but nonetheless, my baby doesn't rush me. So often she holds me close while I just cry, asking for forgiveness. It is hard for me to do anything else besides cry. I cry for being blind for so many years; I cry for the hurt I put on my woman and my child; and I cry to God, shedding so many tears for pulling me out of a debilitating situation. Now I know he is real. Now I know why my grandma believes in a higher power, and I now know why my mother became a preacher. They have to hold onto the power of good to keep the bad away.

Even though I know General and Boo are dead, my heart still

skips a beat every time the lights go out. Boo said on many occasions I would be the death of him, and when it was all said and done, it was the truth. I owe him a big one for saving my life. I'll never trust a man again, and I pray every day old skeletons from my past don't come back to haunt me.

I'm still in debt to a major conglomerate, Diablo, and the hood entrepreneur, Joe Crack, who I know could double back and split my wig. My face all over the TV screen—they both know I'm alive and well. I walk on eggshells morning, noon and night.

The boys in blue asked me if I wanted to be protected, but I said no because all pigs lie in dirt. I'd be offed in a matter of hours; there's always a crooked cop. Look at that detective assigned to my case. I knew it when I first met his ass that he was foul. Come to find out he got just what he deserved when the world found out how crooked he really was. What happens in the dark will always come to light.

One single shot from his gun killed Boo instantly, but before he went, he caught the detective once in the abdomen and the other shot ripped through the flesh of his left leg. I know he wished he kept his mouth shut on the phone, though because Boo had him on recorder through his cell phone and the cops retrieved it from his dead hand. The death he planned for me got him life times two.

I should've listen to Porsha when she told me to stop watching the news and stop reading the papers, but I couldn't help it. Boo was smart catching the detective with his own tactics. He still got him caught up even though he died. Everything the detective said in the basement would become Boo's voicemail message. The media loved it, and they couldn't stop talking about the ghetto kid that outsmarted the crooked cop.

My name earned fame being linked to the death of my aunt 'cause I was the one who got away. Even though the drugs had taken over my aunt's mind, body and soul, she still was beautiful in the mug shot they splashed all over the news channels and newspapers. The thought of us being young again flashed before my eyes as I remember the day Diane took the now famous picture.

Who knew the first man I would ever sleep with would become a killer, years later killing my aunt and holding me hostage? Trap was a sweetheart, the boy next door and a tormented soul... I never knew who he really was. How did he turn out to be the man he became? Did I really drive him over the edge falling in love with a woman? I'll never know...

"Honey, you're burning the bacon." Porsha comes from behind, grabbing the fork I am cooking with out of my hand. She places a wet kiss on my neck, breaking me out of my trance.

"I didn't burn it that bad, did I?"

"No, but I can tell you were day dreaming again about that situation." Porsha takes over at the stove. She looks at the spread I laid out on the kitchen counter and inhales all the different food smells. "Everything looks so nice and smells so good."

How can I not think about the situation that almost took my life? Every time I look at Porsha or Shame Jr. I'm reminded that the first person I gave it up to killed the father of my child and the brother of my best friend, my wife. How do I live with that? How do I tell her the reason why her brother's dead is because of a man I knew? More than likely, he probably supplied the hot dose of coke Mario OD on as well. If only she knew...

My truth about General and Boo could turn her heart to stone. Then every time she looks at me it will be the look of disgust. She'll regret the day I met her brother, her talking me into keeping the baby and giving me her heart. It can change the love she has for me into hate.

"You're sitting there in a daze again, honey. Would you like me to fix you a plate?" Porsha asks, opening up the cabinet to pull out dishes.

I fissure up a smile. "Yeah, baby, I can eat."

In the next breath, I am bombarded by Kay and her children. For the first time since I've been back, I am happy to see the little crumb snatchers. "Auntie Egypt…" they yell out, putting a smile on my face. Just like every Saturday morning, we all sit at the dining table to enjoy breakfast. I feel at ease, the laughter of the children making all my creepy thoughts disappear for the moment. And the glow about Porsha's face is priceless as she watches me smile.

The shower water runs down my back as I assume the position with my hands holding up the wall. The steam overwhelms the bathroom and makes it easier for Porsha to sneak up on me. I never hear her creep in; I only feel her caress. Her fingertips ease all the tension, putting me in a relaxed state of mind. We embrace each other, sharing an intimate moment without having casual sex. No words are spoken, but our heartbeats have plenty to say, palpitations underneath our embrace.

As I turn the water off, she continues to do her duty of loving me by drying my body with a terry cloth towel. The warmth in her stare as she glides by my pussy-willow makes me tingle, but I can't allow her to touch my sickly forbidden fruit. I back away from her touch, and in an instant, Porsha calms down. She stands back to her feet and pulls me by the hand to the bedroom before pushing me playfully to the bed.

"We need to talk about your mother," Porsha says she climbs on top of me seductively.

"I'm still not ready to see her face to face sweetheart. And no, it's not up for discussion." I push Porsha off of me and grab up the TV remote. "There has to be something good on this morning. Oh, yeah, Saturday morning cartoons."

"I'm getting tired of being in the middle of this baby. I need you to be a woman and take the first step. Say to her what it is you need to say so you both can begin to heal." Porsha comes back with an even sweeter tongue kissing my earlobe.

"I don't know what to say to her or where to start, baby. Flat out I'm afraid she might not love me." I speak to her with my eyes shut, enjoying her hot breath on my spot. I want her to persuade me more and more. Her touch is becoming irresistible. I really don't care at that moment about being tainted, and for the first time, I don't want her to stop.

"Just come to the church with me and we all can pray about it. Can you do that for me?" Now she licks around my belly button, and I'm about to blow. "You never know what might happen, Egypt. You know prayer is strong when you have faith." Her soft kisses are between my legs. She blows ever so slightly over my hot spot. I can't resist.

"Yes, baby, you can have whatever it is you like." I grab a handful of hair, and Porsha knows now that I'm ready for her to touch me in all the right places.

"What did you say?"

"I said yes."

"Do you want me to finish what I started?" Porsha asks seductively.

"Yes... please..."

I stand at the same spot staring at the same double doors of the church where my mother was speaking on that cold, lonely night. Every last decision I made leading up to me getting held hostage in a laundry room comes back full speed until I am outta breath. I can hear the choir singing from the open windows of the building. My feet can't move. All ten of my toes are glued to the ground. I had stood here a time before asking God for a miracle. He sent me on a whirlwind, but it's a miracle I stand here, so now it's time I pay him some respect.

Palms sweaty, I turn the doorknob to open the church door. I walk in, taking a deep breath as I'm approached by an usher.

"Where would you like to be seated?" she asks, handing me a bulletin with a smile.

My stomach turns, but this time not for a hit of crack, however, but for some peace of mind. I start sweating bullets. I should've come with Porsha so I could have some support instead of letting her leave the house without me.

The old woman dressed in black and white ushers me to the last row of the church, and I take a seat. Without any doubt I knew Porsha and Kay sat up front with the kids, tapping their feet to the gospel tunes. My woman went from singing Mary J. Blige to Mary Mary. It's all good, too. I ain't mad at her. The best thing she could've done was invite the Lord into her life. It is a twist of fate how God works in her life, in my life and my mother's, bringing us all together. I sit here in his house alive and well as he has given me another chance. I cursed him, used his name in vain and had no belief that he was real until he rescued me from myself. Things might not have gone so wrong in my life if I would've embraced him long ago. But hey, there's no time for regret. I had to go through the fire to get to my heaven.

The singing finally comes to an end and the preacher reaches the pulpit with his black robe on. Shaking his head while waving his hands in the air, the Holy Ghost is good to him at that moment. I look at my watch. It is exactly 11 o'clock a.m., time for morning worship to start. The congregation ceases all clapping, waiting for the pastor to speak.

"I want to thank the choir this morning for singing such a powerful song. It really hit home for me. Let the church say Amen."

"Amen," the congregation replies in unison.

"Please prepare for special prayer," the preacher says next.

I watch people get up from their seats and gather around the pulpit on their knees. Others stay in their pews and get down on their knees. I look up and spot them both, Porsha and my mother.

Overjoyed marks the expression on Porsha's face when our eyes fall onto one another. I mouth, "I love you," and she does the same. My mother close by turns her head and notices me for the first time. I don't know how she knew it was me, but from the smile she wears and the tears boiling over her eyes, she is sure of it. I stand there, keeping my eyes affixed on their smiling faces. I need them to keep eye contact, giving me the courage to move my feet so I can walk to them.

Butterflies swim around in my stomach. I am very uneasy, but I put one foot in front of the other and begin to move. I keep it up until I am out in the aisle walking towards the pulpit for special prayer. Then suddenly, the smiling faces stop.

That's the last thing I remember before everything went black. My mother, Ms. Lola James-Bloom, was DOA when the paramedics finally got to the scene of the crime, and I came to. The shooter was missing in action and none of the parishioners could give a detailed enough description for the police to proclaim a suspect.

Covered in my mother's blood, I could do nothing but hang my head and stare at her blood on my hands. Porsha told me my mother saved my life when she pushed me to the floor. I cracked my head on the side of the pew, blacking out when I went down, and she caught a bullet straight in the heart, protecting her only daughter from the devil in the black dress. She gave her life to give me mine. Before they covered up my mother's body, I did what I had to do to make things right. I wiped the cold tear still on her face and kissed her cheek.

"I love you, Momma. I always have, and I always will." I felt good saying it as I began to cry. I let out all my hurt at the foot of her body. I gave it all to God.

'You get a pop quiz every day of your life when you live to see another day. Be blessed that you're still here; nobody is promised tomorrow. You never know when the Lord is going to call you or someone you love close to you neither. So live for the moment and always make sure you say what it is you have to say to a loved one.

REST IN PEACE
MS. LOLA JAMES-BLOOM

The End

CPSIA information can be obtained
at www.ICGtesting.com
Printed in the USA
BVOW11s1408040517
483094BV00007B/40/P

9 781478 769743